Appearance
of
Evil

Also by Christopher A. Lane

Eden's Gate

Appearance of
Evil

A NOVEL

Christopher A. Lane

ZondervanPublishingHouse
Grand Rapids, Michigan

A Division of HarperCollinsPublishers

Appearance of Evil
Copyright © 1997 by Christopher Lane

Requests for information should be addressed to:

📖 ZondervanPublishingHouse
Grand Rapids, Michigan 49530

Library of Congress Cataloging-in-Publication Data

Lane, Christopher A.
    Appearance of evil / Christopher A. Lane.
        p.   cm.
    ISBN: 0-310-21567-6 (softcover)
    I. Title.
PS3562.A4842A86   1997
813'.54—dc21   97–27455
                                                  CIP

Interior design by Sherri L. Hoffman

Printed in the United States of America

98 99 00 01 02 03 04 /❖ DC/ 10 9 8 7 6 5 4 3

Dedicated to Jesus
Light of the world
In whom there is no darkness

He will bring to light what is
hidden in darkness and will expose
the motives of men's hearts.

1 CORINTHIANS 4:5

PROLOGUE

IT CAME UPON HER LIKE A SUMMER STORM, suddenly, with unexpected fury: a hideous face . . . hundreds of eyes . . . a tangle of arms . . . a dozen hands reaching toward her . . . hooded figures . . . a circle . . . candles . . . distant voices . . . shouts . . . whispered taunts . . . shadows . . . blood. Everywhere blood.

It was a mind-numbing montage, like something out of a gory horror flick. But even more disturbing was the nagging sense of familiarity, as if these scenes were snatches from events long forgotten.

Ruth Sanders tried to shake off the unholy vision. She tried to dismiss it, to blame it on her diet—perhaps she had eaten something that disagreed with her. She tried to explain it away as a product of her overactive, overly tired imagination. But no rationalization helped.

Slowly, the blurred, choppy, supernatural movie began to fade. But as it did, something dark and vague took its place. It approached her like an animal, like a predator stalking its prey. It seemed to be alive, a nameless, faceless, disembodied entity. She could feel its presence. She could smell its wretched stench. She could hear it mocking her with every hissing breath. It seemed to know her—an old enemy come back to haunt a favorite foe.

Ruth had never dabbled in the occult. As a woman of faith— a born-again Christian—there was no place for ghosts or ghouls in her well-ordered theology. Neither did she believe in omens or portents. So it was with a mixture of skepticism, confusion, and panic that she analyzed the phenomenon she was experiencing.

An eerie silence descended upon her. Then she heard it.

I am coming for your firstborn, a wailing voice sang out, the words echoing as if across a vast, empty space.

Chills rippled down Ruth's spine—and then it was gone. The specter had departed, disappearing just as it had arrived. But in its wake trailed a web of white-hot emotions: dread, despair, and a deep, abiding conviction that tragedy was about to strike. She felt certain that something awful was about to happen, that it was looming on the horizon, rising skyward like a mighty thunder-head, waiting to rush violently into her life.

"Watch out!!"

Ruth looked up to see a concrete embankment hurtling toward them. She spun the wheel, tires screeching as the station wagon swerved and fishtailed, narrowly missing the overpass.

"Are you all right?" Patty asked from the passenger's seat. Her face was pale, her breathing labored.

"I'm fine," Ruth answered shakily, swallowing hard. "I—I'm sorry. I must have been . . . daydreaming."

"I'd rather you didn't. Not when we're doing seventy on the interstate. You want me to drive?"

"No," Ruth told her with a shake of her head. "I just wasn't paying attention."

"If you're getting sleepy—"

"I said I was fine!"

"Okay," Patty said. "You may not be sleepy, but you sure are grouchy," she muttered under her breath.

They rode on without speaking for another five minutes, until they reached the Woodmen exit.

"Do you believe in premonitions?" Ruth asked as noncha-lantly as possible, pretending to be occupied with the task of dri-ving. She pulled into the right-hand lane and took the exit.

"Premonitions?" Patty shrugged. "I guess so. I don't think I've ever had one. Of course, according to Stephen King—"

"Patty," Ruth groaned. She checked her mirror, then pulled into the left-hand turn lane at the first intersection. "Why is it that every time we carpool, you somehow manage to turn the conversation to that trash you read?"

"Trash!" Patty retorted, pretending to be deeply offended. "I'll have you know that in my opinion, King is one of the best authors in contemporary literature. Highly underrated. His books are well written, very exciting, very suspenseful—"

"Very gruesome . . ."

"Sometimes they get a little bloody, sure."

Ruth snorted at this. "A little bloody?" The light changed, and she made the turn, accelerating down the parkway. It was almost 9:30 and traffic was light. Rush hour had given way to the dark, deserted streets of evening.

"Stephen King could be one of the most skillful writers who ever lived," Ruth argued, "but that doesn't mean he's worth reading. All those monsters and demons and vampires—"

"Not vampires," Patty corrected. "That's Anne Rice. She's good too."

Ruth shook her head. "It's just not . . . edifying. I don't see how you can reconcile that junk with your walk with God."

"It's just fiction," Patty replied with a shrug. "Pure escapist entertainment. I read it to relax. You should try it sometime. You'd be surprised."

"For your information," Ruth told her, "I started a Stephen King book once. I did. Back in my unenlightened days. And I didn't find it relaxing or entertaining. It was creepy. Even oppressive. Gave me nightmares." She slowed for a red light. "Now Bodie Thoene. There's a writer. Her historical fiction is well researched, her characters are virtuous, the stories are uplifting and inspirational—"

"And bo-ring," Patty chimed.

Ruth chuckled at this. "How did we ever get to be best friends?"

They shared a laugh as the station wagon crossed another intersection.

"Back to premonitions," Patty said, raising her eyebrows. "You were saying . . ."

"I was just wondering. Do you think it's possible to know that something bad is about to happen—before it happens?"

"Something bad?"

Ruth pulled into the left-hand lane and passed a slow-moving pickup. "You know, an accident or something."

"Like us being plastered into that overpass back there?" Patty asked. "I could see that coming."

"No. I mean . . . have you ever . . . Oh, never mind."

"Do I believe in psychic foresight—sixth sense?" Patty said dramatically. "Like looking into the future and discerning that a calamity is about to occur?"

"Please."

"A sense of foreboding," Patty continued. "A feeling that something evil this way comes?"

Ruth scowled at her.

"Actually," she confessed, "I think it's possible." Patty's face took on a thoughtful expression. "For instance, in one of my favorite Stephen King stories, there was this guy who had these premonitions about—"

"You're impossible."

"Sorry," Patty said with a grin. "Go ahead. You've got this feeling that tragedy is about to strike."

"I didn't say me, personally," Ruth objected. "I was speaking hypothetically."

"Sure you were. So you've got this feeling that tragedy is about to strike. Think the stock market is going to crash?"

"No, nothing like that," Ruth sighed. "It's just . . . Listen, Patty, you know I'm not superstitious. I think fortunetelling, tarot cards, palm reading, tea leaves—it's all a bunch of mumbo-jumbo, not to mention an abomination to God."

"But . . . ," Patty prodded.

Ruth made a left turn, then a right onto a street lined with fast-food restaurants and strip malls. "But tonight, I've been having this strange feeling."

Patty considered this. "Maybe it's Gertie's chicken."

This drew a chuckle. They had both gone straight from work to a potluck meeting of the ladies' group at church. One of the members, Gertrude Hines, had brought a chicken salad. Since Gertrude was a notoriously bad cook, and routinely brought a bucket of Kentucky Fried to such events, whispered remarks had been made regarding the quality of the dish.

"No, I don't think I have food poisoning. Yet."

Laughter.

"It's like . . . I don't know . . . like something's wrong. Maybe it's just fatigue, or stress, or—"

"Or a foul plate of fowl," Patty interjected.

More laughter.

"What—pray tell—could possibly be wrong?" Patty asked, suppressing another round of giggles.

Ruth punched the pedal and they made it through a yellow light. "I'm not sure." She paused, trying to decide how much to disclose. Even though Patty was her closest friend, Ruth still didn't feel comfortable—safe—describing what she had just experienced. Patty might think she was losing her mind. "I think . . . I think maybe it's Zach."

"Zach? What about him?"

"That's what's so disconcerting. I don't know." The humor had evaporated from her voice.

"You're serious, aren't you?"

Ruth nodded solemnly. "I'm worried about him, but I have no idea why I should be."

The station wagon picked up speed, seemingly drawing from Ruth's nervous energy. Her imagination shifted into overdrive, and she began visualizing a thousand horrible things that could happen to her only son—the same sorts of unthinkable disasters that routinely paraded through the head of nearly every single mom on the planet. But now, for some inexplicable reason, they seemed completely plausible.

Patty placed a comforting hand on Ruth's shoulder. "It's your job to worry. You're his mother. That's natural."

"Yeah, but . . ."

"It's probably nothing," Patty continued. "Just a free-floating anxiety. Zach is a great kid. And God isn't about to let anything bad happen to him. Listen, here's what you should do."

"What?"

"When you get home, slip into a hot bath, relax with your favorite Bodie Thoene, and take a couple of Tums."

"Tums?"

"Yeah. That'll cure 'indigestion a la Gertrude' every time."

Ruth smiled at this. "It tasted okay going down," she joked. "But who knows where Gertie got that chicken."

"Probably been in her freezer since the fifties."

"Maybe longer."

"World War II white meat. Mmm-mmm."

They turned into the subdivision and began navigating the maze of curling streets. "You're right," Ruth admitted. "It's probably nothing."

"Zach still playing that guitar of his?" Patty asked, shifting the conversation to emphasize the positive.

Ruth nodded. "Constantly. He formed a group with some of his buddies from church. They perform 'godly grunge'—if you can imagine that. They practice in our garage every weekend. The racket drives the neighbors crazy. They're planning to do street evangelism this summer. Say, did I tell you Zach was asked to lead worship at the youth rally in Denver next month?"

"Yeah," Patty smiled. "That's great. The kid's on fire for Jesus, that's for sure."

"You better believe it," Ruth agreed. She had relaxed slightly, happy to talk about her favorite subject. "And when he isn't making music, he's either reading his Bible or fiddling with his computer. He spends hours linking up with a bulletin-board service on the Internet. He and some of the other teens from the youth group started a 'cyberspace' ministry—whatever that is. They do Bible studies and share the Gospel via computer. Somehow.

"Anyway, I don't know when he finds time for schoolwork. But he does. All A's, one B last quarter."

"So I heard."

Ruth grinned apologetically. "Listen to me brag."

"You have good reason to. He's an amazing kid. Wouldn't surprise me if he wound up being president. Either that or a pastor."

The car rolled through the neighborhood, following the warm pools of light created by the tall, arching street lamps. They were almost home. Ruth's brief, disconcerting glimpse of hell was quickly fading, and with it the threat against Zach. "When Zachary was born, Richard received a word from the Lord," Ruth said dreamily. "I have it written down somewhere. The general theme was that Zach would be like David, a man after God's own heart."

"That's wonderful," Patty said. "You never told me that."

Ruth shrugged.

"Well, I'd say Zach is well on his way to fulfilling that destiny."

They pulled into Patty's driveway.

"I wish Richard were here to see it," Ruth quietly lamented.

Patty gave her a hug. "I'm sure he'd be proud." She began collecting her things. "I'll drive tomorrow. Okay?"

"Fine." Ruth smiled. "Tell Fred and the kids hello."

"See you in the morning."

As she backed the station wagon out of the driveway, Ruth felt a cloak of sadness settle over her—the same feeling that always accompanied thoughts of Richard. It always hit her hardest after a long, taxing day. And this particular Thursday certainly qualified as one.

Work had been hectic, a succession of meetings, impending deadlines, and unforeseen setbacks. And despite the fellowship, the get-together at church tonight had been downright dull. As a result, she was depleted, weary—both physically and emotionally. And so her thoughts turned to Richard: the happy times, the difficult times, his face, his smile, the tumor, the operations, his thin, sick body fighting a losing battle . . .

She could still see her husband—or what had once been her husband—lying there in the coffin, his features gaunt and expressionless, his eyes vacant.

I've still got Zach, Ruth reminded herself to fend off the sorrowful memories. Zach had been her lifeline during Richard's protracted illness, her salvation in the heart-wrenching aftermath. He was a tangible expression of God's goodness and faithfulness, the angel who had walked her through a seemingly endless valley of pain. And two years later, Zach was still assisting her through the ashes of Richard's death.

If anything ever happened to Zach, she thought as she swung around the corner and aimed for the driveway in the center of the cul-de-sac, *I couldn't go on.*

Pressing the garage door opener, she waited for the door to clunk and groan its way up. Patty was right, she decided. The "premonition"—despite its impressive special effects—was probably nothing.

Guiding the car into its tight parking space between the bikes and the freezer, she nearly ran over a skateboard. On a typical evening this would have irritated her. Zach had neglected to put it back where it belonged—again. But tonight she welcomed the distraction. Seeing the skateboard reminded her of how much she loved and valued Zachary, and of why she so disliked days like this one: they kept her away from him. Apart from God, Zach was the most important thing in Ruth's life, and it concerned her when her number-one priority was bumped down by work and church functions.

Silencing the engine, she opened the door and realized that she still felt that unexplained heaviness. *Why all this worry about Zach?* she wondered as she got out of the car. *What could possibly be wrong with such a great kid?* She took her purse in one hand, the half-empty casserole dish in the other, and clumsily slammed the door with a hip. As she did, her mind began to assemble an invisible list of answers: school . . . girls . . . peer pressure . . . drugs . . . alcohol . . . There were so many threats in modern society, so many problems that plagued teens these days. But none of them fit Zach. He was well behaved in class—an exemplary student, according to his teachers. He got along with girls but had decided not to "go steady" with anyone until after high school. He was committed to academics and ministry and had pledged to abstain from sex until marriage. Ruth believed him, too. She had never known a teenager with such maturity, such integrity, such a godly character. Of course, she was ever so slightly biased. But even so, Zach didn't engage in any of the life-endangering habits of his peers—he didn't smoke, drink, or do drugs—and he didn't hang around people who did. He never went out partying, like so many youths, and never violated his curfew. The kid was a saint.

Stepping into the utility room, Ruth glanced at the clock over the washer: 9:42. *How am I supposed to be a responsible parent,* she asked herself, *when I'm never even around to see my son?* A well-placed foot slammed the door. Most days, it was the same story: gone when he woke up, gone when he came home from school—and tonight, had it been twenty minutes later, he would already have been in bed and she would have missed seeing him altogether.

What kind of life is that for a teenager? she chided. *He's leading a parentless existence. And at a critical time in his life, a time when he needs the most support.*

"I'm doing the best I can," Ruth muttered, blinking away the dreary cloud of self-condemnation. She eyed the dining-room table. An empty cardboard pizza container sat open on it, further evidence that Zach could fend for himself. The kid was nothing if not resourceful. If Mom wasn't around for dinner, he'd simply whip something up himself—or give Domino's a call.

Probably even paid with his own money, she thought. No need to worry about Zach. He could take care of himself. In fact, half the time he was taking care of her.

Good old Zach. If all else fails, I've always got him. And he's got me.

The living room was dark. Ruth took that to mean that Zach was holed up in his room plinking on his guitar or hacking away at the computer.

As she made her way down the hall she felt—rather than heard—the dull pulse of bass emanating from Zach's stereo. Thankfully, he never cranked it up to full volume. That probably would have demolished the house. But no matter how quiet the level, that bass could still be felt.

She paused for a moment outside his bedroom door, listening. A conglomeration of distorted, electronic sounds met her ears. Grunge, she decided. She couldn't quite make out the lyrics, but she knew they must have something to do with God. Zach's music always did.

Rapping gently, she waited to be invited in. When there was no response, she tried again, slightly harder.

"Zach?"

Nothing—just more thumping bass.

He can't be wearing headphones, she thought. *Maybe he fell asleep.*

She tried one final time before twisting the knob.

"Zach?"

As the door swung open she saw exactly what she expected to see: a floor littered with CD cases, an open Bible, several textbooks, pads of paper, pencils, and an assortment of socks and other discarded clothing. Zach's electric guitar was propped against the chair at the desk. His computer was running, the screen filled with colorful flying fish.

In the split second that it took her eyes to move from the cluttered floor to the far corner of the room, the sense of fear fell upon her with renewed force. As it did, the room immediately took on a smoky appearance, as if a thin fog were sweeping from window to door. Ruth's knees wobbled, threatening to buckle.

Before she could study this transition or recognize that the usually bright, inviting bedroom was now awash in animated shadows, evidence that a host of otherworldly squatters had claimed the space as their own habitation and were now unwilling to depart—she saw him.

The body hung motionless, the head leaning forward awkwardly, held aloft by a taut guitar cord. The legs were rigid, the feet turned in toward each other. The eyes were open, but the pupils were empty and unfocused. The face was contorted, the brow furrowed, the lips curled down in a grimace of agony. The skin had taken on a ghostly gray, almost purple tint.

And the chest . . .

The shirt had been removed and a symbol carved into the skin over the heart: a long vertical line and a shorter horizontal, like an inverted cross. A half-moon arc decorated the intersection of the two lines. Blood trailed from the tattoo, forming a snakelike pattern down the abdomen, and dribbling in dark lines along the left pant leg before dropping to a blotch on the carpet below.

The room began to spin. Ruth grew lightheaded, tottered, then fell to the floor. Wavering on all fours, her limbs trembled as waves of pure, undistilled terror swept over her.

Her brain was paralyzed, unwilling to process the information her eyes were gathering. It refused to accept the hideous sight as reality and threatened to blackout. Incapable of gathering the breath to scream, she let out a small, mournful cry, her eyes fixed on the noose that suspended her son between heaven and earth. The last vestige of hope rose from the depths of her soul, and she silently willed the cord to release him. But it did not.

As her nervous system threatened to shut down and she drifted into shock, Ruth noticed the lyrics of the music for the first time. A gritty, male voice was shouting through a blaze of distorted guitars:

> You can run, but you cannot hide.
> The master has come for your suicide.
> Come on, do it! Put your head through it!
> Life is a lie! Just swing . . . and die!

Ruth's faith evaporated. Her arms and legs gave way and she fell forward, rolling into a supine position beneath the body of her only son, beneath the lifeless corpse that had held her greatest source of joy in all the world. Unable to move, unable to call for help, unable to turn her gaze away, she stared up in horror. As she did, her mind managed to form a one-word question, the same question that would plague her for the rest of her life. And it was directed to the very throne of heaven.

Why?

ONE

FEDERAL BUREAU OF INVESTIGATION
TRANSCRIPT OF PRISONER INTERROGATION

Subject: Dr. Craig P. Hanson

Date: 4/10/97

Charges: Thirteen counts cruelty to animals
         Two counts sexual/physical abuse of minors
         One count first-degree murder

This transcript is the property of the Federal Bureau of Investigation. It may not be duplicated in any form without the express, written consent of the U.S. Department of Justice.

Description of arrest: Subject was apprehended at his home at approximately 5:30 A.M., Wednesday, April 9, 1997. Subject did not resist arrest.

Description of interrogation: Subject was questioned for eleven hours over the course of two days (April 9/April 10). The interrogation was recorded on audio cassette.

NOTE: Subject waived right to an attorney.

Disposition of case: Case closed.

Transcript of Craig P. Hanson Interrogation—FC-254/34 (p. 29)

  INT: So you're ready to confess?
 SUBJ: As ready as I'll ever be.
  INT: Please state your full name, your age, and your
       occupation.
 SUBJ: Again? Craig Patrick Hanson. 39. I'm a clinical
       psychiatrist.
  INT: Do you understand the charges against you, Dr.
       Hanson?
 SUBJ: Yes.

```
INT: And you understand that you have the right to have
     an attorney present?
SUBJ: Yes. Can we just get this over with?
INT: All right. Tell us what happened.
SUBJ: On the evening of February 22, 1996, I broke into
      a home at 1937 Benson Road. I strangled a teenager
      by the name of Zachary Sanders with a guitar cord.
      Then I carved a satanic symbol into his skin and
      hung him—to make it look like a suicide. How's
      that?
INT: Is that the truth?
SUBJ: Of course.
INT: What about the other charges?
SUBJ: I did those things too. I abused my daughters,
      forcing them to participate in satanic rituals.
INT: And the animals?
SUBJ: I used cows, goats, dogs, cats . . .
INT: Sheep?
SUBJ: Yeah, sheep too. I used them to perform satanic
      rituals.
INT: That's it? No remorse? No explanation for why you
     did it?
SUBJ: I confessed, didn't I? You got what you wanted.
INT: Okay. Now let's talk specifics.
```

"Ever been to Super Max, Ms. Gant?"

Susan looked up from the transcript. "No."

The two U.S. marshals shared a smile.

"But I've been to the prison in Corvallis," she offered from the backseat. "I clerked with the public defender in Portland. We saw our share of tough guys."

"Not the same," Campbell said, shaking his head. He put his foot down and the Dodge rocketed past a diesel truck that was struggling up Highway 115.

Probably not, Susan thought. Marshal John Campbell looked like someone who knew what he was talking about. He was a husky man, around fifty, black, with a seriously recessed hairline. His low, baritone voice demanded immediate respect, and the size of his frame told the world that he could hold his own in a scuffle. His partner, Tony Rosselli, was shorter and even stockier—a fireplug with no neck to speak of and thighs the size of Susan's waist. A real muscle pig. He wore his hair in a crew cut and couldn't have been much more than twenty-one.

"Nothin's the same as the Max," Tony told her solemnly. He twisted in the seat to face her. "They call it Alcatraz of the Rockies."

"Is that right?" She hadn't heard that particular nickname.

"Yep," Tony nodded. "You ain't seen a prison till you've seen Super Max. Not the kind of place for a lady. 'Specially a lady like you."

Susan watched as Tony offered his most charming grin, then quickly surveyed her overall appearance. She'd checked it carefully in the mirror herself before she left her apartment, anxious for some reason to make a good first impression: shoulder-length blond hair, blue eyes, smooth skin, high cheekbones. She was conservatively dressed in a dark blazer and skirt. Still, Tony's eyes paused at the curve of her blouse, then darted down to her hips. She could almost see the wheels turning beneath his flattop.

"You could've been a model," he said, his expression just one step removed from a leer.

"I was for a while," she told him, wondering if he was about to start drooling. "Helped me pay for law school."

"You married, *Ms*. Gant?"

"Tony . . . ," Campbell warned.

"Just asking," Tony sighed. He turned around and frowned at the windshield.

"We just want you to be prepared," Campbell explained, returning the conversation to a more professional level. "Super Max is a hellhole. Makes other federal pens look like country clubs."

"The most dangerous prisoners in the United States are housed here," Tony added proudly. "Members of the Medellin drug cartel, guys from the neo-Nazi group The Order, the New York Trade Center bombers, John Gotti—serious people."

"So I've heard."

"It'll take us a good thirty to forty-five minutes just to get in. And when we finally do . . ." His voice trailed off.

"What?"

The marshals glanced at each other in conspiratorial fashion. "What?"

"Well," Campbell said, "this client of yours—he's not exactly a choirboy, if you know what I mean."

Susan did. According to the case notes, Dr. Hanson had been convicted and sentenced to death for committing a wide array of heinous crimes. Strangely enough, it wasn't the murder of a teenage boy or the unconscionable abuse of his daughters that had brought the wrath of the federal government. It had been Hanson's mistreatment of animals. Each of the thirteen mutilations was a felony, and since they had been carried out in four separate states, that made them federal offenses. Taken as a whole, his crimes made Hanson a prime candidate for a private suite in the U.S. Penitentiary Administrative Maximum in Florence, Colorado.

"Yeah," Susan said. "I understand he's an interesting guy."

The marshals snickered at this.

"Oh, he's interesting all right," Tony snorted.

" 'Certifiably' interesting," Campbell agreed.

"Not according to his psych eval," Susan told them. "The docs gave him a clean bill of health. He's not crazy."

"Yeah, well," Campbell grumbled, "anybody who could kill a kid like that, notch a satanic symbol in his chest, and abuse his little girls . . . In my book, he's a nutcase."

"Loony tunes," Tony added. "A real sick puppy."

"And he's right where he belongs," Campbell concluded.

Susan didn't respond. The point wasn't worth arguing. But according to the medical experts, Hanson had been competent to stand trial two years ago. That didn't mean that he wasn't a cold-blooded killer, a man with no sense of right and wrong and no respect for human life. It just meant that he wasn't clinically insane.

None of that mattered, of course, because this was a junk case. A no-winner: the final hearing for a death-row inmate. The appeals process had been exhausted—or more accurately, allowed to lapse. Hanson had chosen not to appeal, and this hearing was merely a formality on the road to his execution. The verdict had been handed down twenty-six months earlier. It was now up to a judge to set a date. Hanson would be dispatched by lethal injection. That much was certain. The only question was: When?

Susan was well aware that the outcome of the case was predetermined. She also knew why it had been handed to her. Hanson had fired his lawyer at the last minute. And since the government guaranteed legal representation to all citizens, she had been assigned to walk the case through its final days. It was a simple task that even a new grad could have handled. But it was important to Susan because it represented her first bona fide solo flight. She had been complaining long and loudly to her supervisor, Jack Sherman, about never seeing any court time, about always playing a supporting role to the rest of the staff. The pitiful diatribes about spending all that time in law school just to become a glorified gofer had apparently paid off. Jack had finally decided to give her a shot at prime time.

This was it. This was her chance. For the first time since graduating at the top of her class at the University of Colorado, the first time in five years—three of which had been spent laboring away in obscure research libraries in and around Portland—for the first time in her budding career she was about to assume the position of chief counsel on a legal case. Too bad it was a throwaway. Still, she was young and idealistic, just naive enough to believe that she might somehow make something of it: find a new angle that others had failed to consider, discover a buried precedent or a missing piece of evidence that the FBI had overlooked, file a last-ditch petition to prolong Hanson's life, convince the judge that Hanson wasn't such a bad guy after all . . .

Theoretically, she could work magic, turning this lost cause into a surprise victory. Realistically, the case was a foregone conclusion, a mundane chore. Still, it was something to cut her teeth on.

Susan glanced out the window. They were skirting the edge of the Wet Mountains, following the highway up the Arkansas Valley. The scenery was spectacular, some of the most stunning in North America. Not the sort of place you expected to find a maximum security prison facility.

"Ever met a Satanist before, Ms. Gant?" Tony asked. He poured coffee from a thermos and handed Susan the first steaming cup.

"Thanks." She took a sip. It was warm, not hot, and tasted watery. "No, can't say that I have."

And I'm not sure I will today, she thought, but didn't say it. Maybe Hanson was a practicing Satanist—some sort of high priest, as the Feds had asserted. And then again, maybe he wasn't. Maybe he was guilty of conducting midnight rituals, of mutilating cattle and sheep, of abusing children as part of some bizarre pagan rite. Or maybe he wasn't. That was why she was making this trek. To talk to Hanson and—hopefully—answer a few of those questions firsthand.

"Well, you're in for a treat," Campbell deadpanned. "A real treat."

"Yeah, I'll bet."

"'Course, representing a Satanist," Tony said, "an adolescent-murdering child molester—you won't win any popularity contests. The children's rights folks and the concerned parents back in the Springs won't like it. You could get some angry phone calls. Maybe even a few threats."

"It's too slow," Campbell complained. "That's what's wrong with our justice system. There shouldn't *be* any appeals. There shouldn't be any waiting period. Once a guy is tried and convicted, they should sentence him, lock him up—"

"And throw away the key," Tony threw in.

"And when they put somebody on death row, a scumbag like this Hanson, for instance," Campbell continued, "they should quit stalling and just do it: jab the guy and push the plunger. Seven minutes later, the whole mess would be over."

"Sayonara Satanist," Tony said.

"Save the taxpayers a lot of money," Campbell noted dispassionately.

Susan tried to ignore them, silently hoping that there wouldn't be a John Campbell or a Tony Rosselli sitting the bench. Things were already grim enough.

TWO

SUSAN TOOK HER SEAT ON THE VISITOR'S SIDE of the barrier and breathed a sigh of relief. Passing through security had been every bit as rigorous as the marshals had promised. She had been searched from top to bottom three times, gone through an intricate series of metal detectors, and been briefed on procedures a total of four times. She was ready to call it a day and head back to Denver—and she hadn't even met her client.

Two minutes later, the bolt on the door at the far end of the large visitor's area slid back with a thunderous clank. It creaked open and a battalion of guards began filing into the room. Near the center of the cluster, behind a row of men who looked like former football stars, a small, slight man loped along, his hands and feet wrapped in manacles. When the entourage finally parted, allowing the prisoner to approach a solitary chair on the other side of the Plexiglas barrier, she realized that he wasn't particularly short or thin. He was above average height—about six foot—and weighed maybe 175 pounds. But he looked tiny compared to the hulking brutes that shadowed him.

Campbell and Rosselli had taken up residence ten feet behind Gant in the row of chairs lining the back wall. She wasn't sure why they were in the room at all. Probably another security precaution. Whatever the reason, they distracted her. She could *feel* them back there, and though she couldn't quite make out the words, she could hear them mumbling back and forth. Making wisecracks and snide remarks about Hanson, she guessed.

After warning them with an icy stare, Susan turned around and found herself face-to-face with her client: Dr. Craig Hanson. He was sitting, his face emotionless, waiting for the meeting to begin.

Susan studied him for a moment, taken aback by his appearance. He looked normal—dangerously normal. No wild-eyed expression. No unruly hair. No long, scruffy beard. The guy was actually rather handsome: light brown hair, smooth features, a likable face—closer to Harrison Ford than Charles Manson. And even with chains dangling from his limbs and clad in bright orange coveralls, he had a studious, educated look—like a professor or even a lawyer.

"Good morning, Dr. Hanson," she said through the intercom. "I'm Susan Gant. I'll be representing you in next week's hearing." She spread a stack of file folders out on the desk in front of her and took up a yellow legal pad and pencil. "Now, I'd like to start by asking you a few—"

"I'm innocent, Ms. Gant."

Susan looked up. His voice was calm, his face serene. He seemed sincere.

"Well, Dr. Hanson," she sighed, "that's what I'm here to help you prove."

"Call me Craig. My life is in your hands. No sense being formal."

Susan nodded. He had a point. "Okay, Craig. You can call me Susan."

"Susan," he said, looking directly into her eyes, "I'm innocent. I mean it. I'm really innocent."

She paused. Every inmate in every prison on earth feigned innocence. "Great. Now, let me—"

"I was framed."

"For the murder, for the child abuse, for the mutilations—what were you framed for?"

"All of it. It was a setup. They framed me."

Campbell and Rosselli apparently overheard this because a new round of snickers broke out.

"They?" she asked, trying to ignore the marshals. "Who's they?"

Hanson stared at the desktop for a moment. Then he rubbed his eyes.

"Are you familiar with Job?"

"Excuse me?"

"Job. It's a book in the Bible."

Susan shrugged. "Sort of. It's about a man who had a hard life."

"It's the story of a godly man who became the focus of a heavenly wager," Hanson clarified with a thin smile. "You see, Job's life was without blemish. Spotless. Clean. He was God's pride and joy. Everything was going along just fine—then the devil showed up. He heard God boasting about Job and issued a challenge. Good old Job wouldn't be quite so good, the devil argued, if his life wasn't so rosy. A tragedy here, a sickness there, and this same Job would do a 360 and curse God. Or so the devil claimed."

He stopped, adopted a thoughtful expression like an orator about to make an important point, then continued. "The gauntlet was thrown down. And God, not being one to back down from a dare, agreed to let the devil 'test' Job. That's when the fun began.

"In an instant, Job was reduced to nothing. His children, his possessions, his health, all stripped from him in the blink of an eye. Overnight, his life became a nightmare."

Susan watched her client through the partition. Maybe the marshals were right. Maybe he was loony tunes.

"Some scholars believe the account is an allegory of the human condition."

"Is that right?" Susan nodded, pretending to be interested. "Mr. Hanson, if we could get started, I'd like to ask you about—"

"I used to think so too. I used to think it was a fable that underscored the suffering we all experience."

Susan waited, knowing there was more.

"But now I know better."

"How's that?"

"Now I know that it was real."

"What was?"

"Job's life."

"And how do you know that?"

The smile returned to Hanson's face. "Because I've lived it. I am the twentieth-century incarnation of Job. For some reason, God allowed the devil to touch me. And I have lost everything."

Glancing down at the file, Susan took stock of the "everything" Hanson had lost: job, wife, daughters, freedom. Well, he was right—that was just about everything a person could lose. And unless she succeeded in pulling a rabbit out of a hat, in a few short weeks he would lose his life.

"But as you mentioned," she pointed out, "Job was a saint. His tragedies were not self-induced."

"Neither are mine."

Susan considered this, her brow furrowing. "Are you trying to say that you were minding your own business and suddenly this whirlwind of violence and mayhem swept over you?"

"I'm trying to say I'm innocent."

Susan frowned at him. She was growing tired of this circular conversation. "Dr. Hanson."

"Craig," he corrected.

"Craig," she said with a frown. "Did you kill Zachary Sanders?"

"No." The answer came without hesitation.

"Then why did you confess?"

This time Hanson had no reply.

"Why did you confess?"

His jaw tightened and began to twitch. "They threatened me."

Susan suppressed a groan. Back to *they* again.

"They threatened my family," he added. "My wife and my girls."

"Who? Who threatened you?"

His response was a heavy sigh.

Susan massaged her forehead, feeling a headache coming on. "You didn't kill Zachary Sanders?"

"No."

"Then how did he die?"

"At the end of a guitar cord."

"Suicide? Is that what you're implying?"

Hanson shook his head. "Oh, no. Zach was murdered. I'm sure of that. But I didn't do it."

"But you confessed to it."

"Yeah." He nodded. "And I was coerced into pleading guilty."

Something didn't make sense. "If you were threatened into a confession," Susan asked, "then why are you attempting to retract it now—when it's too late to appeal? Aren't you still intimidated by *them?*" She did her best to make it sound unpatronizing, but it came out patronizing anyway.

"I'm not afraid anymore," Hanson told her. The warmth had evaporated from his expression. "Not of them. Not of this place." He motioned to his surroundings. "I'm not even afraid of death."

"Bet that long walk to the needle will put the fear back into him," a voice behind Susan said.

Thankfully, Hanson didn't seem to hear it. "I have nothing left to lose," he continued. "And everything to gain."

Susan glanced down at the files spread in front of her. "From what I've seen, Craig, the prosecution had a strong case against you. Even without the confession, there's still a considerable amount of evidence: fingerprints, witnesses . . ."

"I was framed."

"So you said." Susan was getting frustrated. "Help me here, Craig. Why should I believe that you were framed? Better yet, why should a jury believe you were framed?"

Silence.

"Craig . . ."

His lips curled down into a scowl. "For one thing, I wasn't even living in Colorado Springs when Zach died."

Susan waited for more, but Hanson seemed to be finished. "That's it? That's your defense?"

"That's it."

"According to the trial records, witnesses placed you in Denver on the day the Sanders boy died. Isn't that right?"

"Yes."

"So that puts you in the vicinity. And you didn't have an alibi?"

"No. But I didn't have a motive either."

"I read your confession," Susan told him. "You had a motive."

"It was a pack of lies," Hanson responded tersely. "I said what they wanted me to say."

Susan made a note, then asked, "Why were you in Denver?"

"Business trip. I take them all the time—or at least I used to."

"You're a psychologist, right?" Susan asked without looking up.

"Psychiatrist," he corrected. "I was in Denver to attend a symposium."

"No one was with you or saw you on the night in question?"

"No. The evening session was canceled because the speaker was ill. I went to my room, watched a little television, and went to bed." He turned in his seat and gazed vacantly at one of the guards. "But there were hundreds of other people at the same conference—for that matter, there were literally millions of people in the Denver/Springs area. I'll bet plenty of them didn't have an alibi either."

"But they're not in prison now, convicted of murder. And you are," Susan pressed. "Why did the FBI single you out?"

"I was framed."

Susan sighed. Back to square one. She began fiddling with an errant strand of hair, trying to figure out a way to get this guy to open up. "Okay, Dr. Hanson—*Craig*—let's say, for argument's sake, that you're telling me the truth, that you were framed. You never murdered anybody, never abused anybody, never sliced and diced animals—so why were you framed?"

"Because they needed a scapegoat."

"*Who* needed a scapegoat?"

He looked at her for a long moment, then closed his eyes and let his head sink forward.

"Come on, Craig. If you expect me to help you, I've got to know the details. If you didn't do it, then who murdered Zachary Sanders?"

"I'm not sure," Hanson said. "Besides, it isn't about murder."

"Then what is it about?"

Hanson suddenly looked very tired. "It's about a conspiracy. It's about wolves in sheep's clothing. It's about evil spirits and enemy attacks and demonic strongholds. It's about spiritual warfare being waged in the heavenlies. It's about a man by the name of Craig Hanson being made to follow in the footsteps of Job."

Great, Susan thought. *More vague religious allegories.*

"I don't expect you to believe me," he confessed sadly. "My last attorney certainly didn't."

"Is that why you fired him?"

Hanson ran a hand over his face, then stood up. "This is pointless."

The guards converged on him, pressing him back into the seat.

The room was silent for nearly a minute.

"Okay, Craig," Susan finally said, taking a deep breath. "You're right. I don't believe you. Change my mind. Convince me."

Hanson shrugged at her and shook his head, as if there was no hope.

"I'm here and I'm willing to listen to your side of the story." She leaned towards the Plexiglas partition, her attention focused on Hanson.

Instead of meeting her gaze, his eyes began to scan the wall behind her. "It's been like a bad dream," he said in a voice just above a whisper. "A bad dream that I can't wake up from."

The calm exterior broke and Hanson's eyes teared up.

Susan turned to a fresh sheet on the legal pad. "Start at the beginning, Craig. Take your time. Tell me everything."

"The beginning," Hanson muttered, sniffing. "The beginning. I suppose that would be when we left St. Louis."

"Why did you leave? What brought you to Colorado Springs?"

"Sam."

"Who?"

"My wife, Samantha."

Susan jotted a note. "She wanted to move to the Springs?"

"Not the Springs specifically." Hanson leaned back in the chair and wiped his eyes. The brief surge of emotion had passed. "She just needed a change."

Susan continued scribbling, listening.

"Sam's prone to depression," he explained. "Sounds crazy, right—a head doctor's wife suffering from the blues? But she has a family history of depression: her mother had it, her grandmother had it . . . Sam's problem is relatively mild, but chronic. We've tried therapy, drug treatment, prayer—nothing seems to work.

"Except change. For some reason, change helps. Don't ask me why. It shouldn't. Change is stressful. It often induces depression in other people. But for Sam—well, it just helps. My guess is it has something to do with the newness factor—new town, new house, new church, new places to shop, new friends . . . Of course, the newness wears off eventually, in a matter of months, sometimes weeks or even days. And so does the antidepressant effect. But for a while, it works.

"So, we moved a lot—for Sam's sake. Mostly around eastern Missouri. That's why we left St. Louis. That's why we headed West. One of the reasons, anyway."

THREE

WE MADE THE CREST OF MONUMENT PASS AT 7:13 P.M.
on October 3."

Susan looked at him, surprised that he remembered so precisely.

Hanson laughed. "The girls etched it into my memory. They were fighting. They'd been fighting incessantly for nearly nine hundred miles."

"Is that it? Is that Pikes Peak?"

"Of course not, dweeb-face. We aren't there yet. That's just a regular old mountain."

"It is not. It's Pikes Peak. Isn't it, Daddy?"

"Pikes Peak is taller than that, dweeb-face."

"Huh-uh."

"Is too."

"Mommy!"

"Girls . . ."

"Only a dweeb-face would think that's Pikes Peak."

"I'm not a dweeb-face! Mommy!"

"Girls!"

"The last sign said Monument Pass, so that couldn't be—"

"It is!"

"Is not!"

"Girls!"

34

"Hey!" Craig's voice thundered through the Jeep Cherokee. "Item number one, yes, Emily, that is, in fact, Pikes Peak."

"I knew it!"

"No you didn't, dweeb-face!"

"Did too. And look at the clock. It says 7:13. I was closest. I guessed we'd see Pikes Peak at 7:34."

"I was closest! I guessed 6:53."

"You did not! You guessed 6:47."

"But I changed it, remember?"

"No you didn't."

"Did so!"

"Did not!"

"Did so, dweeb-face!"

"Mommy, Rachel called me a dweeb-face!"

"Girls . . ."

"Hey!" Craig scowled into the backseat. "Item number two, Rachel Ann, stop calling your sister dweeb-face."

Rachel muttered something under her breath.

"Item number three . . ." Craig leaned across the front seat and kissed Samantha on the cheek. "Ladies, I'd like to welcome you to our new home. Pretty ugly, huh?"

The sun had just set behind the southern end of the Front Range, and the long line of sharp peaks was backlit by a soft pink light. Pikes Peak took center stage, a majestic, snowcapped pinnacle reaching high into the sky, dwarfing its smaller neighbors. To the east, the sky darkened from orange to indigo to a deep purple on the distant horizon.

"You didn't know that was Pikes Peak," Rachel jabbed.

"Did too. I looked it up in the Colorado book Mommy got me."

"As if you could read."

"I can! Mommy!"

"Girls . . ."

"Hey!" Craig glared at Rachel, then at Emily. "Item number four, you girls need to stop bickering before your mother and I lose our minds."

Emily and Rachel both stuck out their bottom lips, prepared to pout.

"It's been a long day," Craig explained, "we're all tired, we're hungry. Just mellow out. We'll be at the hotel in a few minutes."

"Will it have a pool?" Emily wanted to know.

"I'm sure it will," Craig told her.

A squeal erupted from the backseat.

He looked at Samantha. "Well, what do you think?"

"Looks okay," she answered without enthusiasm.

"Okay?" Craig examined her face. It was drawn. There were dark rings beneath her eyes, and her lips were turned down in a hopeless, listless frown. It was an expression he knew well; it meant that she was riding the emotional elevator to a lower floor.

"Come on, honey," he tried, knowing from experience that no amount of positive talk would pull her out of it. "You're going to like this place."

"I hope so," she sighed.

He gave her shoulder a squeeze. "This is the best thing that's ever happened to us. Everything's new. A chance to make a fresh start."

The frown on Sam's face became more pronounced, as if she were about to cry. "I hope so."

"We're going to like it here, aren't we, girls?"

"Yeah!" Emily and Rachel shouted in unison.

"We'll wind up settling down, probably spend the rest of our lives here."

"Mmm . . . ," Samantha grunted.

"Tomorrow while I'm at work, you and the girls can start house hunting. It'll be fun."

"Fun!" Sam was suddenly animated and angry. "Craig Hanson, I have hunted for six houses in six different cities in the span of thirteen years. The first couple of times, sure, it was kind of fun. But now—now I'd do almost anything to trade places with you. I'd give my eyeteeth to go to that clinic of yours in the morning, sit at your new desk, and listen to a new group of wackos whine and moan about their problems. You'll have instant colleagues, instant friends, an instant social network. Me? I'll be enrolling the girls in school and riding around all day with a realtor, listening to her try to sweet-talk us into more house than we can afford, enduring the hard sell, doing walk-throughs on houses that are either way out of our price range, or such run-down shacks that you couldn't pay us to live in them. And I won't make a single friend for months."

Craig took a deep breath, determined not to lose his cool. "First of all, they aren't wackos. They're patients. Second, they're supposed to have an excellent school system here. One of the finest in the nation."

Sam blew air at this.

"Third, I'll bet you find a great house right off the bat."

"Right," Sam scoffed. She had already retreated into her cocoon of melancholy.

"Seriously. You never know. The very first home might be the one."

"Mmm . . ."

"And fourth, I hear the people out here are very friendly and easy to get to know."

She was no longer listening.

Craig's patience was growing thin. Despite Sam's state, there was only so much pessimism he could take. "Listen, I happen to believe that we're here for a reason, that God wants us here, that I'm supposed to be working at this clinic. I actually think this is part of his plan for us—that he has good things in store for our family. It's called faith, and it wouldn't hurt you to exercise a mustard seed's worth of it."

He watched her, wondering whether she would swing back
in a rage or allow his admonishment to become a springboard to
a more even keel. For a long moment, she seemed to vacillate.

"You're right," she sighed. "I'm sorry. Usually I'm excited
about moving. But this time . . . I don't know why, but I just . . .
I have a bad feeling . . ." Her words trailed off, and tears began to
trickle down her cheeks.

Craig put a comforting arm around her. "Don't worry, honey.
Everything's going to be fine."

"I hope so," she sniffed, attempting a smile. "I really do hope
so."

FOUR

"IT WAS BAD FROM THE START," HANSON LAMENTED. "At least for Sam. The move seemed to push her over the edge, deeper *into* depression instead of out of it. I had to sedate her the night we arrived." He paused and shook his head slowly. "She wound up spending almost as much time down at the clinic as I did."

"Tell me about the clinic," Susan prodded. She glanced at her files. "You were hired by . . . Trinity Institute?"

Hanson was staring at the wall above her head again. "The Trinity Institute of Psychiatric Therapy. Everybody calls it 'The Institute' for short. It's a branch of Trinity Ministries International—an outgrowth of Trinity Christian Fellowship."

"The megachurch?" Susan asked. She had read about Trinity in the Denver paper. According to the article, it boasted close to seven thousand members and was growing by leaps and bounds.

Hanson nodded. "The Institute is the brainchild of Dr. William Bayers, arguably the finest mind in Christian psychiatry. He assembled a top-notch staff and designed a progressive program employing an intelligent, balanced treatment that integrated first-class psychological techniques and philosophies with prayer and Christian principles. It was a unique, truly holistic approach that not only made sense but produced impressive results.

"Anyway, the Institute had the perspective and setting I'd been looking for. Until then, I'd worked at secular hospitals and mental institutions. My hands had been tied in terms of dealing with spiritual issues—which can often be at the root of emotional and physical problems.

"So the Institute was the perfect environment for me. Or so I thought."

"What do you mean?" Susan asked, looking up from her pad.

"I mean that I could tell something was wrong my very first day at the clinic."

"Grant Singer, at your service."

Craig had just parked his car and barely cracked open the car door. "Craig Hanson," he said, shaking the hand extended towards him.

"Oh, I know who you are, Doctor." Singer nodded enthusiastically, helping him out of the car. "It's great to have you on staff."

"Well, I'm glad to be here," Craig answered, wishing he could think of something less trite to say. Briefcase in hand, he followed Singer toward the main entrance.

"Have you met Bill yet?" Singer asked, holding open the glass door.

"Bill?"

"Bill Bayers, chairman of the clinic."

"Oh, Dr. Bayers, sure. I interviewed with him. He's impressive. Quite a reputation."

"You'll like him," Singer assured. "He's easy to work for. A hands-off kind of guy."

"Sounds good."

Singer led him down the hallway to the elevator. "Your office is on the second floor. Two doors down from mine."

"Great."

"I hope you're ready to dive in." Singer grinned. He punched the arrow pointing up and the elevator door opened with a ping. "The fella you're replacing, Sid Binker, just started his sabbatical Friday. So you've got a complete caseload."

"Great."

Singer pressed the round button marked 2 and the door closed. "I think your first patient is at nine."

"Seriously?"

Singer checked his watch. "That gives you an hour and a half to get your bearings."

The elevator lurched to a stop and the door slid open. "This way," Singer said. And he strode through a reception area.

Craig trailed after him, feeling like a lost dog.

"Say, Marge?" Singer looked at the woman seated at the desk. "What time is Dr. Hanson's first patient? Nine, isn't it?"

Marge used her pointer finger to touch one of a dozen colored squares on her computer screen. The screen flashed and a new set of squares appeared. "Ah—no. Actually, it's an eye-opener."

"Eight o'clock? Ouch!" Singer pretended to be in pain. He looked hard at Hanson. "I'd say your first order of business is to get on Marge's good side. She's in charge of scheduling." He smiled warmly at Marge. "She doesn't schedule me till nine. The darling. Be nice to her, bring her flowers once in a while—in other words, shamelessly kiss up to her—and maybe she'll do the same for you."

"I like roses," Marge said, offering them both a wicked grin. "Your schedule and patient files are on your terminal, Dr. Hanson," she told him politely.

"Terminal?"

"We're high-tech here," Singer boasted. "Bill is into automation. Everything's computerized. Even the treatment sessions."

Craig looked at him, wondering how a session could be computerized.

"You'll get the hang of it," Singer assured him. "It's all voice and touch activated. Tutorials are built in. No typing skills necessary." Here he paused to chuckle. "Before long, your desktop terminal will be your best friend."

"Incidentally," Marge added with a warm smile, "welcome aboard. We're pleased to have you at the Institute."

"Thank you."

Singer stepped into the hallway and aimed a thumb at the closest door. "There you go. I'm down here." The same thumb pointed further down the hall. "If you have a problem, don't hesitate to pop over. Bill should be by later to give you the new employee speech and a brief orientation."

"Okay," Hanson nodded, reaching for the doorknob to his new office.

"Say, if you're free for lunch, why don't you let me take you out. My treat."

"Okay, sure. Sounds good."

"Well, I'll let you prep for that eye-opener." Here his face took on a lopsided smile, as if to say *better you than me, pal.*

———————————

"You make it sound like all this happened yesterday," Susan interrupted. "How can you recall all the details?"

Hanson shrugged. "You don't forget your first day at a new job. Especially this new job."

———————————

The office was impressive. It was larger than he'd expected, and well furnished. Everything looked new, and everything, aside from a weird abstract next to the window, suited his taste: the medium-sized oak desk, the comfortable leather armchairs, and the handsome leather couch. Built-in bookshelves lined most of two walls, and out the double-wide picture window was an impressive view of Pikes Peak. Not bad. Not bad at all.

He set his briefcase down behind the desk and tried out the chair. It felt good. Just the right height and padding.

"Coffee?"

He looked up to see Marge standing in the doorway, holding a tray filled with attractive mugs bearing the Institute's logo.

"I'd love some."

Marge presented the tray, offered cream and sugar—which Craig refused—and then retreated.

"Black . . . Dr. Hanson likes his black," she mumbled as she left.

Leaning back in the chair, Craig examined his new computer. A run-of-the-mill PC, apparently, no different from his Packard Bell back home, except for the tiny, rainbow-colored symbol decorating the base of the monitor: an apple with a bite out of it. He leaned over to turn it on.

"Good morning, Dr. Hanson," a synthesized voice greeted, before his hand had reached the switch.

Craig stared suspiciously at the screen. It had come to life of its own accord, a swirl of colors erupting in intricate patterns. In the lower left corner, just out of the range of the screen saver, were the words: "System Operational."

"Would you like to view your appointment schedule?" the voice asked.

"Sure."

"Please define this term. Is it affirmative or negative?"

"Affirmative."

"Sure," the computer repeated in a voice that resembled Hanson's. "Affirmative."

There was a whirring sound as the hard drive went to work.

"Please enter your security code and password, Dr. Hanson," the voice told him.

Craig frowned at the screen. Code? Password?

There was a tap at the door.

"Come in."

It was Marge. "I'm sorry about that. I completely forgot to mention the security barriers."

"How did you know that I was—"

"My computer told me," she explained. Then she noticed the look on his face. "Don't worry. I won't always know what you're up to. No one can eavesdrop once you're up and running. The system is programmed to ensure patient/therapist confidentiality. It's just that, since this is your first day and your data branch is new, the system alerted me that someone was attempting to enter virgin territory."

Craig looked up at her, not sure he understood what she was trying to say.

"Ask the computer for help. It will assign you a random code and password."

"It will?"

She nodded, smiled, and left.

Whatever. Craig pursed his lips. "Help," he said, feeling rather foolish talking to an inanimate object.

"How may I help you, Dr. Hanson?"

"I need an access code and a password," he told it.

"Of course," the voice replied politely.

Two seconds later a number appeared on the screen: *22763AHD.* Below it was a word: *Stallion.*

"Please memorize these," the computer instructed. "You will be issued a new code and password each week. I do not advise writing them down."

Tough, Craig thought, scribbling the number and word on a Post-it.

"Okay . . . Now I want to open my schedule."

"Please enter your code and password, Dr. Hanson."

"But I just—"

"It is still a necessary security precaution," the synthesized voice explained.

Craig shook his head at the thing. Nothing like a smart computer. "22763AHD," he read from his Post-it. "Stallion."

The hard disk whirred, and a split second later a collage of colors and rectangles presented itself. At the top of the screen, bold type declared this to be: Dr. Hanson's Schedule, October 4.

He studied the information. Patient names . . . reference numbers . . . note time . . . It was all there.

"How do I—"

"You may access patient files by voice or touch command," the computer explained, somehow anticipating his question.

He reached up and tapped the first slot.

The schedule suddenly disappeared, replaced by a menu.

"Session notes . . . MRT unit . . . Chart . . . ," he read, running his finger down the list.

The computer chirped at him. "Please select one item at a time, Dr. Hanson."

He sighed, already sure that he and this electronic box were not going to be "best friends," as Singer had promised.

"Chart," he barked at it.

A patient chart magically appeared. It looked just like a regular old-fashioned chart, except that it was encased behind the glass screen. Hanson scanned the information, using his forefinger to scroll down the page.

Female. Single. Forty-two years old. In therapy for twenty-four weeks. Under the care of Dr. Sidney Binker—the man Hanson had replaced. Binker had diagnosed the patient as suffering from SRA—satanic ritual abuse. A paragraph later, Hanson found the catalyst events that had apparently caused a sudden manifestation of what Binker assumed were repressed memories: two recent deaths in the family.

He scrolled on. Not finding what he was looking for, he opened the Sessions file. Craig was amazed at the detail. Somehow, the computer had recorded and transcribed each and every session. Incredible.

Binker's closing comments were there as well. His predecessor had tracked the patient's progress, recording significant issues and citing breakthroughs, with thorough, concise notes. Still, after scrolling through nearly a half-dozen sessions, he hadn't found anything to suggest that the patient was an SRA victim.

There. In session 8. Binker had entered a note in the space designated for comments. It said simply: "Patient has experienced flashback episodes."

Craig scrolled forward, looking for other telltale signs that would have alerted Binker to the possibility of ritual abuse. He found a note about the patient's fear of horror films and novels. There was another that talked about a nightmare. A third made reference to a midnight encounter with a demon. Another mentioned a fear of enclosed spaces.

Taken as a whole, these bits of information seemed to suggest a childhood trauma, possibly even a scarring sexual event. But SRA?

He reached session 24 and paused. There was a tiny V encased in a small square down in the bottom corner of the note.

"Wonder what that is?" he muttered.

"You have a question, Dr. Hanson?" the computer asked helpfully.

Well, now that you ask . . . "What's that square with a V in it?" He tapped the icon.

"That is the designation for a video notation. Would you like to view it?"

"Sure."

The hard drive whirred. Suddenly a face—Dr. Binker's, Craig assumed—appeared on the screen.

"The patient has exhibited classic characteristics of an SRA survivor," the talking head announced in stereo sound. "Therefore, I plan to take her into the MRT unit next week in order to confirm the diagnosis and begin confrontation treatment."

"What's the MRT unit?" Hanson wondered aloud.

"I am sorry, Dr. Hanson," the computer replied. "I do not have the capacity to answer your question. Please avoid abbreviations, define your terms more clearly, and explain your question."

"Never mind."

A tone sounded. "Your eight o'clock appointment is here, Dr. Hanson," the synthesized voice told him.

"Nothing like being totally unprepared," he mumbled.

"Please repeat your statement, Dr. Hanson. I was unable to—"

"I wasn't talking to you. Leave me alone."

"Yes, Dr. Hanson." The screen went blank.

There was a tap at the door. Craig made a mental note to ask Singer about the MRT unit, then rose to answer it.

FIVE

"AND THAT'S THE FIRST TIME YOU MET HER?" Susan asked, furiously scribbling notes.

"Yeah." Hanson nodded.

"Okay." She paused to survey her pad. "Tell me about this SRA business. What is satanic ritual abuse?"

"Good question," Hanson retorted. "Unfortunately, I don't have a good answer for you." He paused, thinking. "By definition, it's a post-traumatic syndrome experienced by patients who have been victims of ritual abuse."

"And what constitutes 'ritual abuse'?"

Hanson took a deep breath. "Okay. The scenario goes something like this. There are these groups running around, transgenerational cults who engage in secret ceremonies that honor Satan. They're closet devil worshipers. They go to the office by day, engage in sick religious festivals by night."

"Why is it that these cults aren't ever exposed? I haven't noticed the FBI breaking up any secret rings of Satanists. How do they remain secret?"

"Code of silence," Hanson explained. "They threaten their members with death and torture. And they invoke potent forms of brainwashing."

The skeptical expression on her face changed to one of disbelief.

"Anyway," Hanson continued, "these ceremonies involve unthinkable, barbaric acts of violence: sacrificing animals, gang-raping women, burying people alive—"

48

"Burying people alive?" Susan gasped.

Hanson nodded. "And that's just a sampling. The list of atrocities goes on and on."

"That's—that's horrible," she said, making a face.

"Yes, it is," Hanson agreed. "And as a result of these abuses, the victims suffer severe, debilitating emotional and spiritual damage. In order to deal with the trauma, they tend to bury the memories deep in their subconscious. It's called 'going numb.' The clinical term is 'dissociation.' The victims move away from the event, psychologically distancing themselves from it. They basically deny and hide the experience, pretending that it never happened, until they reach a place where they can recall and deal with it in a safer environment—usually decades later, as an adult. It's a survival mechanism."

Susan shook her head in disgust. "How common is SRA?"

Hanson shrugged. "I have no idea. I'm not even convinced that it exists."

"But you just said—"

"You wanted to know what it was. That's it. Whether it's a reality or a myth is another thing altogether."

Susan considered this. "You think it's contrived?"

Hanson shrugged again. "It's anybody's guess. I won't go so far as to say it's a complete farce. I've seen a few cases that were probably genuine. But even those lacked any hard evidence. I don't doubt that there are some bizarre religious groups out there engaging in sexual/violent rituals. But I have a hard time swallowing the idea that there is a permanent infrastructure of satanic cults that practice this behavior on a regular basis.

"My theory is that many so-called SRA survivors were subjected to more 'common' forms of abuse—incest, rape, various forms of physical and emotional mistreatment. Though these abuses are not 'satanic' in nature, they are nevertheless traumatic and can cause serious psychological wounds. Therefore, the victim turns to evil metaphors in order to deal with the pain.

"There's one thing I'm certain of: SRA has become a pop psychology phenom—a catchall for nearly every emotional problem that comes through the door. If you're suffering from any form of codependency or addiction, if you have dysfunctional relationships or intense phobias, there are therapists out there who are ready to slap an SRA label on you. It's a vague syndrome at best anyway, so it can be applied to nearly everyone with equal success, thereby alleviating patients from personal responsibility. It's always nice to have someone or something to blame for the way you are. And it's especially handy when that someone is Satan.

"The scariest thing about it is that the entire recovered memories movement is feelings oriented."

"Feelings oriented?"

"Yeah. If you feel bad, then someone probably did something bad to you when you were little. You just don't remember it. In fact, not remembering the abuse is sometimes considered proof of abuse—or so the misguided logic goes. And the way you feel dictates the direction of your therapy. The therapist starts to dig, looking specifically for a buried event that could be causing the emotional distress. With a bit of creative prodding, a little hypnosis here, some prayer therapy there, several leading suggestions—suddenly you gain access to this cache of repressed memories. And coincidentally, they all point to SRA.

"Both sides of the controversy have been documented," Hanson told her. "I could recommend some books."

"Okay." She listened as he listed off a dozen titles. When he was finished, she examined her pad again. "So Ruth Sanders was an SRA victim?"

"They're called survivors," he clarified. "And yes, she seemed to be. At least from Dr. Binker's notes."

"Did you disagree with his diagnosis?"

"Not at first. But later, when I had a chance to review the entire case, I changed my mind."

"Why?"

"I've got this case that's perplexing me," Craig began.

"*Perplexing* you?" Singer interrupted. "You've only been here a couple of weeks."

"Almost a month."

"Whatever. Not long enough to be perplexed. Bothered. Vexed maybe. Even in a quandary. But not perplexed."

Craig frowned at him. Singer was turning out to be a real smart aleck. A friendly smart aleck, but a smart aleck just the same. They had agreed to meet at Starbucks after work for a latte, something that was quickly becoming a habit.

"Okay," Singer relented. "What's the problem?"

"It's this female patient."

Singer started nodding. "She's got a crush on you."

"No."

"You've got a crush on her—that's even worse. Separated from some gorgeous young thing by a stuffy old set of professional ethics."

"No." He squinted at Singer. "Besides, I'm a Christian, so—"

"Yeah, yeah, so am I." Singer frowned. "Then what is it?"

"Shut up and I'll tell you."

Singer sipped his latte glumly.

"It's one of Binker's people. Diagnosed SRA."

"That's a tricky one. Most overused diagnosis going nowadays."

"Exactly. So I've been reviewing the notes. And I'm not sure I see it."

"Why not?"

"I don't know. The symptoms are just too vague."

"Flashbacks?"

"Yeah." Craig nodded. "But I have to wonder if Binker helped manufacture them."

"Possible. Doesn't sound like Binker though. He was good. Did he do a Minnesota Multiphasic?"

"Yeah. He ran the MMPI her first week. Used art therapy too."

"And?"

"I wouldn't call any of it conclusive. The Personality Inventory showed some SRA tendencies. But nothing cut and dried. And the art . . . It was dark, blacks and reds. But the woman lost a husband and a son in a three-year period. I'd be surprised if her drawings *weren't* morose."

"Body memories?" Singer asked. "Any strange scars or weird physical sensations?"

Craig shook his head.

They both sat there, staring out the window at the deepening twilight.

"Has she been in the MRT unit?" Singer finally asked.

"With Binker."

"You haven't had her in there?"

"No."

"Why not?"

Hanson shrugged. "I don't know. I'm just not comfortable with it yet. I feel incompetent in there. Besides, I'm not certain it achieves any practical results. I need to read up on it in the journals."

"It's not that complicated. And even if you don't have the slightest idea what you're doing, the patients will never know."

"Maybe not."

"As for results, I can testify that the unit works."

"Really?"

"You bet. It's the best thing since the twelve-step program."

Craig frowned at this, not sure he knew enough about MRT to make an intelligent analysis.

"What about this lady's therapy journal?" Singer asked.

"Journal?"

"Yeah," Singer nodded. "You've been through it, haven't you?"

"I'm not sure she has one."

"Of course she does," Singer snorted. "Every patient at the Institute keeps one. They have to. It's part of their therapy contract. No diary, no treatment."

"I never heard anything about that."

"Trust me, it's policy. The administration claims it's for therapeutic purposes—you know, that keeping a journal helps people work things out, blah, blah, blah. Personally, I think it's PR motivated."

"PR?"

"Sure. When a patient makes a miraculous recovery, then the Institute can pull out quotes from the diary—with the patient's written consent, of course—and show the world just how bad off they were pre-cure."

"I'll have to ask my patient about—"

Singer shook his head. "It's on your computer."

"It is?"

"Yeah. Marge scans everybody's diary once a week, loads them directly into the system. I'm surprised Sam didn't mention it."

Hanson shook his head. His wife hadn't spoken much about her therapy sessions—good, bad, or indifferent.

"How's she doing, anyway?"

"The same."

"That's tough."

They sat in silence, watching foot and vehicular traffic pass by outside.

Taking a last slurp of his latte, Craig rose to leave. "I'd better get going. Catch you later, Grant."

"Where you off to?"

"Back to the Institute."

Less then twenty minutes later Craig was sitting behind his desk, talking to his computer.

"Show me Ruth Sanders's file."

"Please enter your security code and password, Dr. Hanson."

Craig complied, reading them from the Post-it in his top drawer, then waited as the hard drive went into action. Moments later a menu appeared. Chart, Sessions, Billing, Text . . .

"Where's her diary?" he muttered.

"Choose Text," the computer told him.

He obeyed, tapping Text with his finger.

Suddenly a book appeared on the screen. It had a burgundy cover and was inscribed with ornate gold letters: Ruth's Diary.

"Open," he commanded.

The cover swung back, just like a real book. Inside were pages bearing a neat cursive script.

Craig scanned the first few entries. They dealt with surface feelings, occasionally alluding to the death of her husband. The son, Zachary, wasn't mentioned.

Turning pages by touching a tiny icon of an open book, he perused the material. More general feelings. The sort of thing you would expect from a grieving woman who was starting therapy and had been asked to record her emotions. Journaling was difficult for some patients. Especially at first. It took time to allow yourself to be honest, to pour out your innermost thoughts, chronicling mood swings, disturbing memories, and raw wounds hidden below the polished exterior of normalcy.

After speeding through a half-dozen entries, Craig found one that referred to a flashback. It was only a fragment, pieces of feelings and a brief but nightmarish vision of a demonlike figure. It was significant not because it suggested the possibility of post-traumatic stress disorder (PTSD)—it would take more than a single episode to evidence something so serious—but because of when it occurred. According to Sanders, she had experienced the flashback on the way home, the night she had found Zachary dead. She was retelling it now, months later, in her journal, probably because it felt like a safe place to do so. She was learning, as many patients did, that a diary is the world's best listener—never judgmental, never condemning, always ready to hear any and everything on your mind.

A possible primer, Craig thought, scrutinizing the entry. SRA survivors commonly experienced flashbacks and dreams before recovering memories of abuse. These phenomena were thought to be a way in which the unconscious nudged the conscious mind, gently signaling that it was time to face the forgotten events.

Three entries later, Sanders returned to Zachary, spending a paragraph on how his death had affected her. It was clear that she was slowly coming to grips with his death and the grief associated with it.

The next entry was more detailed. The following one, even more so. Craig read the account with both a professional interest and a morbid curiosity. From Sanders's perspective, Zachary had been almost godlike, a flawless child who had matured into a flawless teen. She told of his commitment to Christ at the early age of nine, of his ever-expanding love for Jesus, of his constant, insatiable hunger for God. According to Sanders, in recent years this quest had taken the form of music and computers. Apparently, Zachary had been something of a virtuoso on the guitar, and a talented hacker—the equivalent of a virtuoso—on-line.

The entry ended with Sanders asking the eternal question: Why? Why had Zach killed himself?

Craig had seen Sanders five times since his arrival at the Institute. But she had yet to even speak Zach's name, much less talk about the suicide. It was too early in their doctor/patient relationship to expect that. Craig was going slowly, building trust, being careful not to push her too hard, too fast. He would let her choose the pace and control the subject matter until she felt comfortable dealing with Zach's death.

So the information he was gleaning from the diary was fascinating. Zach had committed suicide—Craig knew that much from Binker's notes. But as for the details . . .

The next entry was long and explicit, a written catharsis. Sanders had put the entire evening—the evening of Zach's death—on paper: her feelings, her memories, the experience, even the scene of the suicide itself.

Craig cringed at the account. Sanders described Zach's pale, lifeless face, his eyes, the way his body hung from the guitar cord, the satanic emblem carved on his chest—just reading it made Craig slightly nauseous. He could only imagine how writing it had made Sanders feel.

In the next entry, Sanders seemed to regress. She was back to denial, questioning why the tragedy had occurred, even questioning whether it had happened at all. She had penned an emotional essay extolling Zach's virtues, claiming that he was neither inclined toward nor capable of taking his own life. She even went so far as to suggest that Zach had been murdered.

Craig shook his head. Then an idea struck him. The satanic symbol on Zach's chest—did that have something to do with Binker's diagnosis? Craig had initially wondered if Binker had *moved* Sanders toward the concept of SRA. But maybe it was the other way around. Maybe Sanders, unable to accept Zach's suicide, had convinced first herself and then Binker that someone else had killed him. But the devil?

The following entry answered some of Craig's questions. Once again, Ruth described the scene in Zach's room the night of his death, but this time in more detail and almost clinically, without emotion, listing the facts of her son's death like a detective discussing a case. A heavy metal CD espousing suicide had been found playing on Zach's stereo. Zach's body had been defaced, an inverted cross etched over his heart. He had hanged himself. The CD, Sanders said, was not Zach's. He owned only "godly grunge"—not worldly, devilish music. The symbol, Sanders explained, was a sign found on victims of satanic sacrifice. She had obviously done research into the subject. As for the guitar cord with which he'd been hung, Sanders had no explanation. But she once again insisted that Zach had been a happy, healthy, well-adjusted kid with a strong faith and solid sense of right and wrong. In other words, he never would have committed suicide.

Craig reread Sanders's argument. It was clear, logical—frankly, it made sense. But that was to be expected. Zach's suicide had clearly taken her by surprise. Now she was trying to deny or rationalize or explain it away as something other than what it was. That was a natural reaction to an unexpected trauma, the mind's attempt to soften the blow.

That's the way teen suicide usually is, Craig thought. *Parents are often oblivious to the signs that their teenager is in trouble—until it's too late. And then they have to figure out a way to deal with the indescribable pain, the shame, and the guilt that plagues them, causing them to wonder if it was their fault, if there was some way they could have prevented it.*

Craig skipped over two more entries that discussed trouble Sanders was having concentrating at work. Then he stopped. The next entry was like something out of a horror film.

I was standing at the top of a flight of stairs. There was light above me, darkness below. I remember I didn't want to go down the stairs. But suddenly, someone pushed me from behind. I fell, tumbling down the steps, into the black pit. I got up and tried to go back up the stairs. But they had disappeared. For a long time, I just stood there. Then I heard someone laughing. It sounded like a child. So I began inching my way along. I couldn't see anything. I followed the wall. It was cold and wet. Then I reached a door.

When I opened it, I found a small room bathed in warm, golden light. I looked around and saw that the light came from hundreds of candles that had been placed in a wide circle. There was a group of small children—maybe ten kids—squatting at the center of the circle. They were giggling and playing a game. Jacks, I think. One of them looked up at me and smiled as I approached. I remember the way he watched me . . . There was something strange about his eyes. Then he motioned to me, inviting me into the circle of light. But I hesitated. I was scared. I didn't want to go. Then I felt another push from behind. I tripped and rolled. The next thing I knew, I was on all fours, at the center of the circle. The children were standing now, huddled over me. Except that they weren't children anymore. They were giants in black, hooded robes. And their eyes were on fire. They stared down at me with wicked grins, cackling and howling. I screamed at them. Then one of them pulled out a long, curved knife.

And that's all I remember. Then I woke up . . . thank God.

Susan shook her head at Hanson. "I find it absolutely amazing that you can recount all this without notes." Actually, she was thinking that it was a little too amazing. Was this story for real? Or was this guy making it up as he went along?

"I have a photographic memory," he admitted.

"Must come in handy." Susan jotted that down in the margin. "Okay, so you were looking at Ruth Sanders's diary," she reviewed, "finding some pretty nasty stuff."

Hanson nodded his agreement. "Nasty is a good word for it."

Craig scrolled through the next four entries. They were all the same: graphically violent dreams involving circles, candles, happy children, knife-wielding giants in black hoods and robes, basements, dark holes, feelings of terror . . . The symbolism seemed straightforward, even to a psychiatrist who wasn't big on dream analysis. The circles and candles were like those used in satanic rituals. The children probably represented the facade of normalcy that these cults were supposedly able to maintain. According to some researchers—those who supported SRA therapy—cult members were often respected, upstanding members of the community: doctors, lawyers, accountants, church elders. They seemed regular—even happy—by day, and became bloodthirsty Satanists by night. Or so some people believed. Their gigantic size was a reference to their authority, control, and power over Sanders. Being shoved down stairs could represent an attempt by Sanders's subconscious to move her toward recognition of her memories—memories that had been buried somewhere underground. The fear—that was the emotion that was keeping her from facing the memories. It could even have been a sign of cult programming, a cue to ensure her silence.

Sure enough, immediately after the dreams in Ruth's journal, Craig found the memories themselves. They were even more vivid, naming dates, locations, even members of Sanders' own family that had participated in bizarre and perverse ceremonies. In one such entry, she described being made to watch a human sacrifice—a baby being murdered. In another she was buried alive in a coffin. In another she was forced to participate in the mutilation of a cat. In another, she was threatened with death if she exposed the cult, and an inverted cross was carved into the skin above her heart.

Craig read the entries with a mixture of horror and skepticism. There was something about it . . . Something about the way Sanders had moved from grief over her son's death to acknowledgment that she was an SRA survivor. The transition was too abrupt, too severe. The progression seemed to have taken place at high speed, on fast-forward. SRA victims didn't go from no memories on Monday to full-blown memories by Friday. The process of recovering repressed memories—valid or not—was slow and difficult, often requiring years of therapy to accomplish.

And another question plagued him. Why hadn't Binker referenced these diary entries in his chart notes? The man seemed thorough. According to Singer, Binker had been competent. Craig suddenly wondered why Binker had decided to take a sabbatical. Why now? Why walk out on a full caseload? Wouldn't you see at least some of your more serious patients through to healing?

Patients like Ruth Sanders, for instance. He decided to find out why Binker had left. Maybe giving Binker a "sabbatical" was a quiet means of dismissing him, or a nice way of saying that the guy had had a nervous breakdown.

Craig noticed a blinking icon at the bottom of the screen. It was the box with the tiny V inside.

"Let me see the video notation," Craig told his computer.

The hard drive whirred and Binker's face appeared on the screen.

"It has now become quite obvious that SRA is the appropriate diagnosis," Binker said. "I was beginning to have doubts until I took Sanders into the MRT unit." The man shook his head at his unseen audience. "That's what opened the door to the dreams, and soon afterwards, the memories."

Binker disappeared and Craig found himself staring at a fresh page from Sanders's diary.

"The devil is after me," the account declared. The handwriting was ragged, uneven. It bore little resemblance to the neat cursive of the opening entries. "He already came for my son. Now he's coming for me."

Craig sighed at the pronouncement. What was it about the MRT unit that had so accelerated Sanders' memory recovery process? He decided that it was time to find out.

SIX

"WHAT'S THE MRT UNIT?" SUSAN ASKED. NOW ON her second notepad, her hand had begun to tire, and she was silently wishing the authorities at Super Max had consented to the use of a tape recorder. But around here, rules were rules.

Behind her, Campbell was lazily reading the newspaper. Next to him, Rosselli had dozed off.

"MRT stands for Memory Reconstruction Therapy."

Susan shrugged at this. "Which is . . . ?"

Hanson shrugged back. "An advanced therapeutic modality." When the puzzled look on Susan's face didn't change, he added, "A high-tech toy. It's been nicknamed the 'Memory Playground.' Kind of an advanced, psychiatric video game. Cutting-edge technology. Came out in experimental form about six months before I arrived at the Institute. The mental health community is still divided over it. There are so many ethical and moral issues involved. And the testing conducted by the manufacturer is inconclusive, at best." Hanson frowned. "But Dr. Bayers was sold on it from the start. He was convinced that it was an invaluable tool— the greatest therapeutic innovation of the past century.

"I'm still not convinced. But then, that's me—I'm rather conservative. I like to see the results, read the literature, familiarize myself with the studies before I buy into something. Other people, like Dr. Bayers . . ." He lifted his hands in a gesture of befuddlement. "There's always someone willing to try the newest gadget. And there are always those who want that gadget to be a miracle cure, even if it turns out to be Pandora's box."

"So . . . what exactly is Memory Reconstruction Therapy?" Susan tried again.

"It's based on VR technology," Hanson explained, stroking his chin. "Virtual reality." He smiled. Apparently he found her lack of familiarity with the jargon slightly humorous. "You've seen the VR sets that let you play 3-D games in a manufactured, 'virtual' environment, right?"

Susan nodded. "They're using that equipment in schools now."

"Kids take field trips to anywhere in the world—and well beyond—without ever leaving the classroom," Hanson told her. "Med students carve up virtual cadavers. Residents can practice for tough ops on virtual patients. Air traffic controllers use VR in most major airports now. They just slap on the equipment and start guiding virtual representations of real airliners in a 3-D flight space. I have to admit, from what little I know about VR, the practical applications seem limitless."

He paused and stretched his neck. "Well, some VR tech in a computer lab somewhere came up with this brainstorm: Why not make a unit that could help facilitate therapy by recreating troubling situations and memories in a safe, virtual environment?"

"I'm not following you," Susan admitted.

"Back in the early days of VR, they used it to treat phobias. The technology was crude, compared to today. But it was effective. For instance, you could help a patient overcome a fear of heights by placing them on a virtual bridge and—over a series of sessions—have them look over the edge, take steps onto it, cross it, etc."

"And that worked?"

"Quite often."

"And the MRT unit is like that?"

"Much more advanced. Though you wouldn't know it from the looks of the unit itself. The MRT is just this small room crammed with electronic equipment. Almost like a storage closet.

Very unassuming, really. There's a miniature mainframe computer, several racks of gear—gloves, glasses, even a full suit—and this laser platform. The platform looks like a square treadmill, with tiles that move when you walk on them. You don't go anywhere. You just walk in place—kind of like a moving sidewalk. And there's this network of cameras and lasers surrounding the platform. They capture and record your body position and movements at split-second intervals, instantly relaying this information into the virtual environment."

Susan had stopped scribbling. She was looking at Hanson, trying to make sense of this.

"It sounds complicated," Hanson agreed. "But it isn't. It's all tutorial-assisted by the computer—just like the individual terminals. All you do is follow the directions."

───────────────

"Please activate visual and touch-sensitive peripherals," the synthesized voice said.

Craig stood examining the "peripherals." The glasses were more like goggles, dark lenses surrounded by rubber that fit right up against your face. The gloves were strange-looking, dull silver that resembled the mail worn by a knight. He wasn't sure he wanted to put any of it on—and he was certain he didn't want to don the full suit. So he had asked the computer to lead him through what that machine called a "partial reality simulation."

"Please activate visual and touch-sensitive peripherals," the voice repeated.

It was seven in the evening. The Institute was empty, the offices deserted. There was no one there to laugh at him. No one to correct or criticize. It was the perfect time to give the MRT a test drive. If he crashed, big deal.

Craig pulled the gloves on. As he did, he realized that there were no wires connecting them to the mainframe. For that matter, there weren't any trailing from the goggles either.

"Must be a cordless setup," he muttered to himself.

"Do you have a question, Dr. Hanson?" the computer asked.

"Yeah. Where are the cords?"

"Cords?"

"The connections from the glasses and gloves to the—to you."

"The peripherals are cellular, Dr. Hanson. The receiver and transmitter chips do not require physical connections."

"Like I said," he muttered, "cordless."

"Do you have a question, Dr. Hanson?"

"No," he grunted. "I mean yes." He slipped on the goggles and the room disappeared. "What do I do now?"

"Please mount the platform."

Hanson laughed at this. He couldn't see his own hands, much less the platform. Pulling the goggles up, he stepped onto the platform, at the center of the tiles. Then he repositioned the goggles and stared into the black void.

There was a brilliant flash of light. Then darkness. Another flash. Darkness. More flashes. "The laser-directed scanning system is now recording your spatial dimensions," the computer said. "Please remain still for the next twelve seconds."

Craig stood there, feeling stupid. He could imagine what he looked like: a geek in a Lone Ranger mask and Sir Lancelot gloves. This was the next wave of technology?

The computer chirped, and a new world sprang into existence, a full-color world with an eerie three-dimensional plane. Craig was no longer blind, he could see the room around him— a large, brightly lit room washed in a spectrum of pastels.

He moved his head from side to side, then up. Everywhere he looked, he saw color and light. The room, a room he knew to be composed of artificial matter, looked tangible. There was something slightly cartoonish in the angles and perspectives. But his brain was reeling, telling him that what he was experiencing was real.

Raising his right hand, he reached out and touched the wall closest to him. It was hard, like a wall should be. He bent and tapped the floor. Hard. There were even grooves between the tiles.

"Do you require an escort, Dr. Hanson?"

He lifted his head and saw a face hovering across the room, next to the only door. The face had two eyes, a nose, and a mouth, yet its features were smooth and indistinct. It looked as if it had been fashioned out of metal, more of a robot than a person.

"Who are you?"

"I am your guide, if you require one," the face answered with a smile.

"I'm trying out the system," Craig told it suspiciously. There was something about the disembodied face that sent shivers up his spine. "Are you part of the tutorial?"

The face nodded.

"What do I do now?"

"You may exit the system," the face answered. "You may initiate a reconstruction. Or you may view a demonstration."

The demonstration sounded relatively safe.

"Demonstration," Craig said. "Say, what's behind that door?"

The face smiled again. "You are about to find out."

The door swung open and the face flew through it, vanishing into a rectangle of blue/gray static.

"Please follow me, Dr. Hanson."

Craig groaned at this, not sure he wanted to. Besides, he didn't know how to get from one end of the room to the other. He took a tentative step. The door seemed slightly closer. He took another step, then another. A dozen steps later he had reached the door. But he still couldn't see through it. The space in the doorway looked like a television set after the station had signed off.

"Follow me," the face called from beyond the door.

Craig hesitated. Then he remembered that this was all fake, an electronic mirage.

"I'm coming," he replied, stepping through the portal.

The next room materialized. It was a long, windowless hallway. The face was floating at the far end of the hall, waiting. As Craig moved toward it, he noticed that the hall was lined with doors.

"What are these?" he asked, pointing to the first doorway.

"Memory Reconstruction Demonstrations," the face answered. "Each room represents a specific phase of therapeutic treatment."

Craig reached for the first door and was amazed to find that the knob felt solid. He turned it and pushed the door open. Inside, he found himself back in the MRT unit. A faceless, mannequin-like figure in a white clinician's jacket was assisting another face-less figure—one that appeared to be a woman—onto the platform. The former was explaining to the latter the benefits of the unit.

"You will find this experience quite remarkable," the first said. "It simulates your trauma—only as much of it as you feel comfortable with, of course—in a nonthreatening, totally safe environment. At no time will you be in any danger. And you may end the session whenever you feel ready."

The "patient," wearing goggles and gloves, nodded her consent.

"Good, then let's get started," the "doctor" said. And he began to lead her in a meditation exercise. She was instructed to breathe slowly in, then out, inhaling peace and good feelings, exhaling worry and negative energy. The doctor then had her concentrate on various body parts, isolating and cleansing them. Finally, he focused on her mind, drawing her to a state of full relaxation—something akin to a trance.

As the woman stood there, breathing deeply, focusing all of her inner energy on breaking through a "wall of memories," the lasers finally began to flash, the cameras jinking and jiving, recording her body position. Then the scene froze. It looked like a 3-D video that had been put on pause.

"What happened?"

"To continue the demonstration, Dr. Hanson," the face said, "please move to the next room."

Craig did, watching the face out of the corner of his eye as he did. The next room turned out to be just like the first room—empty except for a door. Then a figure materialized—the same faceless female that he had just left in the last demonstration. She stood looking at the room, turning her head to take it all in.

"Are you ready to begin?" It was the metal, robot face.

"Yes," the woman said.

"Please describe the specific memory or trauma you wish to confront."

The woman paused, then began to relate a childhood incident of abuse, explaining how her drunken father had verbally berated her, then beaten her with a belt.

The face kept asking for more details and the woman kept supplying them: the time of day, the way the room was decorated, what her father looked like, the tone of his voice, the feelings the event had produced in her . . .

When the interview was over, the face led the woman through the door.

"To continue the demonstration, Dr. Hanson," the voice said, "please move to the next room."

The demonstration was interesting, but Craig was getting tired of traipsing from room to room. There had to be a more efficient method of presentation.

When he reached the next room, it was blank. There was no color or sound. Just the woman standing in the middle.

"Are you ready to begin?" the face asked her.

"Yes."

The room went dark, then blinked back into being. This time it looked like the bedroom of a small child: toys scattered on the floor, dolls on a shelf, a flowered bedspread—just as the woman had described earlier. A moment later, there was a stomping sound. A fist pounded against the door, and a man entered the room. His face was cloaked in shadow, but he was large, very muscular, as the woman had said. And he was staggering, obviously drunk.

Craig watched as the man shouted at the woman, slurring his words, then pulled off his belt and struck her. The abuse continued, following the pattern and scenario set down by the woman.

Suddenly it was over and the woman was back in the MRT unit, the doctor at her side. He helped her out of the goggles and gloves and led her to a chair. Then, in a soothing voice, he began asking her questions. It was not unlike a debriefing session: probing for answers, while continually reassuring her that she was safe.

Craig left the room. The face was waiting for him back in the hallway.

———————————

"Wait a minute." Susan held her hand up. "You can still recall all the details? The images you saw in the MRT? The specific demonstrations? Everything?"

Hanson nodded. "I told you. I have a—"

"Oh, that's right," she said rather glibly. "A photographic memory."

He glared at her. "You don't believe me, do you? You think I'm making all this up."

"No, it's just that . . ." She sighed heavily. "Never mind. Keep going."

Frowning, he continued. "So anyway, then I asked the face what I was supposed to do now."

———————————

"You may exit the system," the face said. "You may—"

"Do you record patient sessions? Real ones, I mean. Not demonstrations."

"Yes."

"Can I call up a specific session from a specific patient?"

"Yes."

Craig waited. "That's what I want to do."

"Please enter your password and code, Dr. Hanson," the face said.

Craig sighed at this. "I already did. That's how I got into the system."

"Please enter your password and code, Dr. Hanson," the face repeated.

"Okay," he groaned. Then he realized that he couldn't see the slip of paper he had written them on. It was in his wallet, and he was wearing those blasted goggles.

He tried three times before he got it right.

"Please enter the patient's name," the face said, still staring down at him from the end of the hallway.

"Sanders. Ruth Sanders."

"Accessing," the face said. "Session number?"

Craig considered this. "I'm not sure."

"Session number?"

"How about . . . one," Craig tried, for lack of anything better.

The hallway disappeared and Craig found himself back in the MRT unit again. There was Sanders, standing on the platform, her goggles and gloves already in place. He could hear but not see Binker.

"Inhale," Binker was saying. "And exhale. Breathe in the Spirit. Breathe out sin. Breathe in love, joy, peace . . . Breathe out worry, tension, fear . . ."

Sanders was following his directions, breathing slowly, smoothly.

"Imagine yourself in God's presence," Binker continued. "His Word says that by the blood of Jesus, you have been washed white as snow and are now worthy to enter into the Holy of Holies. Picture yourself before the throne. Remember that God is abundant in mercy, that his loving-kindness has no end. It has no boundaries. His love is limitless.

"He is beckoning you," Binker said in a calm, sedate voice. "'Come, my child, and enter into my rest. Know my peace. Let me embrace you.'

"Let him," Binker encouraged. "Let God embrace you. Let him wrap his loving arms around you. Sit on his lap and allow him to hold you."

Sanders was silent, apparently following Binker's directives.

It struck Craig as odd and mildly amusing that Binker was employing this technique for relaxation. It wasn't unprecedented. Scores of other Christian mental health professionals commonly used it. But it was nevertheless ironic. TM—transcendental meditation—and hypnosis were no-no's in Protestant circles. That the MRT demonstration had shown a woman being led through relaxation exercises was probably only because it was developed by a secular manufacturer. The Institute certainly would not have condoned it. Yet a sizable segment of these same Christians saw nothing wrong with practicing a sanitized version of meditative hypnotherapy. And that was precisely what "prayer-based visualization" amounted to. The key to its acceptability seemed to be the substitution of prayer for meditation and positive visualization—involving God—for hypnosis and mind-control techniques.

When Sanders had achieved a state Binker referred to as "enlarged faith"—Christianese for an altered state of consciousness—the unit went into action. The lasers flashed, the cameras adjusted and readjusted. In the next instant, Ruth Sanders was in the entryway room with Craig, the invisible voyeur, at her side. Together they looked up at the face.

"Are you ready to begin, Ruth?" it asked, eyes fixed on Sanders.

"Yes," she said sleepily.

"Please describe the specific memory or trauma you wish to confront."

Sanders paused. "I don't have any specific memories. And trauma . . . I don't know."

"Please describe your feelings at this moment," the face suggested.

"I feel . . . calm, peaceful. On the surface at least. Way down inside, I'm still . . . avoiding the pain, I suppose. I don't want to confront it. I don't want to deal with it."

"Why?" the face asked.

"It hurts too much," she answered, on the verge of crying. "I just want to bury all the hurt. Throw it all in a bottomless well somewhere and never have to feel it again."

The door below the face opened. "Follow me please, Ruth." And the face was gone.

Sanders took a deep breath, then moved toward the door. Another deep breath, and she was stepping through it into nothingness. Craig followed.

It was dark for a few seconds. Then a dim light faded into view. It was a candle. A single candle surrounded by a field of black. Sanders approached it. Suddenly the darkness began to move. It was seething with arms and legs, limbs twisted and tangled. Just beyond the reach of the candle, faces began to materialize: eyes here, a mouth over there, teeth, tongues, sneers . . . And then the mumbling started. There were no clear words, not even succinct voices. Just murmurs and groans, like gusts of wind beating against a rickety old gate.

The light of the candle grew in intensity, revealing a circle of hooded figures. They were chanting something, marching counterclockwise around a small bundle on the floor. The bundle moved. The blanket slipped, and the face of a kitten peered out through innocent eyes.

The light continued to grow. Now the room had taken on a red glow. There was something on the walls. It looked like paint, still wet. It was trickling down, forming vermilion puddles on the concrete floor.

The marchers stopped abruptly. One stepped forward, his face hidden beneath his hood. Reaching inside an oversized sleeve, he pulled something out—a knife. A huge knife with a long, curving blade.

The chanting had fallen away. The room was silent—except for the kitten, meowing softly. The figure nearest the cat raised the knife over his head. As he did, his hood slid back, revealing a mouth filled with long white fangs.

"Stop!"

The shout echoed through the room, causing the scene to ripple, then vanish.

They were back in the MRT unit. Ruth was panting, gasping for air. She tore off her glasses and her gloves, dismounting awkwardly. But before she evaded the view of the cameras, Craig saw the look on her face, the expression of sheer terror.

"Would you like to view another session, Dr. Hanson?" It was the face. Craig was back in the hallway.

"No," he answered, disgusted by what he had just experienced. "How did that—how did that happen?"

"Please rephrase your question, Dr. Hanson. How did *what* happen?"

"How did the computer do that?" he demanded.

"The visual and audio stimuli were generated using a program designed to simulate the actual experience as closely as possible in a safe environment," it explained. "If you were to activate the total-body peripheral, the program would incorporate full olfactory and audio/visual stimuli, as well as various mild pain sensations—"

"Pain?!"

"If sexual or violent abuse is the source of trauma, the program works to recreate those experiences in a safe environment."

Craig shook his head at it all. "But Ruth didn't even describe the scene for you. She said she didn't *have* any memories."

"The program manufactures memories based on the emotions described by the patient and the data supplied by the therapist."

"It does what?"

"If no memories are available, the program generates plausible memories based on studies, research, and treatment of patients suffering from similar disorders."

"How?"

"The emotions are run against a correlation of syndromes and cross-referenced with the diagnosis supplied by the attending mental health professional."

"It 'manufactures' memories?" Craig could hardly believe his ears.

"Yes. Based on a complex correlation of—"

"Enough," he told it. "I want out."

"You wish to exit the system, Dr. Hanson?" the face asked politely.

"Yeah. I want out. Now!" He didn't wait to be directed back through the hall or the room. Instead he ripped off the goggles and left the platform.

"Dr. Hanson," the computer said. "You must enter your password and code in order to activate the shutdown mechan—"

Craig silenced the voice with a firm tug on the power cord. Booting it back up might cause the tech grief in the morning. But at that moment, Craig didn't particularly care.

SEVEN

Y OU'RE SAYING THAT, IN YOUR OPINION, THIS MRT thing is unreliable?" Susan asked.

Hanson looked at her incredulously. "In my opinion, it's a monster. Hypnotherapy is unreliable. Age regression is unreliable. Memory Reconstruction Therapy? I'd say it's downright dangerous."

He paused to let that sink in. "I later learned that all of Sanders's early MRT sessions were computer- and doctor-enhanced. In other words, she didn't have any memories of SRA, so they helpfully filled in the gaps. And by putting her into a suggestive state before starting the treatment—" Hanson shook his head. "That's what caused me to suspect—"

"Ms. Gant?" It was Marshal Campbell. "It's time to go."

"Can you give me just a couple more minutes?" she asked. "We're right in the middle of something."

Campbell looked at one of the guards on the other side of the partition. The guard frowned and shook his head. "Nope," Campbell said. "That's it for today."

She shrugged apologetically at Hanson. "Sorry, Craig. We'll have to start there tomorrow. Okay?"

Hanson nodded glumly. The guards jerked him from his seat and efficiently "assisted" him through the door.

"I wanna go back to Denver," Tony whined. "I've got a date."

"Tony Rosselli: ladies' man," Campbell teased.

"Why can't we go back to Denver?" Tony asked.

Campbell shot a thumb at the backseat. "It's Ms. Gant's show. Ask her."

"Ms. Gant," Tony said politely, craning his neck. "What do you say we head back to Denver? It's not that far. We can drive back down here in the morning."

Susan looked up from her file, absentmindedly. "Huh?"

"I've got a date with this incredibly gorgeous—"

"You mentioned staying in Florence," Campbell said. "Is that still the plan, Ms. Gant?"

She nodded.

Tony's face fell and he groaned as if in pain.

"But you guys don't have to," she said.

"Yes, we do, ma'am," Campbell said. "We're assigned to you— for the duration."

Tony groaned again, this time even more melodramatically.

"Florence has Motel 6 and Travelodge," Campbell announced. "We can be at either one in ten minutes. Got a preference?"

"No. As long as it's not a fleabag."

"Not much choice around here, ma'am."

"Her name's Bambi," Tony said dreamily.

"Bambi?" Campbell laughed. "Sounds like a stripper. Or a hooker."

At the motel, Susan took a quick shower, then pulled on an oversized T-shirt. It felt good to be clean again—clean and away from Super Max. What a depressing place.

She turned on the TV and climbed into bed to review her notes, suddenly wishing she had a bottle of Pepto-Bismol. Dinner had been a greasy hamburger and a bag of soggy fries. Indigestion city. The company hadn't been great either. Campbell and Rosselli had insisted on accompanying her but had spent the entire time talking sports, cars, and women—discussing Rosselli's near miss with Bambi in great detail.

She paged through her notepads, scanning the material. The more she thought about her interview with Hanson, the more it disturbed her. Hanson had turned out to be less of a nut than she had expected, despite the first impression he'd made with his talk of Satan and God and Job. From that point on, he'd seemed relatively sane, even sincere. But was he reliable? Was he telling the truth, or had all of that been an elaborate fiction? And his story—yuck! Devils, hooded characters with knives, horrific flashbacks, grotesque 3-D memories . . . She'd never even heard of satanic ritual abuse before today. And she wasn't sure she ever wanted to again. Unfortunately, she had no choice. Tomorrow it was back to the Max, to pick up where they had left off.

There was a thud outside. It startled Susan until she realized that it had just been a car door. Then she laughed at herself. Her nerves were obviously frazzled. A few more bumps in the night and she'd be pounding on the marshals' door, demanding protection.

She uttered a mock prayer to a God she hadn't spoken to in nearly ten years and returned to her notes. Susan didn't go to church. Not anymore. She had given up that habit sometime in college, when it had become impractical because she wasn't sure where to go and often didn't have the time. Most of her friends had scoffed at the notion of religious affiliation anyway. Slowly, subtly, she had lost all desire for things religious. Her parents, on the other hand, were still almost hyperspiritual. They went to church whenever the doors were open. Throughout her childhood, they had dragged her along. And somehow, she knew that their devotion was more than just an obsession, more than just a bondage to the strict laws of the Bible. They genuinely believed that Jesus was God's only Son, that he had come to earth, died on a cross, and risen to redeem mankind. Susan had believed that once, too.

As she stared mindlessly at the television—at a sitcom she didn't recognize—Susan recalled the night she had confessed Jesus as Savior. It had been at a Sunday evening service. She was ten.

Though she couldn't recall the pastor's sermon, she remembered that it made her feel guilty. Why his words had penetrated her defenses that night, unlike the endless string of sermons on the Sundays preceding it, she had no idea. But for whatever reason, by the end of the service, she was well aware that she was a sinner destined for hell. When the altar call was issued and the congregation began singing a closing hymn, she stepped into the aisle and went forward, following the pastor's persistent urging: to confess her sins and receive Jesus. A few days later she was baptized, promising to serve God for the rest of her earthly days.

Had she really meant it? Probably. At the time. Of course, children often made promises they weren't destined to keep. Was the experience valid? Maybe. More relevantly, was it still valid today? If she died in her sleep, would she wake in heaven, safe in Abraham's bosom? Or would she find herself roasting in the lake of fire?

She set her pad and notes on the nightstand, hoping to set aside these heavy thoughts with them. But as she did, she noticed something on the small shelf, next to the phone book. It was a Bible. Picking it up, she examined the cover. The golden emblem of an earthenware vase told her that it had been placed there by the Gideons. She tried to think of the last time she had cracked open the Good Book, but couldn't.

More out of curiosity than interest, she opened it, choosing a page at random. It turned out to be Psalm 14. *The fool says in his heart, "There is no God."*

I'm no fool, she thought. *I believe there's a God.* The conviction came to her with surprising ease. *We just don't know each other very well.*

She shut the book and put it back on the shelf. Turning out the light, she fingered the remote, and the bright TV screen was transformed into a dull gray square.

As she pulled the covers up around her neck, Susan wondered if maybe it was time she and God got reacquainted.

She could barely breathe. The sides of the box pressed against her, and she could hear something peppering the wooden top: dirt.

She screamed, fought for oxygen, then screamed again. But she knew that no one could hear her. Either that, or they were ignoring her pleas for help.

Minutes passed, hours . . . She lost track of time. The air, what little there was of it, grew stale and thin. Her mind was numb. She couldn't think. She could only wait.

Finally, she heard a sound: digging. She began to hyperventilate. Then she vomited—over and over again.

When the top was lifted off, the light blinded her. She reached up and felt two arms. They wrapped around her and pulled her up. Rescued at last.

But as her eyes adjusted, she noticed the candles, the circle of figures, the blood . . . She gazed up into the face of her savior, confused, terrified. He removed his hood and she screamed.

It was the most hideous sight she had ever beheld: a skull with eyes of fire and a mouth spewing forth writhing serpents.

A bell chimed. The robe-clad onlookers chanted something. The bell chimed again. They all drew knives and leaned toward her. The bell chimed again. This seemed to be their cue. Raising the blades, they moved closer . . .

Ring!

Susan awoke with a start. She was trembling, drenched in sweat, breathing hard. Looking about the room, she tried to orient herself.

Ring!

It came back to her in pieces: Super Max, Dr. Hanson, Florence, Motel 6 . . .

Ring!

She glanced at the clock. 2:17. Who could be calling at—

Ring!

She fumbled with the receiver. "Yes. Hello."

"Susan? Susan Gant?"

"Yes. Who's calling?"

"Are you representing Dr. Craig Hanson?"

"Yes?"

"I have a message for you."

"Who is this? Who's calling?"

"If Hanson walks, I'll come for you."

"What? Who is this?"

"Oh, didn't I introduce myself?" The caller laughed. "The name's Satan. I'm sure you've heard of me. I look forward to meeting you—in hell."

Click.

Susan stared at the receiver. Could she be dreaming? Was the phone call an extension of that awful nightmare?

She toggled the button and dialed Campbell and Rosselli's room.

"Huh," a groggy voice answered. "What is it?"

"This is Susan Gant," she said, feeling foolish yet panicked. "Could you guys come over here?"

"Now?"

She could hear Tony in the background. "Who is it?" He cursed. "It's the middle of the night!"

"Now," she insisted.

"Okay. Give us a second to get our pants on."

Two long minutes later there was a knock at the door.

"Ms. Gant?"

She recognized Campbell's deep voice and opened it.

"What's up?" Campbell demanded. He was wearing a white undershirt and slacks. His gun and holster were in hand. Behind him, Tony—wearing only pants—had a shotgun cradled against his muscular, bare chest.

"I just got a call," she said, noticing that Tony's shoulders were even more impressive minus his uniform.

"So did we," Tony deadpanned with a frown.

"A threat," she clarified.

She was suddenly aware that she was standing there in nothing but a T-shirt, a sweat-moistened T-shirt. But the fear was still with her—the dream and the call combining to produce a state approaching terror—and she didn't care.

Campbell looked at her, then at the phone. "Nobody knows we're here," he thought aloud. "Nobody except the U.S. Marshal's office in Denver."

"What'd they say?" Tony asked, sliding into a chair at the tiny table near the door.

"That if I got Hanson off, he'd come for me."

"Man or woman?" Campbell asked.

"Man."

"Don't suppose he left a name," Tony joked.

She nodded. "He did."

"What was it?" Campbell prodded.

Susan looked at Campbell, then at Tony. "Satan."

"Satan?" Hanson seemed amused by this. He smiled, then began to laugh, causing his shackles to clank. "And what time was it?"

"Two something."

"2:17?"

"Something like that," she said. "I probably shouldn't have told you, but—"

"Probably not!" Campbell's voice chimed in from behind her. His face was buried in the paper, but he was obviously paying attention.

"But I just thought that you should—"

Hanson waved her off. "I'm glad you did." The smile vanished and his expression became stony and serious. Leaning toward the Plexiglas, he whispered, "It's starting."

"What? What's starting?"

"The game."

"Huh?"

"It's the game they like to play. They played it with me, and I lost. Now they're playing it with you."

Susan looked at him questioningly.

"They know that I'm innocent," he explained. "And they know that if I tell the truth, I'll be exonerated. Worse, they'll be exposed. So they have only one recourse."

"And that is. . . ?"

"Fear. They've got to scare you off the case." He paused and nodded thoughtfully. "It'll get worse, of course. And if you don't back down . . ."

Susan stared at him with wide eyes. "What?"

Hanson shrugged. "You're not married, are you?"

She shook her head.

"Any kids?"

"No."

"That's good." He considered this. "Well, maybe it's good. They can't blackmail you, like they did me. But if they can't target your family, they'll have to go directly after you. First, they'll try more threats, phone calls, maybe a letter or two. Then, if you aren't dissuaded, they'll start playing hardball."

"Hardball?"

"Run you off the road some night on the way home from the office. Have you roughed up. These people are not above kidnapping, rape, torture—even murder."

"Hey!" It was Campbell. He had forsaken his paper and was now standing directly behind Susan. "Are you trying to threaten Ms. Gant? 'Cause if you are—"

Tony was suddenly at her side. "We can talk to the guards," he assured Hanson. "They'll see to it that we get some quality time—alone with you, *Doctor*."

"Guys," Susan waved them off. "It's okay. Really. Go back and sit down."

"I wasn't trying to frighten you," Hanson explained. "Well, maybe I was. I just want you to take this thing seriously. I want you to know what you're getting into. If you want out, this is the time. Before things go any further."

"I don't want out," she assured him.

"It could get ugly. It did for me."

"That's what these guys are for," Susan smirked, gesturing to the marshals. "I let the phone call spook me more than I should have. I overreacted. I mean, I woke up from this nightmare and went straight to—"

"Nightmare?"

She shook her head. "It was nothing. Just a—a crazy dream. Probably fast-food induced."

"Tell me what happened in the dream," Hanson said.

"No. We don't have time. Let's get started."

"I want to know."

Susan sighed and began relating an abbreviated version of the night terror.

"Hmm. Interesting," Hanson said when she had finished.

"What do you think it is, Doc?" she joked. "Am I insane?"

Hanson smiled at her, warmly this time. "It could be your sub-conscious trying to tell you something. Or it could be a sign that my description of SRA really bothered you yesterday—especially the part about the Satanists burying people. Then again, it could have been a case of indigestion brought on by a greasy burger."

"Thanks," Susan groaned. "That's a big help." She was actually beginning to like Craig Hanson. He seemed like a nice guy, and somehow he managed to maintain a sense of humor—even on death row. He was a handsome man, and she liked the way he looked at her. That made her nervous. It was against the rules, besides being really stupid, to get involved with any client—much less a convicted murderer.

"Back to business," she said, taking up a pad. "You were telling me about the MRT unit."

"Right."

"What you found there was disturbing."

"Right." Hanson leaned back and stared at the ceiling. "Well, that first night in the unit really got me thinking. I started questioning Binker's judgment on the Sanders's case. I wondered if maybe her SRA memories had been implanted by memory reconstruction. It seemed possible. That led me to reexamine his diagnoses and treatment of other patients. I soon discovered that Binker was one of the biggest proponents of MRT in the Institute. Second only to Dr. Bayers. He sent nearly all of his patients to MRT.

"I went back to the unit several times, always at night when no one was there, to try and settle these nagging questions."

"And did you?"

"The more I investigated, the more confused I became. It became clear that Binker had used the MRT to lead scores of patients to the diagnoses of his choosing. His video notations would mention that he suspected MPD, for instance—multiple personality disorder—and then he would send the individual into the VR environment to confirm it. And what do you know? Since he was the one programming the unit with information, the diagnosis always turned out to be right on the money.

"I also found a number of sealed files in the system. The computer wouldn't let me access them. You have to realize that these were *my* patients now. Yet I couldn't get to their MRT sessions. Even some of Ruth Sanders's memory reconstruction records were out-of-bounds. So I mentioned this to Grant Singer. He told me to take it up with Dr. Bayers."

"Did you?"

"Yes. We met in his office, and I explained the problem. I didn't mention that I was starting to question Dr. Binker's competence. I just said I wanted to access the files and didn't know how."

"What did he say?"

"He told me he would look into it."

"Did he?"

"I don't know."

Susan finished a page and turned to a fresh sheet. "I'm going back to Denver tonight," she told him. "I've only got a week to prep your case. I'll try to get the judge to postpone the hearing. But we can't count on that. So we need to discuss the charges today, to decide how we're going to handle this."

"I'm innocent."

"And you want to challenge the conviction at the hearing?"

"Yes."

"It's not that kind of hearing. It's not an appeal. But if we can gather some new evidence and use your testimony . . ." She paused, thinking. "I don't know. The judge probably won't allow it."

"But we can try?"

"Sure. We can try just about anything."

"Then let's do it. I have nothing to lose."

Susan made a note on her pad. "Okay. Then we need to talk about the murder—and how you were framed for it."

"I'm getting there," he said. "In fact, I'm there."

"You are?"

Hanson nodded. "It was the day after I talked with Bayers. That's when I got the first phone call."

"From whom?"

"From Satan."

EIGHT

"CAN YOU GET THAT, HONEY?"

Craig could hear Sam's voice, but it sounded far away.

"Craig? Can you get that?"

"Huh?"

An elbow bumped his ribs. Then he realized that the phone was ringing. Struggling to awaken, he reached for the night-stand—and knocked the receiver to the floor. When he found it, he held it to his ear and squinted at the alarm clock. 2:17.

"Yeah."

"Mind your own business."

"Excuse me." He was still foggy. "What was that?"

"Mind your own business. If you don't, your family will suffer."

"What? Who is this?"

"Oh, didn't I introduce myself," the voice said with a chuckle. "The name's Satan. I look forward to meeting you—in hell."

Click.

Craig glanced over at Sam. She was asleep already, a peaceful look on her face. Replacing the receiver, he padded down the hall to check on the girls. Emily had shed her blanket, and her stuffed bear had escaped over the side of the bed. He returned the bear and covered her up, then went to Rachel's room. Rachel was fine, snug beneath her comforter, her animals neatly arranged at the foot of her bed.

He peered out the front blinds. Nothing. After gulping down a glass of water, he slipped back down the hall to bed.

Maybe it had been a wrong number, he decided, closing his eyes. Or maybe he had dreamed it. Weird.

The next day the call was forgotten. He hurriedly showered, shaved, and dressed, dodging Sam as she readied herself to drive the girls to school. He could hear the girls fighting from all the way down the hall, something about a doll and several references to dweeb-face. Craig swung by their rooms on the way to the kitchen and ordered them to stop squabbling and get ready for school. Then he started to prepare toast.

Ten minutes later, coffee cup in hand, he bid the girls and Sam good-bye and left for work. It was a short drive in good traffic, but he always took the back roads to ensure that he missed any morning snarls.

A thin mist had settled over the lower third of Pikes Peak, the rest of the mountain reaching high into a cloudless sky. The sun was beaming down, terrifically bright in the thin, high-altitude air.

Halfway to work, Craig noticed a cassette sticking out of the car's tape player. He pulled it out and examined it. No label. He didn't remember any tape being in the car. Maybe Sam or Rachel—no. They hadn't been in his car. He shoved it in and turned up the volume.

"Greetings. Yes, Dr. Hanson, this is your old friend, Satan. Did you sleep well? Did you miss me? I missed you. I just wanted to punctuate that little talk we had last night. Remember: *Mind your own business!* See you in hell."

Craig slammed on the brakes and was almost rear-ended by a Suburban. The driver honked and shouted something as he roared past.

Craig slipped into the parking lot of a supermarket and switched off the engine. He ejected the tape and stared at it. What was all this? Why had he gotten a threatening call in the night? And why was there a threatening tape in his car? Better yet, how did it get there? Had someone been in the garage?

He picked up his car phone and hit the speed-dial button. The line began to ring.

On the second ring he heard Sam answer, "Hello?" She sounded harried. He could hear Emily and Rachel bickering in the background.

"Hi, honey."

"Craig? What is it? We're late."

"Uh—it's—it's nothing. I'll talk to you guys later."

"Okay. Love you." She hung up.

Seven minutes later he was parked in front of the Colorado Springs Police Department, trying to decide whether to report the incident. It was probably just some kook. Maybe even one of *his* kooks—a patient who either wasn't happy with treatment, or who had developed an unhealthy bond with him. That sort of thing happened a lot in the mental health business.

He poked the tape back in, rewound it, and pushed play. He listened as the message replayed. It didn't sound like a patient. In fact, there was nothing familiar about it. Maybe the nut had used one of those voice modulators to disguise himself.

Ejecting the cassette, he got out and went inside the station. Better safe than sorry.

After a twenty-minute wait, he spoke with a clerk. Ten minutes later, he was ushered into an office.

"I'm Detective Rutherford," the man said, extending his hand. "What seems to be the problem . . ." He glanced at the form. "Dr. Hanson. Crank phone calls?"

Craig nodded.

"How many?"

"Just one. Last night."

"Did the caller identify himself?"

Craig opened his mouth, then closed it again.

"He did or he didn't?" the detective prompted.

"He said he was—" Craig's voice sank. "Satan."

"Who?"

"Satan."

"Is that so," the detective said, trying to suppress a smile. "Satan."

"Right."

"Must be long-distance from hell," the detective joked. "Wonder if he's got a Friends & Family discount."

"Ha-ha," Craig deadpanned.

"Sorry," the detective said, still grinning. "I couldn't resist." He surveyed the form. "Says something about a tape?"

"Yeah," Craig replied. "I found it in my car this morning. It's the same voice. A man. But I don't recognize it."

"Mind if I give it a quick listen?"

He handed Rutherford the tape.

"Rod!"

A uniformed cop appeared in the doorway.

"Get me a boom box."

The cop nodded and left. In thirty seconds he returned with a portable stereo cassette player. Rutherford set the stereo in the middle of his desk and loaded the tape. He hit *play* and sat down.

There was silence, then— static.

"Guess I forgot to rewind it," Craig told him.

Rutherford pressed rewind and began drumming the desk with his fingers. When the player clicked, he depressed play again.

More static.

"It's on there somewhere," Craig said with a shrug. "Maybe the other side. I don't know."

Detective Rutherford spent the next five minutes fast-forwarding, sampling, rewinding, sampling, turning the tape over and over again.

Still nothing.

"Looks like Satan vanished," Rutherford smirked, eyeing Craig. "Maybe you got it wrong, doc. Maybe it was Casper."

"Casper?"

"The friendly ghost." He handed the tape back and showed Craig to the door, laughing all the while.

Craig walked out of the station embarrassed and confused. He was sure that he hadn't imagined the message on the tape, nor the call in the night. This was getting truly bizarre. Maybe—maybe the detective had somehow recorded over the message. Yeah. That was probably it. He had mistakenly hit *record* and the message had been erased.

Glancing at his watch as he exited the police building, he sighed. Great—late for his first patient. He jogged across the parking lot and jumped into his Cherokee. The engine revved obediently, and he backed out of the space. Then he noticed a dull thunking noise. The Jeep was listing to the right side. He stopped and hopped out, doing a circular inspection of the vehicle. There it was. The right rear tire was flat. Great. Just great.

He called Marge to let her know that he was going to miss his eight o'clock altogether, and then he began the arduous task of changing the tire. He had to find the jack, locate the spare . . .

He had already gotten black smudges on his white dress shirt in his struggle to remove the flat when he saw the marks: two thin lines running from the wheel to the outer edge of the tire. Tracing them with his fingers, he realized that they were knife marks. His tire had been slashed.

"So then what did you do?" Susan asked.

"What *could* I do? I changed the stupid tire and went to work."

"You didn't report it to the police?"

"Not after the tape incident. They would have laughed me out of the station."

"Did you tell Sam about the call or the tape—or the tire?"

"No."

"Why not?"

"I didn't want to worry her. She was having a hard enough time as it was. So I decided just to let it slide. And for a while, that strategy seemed to work."

"No more calls or threats?"

"Not for a week or so—not until I tried to access those off-limits MRT files."

———————

"You're sure this is okay?"

"Of course I'm sure. The files were locked up by accident. It was a glitch in the security system. Now we need them unlocked."

"So why are we doing this at ten o'clock at night?"

Craig smiled at him. Roger was no dummy. He knew an illegal act when he saw one.

"Are you going to help me or not?" Craig asked.

"Oh, I'll help," Roger said, still hooking his laptop to the mainframe in the MRT unit. "I just want to know the situation here. Should we run if somebody shows up?"

"No. Walk quickly, maybe—in the other direction."

Craig had known when he asked Roger to help him breach the unit that he would say yes. For two reasons. First, Roger and Craig were old friends. Second, it was a challenge. And Roger loved challenges. As a design expert for Phoenix computers, he faced on-line challenges ten to twelve hours each working day. In his off-hours, he surfed the Net, obsessively hacking his way into systems that employed encrypted security barriers—for the sheer thrill of it. The more heavily guarded the system, the better. Craig knew that his friend was one of the best in the business.

"Ready?"

Roger pushed a button on his laptop. "Just a second." He waited for the device to boot up, then began entering command sequences. "Okay. Here we go." More commands. "Hmm . . ."

Craig watched him work, wondering what in the world he was doing. "What should I—"

"Shhh! Let me concentrate." He tapped away, pausing to analyze the screen every few seconds. Ten minutes passed. Fifteen . . . Twenty . . .

"Roger, we don't have all night."

"I'm almost in." Seconds later, his lips curled into a grin. "After all that rigmarole, that's all you got?"

"What? What is it?"

"Well, whoever designed this system put in all sorts of hurdles. Stuff that would deter a novice, I suppose."

"Or a psychiatrist."

"Yeah. But most any hacker could snake through there without even slowing down."

"Whatever you say."

"Ah—tricky."

"What?"

"An invisible fence. Now I have more respect for you. Up till now it was all the standard stuff, generic barriers you can buy down at Egghead Software. And then he gives you this look, like it's an open door. But there's this one last fence that you can't see. And if you aren't careful, you go rushing in, and it sets off a siren somewhere."

Roger tapped away at the keyboard. "Take that. And that."

The mainframe suddenly whirred to life. "Please enter your code and password, Dr. Hanson," the mechanical voice said.

Craig looked at Roger. "Should I?"

"You have to if you want in. It's voice recognition. I could bypass but it would take time. Put on the gear."

Craig reached for the data glove, but Roger shook his head. "I'd use the suit if I were you. We've got one at Phoenix. It's so much more efficient than the glove. Easier to move around."

Craig shrugged and began donning the wet-suit-like outfit.

"Get inside the virtual environment, then give the thing your code and password. You should be able to access anything you want." He started fiddling with his computer.

Craig zipped up the full-body peripheral, then snapped on the helmet and stepped onto the platform.

The lasers and cameras blinked at him, and then he was standing in the artificial entryway.

"I want to access the locked MRT files," he told the computer.

"Please enter your code and password, Dr. Hanson," it repeated.

When Craig did, the door at the end of the room opened. He looked for the floating face, but didn't see it. Stepping into the dancing static, he found himself in the hallway. Except this time it seemed to stretch toward infinity. And instead of a half-dozen doors, there were hundreds or even thousands lining both sides of the hall.

He reached for the first doorknob. It was locked. "Roger!"

"What?"

"The rooms are still locked!"

"Impossible."

"I'm standing here trying to twist the knob."

"Does it have a keyhole?"

Craig bent down and looked. "Yeah."

"Ask for a key."

"Huh? Ask who?"

"Just do it."

"I need a key," he told no one in particular.

Suddenly the face appeared. "Perhaps you should try a different door."

"Roger!"

"Ask for a key. Put it in the form of a question."

"May I please have the key to this door?"

"Of course, Dr. Hanson," the face said.

The key magically appeared in Craig's hand. He inserted it into the door, turned it. The knob twisted. "It's open."

"Told you," Roger said from beyond cyberspace.

Craig examined the room. It was empty. Then he stepped inside. He was instantly met by colorful images, stereo sounds, and physical sensations.

There was an attractive young girl seated on a couch in a living room. She was chewing gum, reading a magazine. The television was blaring. There was a window behind her. It was dark outside. The front door opened and a couple entered. The girl rose to greet them.

"Sorry we're late," the woman said. "The meeting ran long."

"Church meetings always do," the man grunted.

"How were the kids?" the woman asked. "Did they give you any trouble?"

"No. No problem at all. They watched their video and went right to bed. Not a peep."

"That's a relief," the woman said. "How much do we owe you?"

"The usual," the girl replied.

"The usual?" the woman objected, digging in her purse. "But Becky, we're an hour past the time we agreed on."

The girl shrugged. "Don't worry about it."

"You're sure?" the woman asked, extending a roll of bills.

"I'm sure."

"Well, at least let Don drive you home."

"Oh, no. I can walk."

"It's no trouble," the woman said. "Right, Don?"

"Right," he said. "Let's go."

"Thanks so much, Becky," the woman said.

Becky followed Don out to the car. They got in and he backed out of the driveway. They rode in silence for several minutes.

"That's my street," Becky said, pointing behind them. "You missed it."

"Don't worry," Don said. "We'll circle around."

He pulled into a vacant lot and made a U-turn. Then he shifted into park and turned off the engine.

"What are you doing?"

"I think a good baby-sitter like you deserves a special reward," he told her. He slid toward her, trapping her against the passenger door. His hands moved quickly, one sliding around her shoulders, the other grasping her waist. He leaned over and kissed her neck.

"Mr. Hill! Stop it!" She pushed at his arms, but they tightened their grip.

"Shh!" he cautioned. "If someone hears us, you'll be in a lot of trouble. Seducing an older man . . . People frown on that, you know." He laughed and then resumed his assault, unbuttoning the girl's blouse.

Becky began to sob.

Craig watched in disgust. The episode was sickening. And the suit—the full-body peripheral somehow enabled him to feel what was happening. The embrace, the force of Don's attack . . .

Craig backed out of the room and slammed the door. "Oh, my word!"

"What?" Roger wanted to know. "What is it?"

Craig ignored him. "Is that what's behind all these doors?" he asked the face.

"No. Each experience is different," the face explained. "Some involve sexual experiences: incest, rape, bondage. Others involve violence: beatings, shootings, knifings, murders. Others are a combination of traumas, including satanic ritual abuse. The full-sensory peripheral suit allows the wearer to experience these stimuli in a safe, nonthreatening environ—"

"Where did they come from? Where did these episodes come from?"

"They were recorded during patient sessions."

"Are you telling me these are memories?"

"Reconstructed memories, perfected by program enhancement."

"Perfected?" Craig glared at the face. "Why? Why have these episodes been filed? Why are they being kept here? Why have they been 'perfected'? Why were they recorded in the first place?"

"Dr. Hanson, please rephrase your question or—"

Craig ripped off the helmet and began removing the suit.

"What's the matter?" Roger asked.

Craig shook his head. "What a depraved world we live in."

NINE

"WHAT DID YOU DO AFTER THAT?" SUSAN ASKED. "Did you tell anyone?"

"I reported it to Dr. Bayers."

"And . . ."

Hanson shrugged. "He didn't seem concerned. He said that the records were guarded by stringent security barriers and could only be accessed by himself or the attending therapist."

"But what possible use could—"

Hanson nodded. "That's what I wanted to know. But he had a stock answer for that: The memories were filed and kept for legal purposes, in the event that a client turned around and sued the Institute."

Susan's features bunched up. "I doubt that a virtual reality 'memory' session would be admissible in court."

"I'm just telling you what he said. He likened it to a vault or a safety deposit box. The contents were private and inaccessible."

"What about the suit? That sounds—perverse."

"My thoughts exactly. According to Bayers, it's used for therapeutic purposes, during the actual sessions themselves. Apparently it enhances the experience, making it much more convincing—more real.

"The theory behind MRT is that by replicating real-life situations, it enables patients to come to terms with trauma—especially sexual and violent abuse. They feel the assault, yet it is much less intense than the actual event. It's also conducted in a safe environment. The patient can end the session whenever they want to. If it becomes too much for them, they simply call it off and exit the memory."

"And you buy that?"

Hanson shook his head. "No. But there are quite a few therapy techniques that I don't personally subscribe to. You have to understand that Bayers is . . . well . . . he's one of those men who reach the top of their field at a young age, but never quit striving for more."

"Ambitious?"

"That's an understatement. I didn't realize it until I started at the Institute, but Bayers is brilliant, driven, and visionary, to the point of being controversial. Sort of the Bill Gates of psychiatry."

"Lunch." It was Campbell. "You can come back and finish up with the doctor this afternoon."

"I'd rather stay here," Susan said. "We still have a lot of territory to cover. Why don't you guys take a break? We'll keep going. If that's okay with you, Craig."

"Fine."

Campbell groaned at this and began conferring with a guard. "All right. Tony and I will eat in shifts. We'll grab you a sandwich."

"Thanks," Susan said, turning to a new page on the legal pad. Then she checked her watch. "We've got maybe two more hours, Craig. And that's stretching it. Can you sum this thing up by then?"

"I'll try."

"Okay." Susan thought aloud. "You saw the files. You talked to Bayers. He discounted it. What happened next?"

"That's when the harassment started again," Hanson told her. "In fact, it was the same day I talked with Bayers. That night."

"An anonymous phone call?"

"No," Hanson sighed. "Worse."

"How much longer, honey?"

Craig looked up at the clock in the study. It was closing in on eight. There was still a large stack of treatment notes to sort through and synthesize. But it was time for the kids to go to bed.

"I have a good forty-five minutes left," he yelled back at Sam. She was upstairs somewhere. "But I can finish up after stories and songs."

"Good! Rachel and I are up here reading *Perelandra*."

"What about Emily?"

"She wants *The Silver Chair*," Sam called back.

"Where?"

"The Silver Chair!"

"No! *Where* does Emily want to read?"

"In her room! And tell her to get her pj's on first! And brush her teeth!"

"Isn't she already up there?"

"No!"

"Emily!" Craig saved his work and set out in search of his youngest daughter. "Emily!" He found her in the family room, watching *Black Beauty*. The girl was crazy about horses.

"Come on, Em," he said, flicking off the VCR, then the TV.

"Dad!" she complained. "It was right at the good part."

"Yeah, I know. It's always at the good part. Upstairs. Jammies and teeth."

Emily just sat there on the couch, her lower lip extending halfway down her chin.

"Hurry up, Em. You want me to read to you, don't you?"

She nodded.

"If you dawdle, we won't have time."

Emily jumped up, suddenly motivated. She ran up the stairs. Craig could hear her speed-brushing, then slamming dresser drawers. By the time he arrived at her room, she was picking up dirty clothes and tossing them in the hamper.

He sat down on her bed. "Where's *The Silver—*"

A book was thrust into his hands and Emily hopped into bed, pulling the comforter up around her chin.

"*The Horse and His Boy?* What happened to *The Silver Chair?*"

"Rachel read me the last chapter this afternoon," she reported. "Now I'm ready for this one. And it's about a horse," she added with excitement in her voice.

"Okay." Craig paged to the first chapter. "'How Shasta Set Out on His Travels.'"

"Who's Shasta? Is that the horse?"

Craig put a finger to his lips. "Let's wait and see." He cleared his throat. "'This is the story of an adventure that happened in Narnia and Calormen and the lands between, in the Golden Age when Peter was High King in—'"

"What about the horse?"

"Be patient, Em.'—when Peter was High King in Narnia and his brother and two sisters were King and Queens under him.'"

Craig managed to read to page eleven—and most importantly, introduce the horse—before Emily nodded off.

"No songs tonight," he whispered, watching her. She looked so innocent and pure. As was his custom, he prayed for her and for Rachel, for their protection, health, and futures. As he was leaving the room, Sam was coming down the hall with Rachel. He gave his eldest daughter a hug and then went back downstairs to the study.

Craig worked for another twenty minutes before he noticed the blinking icon: a miniature E in the upper right corner of the screen—e-mail. He stared at it, wondering who was sending him an electronic message. Who knew his address? The PC wasn't connected to the one at the clinic. In fact, the only reason he had a modem was to access Prodigy—for the kids.

Clicking on the icon, he was rewarded with an envelope. His name and Internet address were printed in the center. There was no return address. He clicked on the envelope and waited as it rotated on the screen and a floating letter opener appeared to open the back. A letter magically came out of the envelope and began to unfold. The creases were still visible when it finished.

He read the note once. Reread it. Then read it a third time. It had to be someone's idea of a joke, a bad one. Either that or . . .

He read it again.

Greetings, Dr. Hanson:

I understand that you have been sticking your nose into my business—again. You appear to be a slow learner, Doc. I tried to warn you. But apparently you didn't take me seriously. Maybe you will this time. I hope so . . . for your family's sake.

                                                    Yours truly,
                                                    Satan

P.S. See you in hell!

Craig could feel his heart beating faster. *For your family's sake?* What was that supposed to mean? He stood and walked out of the study, resisting the urge to run. By the time he reached the stairs, he was sweating. Taking them two at a time, he leaped into the upstairs hallway and took a right toward the master bedroom. The light was on; Sam was lying on the bed watching their small color television.

She looked up at him. "What's the matter?"

He spun on his heels without answering and hurried to the girls' bedrooms. Rachel was still awake, her bedside lamp on. *Perelandra* was propped in her lap. "Hi, Daddy. What are you doing?"

"Nothing, honey. Go to sleep, please."

He entered Emily's room. It was dark. It took a moment for his eyes to adjust. When they did, he breathed a sigh of relief. There was a lump in Em's bed. He stepped over and leaned down to kiss her. But her pillow was empty.

Panic.

Yanking back the covers, he found an assortment of stuffed animals. No Emily.

"Rachel!"

She came trotting in. "What?"

"Where's your sister?"

"I dunno, Daddy."

There was a gasp. It was Sam. She was standing in the doorway, her gaze fixed on the window. The curtains were rippling in the soft breeze.

"What's the window doing open?" Craig wondered aloud.

He stuck his head out and surveyed the roof. Nothing.

Pushing past Sam, he hurtled down the stairs and out the front door. "Em! Emily!" He raced out to the driveway. "Emily!" Then he ran to the backyard. *"Emily!"*

"Daddy?"

It was a tiny, muffled voice and the yard was too dark to identify the source. "Emily? Emily, where are you?"

"I'm in here, Daddy."

Craig stumbled over the leg of the swing set, then kicked the wheelbarrow on his way to the shed.

"Em?"

"In here, Daddy!"

He fought with the door, trying to force it open, then remembered it was locked. After fishing his keys out of his pocket, he worked the lock with trembling hands, finally thrusting the door open.

"Em? Emily!"

"Daddy!" She began to cry, falling into his arms. "I was scared, Daddy."

"Em, what are you doing in here? How did you get outside?"

"The bad man," she explained through the tears. "The bad man—he made me go out the window and then he put me in here. He said I was naughty and I had to be punished." She began to sob uncontrollably. "Was—was I—was I naughty? Was I, Daddy?"

He held her close to his chest. "Of course not, honey. You weren't naughty."

"Is she okay?" Sam was out of breath. Even in the darkness, Craig could see that her eyes were wide with fear. "Come here, baby." She took Emily and cradled her gently in her arms.

"Where's Rachel?" Craig asked.

"Inside. I told her to call 911."

"Good."

"Craig, what's going on?" Sam had begun to cry too.

"I don't know, Sam," Craig sighed, ushering them back to the front of the house. "I don't know."

"What did the police find?" Susan asked.

"Nothing."

"Fingerprints on the window? On the shed?"

"No."

"What about the e-mail? Were they able to trace it?"

"They might have been able to."

"But?"

"But it was gone when we got back inside the house." Hanson ran a hand over his face. "The police wrote the whole thing off as a kid sleepwalking."

"Sleepwalking?"

Hanson shrugged.

"How did she get down from a second-story window? How did she get locked in the shed? How did they explain that?"

"There's a drainpipe—a rain gutter—that runs down the back of the house. You can get to it from Emily's room. They theorized that she climbed down it."

"This is a six-year-old girl we're talking about?"

"And they decided that the shed must have been left unlocked. Em went out there and locked herself in. Child gets mad at parents, climbs out the window, holes up in the shed. That's how it went, according to the police."

Hanson paused, allowing Susan to finish her note.

"Two nights later, Sam was . . . accosted."

Susan muttered a swear word under her breath.

"She was coming out of church. There was this women's meeting. She didn't want to go to it. But I thought it would be good for her to get out and make new friends."

"It was nice to meet you, Samantha," Mrs. Garner said, smiling. "I hope you can join us again."

Sam nodded, humoring the old gal. She actually had no intention of returning. She hadn't wanted to come in the first place. It had been Craig's idea. It would be good for her, he'd claimed. Yeah, right. She had been feeling down in the first place. But now? The meeting had been terribly dull. Hardly anyone had talked to her. Except Mrs. Garner. And she was old enough to be Sam's grandmother.

It was just like their last church, and the church before that. Cliques, cliques, and more cliques. Everyone had their established circle of friends. And there was no room for someone new.

Sam waited until Mrs. Garner had turned away, making small talk with someone else. Then she grabbed her purse and hurried out the door. The night air was cool, a nice change from the closeness of the church building.

She reached her car and was unlocking it when she felt something touch her shoulder. Startled, she twisted around and found herself staring at a man wearing a ski mask. Sam gasped, flattening herself against the car.

The assailant didn't speak. He just stood there, his eyes flitting up and down over her body.

"Here," she said, offering him her purse. "Take it. There's not much money but—"

"I don't want it," the man said. The words came out in a snarl.

"Then what—what do you—what do you want?" she stuttered.

He laughed at her. "I want you."

"Oh, no. No! Please don't hurt me. Please!"

The man drew a knife, the blade gleaming under the streetlights.

"Please," she whimpered. "Please don't hurt me. Please . . ."

"It's not me that's hurting you," he said, waving the knife at her playfully. He drew it across her neck, just a millimeter above the skin. "It's your husband and that nose of his—the one he's always sticking into other people's business."

Sam tried to swallow, but her throat was too dry.

"I've got a message for him." The knife passed over her neck again. "Tell him to keep on digging. We don't mind. But there's a price. A heavy price."

Sam was sobbing now.

"First we'll take Emily. Then Rachel. Then you, Sam." He licked his lips. "Makes me hungry just thinking about it."

He folded the knife and put it back into its sheath, turning to leave. "Oh, one other thing. Tell him I said hello. Name's Satan."

The man trotted across the parking lot, dodging pools of light. "See you in hell!" he called.

Sam sank to the pavement. Leaning against the car door, she held her head in her hands and cried.

TEN

EVENTUALLY, ONE OF THE CHURCH LADIES FOUND HER and called me."

"Was she okay?" Susan asked.

"Define *okay,*" Hanson smirked.

"Was she hurt?"

"Physically, no. Emotionally, yes. What little progress she had made in therapy was undone. The experience sent her into a tailspin. She had to be sedated for a few days, and wouldn't even leave the house for nearly two full weeks. Needless to say, she did not go to the next women's group meeting at church."

"Did you report it to the police?"

"No. There didn't seem to be any point."

Campbell appeared and handed Susan a sandwich. "Another hour or so and they're going to pull the plug."

Susan nodded at him. "Thanks."

Hanson was nibbling on a fingernail. "I should have taken the hint. It was obvious that I had spooked someone with something to hide. But stupid, stubborn me—I couldn't leave it alone. I became obsessed with getting to the bottom of it." He paused and looked at her through the partition. "It made me so mad. The idea that someone could come along and threaten my family."

"So what did you do?"

"I started trying to piece it together, to figure out what it was I had stumbled onto and why it had upset someone. There was Ruth Sanders, her SRA diagnosis, Binker, the MRT unit, the memory bank ... On the surface, it looked like these elements were all disconnected, like a puzzle missing half of its pieces. Then I took another look at Sanders's diary."

"And?"

"There was an entry, one of the more recent ones, that discussed her son. She had mentioned earlier that she didn't accept his suicide, that she thought he had been murdered. Well, in this particular entry, she actually pointed fingers."

"Whom did she accuse?"

"The devil."

Susan looked at him skeptically.

"And a transgenerational satanic cult," Hanson clarified. "Somewhere during the memory reconstruction process, she recovered a memory about the leader of this cult promising her that he would sacrifice her firstborn son. At the time of the pronouncement, Sanders was just a child. But she had been dedicated to the devil, and part of the 'code of silence' programming by the cult was to claim her son when he reached the age of fifteen."

Susan opened a file and began flipping through the pages.

"Don't bother," Hanson told her. "I already checked. Zach was fifteen."

She looked it up anyway. "Yep. Sure was." Susan stared at the information, trying to decide what it meant. "So you're saying Zach was murdered by Satanists?"

Hanson shook his head. "No. That's what Ruth Sanders was saying. I didn't buy it."

"Why not?"

He combed a hand through his hair. "I'm not sure. It was just a hunch. But the more I looked into Zach's suicide, the more I agreed that it didn't make sense. Everything I could find out about the kid indicated that he was just what Sanders made him out to be: well-adjusted, happy, full of life and energy. Not the profile of a suicidal teenager."

"I thought you just said you didn't buy the murder angle."

"I didn't buy the *Satanist* angle," he clarified. "I was having a hard time believing Ruth was an SRA survivor in the first place, so I had serious doubts about Zach dying at the hands of a trans-generational cult."

"Doubts. Such as?"

"It was too neat. Too convenient. Sanders was going along, minding her own business—not even in therapy. Suddenly her son dies. A couple of months later she's recovering full-blown memories of cult abuse, remembering that they had promised to come for her son." He shook his head. "It sounded contrived. I began to wonder if Binker and his MRT sessions hadn't generated the entire scenario. I also began to wonder if Ruth was being used as a pawn, if the whole ritual abuse business was a cover-up."

"A cover-up? For what?"

"For whatever it was that got Zach killed." He paused and began rubbing his forehead as if it ached. "So Roger and I . . . we . . . we broke into Ruth's house."

"You what!"

"We were looking for evidence, anything that might tell us what had really happened to Zach."

"But the police had already done that."

"The police had concluded that it was suicide. They basically shut the case before it was ever open."

"So you committed a burglary?" Susan looked at him through wide eyes.

Hanson shrugged. "It seemed like the thing to do—at the time."

"We could get into big trouble for this. You know that, don't you?"

"Shh! Keep your voice down."

"You sure she isn't home?"

"She's got group therapy this evening with Dr. Bayers. Won't be back until around nine."

"I can't believe I'm doing this. Hacking is one thing, but . . ."

Craig examined one of the basement windows. Locked. He checked three more, then—bingo. "Here." He yanked out the screen and handed it to Roger.

Roger refused to take it. "We're not wearing gloves. What about fingerprints? We should be wearing gloves."

"Roger, we aren't going to steal anything. Just look around a little." He tried to hand him the screen again.

"Just a sec." Roger sat down on the grass and took off his shoes, then his socks.

"What are you doing?"

"You want to go to jail—fine. But I have no desire to do time for this stupid stunt." He slipped the socks over his hands, then put the shoes back on his feet.

Craig slid the glass back and scooted through the small square, into the dark basement. Roger followed, awkwardly squeezing through the window.

"We should have brought flashlights, too," Roger muttered. "What if she has a dog?"

"I didn't see any piles in the yard, Sock Man," Craig observed sarcastically. "I doubt she has a dog."

"Better not," Roger grumbled. "What are we looking for, anyway?"

Craig ignored the question. "Come on." He led his nervous partner-in-crime up the stairs, into the kitchen. "That way," he pointed down a hall.

They peered into the bathroom, then the master bedroom, before locating Zach's room. It was messy and contained a menagerie of pop culture memorabilia, as if a teen were still in residence. Not uncommon, Craig thought. Parents often preserved a child's room after the child's death. It became something of a shrine.

Flipping on the light, they surveyed the contents: stereo, electric guitar, desk, PC, bookshelf filled with Bibles and study materials. A poster on the wall over the bed showed several long-haired musicians frozen in frenzied performance. The caption read: *Jammin' for Jesus.*

Craig opened the top drawer of the desk and rifled through it: pens, pencils, a capo, money, gum, guitar picks, a couple of CDs. The second drawer had a stapler, scissors, a strange-looking device that Craig assumed had something to do with increasing finger strength—probably for playing the guitar—paper clips, and a miniature dictionary. The last drawer was crammed with music manuscript pads bearing hand-scribbled musical notations.

"Nothing here," Craig said. "Try his PC."

Roger turned it on and waited as it booted up.

"Take those off your hands," Craig ordered. "You look ridiculous."

"Ridiculous but safe." Roger flexed his hands inside the tube socks. Then he took the mouse in a fingerless paw. "Let's see what old Zach was up to."

He worked quickly, opening files and scanning material. "Hmm . . . Not bad."

"What? What did you find?"

"The kid was into 'gramming. Pretty good, too."

"What do you mean?"

"He wrote some of his own programs. Utilities, desk accessories. Nice stuff. Even set up a custom BBS."

"BBS?"

"Bulletin Board Service—on the Internet. Lots of interesting little bells and whistles too. Interactive perks and things. Kid would have made a great hacker."

"I got the impression he *was* a hacker."

Roger shook his head. "Nah. Hacker has become a generic term for anybody who knows his way around a keyboard. But bona fide hackers are out there, on the edge. They're renegades, the outlaws of cyberspace, always looking for a good security rush." He paused, examining the screen. "Zach . . . he was a creative kid. Talented. He put his knowledge to practical use—like this sophisticated BBS."

"So you're telling me he wasn't dredging through anybody's secret stuff?" Craig asked. He was huddled over the terminal, watching Roger peruse the material.

"I doubt it. Unless he snaked out something by accident. Let's check." Roger plucked at the menu and a screen full of codes appeared. Another pluck and a list of dates lined the far right-hand edge. "Internet. Internet. Local. E-mail. Internet. Local."

"What are these?" Craig pointed to a series of duplicate codes dated the day before Zach died.

Roger chewed at his lip for a moment. "Internet addresses." He pointed to another set of similar codes. "Look how similar this address is."

"Yeah."

Roger entered one of the codes. "This one's the Trinity Fellowship BBS."

Craig stared at the screen. "He called the church all the time, didn't he?"

"Yeah. Almost every day. But this other one . . . I wonder . . ."

"You think he called it by mistake?"

Roger shrugged. "Maybe." He clumsily entered the code, his fingers bound in cotton, and called up the address. A graphic appeared on the screen: a woman sitting in a sexually suggestive position, wearing only lingerie. Her lips were ruby red, her face caked with makeup. Long black hair flowed over her shoulders. She looked like a centerfold pinup. Behind her was a cartoonish gremlin figure with a mischievous grin. He was all red, with horns jutting up from his head, and a long, pointed tail. The gremlin held a pitchfork in one hand and looked as if he were about to jab the woman. The colorful logo at the bottom of the screen said: Satan's Cybersex City—erotic experiences in a safe-sex environment.

"Looks like junior did a little partying before he died," Roger smirked.

"Zach wasn't the partying type," Craig argued. "And the codes are so similar. It had to be a mistake."

"The first time, maybe," Roger frowned. "But when a fifteen-year-old finds a porn address on the Internet, and then calls it six more times . . ." He traced the list of codes with his finger, then shook his head. "Even if the kid was pure as the driven snow, he still had a growing storm of hormones to contend with."

"Yeah, I guess," Craig grunted. He studied the screen for a moment, then gestured toward the porn queen. "Can you get us inside?"

"Craig! I'm surprised at you. And you call yourself a Christian?" Roger started laughing.

Craig glared at him. "I mean, can you find the source—the company that runs this service? You said Zach was talented enough to be a hacker. What if he dug into this and found something?"

"Like what?"

Craig shrugged. "Can you do it or not?"

"Of course I can do it," Roger snorted. "Give me a minute."

"Wait." Craig paused, thinking.

"What?"

"Let's take a look at what this 'Cybersex City' has to offer."

Roger raised his eyebrows and chuckled. "Ooh-la-la!" When he activated the icon, the grin on the devil's face grew and the bimbo winked at them. Then both characters disappeared. A menu spilled onto the screen, each item listed next to an oversized pair of full, red lips.

"Good grief," Roger groaned, looking at the selections. "What'll it be, Craig? 'Pete the Pedophile'? 'When Mommy

Wasn't Looking'? 'Sisters N Secret'? 'Sam and Martha Do S&M'? 'Adventures with the Baby-sitter'?" He poked a sock-clad hand at his mouth and pretended to retch. "What sort of sick, perverted minds come up with this smut? It's repulsive. I mean, 'Pete the Pedophile'?"

"'Adventures with the Baby-sitter,'" Craig said.

"Huh?"

"Open it up."

"You've got to be kidding!"

"Just show it to me, Roger."

Roger sighed dramatically, then complied, calling it up. "I'll have to bill it to my PC address at home so that we don't start a postmortem account for Zach. I just love to help support the burgeoning cyberporn industry."

"Bill it to mine and stop complaining," Craig told him. He gave him the address of his computer at the Institute.

The menu vanished and a scene flashed onto the screen. A pretty teenage girl was sitting on a couch, chewing gum, paging through a magazine. The television was on. The front door suddenly opened and two people stepped inside: a man and a woman. The girl stood up, tossing the magazine aside.

"Sorry we're late," the woman said. "The meeting ran long."

"Church meetings always do," the man grunted.

"How were the kids?" the woman asked. "Did they give you any trouble?"

"No. No problem at all. They watched their video and went right to bed. Not a peep."

"That's a relief," the woman said. "How much do we owe you?"

"The usual," the girl replied.

"The usual?" the woman objected, digging in her purse. "But Becky, we're an hour past the time we agreed on."

The girl shrugged. "Don't worry about it."

"You're sure?" the woman asked, extending a roll of bills.

"I'm sure."

"Well, at least let Don drive you home."

"Oh, no. I can walk."

"It's no trouble," the woman said. "Right, Don?"

"Right," he said. "Let's go."

—————————

"It's the same," Craig observed.

"Huh? What's the same?"

"It's exactly the same." Craig shook his head.

"What are you talking about?"

"Turn that off," Craig ordered, frowning at the scene.

Roger used the mouse to end the scenario and the menu reappeared. "Now do you mind explaining?"

"The Institute. They're using the MRT technology to create and record 'memories' of sexual abuse and then . . ." He paused, shaking his head.

"And then what?"

"Then somebody is selling it over the Internet."

Roger stared at him incredulously. "You're kidding. No way. Are you sure this is exactly the same thing you saw in the VR unit?"

"I'm positive." He gazed at the menu, still shaking his head. "Talk about unethical. And immoral."

"Not to mention illegal."

"What's this?" Craig asked, pointing to a miniature pitchfork positioned at the bottom right corner of the menu.

Roger shrugged and clicked on it. Another menu appeared bearing more titles: "Dabbling with Demons," "Ring Around the Virgin," "Initiating the Innocents," "Grave Robber's Holiday," "Burying Baby," and more.

"Gross! What kind of sociopath would—," Roger wondered aloud.

"Call up 'Initiating the Innocents.'"

Roger muttered something under his breath and used the mouse to choose the title.

Moments later a new scene flashed onto the screen. It was another room, this one dark except for a circle of candles. The floor appeared to be concrete. A half-dozen figures clothed in black robes and hoods marched around the candles, chanting quietly. Their shadows danced on the walls, rising and falling as the candles flickered. Another figure entered the scene, this one bearing two bundles, one under each arm. He set them at the center of the circle, then joined the others. The bundles rocked slightly. Then a cry arose. The cry of a baby. After two more counterclockwise rotations, the group of marchers stopped. One of them entered the circle and removed the blankets. The two infants wriggled and squirmed on the hard, cold floor. The onlookers began to converge, throwing back their robes. They were all naked, all men.

"Enough!"

Roger jabbed the mouse and the scene was gone.

Craig wiped at the sweat that was trickling down his brow. "Now ... find out who sells this ... this ..."

"Garbage?" Roger offered, swallowing hard. "Demonic porn straight from the very bowels of hell?"

"That's an apt description," Craig agreed.

Roger worked the mouse with his cotton paw. "These folks— whoever they are—they should be locked up. Better yet, they should fry."

"One of these days, they will—literally," Craig assured him. "They'll be popping and sizzling in the lake of fire. But until then, we need to do something, to make sure they aren't walking around loose."

"Let's see who *they* is." Roger began entering codes. He pulled a floppy disk from his pocket, slid it into the drive, typed, waited, typed some more.

"Hurry up," Craig urged. "We don't have all day."

"Hang on." Still working the keyboard, he shook his head in frustration. "These folks know how to cover their tracks. We're talking professional here. I haven't had this much trouble since I hacked the mainframe at NASA."

Ten minutes later he succeeded in breaching the security barriers erected within "Satan's Cybersex City," and the name of the parent company appeared on the screen.

"Whoa," Roger observed, shaking his head.

Craig stared at the name, stunned. "It makes sense," he muttered. "In a crazy, bizarre way, it all makes sense."

ELEVEN

T HE INSTITUTE?" SUSAN HAD STOPPED WRITING AND WAS looking up at Hanson. "The Trinity Institute of Psychiatric Therapy? That's the parent company for Satan's Cybersex City?"

Hanson nodded, expressionless.

Susan's mind struggled. It was so unlikely. The Institute was using high-tech equipment to record patient traumas—"memories" which, according to Hanson, were led, directed, and in some cases, wholly fabricated. That alone was unethical. They were then turning around and marketing these same traumas as "entertainment" via the Internet to cybersmut consumers. That was illegal. Zachary Sanders had apparently stumbled onto the operation. And someone had . . . had . . .

"Are you saying that Zachary Sanders was murdered? That someone at the Institute killed him and made it look like a suicide, in order to cover a cyberporn conspiracy?" It sounded ludicrous when she said it out loud.

Hanson nodded confidently, as if this were all self-evident.

"Ruth Sanders was . . . 'directed' to a diagnosis of SRA victimhood as part of that cover-up?"

Another nod.

"And you were framed because you got curious about the MRT unit and started digging up the operation?"

"Right."

No wonder Hanson's last attorney had questioned his client's credibility. Susan spent the next two minutes making notes, drawing arrows, and marking important sections with stars in an attempt to commit the bizarre scenario to paper.

"What about the fingerprints?" she asked, still writing. "They were a key piece of evidence in the case against you. They placed you inside Zach's room."

"I just explained that. I was there all right. But months after the fact."

"The police didn't take prints at the scene when they found Zach?"

Hanson shook his head. "They didn't bother. In their eyes, it was clearly a suicide. Whoever killed Zach made it look convincing."

"But they went back and fingerprinted when you were accused?"

Hanson shrugged. "I assume so. Things got pretty confused after Roger and I established the link between the cybersex service and the Institute."

"What do you mean?"

"Well, for one thing, twelve hours later, I was in jail."

"Honey?"

Craig mumbled something and rolled over.

"Honey?" Sam tried again. "I think there's someone at the door."

"Huh?"

"The door. Somebody's at the door."

Craig rubbed his eyes and squinted at the clock. The luminescent numbers said: 5:27. Thirty-three minutes until the alarm was set to go off. The sweetest sleep of the entire night.

"This better be good," he grumbled, tossing back the sheets.

His robe wasn't behind the door so he quickly pulled on a pair of jeans and a T-shirt. Padding down the hall, he worked his teeth with a dry tongue. He was suffering from a severe case of dragon mouth, the result of the jalapeno burgers Roger had insisted they indulge in on the way home from their "investigative" work the evening before.

When he reached the landing he finally heard what Sam was talking about. Someone was knocking at the front door. The knock sounded urgent, and as he descended the stairs he heard a voice.

"Police! Open up!"

Craig felt his heart start to beat faster, and his groggy mind scrambled to figure out why they were beating on the door. Maybe one of the neighbors had been burglarized. Maybe there was a fire. Maybe—he suddenly thought of the girls and wished he had thought to check their rooms before coming downstairs. If the police hadn't been so insistent, pounding, calling out, pounding, calling out, he would have turned around and gone back up the stairs to make sure they were safe.

He was approaching the entryway, a good five paces away from the door, still thinking about Rachel and Emily, when there was a tremendous crash. It seemed to rock the entire house. A second crash ripped the door from its hinges and sent it hurtling through the air. Craig froze, covering his head with his hands.

Before he could fully comprehend what was happening, a squad of policemen scrambled into the house, shouting, guns raised.

"Down! Get down on the ground! Face down! *Now!*"

Craig sank to his knees, disoriented. Before he could fully comply with the order, something hard impacted the back of his neck and he found himself nose-down in the carpet. Pain radiated down his back and arms and stars filled his vision. Unseen hands pushed and pulled at him, forcing his wrists behind his back, into a pair of tight handcuffs. He was briskly searched, then yanked to a standing position.

Blinking, he examined his captors in disbelief. Some of the cops were already filing out of the house, breathing hard and laughing as they went.

"You're making a mistake," he told the half-dozen officers still huddled around him.

They ignored him. One of the men launched into the Miranda, relaying the words at such a rushed pace that they ran together into a long, indistinct blur.

" . . . anythingyousaycanandwillbeusedagainstyou . . ."

Craig looked up and saw Sam standing at the top of the stairs in her robe. Her eyes were wide with dismay, her mouth hanging open. Rachel and Emily appeared in matching Barbie pajamas, their hair tangled and mussed from sleeping. Each girl clung to one of Sam's legs.

He started to speak to them, to offer an explanation, a word of encouragement. But he could think of nothing to say. There was no rational explanation for this—he had no idea what was going on.

When the explanation of his rights had been completed, the officers bullied him out the door and dragged him down the porch and along the sidewalk, toward a waiting patrol car.

"I love you!" he finally yelled back to Sam and the girls in desperation. "I love you!"

"No warning whatsoever?"

"Nothing," Hanson replied. "They just broke in, cuffed me, and carted me off."

"What was the charge?"

"They didn't tell me until I was downtown at police head-quarters."

"Name?"

"Dr. Craig Hanson."

"Age?"

"Thirty-nine."

"Place of birth?"

"St. Louis, Missouri."

"U.S. citizen?"

"Isn't that a little redundant?"

The officer behind him gave his head a slap. "Don't get smart."

"U.S. citizen?" the clerk repeated.

Craig nodded.

"Place of residence?"

He continued answering the questions for another five minutes, giving the clerk basic background information that he was certain the police already had.

"Take this, step behind the line, and turn this way," the clerk said, handing him a message board bearing his arrest number.

Craig followed the instructions. The instant he faced forward a terrific flash went off, blinding him.

"Turn to the right."

He did, and before he could blink away the last flash, there was another burst of light.

"Check this and sign the bottom."

"What is it?"

"Personal effects list," the clerk told him without even a hint of cordiality.

Craig checked it. The list was a short one: blue jeans, cotton T-shirt, Casio digital watch, gold wedding ring. He signed.

"This way," the officer behind him grunted, tugging at the shoulder of Craig's blue, county-issue coveralls. The man was a brute, just like the rest of the officers roaming the halls: tall, almost obscenely muscular, with an attitude. The overall impression was one of intimidation. These people were not to be crossed.

He was led down a series of corridors into a small room. It contained a table, three chairs, and a large wall mirror.

"Sit," the officer said. He glared at Craig, then left, locking the door behind him.

Craig sat there for what seemed like an eternity, staring into the mirror, wondering if it was a two-way device and wishing he'd had a shower and a shave. Just when he had begun to wonder if he had been forgotten, the door swung open and three plainclothes detectives stepped into the room.

"Dr. Hanson," one of them greeted, taking the seat directly across the table from him. "I'm Detective Brooks." He slapped a file folder on the table. "These are Detectives Hoover and Lewis." Lewis nodded, leaning against the wall. Hoover took the remaining chair, frowning.

"Smoke?" Lewis asked. The lanky detective fished a pack out of his sports jacket.

Craig shook his head.

Brooks leafed through the folder. He suppressed a belch, withdrew a pen, and made a note. The dress shirt beneath his suit coat was stretched to the limit by a sizable beer paunch, the buttons straining to hold their ground.

"What's this all about?" Craig finally asked.

"You call a lawyer yet?" Lewis asked.

"I don't need a lawyer. This is all a mistake. You've made a big mistake."

"It's no mistake, Doctor," Brooks sniffed.

"I'm sure it can be cleared up if you'll just tell me what's going on."

Silence.

"Why am I here? Why was I dragged out of my house at the crack of dawn?"

Brooks looked up at him, a serious expression on his round, fleshy face. "Dr. Hanson, you've been charged with first-degree murder."

Craig tried to swallow, but the lump in his throat wouldn't budge. "With what?"

"First-degree murder," Lewis repeated between puffs from his post along the wall.

"Where were you on the evening of Thursday, February 22, 1996?" Hoover asked. He was a small, balding man with a pinched face who looked as if he was suffering some sort of physical discomfort.

"February 22nd?" Craig's brain raced to remember. "I don't know. I was . . . I guess I was home . . . in St. Louis."

"You don't sound very sure," Brooks said.

"Well, that's almost a year ago, I can't be . . . Wait a minute."

"Yes?" Hoover prodded, leaning forward.

"February 22nd? I think . . . Yeah, I was at a convention. In Denver. At the Tech Center. That's right. NAMHP conference."

"What?" Brooks asked.

"National Association of Mental Health Practitioners. It ran from Wednesday through Saturday noon."

"You can verify that?" Lewis asked through the cloud of smoke.

"Sure. I've got the CME certificates—the continuing medical education certificates. My employer in St. Louis has all the receipts."

Brooks wrote something down, then shot a glance at the mirror. "Can someone verify your whereabouts on the night in question?"

"I just told you—"

"Is there someone who attended the conference," Brooks clarified, "who can vouch for your attendance on the evening of Thursday the 22nd?"

Craig thought about this. "Yeah. I suppose so. I'd have to call around, but . . ." He paused. "Thursday night?"

"Right."

"I don't think there was a general session that night," Craig told them. "No, there wasn't. It was canceled. I went to the afternoon session."

"What time did the afternoon session end?" Brooks asked.

Craig shrugged. "Seems like . . . three. Maybe three-thirty."

"Plenty of time," Hoover told his colleagues.

"Plenty of time for what?"

"Were you with anyone that evening?" Brooks continued.

"Not that I can remember. I think I went to my hotel room, watched a little TV, and went to bed."

"What about dinner?" Lewis asked, lighting another cigarette from the waning butt of the first. "You eat with anybody?"

Craig shook his head. "I don't think so. I think I ordered room service."

Hoover snorted at this, and a thin smile crossed his pained face.

"Who am I supposed to have murdered?"

"Zachary Sanders," Brooks said, reading the name from a sheet in the folder.

Craig's mouth fell open. "That's the son of one of my patients! He committed suicide!"

"At least it looked that way," Hoover sneered.

"But . . . I . . . I didn't . . . I . . . ," Craig stuttered.

"No alibi," Brooks said, making a note. "And subject was in the vicinity."

"But I was in Denver at a conference," he pled.

"And could have easily driven down after the afternoon session and done the job," Hoover said. "What's it take, an hour from the Tech Center to Briargate?"

"Less if you speed," Lewis said.

"I didn't even *know* Ruth Sanders then, much less her son." He shook his head. "This is a farce. It has to be some sort of joke. It's a joke, right?"

Lewis took a long draw on his cigarette and then leaned over the table. He pulled something out of the folder and tossed it at Craig.

It was a sheet with a series of black, swirling marks: fingerprints.

"What is this?"

"The prints on the left were lifted from Zachary Sanders's bedroom," Lewis said, tapping ashes on the floor. "The ones on the right are yours, Dr. Hanson, from when you were booked earlier today. You don't have to be an expert to realize that they match."

Craig shook his head. Roger's socks had seemed like such a silly precaution at the time. "I broke in."

"So you did it?" Brooks said, suddenly animated. He began scribbling notes. "You murdered the Sanders boy?"

"No. I mean I broke into Ruth Sanders's house. Just yesterday. To try to figure something out. Related to her treatment."

Brooks glanced at Hoover, then at Lewis.

"If I were you, Doctor," Lewis offered, "I'd get a lawyer."

"I don't need one! I didn't do anything!"

The room was silent for a full minute.

"Why me? Why did you come after me?"

"Should I tell him?" Lewis asked.

Brooks shrugged. "Go ahead."

"We got an anonymous tip."

Craig stared at them, incredulous. "An anonymous tip?"

Lewis nodded.

"Isn't that a little . . . convenient?"

"Sometimes tips are the difference between apprehending a criminal and losing him," Hoover said, sneering.

"But a tip? That's just not—it's not enough to justify an arrest," Craig argued.

"No," Brooks agreed. "But when the tip leads you to a suspect with no alibi who was in the vicinity . . ."

"And whose fingerprints were all over the crime scene," Hoover pressed.

Craig groaned and covered his face with his hands.

Lewis took a long draw on his cigarette. "Bet that lawyer is starting to sound pretty good right about now."

"What about Roger?" Susan asked. "He could have confirmed the break-in and helped explain the fingerprints."

"I didn't think about that at the time," Hanson said, shaking his head. "I was in shock. It all happened so fast. And they just left me there in that room for . . . I don't know how long. Every so often the Three Stooges would reappear and ask the same questions all over again.

"After about eight hours of that, I finally called a lawyer." Hanson shook his head in disgust. "Guy turned out to be a putz. His first word of advice was to plead guilty. Said he might be able to plea-bargain the charge down to second degree. The jerk!"

"What about the interrogation sessions themselves? Did they coerce you into a confession?"

"No. The Stooges were as polite as could be. I think they were just trying to wear me down, waiting for me to make a mistake, to get my story mixed up. I wasn't about to give them the satisfaction. And I wasn't about to admit that I did it—since I didn't." He paused and stared at the desktop. "I changed my mind on the second day."

"What happened then?"

"That's when the note came."

"Rise and shine!"

Craig opened his eyes and found himself looking at a wall made up of gray steel bars. A section of the wall slid sideways and two uniformed men stepped through the gap.

"Let's go, Sleeping Beauty!" one of them said, kicking Craig's feet.

He sat up and realized that the thin, lumpy mattress had left his back full of kinks. His temples were beating out a cadence worthy of John Philip Sousa.

The other officer wrenched him up and slapped a pair of cuffs on.

"Where are you taking me?" Craig asked as they pushed him out the door and down the block of cells. The place seemed to be full to capacity, each cell holding one or more criminals.

"Interrogation," one of them said.

"Not again," Craig groaned.

"Wouldn't have to bother with it if you'd just confess," the other joked.

The trio navigated through a series of barred gates, past several sleepy-eyed guards, before reaching the interrogation room. Craig was shoved inside.

"Here." The bigger of the two officers stuffed a slip of paper into the pocket of Craig's coveralls. "Read it and weep." His partner laughed at this as they slammed the door shut. The bolt clicked, registering that it had been secured.

Craig glanced around. Same room, same chairs, same mirror. Stepping to the mirror, he pressed his nose against it, wondering if he were being watched. Probably. He felt the urge to curse at the hidden voyeurs, to tell them what they could do with their trumped-up murder charge. Instead, he took his customary seat and waited.

Ten minutes later, when nary an interrogator had showed—maybe the Three Stooges forgot to set their alarm clock—he dug the slip of paper out and read the message:

Dr. Hanson:

I warned you. I told you to back off. But you wouldn't listen. Now look where you are. It's a pity, really. And you have only yourself to blame.

It may interest you to know that at this moment, Sam, Rachel, and Emily are being watched. In fact, I am writing this on your personal computer, having just come downstairs from checking on "the girls." You'll be glad to know that they are sleeping peacefully. If you refuse to cooperate, however, they will soon be sleeping for eternity.

It's very simple. Their safety depends on you. Fight this charge and they will pay. Show this note to the pigs, and

I will inflict upon the Hanson women a pain so horrible they will wish they had never been born.

The choice is yours, Craig. Confess to the murder of Zachary Sanders—and any other charges the authorities come up with—and all will be well with your girls. Dare to plead innocent and Sam, Rachel, and dearest Emily will know my wrath. They will be mine . . . forever.

Yours truly,
Satan

P.S. See you in hell.

Craig held his breath. He read the note once, reread it, and was about to go through it again, when the door opened. In came the Three Stooges.

"Morning, Doctor," Brooks said without a smile. He took his usual seat, as did Hoover. Lewis struck a match and sucked on a Marlboro.

"You want your lawyer?" Lewis asked, smoke trailing from his lips.

Craig shrugged, then shook his head. "What's the point?"

Hoover smiled at Brooks. "Do I detect a crack in the armor, Doctor?"

"What's it gonna be?" Brooks asked, opening up the file. "You gonna fight us today, Doc? More of the wrongly accused victim routine? Or are you ready to level?"

"We have better things to do than hang out in here asking you questions that we already know the answers to," Lewis said.

"Start today off right," Hoover pressed. "Tell us the truth."

Craig looked at the detectives. Their faces seemed larger than life. The smoke from Lewis's cigarette gave the room a surrealistic quality, dancing in spirals and playing with the light. He suddenly found it difficult to breathe, the walls edging toward him.

He thought about the charge, about the note, about his family. He could see Sam. He could feel the touch of her skin against his, the softness of her hair. After nearly twelve years of marriage, he was still desperately in love with her. He could see Rachel, his firstborn. Emily, the baby. He could hear them giggling, racing up and down the stairs, bickering over their dolls, whining, demanding to be read to.

"First-degree murder," Hoover said ominously. "Confess and the judge might be lenient—especially for a family man like yourself. But fight it . . ."

Lewis blew a long breath of smoke into the air. "I've seen cases like this get the needle."

"Well?" Brooks asked expectantly. "How about it, Doc?"

TWELVE

"YOU DIDN'T SHOW THEM THE NOTE?"

Hanson blew air at this, implying that the answer was obvious. "How could I?"

Susan shrugged. "What if 'Satan' was bluffing?"

"I couldn't afford to find out. I was too scared, too helpless. All I could think of was Sam and the girls."

"So you confessed?"

He nodded solemnly.

Susan paged through her pad. "If a guard handed you the note . . . that means the police had to be in on it."

Another nod.

Susan sighed. This conspiracy business was getting out of hand—too big and too improbable. "I know there are some crooked cops running around, but—"

"I'm just telling you what happened." He looked into her eyes. "You don't believe me, do you?"

"To be honest . . ." She paused, frowning. "I don't suppose you know the guard's name?"

"No. But I do know that Trinity has connections."

"Connections? What do you mean?"

"Clint 'Eastwood' O'Connor."

"Never heard of him."

"Been a member for twenty years, according to the membership directory. And he's close friends with senior pastor, Jim Riley."

"So?"

"So he's also known as Police Commissioner O'Connor. He's been the head of Springs PD for the past decade or so."

Susan wrote down the information, still not convinced the police would be involved in a frame. She now had a headache and was ready for this to be over.

"What about the animal mutilations?" she asked, rubbing a temple.

"That's where the FBI came in. Up until that time, I was a local problem. But about two hours after I 'confess,' the Feds show up claiming I've been slicing and dicing livestock and pets all over the countryside—Idaho, Wyoming, Montana, Colorado, Texas . . . Since I've already admitted to a 'satanic' murder, I'm the odds-on favorite for mutilating these animals. Satanists do that sort of stuff, you know. And since the mutilations were felonies and were committed in various states, the whole thing is suddenly a federal case. The next day, I'm trucked to a federal holding pen and my lawyer informs me that if I'm convicted, I won't go to the state pen, I'll do my time at Super Max."

"It's a heart-wrenching story," Susan said, only half meaning it. "But now you've got the FBI in on the cover-up. The Federal Bureau of Investigation is helping Trinity and the police Watergate a computer sex scheme . . . I suppose the Director of the FBI is also a member of Trinity."

Hanson glared at her. "I was skeptical too. But the FBI didn't have anything on the murder. They just had those pesky animal mutilations, and they wanted to clear them up. I'm not saying they were in on the conspiracy. Just that they were looking for someone to pin the ritual sacrifices on."

"Did you confess to the mutilations?"

"Not at first, but eventually I thought, why not? The note did say I was to confess to whatever I was charged with. And I'm destined to spend the rest of my life behind bars anyway. Assuming I didn't get the death penalty—which I did."

Susan finished recording the information, then looked up. "Okay, let's say I give you the benefit of the doubt. Let's say the murder was a setup. The mutilation charges were the result of some overzealous Feds out to close a case. That still leaves the child abuse charges."

Hanson's lower lip began to tremble as he fought off a wave of emotion. He tried to say something but couldn't. Thirty seconds later, he had composed himself. "It wasn't enough to slander me, to make me commit hara-kiri with a false murder charge. They had to twist the knife."

"Where are we going?"

"Shut up and keep moving."

Craig obeyed, not wanting to feel the guard's billy club on the back of his head. They soon reached a small, dimly lit room. It was the same type of room in which he had met with his lawyer countless times over the past weeks.

A handsome man in a well-tailored suit entered. "Lose the cuffs," he told the guard. The guard complied, gave the man a quizzical look, then left the room.

"Dr. Hanson," he said cordially, extending his hand. "I'm Agent Reynolds, the Chief Investigator on your case."

Craig shook the man's hand and watched him sit down, wondering what new crime he was about to be charged with. Another murder? A series of murders? Maybe Craig was a serial murderer and just didn't know it yet.

"I have something to discuss with you," Reynolds began, leafing through a ream of paper. "But first I should advise you that you are entitled to have your lawyer present."

Craig scoffed at this. "It won't matter."

"Good. Then sign this and we can get started." He pushed a paper and pen toward Craig.

The paper turned out to be a disclaimer stating that he had forgone the right to counsel in this meeting. Craig signed it.

"Now, I need you to read through this material and—well, read it first, then we can talk about it."

Craig accepted three file folders worth of material.

"I'll get us some coffee." Reynolds rose, signaled to the guard, and left.

Craig examined the first folder. It was marked simply: Emily Hanson. His heart sank and he quickly checked the others: Rachel Hanson, Samantha Hanson. Were they dead?

Flipping open Emily's folder, he was relieved to find something other than a death certificate. It was a chart. A psychological chart. From an examination conducted at the Institute. According to Dr. Grant Singer, Emily was suffering from extreme stress. She had experienced nightmares and was falling behind in school. Singer rightly concluded that these were symptoms of trauma, most likely the sudden and unusual loss of her father. The doctor recommended therapy. The note was dated sixteen days earlier—nearly a month after Hanson's initial incarceration.

Craig wiped away a tear and continued perusing the contents of the folder: more notes from Singer, records of counseling sessions, accounts of play and music therapy sessions—two-thirds of the way through the material he saw a handwritten note. Singer had scribbled it in the margin.

Because of Emily's inconsistent, sometimes radical behavior—swift and severe changes in mood and personality—I have begun to suspect MPD. The question is, was the trauma of losing her father to prison sufficient to produce the development of alters?

Alters? Alternate personalities? Craig's mind began to race. Multiple Personality Disorder? Emily? That was impossible. MPD was the result of extreme sexual and violent abuse. Emily had never been—

Two pages later he saw another three-letter abbreviation. "No!" he shouted, following the denial with a thundering curse. *"No!"*

"Emily fits the criteria for multiple," Singer's note said. "And upon interviewing her concerning trauma, I have concluded that she may be an SRA victim."

Craig threw the folder onto the table and picked up Rachel's. His fingers flipped through the pages, his eyes scanning. Halfway through the stack he found it: MPD. Six pages later: SRA.

"Rachel's condition, combined with her sister Emily's," Singer wrote, "causes me to wonder if we may be dealing with a transgenerational cult. I plan to explore this in the MRT unit, and to question the mother."

He slapped the folder down and took up the third. Sam's was thicker than the others. It tracked her history of depression. But a hundred pages into the folder, Singer took up the familiar chant: possible MPD.

Craig gathered up the folder and was about to throw it at the wall in disgust when he lost his grip and the contents spilled onto the floor. He looked at the paper, not about to bother retrieving it. Then he glanced down at the folder. There was one page still intact, the last page. It was the final section of Singer's closing comments. Craig read it with a growing sense of horror.

While Samantha's condition is quite complex and therefore much more difficult to diagnose, Rachel and Emily Hanson appear to be victims of satanic ritual abuse. After repeated sessions in the MRT unit, I have discovered that they were both victimized by the same individual—the leader of a highly secretive cult. By their own admission, their abuser was their own father, Dr. Craig Hanson.

Reynolds returned bearing two Styrofoam cups. He paused, looking at the mess on the floor, then set a cup in front of Hanson.

"Ready to talk?"

"We have nothing to talk about."

"I thought the Institute was fully computerized," Susan said.
"Huh?"

"I thought everything at the Institute was on computer," she
repeated. "Notes, session records . . . You told me Singer was big
on that."

"He was."

"Then why would he write out his notes longhand? And why
would the Institute issue the folders loose-leaf instead of on disk?"

"I have no idea. Except that I didn't have access to a computer in prison. And they wanted me to see the material." He
shrugged. "So they documented these three patient files the old-
fashioned way."

"I guess Grant Singer isn't exactly your friend any longer."

"You guess right."

Susan scribbled a note. "Your daughters. They testified that
you abused them?"

Hanson nodded. "They told the jury about their dreams, their
flashbacks, about their memories of Daddy putting on a black robe
and—" His voice broke and tears filled his eyes. "I haven't seen them
since," he choked out. "They think I hurt them. They think I'm a
closet cult member. They think I murdered that boy and carved a
satanic symbol on his chest. They're afraid to visit me."

He covered his face with his hands, his body shaking. "It was
Satan."

"What was?"

"All of this," he replied, wiping away the tears. "He did this."

"Satan?" she asked. "The one who made the threatening calls?
The one who sent you the note?"

Hanson shook his head. "No, I mean the devil himself. He's
behind this."

"Time to go, Ms. Gant," Campbell told her. He was standing
behind her chair, a looming giant.

Susan breathed a sigh of relief. It made her uncomfortable
when Hanson started talking about invisible demons and evil

ghouls. And she was ready to leave Super Max, to get back out into the real world.

"You've got to show that the police were negligent in their investigation," Hanson blurted out, realizing that he had just run out of time. "Prove that they mishandled evidence. Without a confession or fingerprints, their case is paper-thin.

"Then get in touch with Roger. He'll help you confirm the cybersex operation. And you can subpoena records from the Institute—show a pattern of 'moving' patients to SRA diagnoses. Get hold of Ruth Sanders's file—especially her diary.

"Have Sam and the girls evaluated at a neutral clinic. I think a good psychiatrist will blow holes in Singer's simplistic theories and expose his suggestive therapy techniques."

Susan nodded. She had already thought of a similar strategy. Unfortunately, there wasn't time to accomplish it all. She would have to pick and choose the most important elements.

"I'll keep in touch and let you know how it's going," Susan assured him. "Until then—hang in there, Craig."

The guards reached for Hanson, lifting him from his seat. The shackles clanked and rattled as they moved toward the exit.

"One last thing, Susan," Hanson called out. "Whether you believe it or not, this is a spiritual battle. It won't be won or lost in the courtroom. The outcome will be decided up there." He gestured toward the ceiling with his head. "In the heavenlies."

The guards ushered him toward the door.

"Read up on spiritual warfare!" he shouted from the door. "And if you don't already have a Bible, get one!"

The door slammed shut.

"Told you the guy was fruit loops," Tony said.

"Get a Bible?" Campbell snickered. "He's the one who needs a Bible. The pervert."

Susan gathered her pads and folders. "Let's go."

THIRTEEN

Jack . . . NO . . . NO, THAT'S NOT WHAT I'm saying. What I'm saying is I need more—" Susan waited as her supervisor, Jack Sherman, told her a second time why the hearing date in the Hanson case was set in stone.

"I realize that, Jack. But come on. The guy's attorney was sacked a few days before the hearing. And now Hanson's retracting his confession. This is a whole new—"

Sherman cut her off, launching into his third rendering: Hanson was on death row. His appeals had been allowed to lapse. The judge on the case—James T. Humphries—was an old-line conservative, and he was sick and tired of death-row inmates stringing out the inevitable for years, even decades, gobbling up taxpayers' money. Humphries was up for reappointment and was not about to let a professed murderer, child molester, and animal abuser milk the system for an extra month. Hanson's time was up. He could tell his tale of woe to the judge, then face the needle. Sherman's advice: Stick with the guilty plea and get it over with.

"He may be innocent."

Sherman scoffed at this, reminding her that all convicts were "innocent."

"I'm telling you I need time, Jack. I'm not talking about months. I'm talking weeks. Surely if we tell Humphries that Hanson fired his attorney and—"

Humphries, Jack explained impatiently, already knew and didn't much care.

"The trial is set for one week from today," Susan said. "One week, Jack. I can't be expected to put this thing together in one week. I need at least six, and that's not enough."

The chances were slim of the judge extending it a single day.

"An extra couple of weeks? Even Humphries can't be that stingy."

More moaning about how unlikely it was.

"I'll file and see what happens. Talk to you tomorrow, Jack."

She flipped the phone shut and stared out the left-hand window at the Front Range. She and the marshals were traveling north on I–25 at a speed well in excess of the limit. Even the Dodge seemed anxious to get away from Super Max.

"Don't tell me you really think Hanson's innocent," Tony groaned from the front passenger seat.

Susan didn't answer. Her mind was busy outlining a plan of attack. She withdrew a pad from her satchel and started jotting notes.

"Doesn't matter what she thinks, Tony," Campbell said, frowning. He was changing lanes, navigating through slower traffic. "She's a defense attorney."

"Oh, that's right," Tony said in a patronizing tone. "She's on *his* side."

"I'm not on anyone's side," she replied, still working on her to-do list.

"Guilty or not, it's her job to get him off the hook," Campbell continued, cutting off a semi in his attempt to move around a plodding RV that was blocking the fast lane. "She'll try to find some loophole in the law and slip Hanson through it." He snorted and shook his head. "Nothing personal, Ms. Gant, but that's one of the reasons I'm not big on lawyers. They're always on their client's side, not the side of justice or truth."

"You're confusing me with F. Lee Bailey," she shot back. "The Public Defenders Office isn't a private firm. We don't have fat-cat clientele or enormous salaries. We defend people who can't afford or for some reason don't have access to representation."

"Sounds a little like the Peace Corps," Tony joked.

Susan ignored him. "Anyway, if I were you, I wouldn't worry about Hanson walking away from this. I've got a few short days to pull things together for his defense. In answer to your question, Tony, yes, I think it's possible that he is innocent. But proving that in court—that's another matter altogether."

She flipped the phone open again as they passed Castle Rock. The stone monolith was bathed in late afternoon sunlight.

"I understand where you're coming from, Ms. Gant," Campbell said. "Personally, I think you're a nice young lady who just wants to help people. But you have to put yourself in our shoes. We go around chasing criminals, tracking them, setting up stings, doing everything we can to apprehend these scumbags. And when we finally do, we feel pretty good about it. Makes the world a safer place and all that baloney.

"But, half the time, when we get the scum to court, some mouthpiece comes along and gets them off on a technicality—say a breach of search and seizure. Everybody, judge and jury, knows the guy's guilty. But we have to let him back out on the streets. Just doesn't seem fair."

Susan considered this as she punched in a phone number. "The justice system in the United States isn't always fair, Mr. Campbell. It's imperfect. It can be stretched out of shape and subjected to serious abuse. But generally, it works. Sometimes the bad guys get off. Sometimes innocent people do time. But for the most part justice is served."

"Yeah, well," he grunted, "that's all well and good, but . . . You have any kids?"

Susan shook her head. "I'm not married. Sarah Johnson, please," she told the person who answered the phone.

"Well, I'm married," Campbell told her. "And I've got four kids. Two of them are teenagers. I have to tell you, the idea of seeing one of them hanging from a rope, skin sliced up by some wacko's knife—it makes me ill."

Susan didn't respond. Campbell was right. It was a sickening thought—especially for a parent.

"And the idea of sending my two younger kids to a psychiatrist and having him abuse them in some perverted, satanic rite, that doesn't set too well with me either."

"He didn't abuse someone else's, he abused his own—"

"Aha!" Tony nearly shouted. "So you think he did it!"

"No. I was just trying to explain that he isn't accused of kidnapping kids off the street or abusing patients."

"Yeah," Campbell groaned, "he did it to his own children. There's a comforting thought."

"I shouldn't even be talking about this," Susan mumbled. "Paul?"

"Yeah. Who's this?"

"Susan."

"Oh, sorry. I didn't recognize your voice."

"I'm on my way back from Florence. Listen, I'm going to file for a continuance in the Hanson appeal, so—"

"So you want me to prep the papers," Paul said.

"If you don't mind."

"If I don't *mind?* Susan, you've got to be more assertive. You're the lead on this Hanson thing, right?"

"Right."

"And I'm a lowly paralegal at your beck and call. You don't ask, you tell."

"You've been working in the PD's office for a decade, Paul. I just got there."

"Doesn't matter. Try it again."

"What?"

"Tell me to have the papers on your desk by tomorrow morning or you'll have my neck."

Susan laughed. "On my desk by eight or you're dead meat. How's that?"

"Not bad. Anything else?"

"I'll have plenty of legwork for you tomorrow."

"Good. See you then."

Susan punched the button, then dialed a new number. "Cindy?"

"Susan? Where are you?" Her voice was veiled by a wall of static. "Sounds like long distance."

"We're down at Castle Pines. But I wanted to catch you before you left for the day."

"What's up?"

"I've got a favor to ask."

This elicited a groan. "What is it?"

Susan tried to decide how to word it. "Um . . ."

"Susan, what is it?"

"You took acting in college, right?"

There was a long pause. "For a quarter. In my freshman year. Why?"

"I think I may have a use for it."

"Is that right?" She sounded skeptical.

"Can you meet me at Starbucks in the morning? Say 7:30. We could discuss it then."

"Starbucks? Must be some favor. Okay. I'll be there."

Susan flipped the phone shut and watched as they topped the hill and the Denver skyline came into view. The sun had ducked behind the mountains and dusk was quickly falling, transforming the layer of smog into a deep, purple haze.

"I don't know," Tony was grumbling. "I tried calling her from Florence last night, but . . ."

"But what?" Campbell prodded.

"But she wasn't in. I think she got tired of waiting around. Figured I stood her up and went out without me."

"You did stand her up, Tony," Campbell pointed out.

"I didn't mean to." He paused. "Do you know how long it took me to get a date with Bambi?"

Susan chuckled at this, and Tony turned and glared at her. "Sorry, Tony. It's just . . ."

"What?"

"Come on—Bambi?"

She and Campbell shared a laugh.

"You wouldn't laugh if you saw her," Tony said. He performed a long wolf whistle. "Wow. She's a looker."

"Looker with an 'h' from the sound of her name," Campbell joked, punching Tony's shoulder.

More laughter.

Twenty minutes later they exited the freeway and pulled into the Park & Ride. Rush hour having come and gone, Susan's Subaru was one of only a half-dozen cars left in the lot.

"Thanks, guys." She collected her gear and popped open the back door.

"Hang on," Campbell said. Pulling his wallet from his jacket pocket, he extracted a card and handed it to her. "If you need any-thing—"

"If the bogeyman calls up in the middle of the night again," Tony jabbed.

Campbell glared at him. "If you need anything, give us a call. Twenty-four hours a day. Okay?"

Susan nodded, smiling at Campbell. He suddenly reminded her of her father.

"And about those 'defense attorney' cracks I was making— sometimes my mouth engages without my brain."

"Don't worry about it."

Tony hopped out of the car, helped her out, and walked her across an empty parking spot to her car. "Want us to follow you home, Ms. Gant?"

She started to tell him where to go and what he could do with his 'bogeyman' talk. But the expression on his face changed her mind. He was serious. The joking young man had disappeared, replaced by a professional law enforcement officer. "It's no problem," he added, glancing into the backseat of her Subaru.

"No. I'm not going straight home."

"We can. It's no trouble."

"It's our job," Campbell called from the driver's seat.

"I'll be fine, guys. Thanks."

"Yes, ma'am," Tony nodded, backing away.

"Good luck with Bambi," she teased.

The marshals waited, watching from inside the Dodge as she unlocked the door and got settled. When she triggered the ignition, they honked, waved, and screeched away across the parking lot.

Susan watched them go—a part of her, the little girl deep inside, wishing she had agreed to let them see her home. Hanson, his tale of satanic intrigue, and the late-night call she had received in Florence had resurrected a sleeping fear, a fear that she hadn't known was still there. It was the kind of feeling a child had at night, alone, in the dark—when something went bump. It was irrational, even silly. But it was fear nonetheless, a very basic, potent emotion.

Thoughts of ghosts and spooks faded as she followed the stream of traffic up University en route to the Denver Public Library. She didn't feel like doing research tonight. She felt like going home, taking a hot shower, and watching TV. But with only a few short days to prepare . . .

She passed the state capitol building, its gold-dome roof shining under an array of spotlights. A few blocks later, she pulled into the parking area of the library. It was an impressive structure, seven stories of limestone—desert yellow, green, and red—and sandstone. A pickup just two spaces from the library entrance was backing out, so she waited and zipped into the slot. Taking out a yellow legal pad and pencil, she stuffed her bag under the seat and got out, making sure to lock the doors. Denver was a relatively safe town, but like any big city, it had its share of crime.

Inside, the library was quiet. She could see only a dozen people. Susan checked her watch: 7:45. No wonder. The high school crowd that stormed the facility around three each afternoon had done its damage and left for the day. Families were home cleaning up dinner dishes, getting kids ready for bed. The only folks visiting the library were serious scholars, doctoral students, bookworms, street people in search of newspapers, and, of course, lawyers.

She set her pad down next to one of a dozen computerized card catalog terminals and stared at the screen, trying to remember the procedure. She had only patronized the Denver Public Library on one other occasion. It was large and luxurious, 91.6 million dollars worth of towers, atriums, and rotundas that housed nearly six million books. Local authorities claimed that it was the eighth largest public collection in the nation. And it boasted numerous high-tech features: Internet on-ramps, reference librarians equipped with radio headsets, even a computerized photography display. But when there was important legal research to be done, Susan visited the Law Library at Denver University. It was smaller, more suited to her needs, and infinitely less confusing.

After a moment's hesitation, she chose "subject," then typed: "Satanic Ritual Abuse." The system reported that there were only three titles. She wrote them down and returned to the menu, this time typing in "Multiple Personality Disorder." Two seconds later the system told her that the library network had no books on that subject. That seemed a little hard to believe. She tried "Repressed Memories." Bingo. Twenty-seven titles. After searching out "Codependency" and "Addictions"—both of which boasted scores of titles—she abandoned the computer and set off into the stacks.

An hour later she approached the checkout counter, her arms loaded with books. Fifteen minutes after that, she was pulling up in front of her apartment building. It was a double-decker brick structure, built in the early fifties, with two rows of apartments, all facing toward the street. Hers was the corner unit on the left end of the ground floor.

The door put up a brief fight, as always, but a series of jiggles and yanks defeated it. When it creaked open, Alexander came running to greet her. She tossed her gear on the love seat and crouched to pick him up.

"How's my baby?"

Alexander purred through closed eyes as she scratched his head.

"Did you think I ran off and left you?"

The purring increased in volume, rippling through the cat.

"Bet you're hungry," she said, putting him down. She was suddenly starving herself. On her way to the kitchen, she grabbed the remote and flipped on the TV. It flashed to life, displaying a sitcom. She poured a fresh supply of dry food into Alexander's bowl, then checked the fridge.

"Looks like slim pickins," she told the cat. After eyeing the empty freezer, she pulled open the door to the refrigerator. She removed a half-dozen Tupperware containers and stood at the sink, stabbing old casseroles, pasta, and a half-eaten burrito with a fork.

When she had consumed all the cold leftovers she could stomach, Susan snatched up her keys and stepped out into the cool night air. A short walk down the sidewalk brought her to a block of mailboxes. She inserted her key, twisted it, and was rewarded with an avalanche of paper. All that in just a couple of days. A cursory look through the material revealed that it was eighty percent junk mail, the rest bills. Except for one letter.

She heard a "meow" behind her and then felt Alexander rubbing against her ankles.

"Back inside, Alex," she said, herding him through the open door as she examined the letter.

The address on the outside was handwritten, but it didn't match that of any friend or relative she could think of. And there was no return address. Ripping it open, she found that it didn't contain a letter at all. Just a sheet of paper with a crude design sketched in red and black: a long vertical line with a shorter horizontal line intersecting it in the bottom third of its length and a semicircle decorating the intersection. She stared at it for a moment, wondering why it seemed familiar. Then it dawned on her.

Opening her satchel, she dug out the Hanson case file and began paging through it. Trial notes . . . charges . . . Hanson's confession . . . There! A description of the murder scene: the Sanders boy hanging from a makeshift noose formed by a guitar cord, with a satanic symbol etched into his chest.

"'An upside-down cross with a half moon,'" she read aloud from the police report. There was no picture, and she made a mental note to find out why not—and to obtain one.

She reexamined the note, then reread the description in the file. They appeared to be the same signs.

More scare tactics, she decided, crumpling the sketch. Then she thought better of it, smoothed the page, and stuck it in her satchel. Might come in handy down the road.

A commercial blared from the TV—a promo for an upcoming episode of *Tales From the Crypt*. Eerie music played as a ghoulish figure with red, glowing eyes cackled at viewers. She looked for the remote, didn't see it, and decided to change the station by hand. After she had censored the creepy advertisement, twisting the knob to another sitcom, she glanced at the answering machine for the first time. The digital display read 4. Sighing, she pushed the button and waited for it to replay.

The first message was from a local charity. There would be a truck in Susan's area next week; did she have any reusable household items to contribute?

The second message was from Jack. He spoke a sentence, then remembered that Susan was down at Super Max and hung up.

The third message was from Don Levy—an old boyfriend who just wouldn't give up. He wanted to know if Susan was interested in attending a concert up at Red Rocks. He sounded pathetically lonely.

She fast-forwarded to the fourth message. The tone sounded and there was nothing. Silence. Finally a voice: "Susan. Welcome home. Did you get my note?" This was followed by laughter and a dial tone.

A chill ran down her spine. She checked the dead bolt on the front door, turned on several more lights, and hunted for Alexander. With the cat in her arms, she replayed the message, listening intently, studying the inflection, the tone, the speech patterns. She was no expert, but she was almost positive that it was the same voice she had heard in the middle of the night in Florence—the voice of "Satan."

Flipping out the tape, she placed it in her satchel and began rummaging around for Campbell's card. When she found it she picked up the phone, pressed in the first three digits, then paused.

No, she told herself, replacing the receiver. *That's just what they want you to do. They want you to freak out. They want you to act like a typical female—to panic, burst into tears, and drop the case. It's just scare tactics.*

A brief prayer escaped from her lips, a request for protection lifted to the Being she had met as a youth but lost touch with in the years since. This case was turning out to be much more than she had bargained for. And she could use all the outside help she could get.

Speaking of help. Susan wrote herself a note to stop by a religious bookstore and get a Bible and some info on spiritual warfare—and dropped it into her purse. When she finished, she noticed that she was trembling.

Taking a deep breath, she made a hasty trip to the kitchen, raided the pantry, and returned to the safety of the brightly lit living room. She sank into the couch, a jumbo bag of peanut M&Ms under one arm, the cat cradled under the other. Munching nervously, clinging to Alexander, she forced herself not to think about Satanists, symbols, phone messages, and most of all about the innocence or guilt of Dr. Craig Hanson. Twenty minutes later, as the investigative reporters of *Dateline* broke a searing exposé on the inherent dangers of airline travel, Susan drifted off to sleep.

FOURTEEN

"AND THIS COLD FRONT WILL COLLIDE WITH THE mass of moist air coming up from the Gulf by late afternoon, bringing thundershowers to the Front Range. Higher elevations may see light snow or hail. In Denver, we can expect . . ."

Susan opened her eyes and glared at the bright-faced, early morning meteorologist, wondering how anyone could be so chipper at such an ungodly hour. She twisted on the couch, groaning. Her back was stiff, her neck ached, and her teeth were coated with a disgusting sugar/chocolate film. She reached for the remote and was about to silence the smiling weatherman when she heard him report the time: 6:52.

Another groan. "I'm late."

Throwing back the afghan, she hurried toward the shower. On the way she fished a couple of Advils out of the medicine cabinet, swallowed them without water, then gave her teeth a cursory brushing.

At 7:15 she was in her car, hair still wet, dodging buses and commuter traffic. According to the radio, the freeway was bumper to bumper, so she stuck to the surface streets, taking University to First Avenue. The digital clock on the dash said 7:34 when she passed Starbucks, hunting for a space along the street. She found one three blocks north and hiked back. When she arrived, Cindy was standing near the front of a line that snaked from the door to the cash register.

"Sorry I'm late," she apologized, short of breath from the trek.

"You look tired," Cindy observed in greeting. "Hard night, counselor?"

"Sort of. Been here long?"

"Five minutes. But we're at an impasse." Cindy gestured toward the cluster of four or five women swarming the register. They were pointing at the wall menu, asking questions and giggling. "Rookies."

"What?"

"Bet you money they've never been inside a coffee bar before. None of them know the difference between an Americana and a cappuccino."

Susan shook her head. "Imagine that." She had no idea what an Americana was but wasn't about to ask.

"We could be here all day," Cindy lamented.

"Bet this never happens in Boulder," Susan said with a grin.

"In Boulder we used to shoot rookies on sight," she joked. "They weren't allowed to even say *espresso,* much less order it."

Susan and Cindy had been roommates at the University of Colorado throughout most of their undergrad and law school years. Susan had chosen the public defender's route and was scraping to make a living. Cindy, on the other hand, worked for a private firm. She lived in a luxurious townhouse in Cherry Creek and drove a Beemer.

"I remember," Susan said. "I didn't dare drink gourmet coffee until after graduation. I was too intimidated."

"You got a late start," Cindy agreed. "But you're coming along nicely. Not like . . ." Her voice trailed off and she glared at the ladies holding up the line. Then she turned and looked at Susan suspiciously. "So? What's up?"

"I need a favor."

Cindy raised on eyebrow. "Must be a big one if you're springing for lattes."

"I wouldn't call it big. Medium-sized, maybe. A medium-sized, extracurricular project."

"Uh-oh." Cindy rolled her eyes.

"What?"

"Well, the last time you had an 'extracurricular project' for me, it involved posing as an insurance fraud investigator. And I wound up implicating your client."

"Jack's client. I was just doing the legwork."

"Whatever. Please tell me this doesn't involve a scam."

Susan gave her a half smile and started to say something, but the "rookies" finally finished ordering and stepped aside.

"Can I help you?" the young clerk asked.

"Grande mocha and a cinnamon roll," Susan answered. "What do you want, Cindy?"

"Same. Only make my mocha a triple."

Susan gave her a surprised look.

"Hey, if I'm going to be part of one of your cons, I'll need all the energy I can get."

When their drinks were ready, they took a seat at a table next to the window and began watching the sidewalk traffic.

"I'm waiting," Cindy said, sipping.

"Okay." Susan opened her satchel and pulled out a notepad. "I've been assigned to the Hanson case."

"Hanson? As in Dr. Craig Hanson, the murdering Satanist?"

"That's the one. I just finished a two-day interview with him, during which—"

"Ugh!" Cindy made a face. "It must have given you the willies to be in the same room with that maniac."

"He's not what you'd expect. He's . . . kind of regular. Not that bad."

"Not that bad? The guy's a psychopath!"

Susan sighed. "Do you want to hear this or not?"

Cindy nodded, pretending to zip her lip.

"Anyway, I'm preparing his final hearing. I've only got a week—unless I can get a continuance."

"A week?" Cindy made a face.

"He fired his lawyer at the last minute."

"Who's the judge?"

"Humphries."

"Ow!" She flinched, as if she had just touched a hot iron. "Good luck getting any slack from that man. He's a bear. Especially when it comes to death-row inmates."

"So I've been told. That's why we've got to work fast."

Cindy took a bite of sweet roll, then a gulp of coffee. "And my role will be . . ."

"I'm getting to that." She spread her notes out on the table. "Hanson is a psychiatrist. He worked at a place called the Trinity Institute of Psychiatric Therapy. What I need is the inside scoop on this place."

"Subpoena their files," Cindy suggested.

"I plan to. And I'll be interviewing some of the doctors there. But I need you to get in and get an unobstructed look, without them knowing about it."

"Hold on," Cindy chuckled. "I don't do burglary."

Susan shook her head. "No, no. Nothing like that. I just want you to analyze their therapy techniques."

Cindy stared at her, obviously confused.

"I need you to pretend to be a patient."

"A mental patient?" she nearly shouted. "You want me to act crazy? You can't be serious."

"I am. Hanson was convicted of three felonies: first-degree murder, child abuse, and cruelty to animals."

"That's sick!"

"He says he's innocent."

"Innocent! Susan, the guy confessed!"

"He claims he was framed and that he was coerced into confessing."

"Oh, now there's a surprise."

"So I have to dismantle those three prongs of the Feds' case."

"How are you going to defend the murder charge?"

Susan looked at her, started to explain, then thought better of it. "It's complicated. Anyway, in order to disprove the child-abuse aspects, I have to show that the Institute misdiagnosed Hanson's daughters, that they used faulty techniques in discovering—or recovering—memories of the alleged events."

"That won't be easy."

"No, it won't. But Hanson told me that the docs at the Institute have a propensity for moving patients toward certain popular diagnoses. Sometimes this may be unconscious—a preconceived tendency. Other times it could be more purposeful."

"And you believe him? You believe a murdering Satanist?"

Susan glared at her. "Cindy, I've been assigned to defend him. Granted, he's been convicted of some nasty stuff, but I am bound by oath to do my best to represent him. He says he didn't do it— didn't murder anyone, didn't abuse anyone. It's my duty to check it out and try to build a defense."

"Yeah, yeah, I know." Cindy took another sip of coffee. "I thought I read that his appeals were exhausted."

"They are. He let them expire. And at next week's hearing, the judge will probably set an execution date. But you know as well as I do, Cindy, it's never too late to introduce new evidence."

Cindy frowned, considering this, then asked, "So why don't *you* pretend to be a wacko?"

"I have a case to prepare. Besides, they'd spot me. I'm sure they've been informed that I'm assigned to Hanson's case."

"I've got cases too, you know. You expect me to drop everything and have myself committed?"

"No," Susan said. "I just want you to go in for outpatient therapy."

Cindy blew air at the window. "I don't know . . ."

"It's simple. A couple of couch sessions. That's all."

"And why do I need a therapist?"

Susan smiled. Pulling two books from her satchel, she pushed them across the table toward Cindy. "Because you're an SRA survivor."

"A what?"

"A victim of ritual abuse."

"Never heard of such a thing."

Susan shrugged. "Apparently it's the up-and-coming syndrome—kind of like codependency a few years back."

"Codependency I've heard of," Cindy said. She flipped open one of the books and scowled at the headings, mumbling them aloud: "Repressed memories . . . multiple personality disorder . . . transgenerational cults . . ." Her face twisted into an expression of extreme distaste. "This is too weird, Susan."

"All you have to do is read up on the symptoms and act accordingly." Susan opened the other book to a bookmark and displayed two pages marked: "Symptoms of Ritual Abuse."

Cindy scanned the list. "Sleep disorders, panic attacks, unusual scars, gynecological maladies . . ." She paused a quarter of the way down the list and looked around to ensure that none of the other patrons were listening. "Bizarre," she sighed, turning the page. "Behavioral indicators," she read. "Self-mutilation, chemical dependency, suicidal tendencies, eating disorders, sexual dysfunctions . . ." She shook her head and turned another page. "Psychological indicators: obsession with the occult, claustrophobia, extreme paranoia, demon possession . . . *Demon possession?* Obsession with fire, blood, death, pornography, violence . . ." She stared at Susan with wide eyes. "This is disgusting!"

Susan nodded her agreement.

"And you want me to pretend to be one of these lunatics?"

Another nod.

Cindy looked out the window for a long moment. "If anyone else asked me to do this . . ." She finished her latte in a gulp, then sighed melodramatically. "When do I start?"

"Today. Give the Institute a call. The number's in here." She removed a folder from her satchel and handed it to Cindy. "Tell them your problem. They'll schedule you for an entrance interview. Request Dr. Grant Singer and push for this week. Explain to them that you weren't making any progress with your last therapist."

"Who do I say was my last therapist?"

"I hadn't thought of that." She paused. "Say you're from out of town. Say you just moved here. I don't know. Make something up."

"Easy for you to say."

"I wish we weren't under such a time crunch. But we are. So we've got to get you in for a session, hopefully two, before the trial."

"We?" she asked sarcastically.

Susan ignored this remark. "You can start studying your character tonight. Can you meet me here again tomorrow—same time?"

Cindy nodded glumly.

"You'll need a miniature tape recorder." She scribbled a note.

"I'm going in wired for sound?"

Susan shrugged. "I need evidence and I need it fast."

"It won't be admissible in court."

"Maybe not," Susan argued. "But it'll be a wild card I can use against the Institute. And with your testimony—"

Cindy shook her head. "This is crazy. What if I don't get in? What if I'm not convincing?"

"If you don't get in, you don't get in. But I think you will. I've seen you in action. You're good."

"Yeah, maybe," Cindy muttered.

"According to Hanson, the docs at the Institute are ready and willing to treat anybody who even remotely resembles an SRA victim. Display a few symptoms and they'll have you recovering memories of ritual abuse in no time."

"Do you believe him? Do you really think Hanson's innocent?"

Susan drew a deep breath. "I don't know. He seems sincere. But . . . who knows?"

FIFTEEN

WHEN SUSAN ARRIVED AT THE OFFICE, THE PAPERS for the continuance were waiting on her desk as promised. She examined them briefly, judged them to be in order, then signed in the appropriate slots.

She was picking up the phone to call Paul when she heard a rap at the door, followed by, "Those look okay?"

Paul Washburn was in his late forties with graying hair and the distinguished look of an attorney. Susan had often wondered why he had never gone to law school, choosing instead to be a paralegal: the designated grunt of the legal system.

"They look fine." She extended the papers toward him. "File them."

A look of surprise washed over Paul's face. "Yes, ma'am." He offered a mock salute. "And may I convey my sincerest condolences."

"Hmm?"

"Judge Humphries. It doesn't get any worse than that."

"You don't think he'll grant the extension?"

Paul frowned and shook his head slowly. "Getting a continuance on a death-row case from Humphries is like squeezing blood out of a turnip—only harder. Anything else I can do for you while I'm running to the courthouse?"

"Yeah. On your way back, how about picking up the Hanson files from the DA's office?"

"Oops. That was a question."

"Pick 'em up!" she ordered sternly, then laughed.

He saluted again before leaving.

Susan spent the next hour looking up phone numbers, placing calls, and getting absolutely nowhere. Ruth Sanders was not at home. Susan left her name and number on the answering machine, then tried Sanders's workplace. According to the receptionist, Ruth was unable to come to the phone. Susan left a message.

Roger Thompson wasn't home. And he was away from his desk when Susan called his extension at Phoenix Computers. She left messages at both locations, one on a machine, the other on voice mail.

In St. Louis, Samantha Hanson was not in. Susan talked to Mrs. Mitchell, Samantha's mother, who made it clear that her daughter did not wish to speak with anyone associated with Craig Hanson and informed her that Sam had filed for divorce.

Grant Singer was with a patient and could not be disturbed. Susan left a message with his secretary and hung up the phone in frustration, muttering a curse.

"Problems?"

She looked up and saw Jack Sherman standing in the doorway.

"Mind if I come in?"

Susan nodded toward a chair. "A week is—it's impossible, Jack. I can't be expected to put together anything substantial in a week."

"Did you file for the continuance?"

"Yeah. But everyone and his dog has already explained to me that it won't be granted."

"Told you."

"I know. But I need time."

"What for, Susan? The case is straightforward."

She shook her head. "No, it's not. Hanson is retracting his confession. And the confession is the foundation of the case against him."

"So put him on the stand," Jack suggested. "Let him tell his side of the story to the judge. He can plead innocent if he wants to. Fine. It's still a simple matter of his word against the FBI and the Colorado Springs Police Department. He either elicits sympathy and is miraculously released, or Humphries slams the gavel and they give him a shot."

"That's the problem. His testimony isn't enough to overturn the original verdict. I need to discredit the evidence and testimony against him. I need new evidence. I need new witnesses. And I need time. Lots of time."

Jack smiled at her. "I understand what you're doing. This is your first case, your first chance to shine. But don't worry. There'll be plenty of others. You can't try to be Ms. Superlawyer in the closing moments of a no-win case."

Susan started to argue, but he waved her off. "If Hanson had just been apprehended, if this was his first trial, things would be different. Even a stodgy old federal judge like Humphries would be sympathetic. But it isn't. This is dusk. Face it—Hanson's time has run out. And consequently, so has yours."

"I'm not going to lie down and let them steamroll this case," she warned.

"Who said anything about lying down? Gather your evidence, interview witnesses, do what you can in the few days you have. Just don't kill yourself worrying about putting the perfect defense together. Even the perfect defense might not be enough to save Hanson."

"Ever considered running for a federal judgeship, Jack?" Susan remarked sarcastically.

Jack laughed, then rose to leave. "I'd have to practice long and hard to be as heartless as Humphries."

"I can't wait to meet His Honor," she snipped.

Susan spent the rest of the morning in the office's small law library, searching for a precedent that would convince Judge Humphries to grant the continuance—for anything, in fact, that might place her client's change of heart and plea in a more favorable light. Not finding either, she gave up and left for lunch.

After doing the drive-through routine at Taco Bell, she headed for a nearby strip mall that, according to the yellow pages, was home to a Christian bookstore. There it was: The Father's Heart. She parked, went inside, and was immediately greeted by an elderly clerk.

"If there's anything I can help you with, just ask," the woman offered, smiling.

Susan nodded and began browsing. The shelves were arranged by subject: best-sellers, family issues, fiction, children's, missions, evangelism . . .

"Do you happen to have anything on spiritual warfare?" Susan finally asked.

The woman led her into the middle of the store. "This area," she gestured to two large racks. "We also have some related books down here," she pointed. "In the cult and occult section."

"Great. Thank you."

Susan looked over the titles. Apparently spiritual warfare was a hot topic. There were somewhere in the neighborhood of fifty, maybe seventy-five different books, all claiming to give you the basics of how to conduct spiritual warfare. Susan chose two guides that looked promising. In the occult section she found a biography by a woman who claimed to have been ritually abused in a transgenerational cult. That might be helpful for background information. Then she went to check out.

"Have you read *This Present Darkness*?" the woman asked as she scanned the books.

Susan shook her head.

"It's a novel, but it sheds some interesting light on spiritual warfare."

Susan nodded politely, thinking to herself there would never be time to dredge through all of these books before the trial date—even if she didn't have a case to prepare.

The woman stepped out from behind the counter and retrieved a book from a nearby display. "Here you go."

Susan paid and left, depositing the books unceremoniously in the backseat of the Subaru. Then she suddenly remembered Hanson's last words. Did she have a Bible in her apartment? Doubtful.

Trudging back into the store, she enlisted the woman's help in picking out an inexpensive study Bible that claimed to be translated into "modern-day language."

Armed with enough material to last an avid reader several months, and feeling somewhat foolish for purchasing a Bible to prepare for a case, she returned to work and found three cardboard file boxes stacked in her office, marked "Hanson." There were also several messages.

Roger Thompson had returned her call. So had Ruth Sanders. Nothing from Grant Singer. She tried Singer first and was told that he was once again with a patient. Then she called Ruth Sanders.

"Hewlett Packard of Colorado Springs," a perky voice answered, "how may I direct your call?"

"I'd like to speak with Ruth Sanders, please. She's in the bookkeeping department."

"Just a moment."

Certain that she was about to hear, once again, that Sanders would be unable to come to the phone, Susan was mentally preparing the message she would leave, when a voice answered: "This is Ruth Sanders."

"Ms. Sanders? My name is Susan Gant. I'm with the public defender's office, and I was wondering if—"

"Are you representing Dr. Hanson?"

"Yes, I am. I'm handling his appeal. And I would certainly appreciate it if you would allow me to talk with you."

Silence.

"Ms. Sanders? Are you still there?"

"I'm here," she replied in a voice just above a whisper.

Susan had expected anger, even bitterness. But instead, Sanders sounded sad, as if she were on the verge of tears.

"I understand how difficult this must be for you," Susan said.

"Do you?" Sanders was crying now. "Do you really under-stand? I lost my son. My only son. And the one person I trusted to see me through the pain of that event, the one person I con-fided in, the one person I looked to for help—he turned out to be my son's murderer."

Susan didn't know what to say.

"They're about to set his execution date, aren't they?"

"Yes."

"Fine. I'll talk with you. As long as this is the last time. I can't go on like this, reliving Zach's death, describing it over and over to the FBI, to the district attorney, to Hanson's lawyers. I have to move forward. If I don't, the healing process will never start. I have to put it behind me. I just want it to be over."

"Can we get together tomorrow?"

"I suppose. I have to work. But maybe at lunch. I have an hour at noon."

"I'll pick you up." Susan listened as Sanders told her how to find her workplace, bid her a sympathetic good-bye, then hung up.

Instantly, the phone rang again.

"Susan Gant," she answered, hoping it was Singer or Thomp-son.

"I understand that you're handling Craig's appeal," a voice said.

"Who am I speaking to?"

There was a pause. "Samantha Hanson."

Susan found it difficult to mask her surprise. "Samantha? I . . . I didn't think . . ."

"I know. My mother never liked Craig. And after all he put me and the girls through, she's convinced he's the devil incarnate. I guess I'm inclined to agree. Did she tell you I'm divorcing him?"

"Yes."

There was a long sigh on the other end of the line. "So what do you want?"

"I'm preparing to defend your husband, and I was hoping to talk with you."

"I'm listening."

"In person, if possible."

"I'm not coming there."

"I wouldn't ask you to. I can fly out. Would Saturday be convenient?"

Another long sigh. "I guess. But the girls are off-limits. You can talk to me, but not to them. They've already been traumatized enough."

"Agreed."

When she had finished talking with Mrs. Hanson, Susan punched a button on the phone and called Paul.

"Book me on a flight to St. Louis."

"Hey, you're really getting into this 'executive order' thing, aren't you?"

Susan laughed. "You shouldn't have gotten me started."

"When do you need to be there?"

"Saturday afternoon. See if there's a morning flight with an evening return. I need to be back here Sunday morning."

"Will do." And he hung up.

After a trip to the Coke machine, she closed the door and took a seat on the floor, next to the file boxes. Pulling off the tops, she tossed them aside and began wading through the DA's case: FBI reports, CSPD reports, statements from witnesses, another copy of Hanson's confession . . . After an hour and a half she had discovered nothing new or novel. The prosecutor's case still hinged on the confession. Without that, nearly everything became circumstantial. Of course, showing that the DA's case was weak would not help Hanson now. She had to prove his innocence beyond the shadow of a doubt. Hanson had left "innocent until proven guilty" territory upon conviction. Now he was merely treading water, hoping for a miracle.

Susan found the statements made by Ruth Sanders. No accusations against Hanson. Just simple descriptions of her son's death—the crime scene, the time, a few other details. Susan looked for Sanders's diary. It wasn't in the first or second box. Thirty minutes later she had determined that it wasn't in the third either.

She made a note. Tomorrow when she went by to talk with the DA—to discuss the confession and to argue in vain that without it there was no case and that Hanson should be exonerated—she would ask about the diary.

At around four she took a break and called Singer and Thompson. Reaching neither of them, she tried Dr. Bayers. Miraculously, he was in and took the call.

"My name is Susan Gant, and I'm representing Dr. Craig Hanson in his appeal," she explained. "I was wondering if I could meet with you to discuss his case."

She waited, expecting him to decline.

"Certainly, I'd be glad to meet with you, Ms. Gant."

Susan was speechless. "Great . . . uh . . . let's see . . . I'll be down in the Springs tomorrow. I don't suppose you'd be available around two?"

"That would be fine."

"All right then . . . uh . . . I'll look forward to seeing you." She hung up and pumped an arm in the air. "Yes!"

Time to call her client with a progress report. Getting through to Super Max was simple: she punched in the ten-digit number. Getting through to Hanson, however, was an ordeal. She was questioned repeatedly by various phone jockeys about the nature of her call, each of them reminding her that prisoners could only accept incoming calls on special days at special times. She retorted again and again that she was trying to reach her client, that her client was on death row, and that since his final hearing was only a few days away, he had been afforded special privileges—such as a daily phone call from his lawyer. Ten minutes and a great deal of aggravation later, she was told to wait: Hanson was being summoned to the phone.

She had begun to wonder if the line had been disconnected or she had been forgotten when a voice answered.

"Hello?"

"Craig? This is Susan."

"Oh, Susan. It's great to hear your voice."

"What's the matter? You sound upset."

"I'm just . . . so alone . . . and I'm afraid. I know I shouldn't let the situation get to me. With God, nothing's impossible, right? But after we talked yesterday, there was this attack. I just—I lost hope. I mean, God can save me. But unless he acts—and acts quickly— my days are numbered, Susan." There was a pause.

"Craig?"

"I'm here," he said, obviously choking back tears. "I'm sorry. I know you're doing everything you can, Susan. And I want you to know that I trust you. I can't imagine anyone else I'd rather have representing me right now. We can see this thing through, right? Together, I mean. Whether you manage a miraculous stay or they load up the syringe—" His voice cracked and he began to sob.

"Craig—hey, it's not over yet. Don't give up on me. Okay? Okay?"

"Okay," came the meager reply.

"I just called to let you know that I'm chasing the leads you gave me. I'll be running around the next few days doing interviews, reviewing the trial records, searching for precedents. We're under the gun time-wise, so things are going to get a little harried. But I'll check in with you every afternoon. I promise. All right?"

"I'd like that, Susan. I'd like that a lot. You're all I have left now. You and God."

No pressure, Susan thought. "Hang in there, Craig. I'm with you."

"Thanks, Susan," he sniffed.

"Talk to you tomorrow."

Hanging up, Susan returned to the mess on the floor, a fresh sense of determination flooding her veins. Maybe Dr. Bayers would provide valuable information. Maybe Ruth Sanders would too. And Samantha Hanson. Maybe she would piece together a workable defense yet. Anything was possible.

Poring over the files, her eyes scanned the pages with renewed energy, searching for something—anything that might help steer Craig Hanson away from the desperate fate awaiting him at Super Max.

SIXTEEN

IT WAS AFTER SEVEN WHEN SUSAN FINALLY GOT home. She was hungry, tired, and in no mood to read the library of religious literature she had brought with her. Dumping the load of books on the couch, she rubbed her stinging eyes. Alexander purred a greeting at her ankles. She picked him up and went to the kitchen, flipping on the TV on her way through the living room.

The freezer and refrigerator were still nearly empty—they had not miraculously replenished themselves in her absence. The pantry contained no real food, nothing even remotely nutritional: gummy bears, M&Ms, Oreos, and two half-empty bags of chips. She pulled out one of the sacks and began munching broken Dorito shards. After feeding Alexander, she dug the phone book out of the cabinet and began paging through the restaurant section. There—Domino's. She dialed and ordered a large Canadian bacon with pineapple.

There was nothing on TV—*Seinfeld* was a rerun—so she rewound the videotape in the VCR. She had programmed the device to record *Frasier* while she was in Florence. Or so she hoped. Nothing was ever a sure thing where a VCR was concerned. After fast-forwarding through a host of commercials, she arrived at the opening credits of *Home Improvement*. *Home Improvement?* Whatever. Apparently she had misprogrammed it. But a sitcom was a sitcom.

The show was nearly over and she had begun to wonder if the Domino's delivery person had gotten lost, when the picture went blank. She fiddled with the remote, pushed rewind, pushed fast-forward, pushed play. Still nothing—no color, no static, no sound, just a dull gray screen. Had the TV gone out? Or had the VCR screwed up the recording? She was about to get up and check when the screen blinked and a face suddenly appeared. It wasn't a human face. It was a featureless silver mask with bulging, red eyes and a thin, metallic mouth. It reminded Susan of something from a sci-fi movie. She assumed it was a promo for some new show—until it began to speak.

"Consider this your final warning, Ms. Gant," the hollow, robotic voice said.

Susan stared at the face, shocked.

"If you insist on pursuing Dr. Hanson's outlandish claims, we will respond with appropriate force. Dr. Hanson regretted his decision to expose us. You will too." There was a pause. "Incidentally, now you can tell your friends that you've seen the face of Satan." The voice trailed off in cackling laughter.

The picture blinked again and the closing credits of *Home Improvement* rolled down the screen.

Susan didn't move. She sat frozen, fighting off a wave of terror, trying to rationally analyze what she had just seen. What did it mean?

For one thing, it seemed to lend support to Hanson's claims. Someone—Hanson's infamous *they*—was getting nervous. And apparently that someone considered Susan a threat.

For another thing, it meant that an intruder had been in her apartment. Someone had broken in, altered the tape, and slipped out. She rose and examined the door. No marks. No scratches. The dead bolt and knob lock were in working order.

It meant something else too: It was time to call in the cavalry. No sense pretending to be brave. False courage wouldn't protect her from this loony "Satan" character. Maybe he was all mouth—a thinly veiled attempt to scare her off. Then again . . .

She found the card and dialed the office number. When there was no answer, she tried the home number that had been scrawled on the back.

"Hello," a female voice answered.

"I'm trying to reach John Campbell."

"Just a moment."

Susan used the remote to switch off the tape and rewind it while she waited.

"Campbell here," a deep voice grunted.

"Hi, John. This is Susan Gant."

"Ms. Gant." His voice brightened immediately. "Are you all right? Something the matter?"

"No, no. I'm fine. I—well, I'm not exactly fine, John. Actually I'm terrified." She paused and fought back a wave of emotion, determined not to cry.

"What is it? What's wrong?"

"Remember the threat I got in Florence?"

"Uh-huh. Did you get another one?"

"Actually, several."

"Why didn't you—"

"I didn't want to bother you."

"It's no bother. It's our job. I'll give Tony a call. We can be there in fifteen . . . twenty minutes, tops."

"Well, you don't have to do that. I just—"

"Be there in a flash."

Before she could object, the line was dead. She suddenly felt embarrassed, silly for having called Campbell. Chances were this was just a hoax. No reason to waste the time and efforts of two U.S. marshals. But at this point, she was less concerned about looking silly than she was about staying alive. Thanks to Satan, self-consciousness had been eclipsed by an overwhelming drive for self-preservation.

The knock at the door startled her. It had only been a couple of minutes since her talk with Campbell. Not time enough for the marshals to arrive.

Cradling Alexander, she walked to the door, peered out the peephole and saw—the pizza delivery kid. She took a deep breath and slid back the dead bolt.

"Large, thick crust, Canadian bacon and pineapple," he read.

"Right." Susan paid him. "Keep it," she said when he tried to give her change.

"Thanks, ma'am."

She closed the door and rebolted it. Back on the couch she checked her watch, silently urging Campbell and Rosselli to hurry, then opened the pizza box. A small piece of paper was attached to the center of the pie. Thinking it was a receipt, she removed it and set it on the sofa. It wasn't until she had eaten a slice and a half and surfed through several stations on the television that she glanced down at the paper. It wasn't a receipt. It was a handwritten note that read:

I am deadly serious. Your friend, Satan.

Susan spit a mouthful of pizza into the box, then tossed the box to the floor, as if it was on fire. She paced around the room, fending off a panic attack, until Campbell and Rosselli arrived, ten minutes later.

"What's going on?" Tony asked when she let them in. He looked around the room suspiciously, then checked the kitchen and bedroom.

"You look stressed," Campbell observed.

Susan picked up the note and handed it to him.

He frowned at it. "Where'd it come from?"

"If I knew that . . ."

"I mean how did it come? Mail? UPS?"

"Through the window, attached to a rock," Tony joked, returning from his patrol of the apartment.

"In a pizza," she told them.

"A pizza?" Tony chuckled. "What kind? Pepperoni or Italian sausage? Thick or thin crust?"

Campbell silenced him with a glare.

"I ordered a pizza," Susan explained. "When it came, this note was inside the box."

Campbell reexamined the note, then looked skeptically at the pizza box on the floor.

"But that isn't why I called. That happened after we talked. I called because of this." She stepped to the VCR, ejected the tape, and handed it to Campbell.

The marshal looked at the label, then turned it over in his hands. *"Frasier?"*

"I recorded the show while we were up at Super Max. Tonight I was watching it and . . ."

"And . . . ?" Tony prodded.

"Well, it turned out to be *Home Improvement.*"

"Bummer," Tony said. "Don't you hate it when that happens?"

Susan scowled at him. "And toward the end there was this message from . . . Satan."

"*Satan,*" Campbell clarified. He cocked his head, then loaded the tape into the VCR. Susan gave him the remote and the three of them watched as commercials, credits, then *Home Improvement* went speeding past.

"That's a rerun," Tony observed.

In another minute the program ended and the closing credits began to roll.

"Stop," Susan said. "Go back."

Campbell did. More *Home Improvement* segments bordered by commercials.

"It was on there," Susan said. "I saw it. There was this face—"

"Satan's face?" Tony asked. "I always wondered what that guy looked like. Was he red with long pointy ears? You know, like Spock with a sunburn?"

Susan's scowl intensified. "It was on there. He threatened me."

Campbell continued scanning. "I believe you, Ms. Gant, but . . . Well, there's nothing here now."

"Maybe it wasn't on the tape," Tony suggested. "Maybe it was a direct broadcast thing—closed-circuit programming straight from hell."

Even Campbell couldn't resist laughing at this. "I'm sorry, Ms. Gant, but—"

"Take the tape and have it analyzed," she demanded.

"Analyzed?"

"Don't you have a lab or something?"

Campbell shook his head. "You're thinking of the FBI." He ejected the tape and set it on the shelf.

"Anything else?" Tony asked.

"Yeah," Susan said. "Now that you mention it, I had a harassing phone message on my machine and a bizarre note." She went to her satchel and began searching for the items. A minute later she said, "They're in here somewhere."

"Maybe they disappeared too. Invisible ink or something."

"Here." She glared at Tony and handed both items to Campbell.

He studied the note first, examining the envelope, then the sketch inside. "Hmph," he grunted, letting Tony have a look.

"Weird," Tony observed.

"Can we play the tape?" Campbell asked, gesturing toward the answering machine.

"Go ahead."

He loaded the machine and activated it. The messages rattled off: A sales pitch from a local charity, an abbreviated message from Jack Sherman, a proposition from Don Levy . . . The device beeped a forth time, then silence. Campbell let the tape roll. Nothing. There was a final beep, and the machine turned itself off.

Susan looked at them, frowning. "It was there," she muttered. "I swear."

Campbell's face took on a puzzled expression. He popped out the tape, picked up the video, and looked at Susan. It was obvious that he was having a difficult time believing her. Tony was suppressing a chuckle.

"I suppose we could have the Bureau take a look at these," he said. "Mind if I take them with me?"

"Be my guest."

"You want one of us to stick around tonight?" he asked, stuffing the evidence into his coat pocket.

"I'll stay," Tony volunteered.

Susan shook her head. "I'll be okay."

Campbell nodded doubtfully. "If you need us . . ."

"Yeah, I know," she grumbled. "I've got your number. Thanks, guys."

She saw them out and slid the dead bolt into place.

"Maybe the marshals are right," she told Alexander, scratching him behind the ears. "Maybe I'm overreacting. It's probably nothing—an attempt to intimidate me, to make me back off. Whoever's behind it is probably just bluffing. Don't you think so, Alex?"

The cat purred its agreement.

On the heels of that bit of positive self-talk, she flipped on two more lamps, turned up the volume on the TV, and took up her place on the couch.

Glancing at the pizza box, she considered trying another piece. No. Her appetite had mysteriously evaporated. She wasn't hungry for anything, much less toxic pizza. It suddenly occurred to her that she should have had Campbell check it for poison.

Susan picked up one of the books on the sofa next to her: *The Complete Spiritual Warfare Manual*. The back cover contained several glowing reviews from Christian personalities and pastors, praising the thoroughness and biblical accuracy of the book.

Cracking it open, she read the short foreword. More accolades for the author and his comprehensive work. Arriving at the table of contents, she scanned the chapter headings: War in the Heavenlies, The Nature of Evil, The Kingdom of God, Strike Force Jesus, Satan's Strategies, Principalities and Powers, The Standing of the Believer, The Armor of God, Weapons of Our Warfare, The Blood of the Lamb, The Cross of Christ, Strategic Prayer, Overcoming the Adversary.

It was like reading a foreign language. The terms were strange, the phrases unfamiliar. Susan had never heard of "spiritual warfare" before meeting Dr. Hanson, much less things like strategic prayer. Raised in a mainline church, she had been taught that sinners were destined for hell, saints for heaven. God was loving and people, in turn, were supposed to love their neighbors. That was about the extent of her theological training. And after giving up church attendance, she hadn't really given theology a second thought.

In the first chapter, she began reading about a beautiful creature named Lucifer. According to the author, Lucifer had rebelled against God, convincing a third of the heavenly angels to commit mutiny with him. Their punishment had been swift and severe. Lucifer had been relieved of his lofty position—that of "covering angel" in God's presence—and literally thrown out of heaven. He and his followers had been sentenced to spend their days exiled on the third planet from the sun: earth. Since that planet was also home to man, one of God's most glorious inventions, this set the stage for an ongoing battle. God and his prize creation were pitted against Satan—the "Adversary," as Lucifer had come to be called—and his legions of fallen angels.

Susan stopped at the next heading: "Adam and Eve—The First Conflict." After marking her place, she set the book aside and turned her attention to the television. On the screen, the doctors of *ER* were fighting to save a critically injured accident victim. Forty-five minutes later, while the *ER* doctors still struggled to save lives, she fell asleep on the couch.

SEVENTEEN

SUSAN HEARD SOMETHING: A DISTANT, FARAWAY NOISE. A tone. Her mind slowly emerged from sleep and fought to classify it. Doorbell? No. Not bright enough. Alarm clock. No. Not nearly irritating enough.

Opening her eyes, she stared at the early morning news team. They were discussing Denver's traffic situation.

The tone sounded again, and she finally recognized it as the phone. Pushing past the books, she reached for the end table, disturbing Alexander in the process. He leapt from the couch and began to meow, demanding his breakfast.

"Hello?" She twisted her arm, checking the time. 6:17. Who on earth . . .

"Ms. Gant? I hope I didn't wake you."

"No," she lied, not sure who she was talking to.

"This is John Campbell."

"Oh. Hi, John."

"I wanted to catch you before you left for work."

"Well, you did."

"I'm sorry. I woke you, didn't I?"

"Don't worry about it, John. What's up?" she asked through a yawn. Sitting up on the couch, she rubbed her eyes and wondered if it was worth the effort to head for the kitchen and start some coffee. No, she was headed to Starbucks anyway.

"We had the Bureau run the materials you gave us."

"Already?"

"Tony and I dropped it by their lab on the way home from your house last night. It's open round the clock. Anyway, we told 'em it was a rush job. One of the guys owes us a favor so—"

"And?"

"And they didn't turn up much. No fingerprints. The envelope was postmarked Denver, but they couldn't determine which station it was routed through."

"Dead end."

"Almost. They did find something interesting concerning the tapes."

"What?"

"There was electrical residue on the video and the answering machine cassette."

"Electrical residue?"

"That's what the techs downtown call it. The way they tell it, audio- and videotapes record images and sounds with electronic patterns and pulses. Even after you erase them, a trace pattern of electrical residue remains. The only way to totally purge them is to use a magnet. Anyway, the techs couldn't reconstruct or recover what you'd lost, but their equipment showed that something had been there."

Susan digested this for a moment. "So I'm not going crazy?"

"No. In fact, the lab report said that whoever produced those messages used a cutting-edge technology—one-pass, it's called. It lets you record on any analog/tape medium in such a way that the recording lasts for only one or two passes through the player machine. You can view or listen to it a couple of times, then it disappears—it's automatically erased by the heads on the VCR or answering machine. At least that's the way I understand it."

"Hanson got a cassette like that. It had a threat on it and when he took it in to the police, the thing was blank."

"That's what concerns me," Campbell said. "This is getting out of hand. Whoever is pressuring you isn't a run-of-the-mill crank. We're talking about a sophisticated, well-planned assault."

Susan sighed into the phone.

"That's why I think it's time to give you some protection."

"What do you mean?"

"Tony and/or I will start shadowing you: follow you to work, follow you home, watch your apartment, hang out around your car to make sure no one tampers with it—you know, a brake job or a bomb."

"A *bomb?*"

"Not likely," Campbell explained. "But you never know when you're dealing with loonies."

"I'll admit I'm nervous," she said. "I slept on the couch for two nights straight—with the lights and the TV on. But I'm not sure I need a bodyguard."

"It's not a request, Ms. Gant. I already talked it over with my superiors. We've been assigned to ensure your safety throughout the duration of the Hanson case. I'm just telling you so we don't spook you. If you look back and see a Dodge trailing you all over town, don't worry. It's just us doing our job."

"I don't think it's necessary."

"Ms. Gant—"

"But I appreciate it, John. I'll feel a whole lot safer knowing you and Tony are covering my back."

"Good. We'll try to stay out of the way as much as possible. If you need anything, just whistle."

"Thanks, John."

She hung up and examined her watch again. No time for coffee now. After feeding Alexander, she slipped out of her clothes and turned on the shower, waiting for the water to make the slow transition from cold to tepid to a temperature bordering on hot. She was certain that the old building still had its original water heaters and pipes.

The phone rang again just as she was about to enter the shower. Grabbing a towel, she raced into the living room and answered it.

"Forget something, John?"

"Sorry to disappoint you, Susan, but this isn't Marshal Campbell."

Susan shuddered. It was the voice—Satan's voice.

"I hope you slept well. Although I don't know how you can manage on that couch."

Panic! The caller somehow knew that she had just spoken to Campbell and also knew that she had slept on the couch. How?

"Incidentally, you have an amazing figure. Those long, luscious legs . . . those firm thighs . . . that trim—"

"Stop it!"

The caller laughed. "Don't be so modest, Susan. Admit it. You're a goddess. And I might add that it's a shame to cover a body like that with a towel. I can hardly wait for you to climb into that steamy shower."

Twisting frantically, Susan checked every window she could see. The shades were drawn. How could he—

"Remember, Susan, if you choose to stay with the Hanson case, I'll be seeing more of you." Another chuckle. "Much more."

Susan cursed at the dial tone, then threw the phone at the couch. She looked around the apartment. Was there a surveillance camera hidden somewhere?

Alexander brushed against her ankles, and she nearly jumped out of her skin.

Taking a deep breath, she tried to calm herself. Maybe the lunatic had just made a series of reasonable guesses. Maybe he *hadn't* seen her without her clothes. Maybe he had merely assumed that she would be taking a shower this morning. And why not? Nearly everyone did about this time of day before going to work.

But that business about sleeping on the couch and talking to Campbell . . .

The phone. Satan had bugged her phone.

She returned to the bathroom, to the shower which was now indeed steaming. But the idea—however improbable—that a psycho was watching her, anxious to drool over her body as she lathered up behind the clear glass door of the shower stall, was too much. Twisting the knobs closed, she clutched the towel around her modestly and began hurriedly applying a thin layer of makeup. Having masked her unwashed skin with perfume and deodorant and reshaped her hair with a cloud of spray, she retreated to the closet, dressing in the dark.

On the expressway, surrounded by miles of rolling steel and smooth concrete, she breathed a sigh of relief. The surface streets would have been faster, but somehow, the traffic made her feel safe. She checked her rearview mirror periodically en route to Starbucks, looking in vain for a white Dodge and thinking that Campbell had been right: This was getting out of hand.

When she arrived at the coffee bar, she found Cindy near the back of a long line of anxious caffeine addicts.

"Where have you been?" Cindy asked in greeting. "I thought you forgot. You look terrible."

"Aw, shucks," Susan responded sarcastically. "You're just saying that."

"Something wrong?"

"Nothing a vacation wouldn't cure."

"I hear that. But I have some news that may cheer you up."

"The Institute?" she asked, following as the line crept forward.

Cindy nodded, grinning. "You would have been proud. I was impressive, if I do say so myself—and I do."

"You got in?"

"Of course. I've got an entrance interview this morning, and the woman I spoke to—Madge, I think it was—"

"Marge."

"Right. Anyway, she tentatively scheduled my first session for Monday."

"Monday?"

"With Dr. Singer."

They drew nearer the register.

"Great. That's wonderful. Oh, before I forget." Susan dug a tiny tape recorder out of her satchel. "Here. Stick this in your purse or pocket or something."

"You want me to tape the interview?"

"Yep. There could be something useful."

Five minutes later, they had ordered and received their drinks.

"How's this?" Cindy gestured toward a table.

"I can't stay. I've got a crazy day ahead."

Cindy frowned at this. "Sure. Get what you want from me, then ditch me." She smiled. "I need to get going too. I'm due at the Institute at nine and then I'm supposed to be in court at 10:30. Should be a nifty trick."

"Good luck," Susan offered as they parted ways. "And thanks." Back in the Subaru, she used her cellular to call Paul. It was only ten to eight, but he was usually in the office by 7:30 or so.

"Paul?"

"Speaking."

"This is Susan. Listen I've got another chore for you."

"I'm listening."

"I need Dr. Hanson's speaking and conference itinerary for the past two years."

"And I can get that how?"

"Contact his employer in St. Louis. The name and number are in the file."

"Done. Anything else?"

"Not at the moment. Thanks, Paul."

At a quarter after eight she pulled into the parking lot at the federal building and sat, sipping her latte, waiting for the DA's office to open. Ten minutes later a Lexus slipped into a spot near the door and a short, overweight man in a dark blue suit emerged—Duane McDermott, the district attorney.

Susan hopped out and hurried to catch up to him.

"Mr. McDermott?"

He turned toward her, obviously irritated and impatient. "Yes."

"I'm the public defender in the Hanson case."

He gave her a once-over, and the frown grew. Apparently she had been found lacking. "And your name is . . . ?"

"Susan Gant."

"Jack put you in charge of the Hanson case, huh?" His lips changed direction, curling upwards. "Lucky us."

Susan wasn't sure what McDermott meant—if the comment was a sarcastic slam at her age and lack of experience or a veiled innuendo concerning her gender and appearance. Either way she didn't like it.

McDermott turned and walked toward the door.

"Mr. McDermott," she said, trotting to catch up. "I'd like to see the evidence in the case."

"That's your prerogative, Ms. Grant."

"The name's Gant."

"Whatever. See the clerk down in records. They open at nine." And he disappeared through the glass doors.

Susan followed. "I was hoping that we could discuss the case."

"What is there to discuss?"

Your attitude, for one thing, Susan wanted to say, but didn't. "Well, you were the lead on the Hanson conviction. Isn't that right?"

"Yes," he replied sleepily, punching the elevator button.

"I thought you might be interested to know that Dr. Hanson has changed his plea."

McDermott smirked at this. "Really? I assumed that an inmate on death row would plead guilty." He shook his head and pressed the button again. "Ms. Gant, for your information, that's what the appeals process is all about. The chief aim is to get yourself off the hook. For whatever reason, Dr. Hanson allowed his appeal opportunities to slip by. Now he's scared out of his mind at the prospect of being injected with a chemical poison. Therefore, he is changing his story at the last minute, on the off chance that he can save his perverted skin. The man's a coward."

"My client has recanted his confession," Susan tried. "He claims it was coerced. That his family was threatened."

"Please," McDermott groaned. The elevator arrived and he stepped on, holding the door open. "This is the same family he abused? Ms. Gant, I am a very busy man. I don't have time for fairy tales. Records is down the hall to your left. First door—you can't miss it. See you at the hearing." He removed his hand and allowed the door to shut.

"Jerk," Susan muttered. She found Records, waited forty minutes for the clerk to unlock the door, then requested the evidence files. The clerk obliged, leading her to a stack of a half-dozen boxes marked "Hanson," and pointing out a small room with a desk where she could work.

When she was seated at the metal table, surrounded by cardboard, Susan lifted the lid of the first container and examined the contents: a collection of manila envelopes, all containing photographs. The outside of each declared it to be an exhibit in the case of the U.S. Government versus Dr. Craig P. Hanson.

Susan tipped the first envelope. Black-and-white 8 x 10s of what appeared to be roadkill slid out. The accompanying information sheet told her that the subject of the photograph was an animal—a calf to be precise—that had been dissected, its blood, liver, bowels, and heart removed. She took another look at it, her mind attempting to reassemble the parts into a baby cow. Unable to do so, she put the pictures back into the envelope.

The next twenty envelopes contained similar photographs—black-and-white portraits of what had once been sheep, goats, calves, cats, and dogs, all mutilated to the point of being indistinguishable from a lump of decaying flesh on the highway.

Susan considered asking for copies of the pictures, but could think of no reason she would need them. Besides, though she hadn't gagged upon viewing them, she wasn't particularly keen on seeing how her sympathetic nervous system would react to a return engagement.

Dredging through the second box, she found a bag containing a curling electrical cord. A wax pencil identified this as the murder weapon used on Zachary Sanders—the noose. She cringed as she inspected it through the plastic, thinking that death by guitar cord was a particularly gruesome way to go. In another envelope she found what she had been looking for: photographs of the crime scene. Even though the Colorado Springs police had originally deemed Zach's death a suicide, they had had the forethought to record the scene with a camera.

The pictures of animal parts had been gruesome but tolerable, largely because they didn't look like what they were. But this . . . Susan stared at the photo, her mouth falling open. She tried to study the surroundings, Zach's room, any clues that the arrangement of the furniture might offer. But her eyes kept returning to the body, to the shirtless form of a teenager: the taut muscles, the smooth skin, the cruel expression on the lifeless face, the symbol—even in black and white, it was clear that it had been carved into the kid's chest with a knife. And the blood, the dark line from the torso to the pants, the dark spot on the floor—

Susan turned her head, retched, then grimaced at the sour taste of bile that filled her mouth. She would need a copy of that photo, despite her reaction to it. Making a note on her pad, she replaced the envelope and went to the next box.

An hour later she had completed a cursory survey of the materials and come to two conclusions. First, this was the most grotesque case imaginable. Second, Ruth Sanders's journal was nowhere to be seen.

After checking with the Records clerk and requisitioning copies of several items, she left the building. On her way across the parking lot she spotted a white Dodge parked on an adjacent street. Susan smiled, resisting the urge to wave at her guardian angels, John Campbell and Tony Rosselli.

EIGHTEEN

THERE WAS A NOTE WAITING ON SUSAN'S DESK when she returned to the office. It said simply: *Dr. Hanson called.*

Interesting, she thought. *How did he get access to a phone?* She made a mental note to ask Campbell about that. There was no point in trying to return the call. She was certain that the folks down at Super Max wouldn't allow Hanson an unscheduled incoming call. He had been allotted greater privileges because of his impending execution, but she was still allowed to phone him only once a day—between four and five P.M.

She checked her watch. It was almost 10:30. Ruth Sanders was expecting her down in the Springs at noon. The trip would take a full hour, possibly longer if traffic was heavy. That left her just enough time to engage in a quick round of phone tag with Roger Thompson and Dr. Grant Singer.

According to Marge, Dr. Singer was with a patient—as usual. Susan left another message, then hung up. It seemed strange to her that Singer hadn't even attempted to return her calls. Perhaps he had been advised not to speak with the defense attorney before the trial. She would ask Dr. Bayers about that.

Shrugging it off, she found Roger's number in her Daytimer and dialed.

"Phoenix Computers. How may I direct your call?"

"Extension 442, please."

"One moment."

As she sat listening to Muzak, Susan went over her schedule for the next few days. After her meeting with Sanders, she would meet with Bayers, then return to Denver and give Hanson a call. If time allowed, she would contact the Springs Police Department and attempt to set up an interview with the three detectives present at Hanson's confession. Maybe she could meet with Police Chief O'Connor as well. But that expedition would have to wait until Monday. Today was already booked up and tomorrow she was flying to St. Louis. She jotted a note, reminding herself to ask Paul about the travel arrangements. Then something struck her. Would Campbell and Rosselli be tagging along—all the way to Missouri?

"Design and development, Thompson here."

"Mr. Thompson? Roger Thompson?"

"Yeah," he answered warily.

"This is Susan Gant with the public defender's office."

No response.

"I'm representing Dr. Craig Hanson."

"Oh." He sounded nonplused.

"I was wondering if we could meet to discuss Dr. Hanson's case."

There was a long silence. "I'm not sure that's such a good idea."

"Dr. Hanson tells me that you helped him breach the computer system at Trinity Psychiatric Institute."

Another pause. "I can't talk right now."

"Then you'll meet with me?"

Thompson muttered something that Susan didn't quite catch. "I suppose."

"What about Sunday afternoon?"

"I don't know . . . I guess."

"I could pick you up. We could grab some lunch or something."

"You know the Chevy's on Arapahoe—down towards Highland's Ranch?"

"Yeah."

"Be there at two."

Click.

"What an amicable guy," Susan sighed.

"Who?"

She looked up as Paul strutted in and slapped an envelope down on her desk. "You leave at 7:10 tomorrow morning. Change planes in Salt Lake."

"Salt Lake?" she groaned. "That's the wrong way."

"The direct flights were all booked. I had to grovel to get you these connections. Anyway, you arrive in St. Louis at 10:50. There'll be a rental car waiting for you. Go to the Hertz counter."

Susan opened the envelope and looked inside. "First class! Paul, we can't afford—"

"It was an upgrade. You're flying coach on the way back."

"You could have been a travel agent."

He polished his nails on his shirt and blew on them. "What can I say? Anything else I can do you for, ma'am?"

"Now that you mention it . . ."

The glib expression on his face disappeared. "What?"

"I may need another ticket."

"What? You're not going to St. Louis?"

"Oh, I'm going all right. But I may have a traveling companion."

Paul raised his eyebrows. "Is there a significant other that you've been hiding from us?"

Susan frowned at this. "He's a federal marshal."

"Ooh. I'm impressed. If I'd known you went for men in uniform, I'd have started wearing my Boy Scout suit to the office."

She laughed at this. "It's purely business. The marshals are flanking me during this Hanson case."

"Oh." He brightened. "Now it's plural. Just how many men are you juggling?"

"One of them may be going to St. Louis with me," she told him, ignoring the remark.

"Tell him to get his own ticket. The public defender's office isn't going to foot the bill."

"Make another reservation—just in case. I'll check with them to see if they plan on making the trip."

"Don't back down, Suzy. Tell them it's Dutch or nothing."

"Get out," she grinned, pointing toward the door.

At twenty till eleven she stuffed her notes in her satchel and left the office. Driving south on I–25, she placed a call on her cellular phone.

"Campbell here."

"John, this is Susan."

"Hello, Ms. Gant. What's up?"

"There are a couple of things I need to talk to you about."

"Shoot."

"First, I'm heading to the Springs for a lunch meeting. I'm just passing—"

"The Tech Center. I know. I'm on your six, about a half-dozen cars back. It's just me. Tony's doing paperwork back in town."

"Oh. Okay."

"What was the other thing you wanted to tell me?"

"I'm going to St. Louis tomorrow. I wasn't sure if you wanted to come or not. You probably don't need to."

"Does it concern the Hanson case?"

"Yes. I'm going out to speak with Mrs. Hanson."

"Then I'm going too."

"Do you really think it's necessary, John?"

"Doesn't matter what I think. Orders are orders. One or the other of us is supposed to shadow you morning, noon, and night until the hearing is history."

"If you say so."

"I do." He paused, then cursed softly.

"What's the matter?"

"I just remembered. My daughter's birthday is tomorrow. My wife is throwing a party."

"What are you saying, John? It'll just be me and Tony?" The tone of her voice made it clear that this was unacceptable.

Silence . . . then, "Tony's got a date with Bambi," Campbell thought aloud. "A second chance at heaven."

"I can go by myself," Susan assured him. "I'll be fine."

"No. We'll work something out," he muttered.

"Okay. Well, my paralegal is taking care of the arrangements. But the Feds will have to cough up the price of *your* ticket."

"No problem. You know where I am if you need me."

"Right." She hung up and returned the phone to its bracket.

Traffic was heavy but flowed smoothly, an odd assortment of businesspeople, campers, and eighteen-wheelers making the north/south trek to the Springs and beyond.

As she passed Castle Rock, Susan checked her speedometer and was surprised to find that she was doing nearly eighty. She considered slowing down to avoid the speed traps always in operation along that stretch. But the traffic flow was moving a good ten miles over the sixty-five-miles-per-hour limit, and she was being "escorted" by a U.S. marshal. Surely Campbell could convince a state patrolman to let her off if she was indeed pulled over.

She was approaching County Line Road, listening to a light rock station, taking in the panorama of natural beauty, when a black sports car sped past. It caught her attention because it had to have been going at least ninety-five. At Monument Pass, however, the car decelerated, as if it was experiencing serious mechanical difficulty. Susan slowed too, unable to pass because a trailer truck was controlling the fast lane. The sports car got slower and slower. The truck got slower and slower, gears grinding, smoke belching from the stacks behind the cab as it struggled to make the steep grade.

Suddenly the truck swerved into her lane and the sports car slammed on its brakes, tires smoking. Susan reacted by reflex, braking and spinning the wheel to the right. The Subaru jinked and skid like an out-of-control sled, lilting first to one side, then the other as it raced down the shoulder at upwards of sixty miles per hour. Slowing, the car swerved to the right and left the shoulder, seemingly of its own accord, bumping and jolting its way across a field of tall brown grass. Susan stood on the brake, riding the vehicle to an awkward halt, the front end bottoming out in a shallow drainage ditch.

Breathing hard, perspiration trickling down her brow, she glanced out the window just in time to see the truck top the pass and rattle off in a final cloud of black exhaust, apparently oblivious to the fact that it had just run another car off the road.

Then she noticed the little sports car. It was stopped on the shoulder not far from her, its engine still running. She couldn't see inside. The windows were too dark. She wondered whether the driver had stopped to offer help or just to collect himself after the close call.

The adrenaline was still pumping through her veins when she stepped out of the car to survey the damage: a tiny new wrinkle in the hood, slightly mashed bumper—otherwise it looked okay. Nothing a body shop couldn't fix. Now if she could get it out of the ditch.

She got back inside and put the gearshift in reverse. The engine roared, the tires spun, but the Subaru didn't budge. Another attempt brought the same result.

The sports car was still there, engine idling. Susan walked over to it, motioning for the driver to lower his window. He didn't. She motioned again. No response.

"I think I may need a tow truck," she told the dark glass. Nothing. She was starting to get irritated when another thought occurred to her: What if the driver had been injured? What if he had suffered a heart attack? Or maybe the driver was a woman and she was losing it, bawling her eyes out.

"Are you okay?" she finally asked.

The electric window came down a crack—not enough to see inside. "I'm okay."

It was a man's voice. It sounded calm and collected. "The question is: Are you okay . . . Susan?"

The window went up and the rear tires squealed, sending the car off in a shower of pebbles and dust.

Susan covered her face, then squinted at the fleeing vehicle, trying to get a look at the license plate. When she did, she swore. It was personalized: SATAN.

Thirty seconds later, Campbell's Dodge screeched to a halt on the shoulder.

"Are you all right?" He ran to her, grasped her by the shoulders, and looked her over.

Susan nodded. "Frightened to death. But all right."

Campbell took a step or two toward her car. "What happened?"

"I'm not sure. This truck veered into my lane and I lost control. But John—there was this other car, this black sports car with dark windows."

"What about it?"

"It came by first, real fast. Then slowed down. So I was stuck behind it and behind the truck in the other lane. And after I went off the road, the sports car stopped, right there," she pointed, "right where your car is now."

"Did you get a plate?"

"That's the scary part. It was a vanity plate that said S-A-T-A-N."

Campbell stared at her for a moment. "Whoever is after you has got some impressive resources. And they're running a smooth, organized, scare-tactic campaign."

"What do you mean?"

"Well, I was stuck in a convoy back there—a few semis had me boxed in. And I'm guessing it wasn't accidental. I'm guessing they blocked me, then went after you. So that means that on this little stunt alone, they had four or five eighteen-wheelers and a sports car." He shook his head. "Then there's that one-pass business . . ."

"I got another call this morning. The guy knew what I was doing. He knew I was about to get into the shower. It was creepy."

Campbell considered this. "Totally out of hand. Come on." He ushered her toward his car.

"What are you doing?"

"Taking you back to Denver. You'll need to file an incident report."

"I have a meeting."

"Cancel it."

"I can't. John, that's just exactly what they want me to do. This meeting is very important to the case."

He sighed at her. "You're either very brave or very crazy. Or both. Tell me about the car. Make, model, year, color . . ."

"I don't know what model it was. Just a sports car. Black. New looking. The kind with a rounded back and one of those airfoil things. It had dark windows. And you know about the license plate."

"Yeah. Probably fake. I doubt someone would be so stupid as to run around claiming to be Satan and have it plastered on his plate."

He stepped over to his car and radioed in the information.

"The state troopers will try to run it down for us," he told her when he returned. "But I'm betting he's long gone. Could have gotten off at Monument and hightailed it toward Black Forest. Could have hit 24 and gone west to Woodland Park. Could have made a run at New Mexico. Or he could be parked in a garage five miles down the road. No way of telling."

"Did you call a tow truck?"

Campbell frowned at this. "Get in."

When she was behind the wheel he gave her instructions. "Put it in reverse and gently press on the pedal—don't gun it. Just press a little, let up, press a little. We'll get it rocking and I'll push you out."

Susan followed his instructions and the strapping man put his shoulder to the bumper. Two minutes later, the car was up on the shoulder.

"Looks roadworthy," Campbell said, crouching to check the undercarriage. "You sure you don't want to go back to Denver?"

Susan shook her head. "I can't. I have to make this meeting. Thanks, John."

She pulled onto the Interstate, then watched in her rearview mirror as the marshal hopped into his Dodge and did the same.

Despite her initial misgivings, Susan had to admit that John Campbell was turning out to be a pretty handy guy to have around.

NINETEEN

RUTH SANDERS WORKED AT THE HEWLETT PACKARD PLANT on the western edge of Colorado Springs. Located just north of the Garden of the Gods, at the foot of Pikes Peak, the large office park/factory facility enjoyed a stunning view of the lower Front Range.

Unlike Denver, Susan reflected as she pulled into the parking area, the air here was clear, the sun unnaturally bright, the sky a deep, high-altitude blue. No smog, no skyscrapers, no traffic snarls. It was like a mountain getaway. As she parked and walked to the entrance, she couldn't help wondering why more people didn't live in "The Springs."

The relaxed, resort atmosphere disappeared when she reached the reception area. A network of video cameras looked down from the ceiling, following her every movement. They turned, motors whirring, as she made her way to a glass enclosure. Behind it, a trio of guards were hunched over a bank of monitors.

"I'm here to see Ruth Sanders," Susan told them through the intercom. She didn't like being watched, and the obvious emphasis on security made her slightly paranoid.

"Name?" one of the guards asked.

"Susan Gant."

The guard checked his clipboard. "ID?"

Susan dug her driver's license out of her purse.

The guard glared at it. Satisfied, he offered a meager smile. "Go ahead." He aimed a thumb at the door.

Susan heard a buzzing noise and pulled the door open. Inside, she found another entryway, this time with a metal detector exactly like those at an airport.

"Step through," a woman in uniform told her.

The device beeped rudely as Susan walked through it.

"Empty your pockets," the woman said, obviously disinterested. "And I'll have to look in your purse."

Susan shrugged. Whatever. This was nothing compared with breaching Super Max. Now if this lady decided to search her . . .

"Step through again."

This time the detector remained silent.

"Who are you here to see?"

"Ruth Sanders."

She checked her clipboard.

"Okay. Wait in there."

Susan stepped into a waiting room filled with couches and hard-backed chairs. Actually, she thought, the place *did* resemble a prison.

Riffling through the magazines on the end table, she selected one and settled in to read.

"I thought you weren't coming."

She set the magazine down and rose to greet Ruth Sanders. The woman was older than she had expected: wrinkled face, graying hair, sad eyes. Or maybe she just looked old. Losing a son might account for the premature aging.

"Hello, Mrs. Sanders. I'm Susan Gant." She shook Ruth's hand. It was cold and limp. "I'm sorry I'm late. I had car trouble."

Sanders nodded at this.

"Do you still have time for lunch?"

"As long as I'm back by one."

"Well, we'll try to be quick."

Susan drove them to a nearby deli. When they had their sandwiches and drinks, she asked, "What can you tell me about Dr. Hanson?"

"He's a devil." She said it in an expressionless voice, as if discussing the weather.

"He was your psychiatrist, wasn't he?"

"Yes."

"Did you have any reason to believe that he had . . . that he was capable of . . ."

"Murder? That he murdered my son?" She shook her head. "Dr. Hanson was the most likable person you could ever hope to meet. Kind, compassionate, caring—that's what makes it all the more horrendous."

"As I mentioned, Mrs. Sanders—"

"You can call me Ruth," she said without smiling.

"Okay, Ruth. As I mentioned, I am representing Dr. Hanson. I'm—"

"What happened to his other attorney?"

"Dr. Hanson fired him."

"Why?"

Susan paused. "Well—it doesn't matter. What's important is that I'm defending Dr. Hanson now. So I'm looking for anything that might help prove his innocence."

Sanders stared at her.

"Do you know of any reason that Dr. Hanson would make a special trip down from Denver, where he was attending a conference, to—"

"To kill Zach? To hang him from the ceiling and scratch a satanic cross over his heart? No, Ms. Gant. I certainly don't. I cannot comprehend why any human being would act in such a way."

Susan realized that this wasn't going to be easy. She tried to think of a way to rephrase the question. "I'm trying to establish that while Dr. Hanson may have had the means to commit this horrible crime, he did not have what we call 'motive.' Motive is what compels someone to act. For instance, a husband comes home and finds his wife in bed with another man. His motive for assaulting that man would be clear: jealousy. A man embezzles funds from the bank he works for. His motive: greed.

"But in this case I've been unable to figure out why Dr. Hanson would want to hurt your son. He claims he didn't even know him."

"Hanson confessed. Isn't that enough?"

"Normally. In fact, it was enough to send him to death row. But now he's recanting that confession. He says he didn't do it."

"Then why did he confess?" The frown on her face trembled.

"He alleges that he was coerced—his family threatened. He had reason to believe that they would be harmed if he did not confess to Zachary's murder."

"But his fingerprints were in Zach's . . ." That was as far as she got. The stoic facade crumbled, and she began to sob.

Susan waited—somewhat impatiently—for the tears to pass. Though she empathized with this woman and her loss, she knew that she was running out of time. In a few short minutes, she would have to take Sanders back to work and would probably not see her again before the hearing.

"Mrs. Sanders—Ruth—let's pretend that Dr. Hanson didn't confess."

"But he did."

"I know," she said. "But just for a moment, suppose he didn't do it. Suppose he was framed. Remember, he doesn't seem to have a motive. Wouldn't it be tragic if Zach's death was avenged by a miscarriage of justice?"

Sanders dabbed at her eyes and tried to sniff the tears away.

"Did Dr. Hanson ever act inappropriately during your sessions at the Institute?"

She shook her head, still sniffing.

"Did he help you progress in therapy?"

A nod and a sniff.

"Up until the day that he was accused of murder, did you ever have any reason to be concerned about his skill as a mental health professional?"

"No."

"What was your attitude about him prior to his arrest?"

Ruth considered this. "I liked him. He was a good listener. And he wasn't pushy—like Binker. Dr. Hanson let me move at my own pace."

"Binker diagnosed you as an SRA victim, didn't he?"

"Yes. And he said I was suffering from multiple personality disorder."

"What did you think about that?"

"I didn't know what to think. I was going to therapy to try and deal with losing Zach. Then Dr. Binker started finding all of these things that were wrong with me. But he was the doctor and I was just the patient."

"Did Dr. Hanson agree with Binker's diagnosis?"

"I'm not sure. I don't think so. He told me that Binker might have assumed some things he shouldn't have. He said he wanted to make a fresh start, to go back to the issues of my husband and my son, then progress from there."

"And you felt comfortable with that?"

"Yes. It made sense to me. Binker . . . he just went too fast. Always pressing me to remember things I never knew I experienced. And that memory reconstruction business—that really bothered me."

Susan phrased her next question carefully. "Did you know that just before your son died, he discovered that the Institute was misusing patient records?"

"Zach?"

"According to Dr. Hanson, Zachary 'hacked' his way into the system. And Hanson asserts that it may have gotten him killed."

Sanders covered her face with a hand, the tears returning. "I just wish this was over."

Susan glanced at her watch and realized that it was. At least this meeting was. Time to get Sanders back.

"I appreciate your taking the time to talk with me, Ruth. I can only imagine how painful it must all be." She wiped her mouth and took a last sip of iced tea. There was still half a sandwich on her plate. Sanders hadn't even touched her lunch.

"Before I drive you back to work, I have another favor to ask. I was wondering if I could take a look at your journal."

"My therapy diary?"

Susan nodded.

It was clear by the look on her face that the idea displeased Sanders.

"Ruth, I'm grasping at straws here. Maybe your diary can help."

"I doubt that."

"You never know. It might just hold the key to this puzzle, the key to Hanson's defense."

"You want me to help you free my son's killer."

"What if he isn't your son's killer? What if he's an innocent man?"

Sanders sighed. "It's in my locker. I'll get it for you when we get back."

They rose and left the deli, making the short drive to the HP facility. Sanders never spoke. She left Susan in the reception area and returned minutes later with an oversized book bound by an attractive multicolored cover.

"Here," she grunted, handing it to Susan.

"Thank you," Susan said, accepting it. But Sanders wouldn't loosen her grip.

"Promise me something."

"What's that?"

"Promise me that justice will be served." She stared into Susan's eyes, then exited through the secure door.

"Justice," Susan muttered to herself as she left the building and climbed into her damaged car. That was a lot to ask from an imperfect system operating in an imperfect world. And the Hanson case—it was anything but perfect. So many loose ends and unresolved questions. But as she drove out of the lot, Susan vowed to do her level best to ensure that justice was indeed served.

The Hewlett Packard facility turned out to be only fifteen minutes from the Institute. With close to an hour to kill before her appointment with Dr. Bayers, Susan sought out a coffee bar, intent upon studying Sanders's diary.

Taking a booth near a window in the deserted establishment, she sipped poorly brewed espresso—Starbucks didn't have to worry about this place stealing their business—and opened the journal. She felt a tinge of guilt as she did this. Browsing through someone else's diary was—well, an intrusion. She was barging into a written record of Ruth's most private thoughts, eavesdropping on the woman's secret hopes, dreams, fears, problems. But Ruth had given her permission, and if it would help Hanson's cause . . .

She examined the first entry, dated March 23—just a few weeks after Zach's death. In it, Sanders explained her state of mind and why she was seeking therapy.

Dr. Binker has asked me to keep this diary. I'm not much of a writer, but he says that by putting my feelings on paper, I will "facilitate the healing process." I'm willing to do anything that will speed that along. I sincerely want to be healed.

First, I suppose I should talk about what happened. My son killed himself. It seems so simple to write those four words. But that phrase is a sword. Every time I say it, every time I think it, it cuts me. The words slice through me, penetrating my heart. I bleed tears when I think of what Zach did.

In some ways, I don't want to cry. I don't want to feel that pain anymore. I want to get over it, to get on with my life. In other ways, I don't want to give it up. I guess I feel responsible for what happened. I should have seen it coming, I should have stopped it, I should have done something. Instead, I went to a ladies' meeting at church.

So I'm beating myself up for not keeping Zach alive, for not giving him a reason to live. There's something else though. It's like he's fading away. I relive the moment I found him daily, sometimes hourly. But it's still fading. I already lost him once. Now I'm losing him again. He's float-ing away. I can't hold on to him. The boy that was my son has changed from a vibrant human being to a gray, dim recollection. Even his memory is slipping away from me. Sometimes, I can't remember his face. I'd rather die than be subject to this torture.

The next several entries were similar: more regrets, more self-condemnation, more anxiety over forgetting the details of her son and his life. Susan was no expert, but to her, Ruth's attitude seemed natural. To be expected. The woman was depressed; she was searching for ways to explain the unexplainable. And she was blaming herself.

At ten till two, Susan closed the book and tossed the remains of her latte into the trash can. It was too bitter and muddy to choke down.

As she made the short drive to the Institute, she tried to decide what she would ask Dr. Bayers. She had a list of topics to probe, but how would she go about it? How would she broach the subject of the MRT unit? How, without completely alienating the man, could she suggest that it was being misused, that some-one associated with the Institute might be illegally marketing memories via the Internet?

She was still considering strategies—the direct approach, the subtle approach, or some middle ground—as she pulled into the Institute's parking lot and slipped her car into a space.

TWENTY

THE TRINITY INSTITUTE OF PSYCHIATRIC THERAPY WAS LOCATED in a modern, attractive office park in Rockrimmon, a well-established neighborhood north of downtown, just west of I–25. The Institute's offices were part of a network of low-rise professional buildings that had been constructed in the early eighties, just before the collapse of the oil industry. Many had stood vacant until the late nineties when growing health care providers—like the Institute—moved in and updated them, quickly gobbling up the space. Now, landing an office in this coveted area was nearly impossible.

Susan looked up at the directory in the entryway, then back down at her notes. Dr. Bayers's office was in Suite 7. But she didn't see a Suite 7 listed.

"Can I help you?"

She looked up; a woman sat at a desk across the room. "I'm looking for Dr. Bayers."

The woman touched the computer screen in front of her. "Ms. Gant?"

Susan nodded.

"Dr. Bayers," the woman said, apparently into the headset she was wearing. "Ms. Gant is here to see you." There was a pause. "I'll send her up." To Susan, the woman said, "He's ready for you, Ms. Gant. Take the elevator to the top—the sixth floor—and go down the hallway to your right. His office is the last door on the left."

"Thanks." Susan summoned the elevator with the press of a button and the door immediately opened. Stepping on, she punched six. Thirty seconds later, she was in the hallway on the sixth floor, following the receptionist's directions. She reached the last door on the left and read the plaque: "Dr. William Bayers, Chairman." Show time.

She tapped on it with her knuckles.

"Come in," came the deep-voiced response.

When Susan opened the door, her first thought was: *Wow!* The office was much larger than she had expected, and much more luxurious. Yards of rust-peppered beige Berber carpet ran away toward a tinted, floor-to-ceiling window, behind which loomed the majestic, snowcapped image of Pikes Peak. It seemed close enough to touch. The other walls were consumed by framed southwestern art and a collection of handsome bookshelves bearing hardbound volumes. An unusual wooden hat rack near the door supported two felt cowboy hats. A long, pine coffee table held a spread of journals and a beautiful Navajo sculpture depicting a half-man/half-eagle creature that was in the process of either taking flight or landing. Three leather couches and a half-dozen leather chairs were arranged at angles, offering visitors a view of the mountain or the library or the occupant's desk. The desk itself was noteworthy: rugged aspen posts supporting a blond aspen top.

"Ms. Gant," the man behind the desk nodded. He gestured to a nearby chair. "Please have a seat. I'll be right with you."

Susan complied. Like his office, Dr. Bayers was not what she had expected. He was younger than he sounded on the phone, younger than she had anticipated the chairman of a mental health facility to be. And better looking. Though Bayers had to be in his early fifties, he had a boyish face, a ruddy complexion, blue eyes, and a full head of hair as blond as his desk. He reminded her of someone . . . of a celebrity . . . of . . . Nick Nolte. No—Robert Redford. That was it. The man was every bit as handsome as Redford.

"Investigate MPD. Recommend starting her on the MRT by the fourth or fifth session," Bayers was saying—to his computer. "Have Marge handle the scheduling and submit the report for review." He paused, looking at Susan but not seeing her. "End notes."

Bayers rose, donned a fresh smile, and extended his hand. "It's a pleasure to meet you, Ms. Gant."

Susan accepted his hand. The grip was firm, the expression on Bayers's face sincere.

"That's a neat little gadget you have there, Doctor," she said, pointing to the computer.

"Call me Bill, won't you?" Bayers patted the computer terminal proudly. "Latest generation of Macs. We run the Hyperdrive AI program."

"AI?"

"Artificial Intelligence," he explained. "No more laborious computer commands. No more scanners. No more transcriptions. You just speak and it acts. Touch the screen, and you've got a patient file. Tell it to go to sleep, and it does."

"That's really something."

"I got into computers in college—back in the dark ages," he said with a chuckle, "when PCs were nothing but a pipe dream. I met Steve Jobs once, convinced him to let me have one of his first Macintoshes back in—'79, I think it was. Couldn't stay away from the thing. Computers have fascinated me ever since."

"Why'd you go into mental health?"

He gave her a lopsided grin. "If I'd known that a high-tech explosion was in the offing, I might not have. I might have majored in computer science. Those guys made out like bandits."

"You've done pretty well for yourself," Susan observed, taking another look at the office.

"Sure. And, of course, psychiatry has its own rewards. Chips and discs and drives don't come into your office and thank you for helping them through a difficult time. They don't express their deepest appreciate for 'curing' them of one of the most debilitating diseases on the planet."

He read Susan's puzzled look and added: "Mental illness. Can I get you something? Coffee, tea, Perrier, something to eat?"

"No, I'm fine, thanks. If you don't mind, I'd like to ask you about Craig Hanson."

Bayers nodded, his expression solemn. "Yes. Craig. A tragedy, really. A terrible thing." He paused. "First, if you have the time, let me give you a quick tour of the facility. Perhaps that will give you a feel for where Craig worked, possibly even answer a few of those questions."

Susan shrugged. "Okay."

He led her down the hall, past other offices, recounting the history of the Institute: how it had begun as a small, nonprofit, amateur counseling ministry in the early days of Trinity Fellowship and evolved into the premiere Christian therapy institute in the nation in a matter of a decade.

"We have here some of the finest psychiatric minds in the world. And with our holistic approach—recognizing that human beings are complex and that their mental dynamics are affected by a combination of physical, emotional, and spiritual factors—we feel that we offer quality care and a standard of excellence that is unmatched."

After visiting two floors of computer-equipped treatment rooms, they reached a door marked: MRT unit.

"This is our Memory Reconstruction Therapy center," Bayers explained, pushing open the door. "The technology employed here is highly advanced and the results are simply astounding."

To Susan it looked like nothing more than an oversized closet. A rack of electronics and tangled wires sat to one side of an empty area. Above them, tiny black devices were attached to the ceiling.

"I actually helped design it," Bayers boasted, grinning. He tapped the rack of metal boxes. "Not technically, but in terms of the production. I helped get the financial backing in place, and I brought together the engineers—mostly ex-Apple employees. We put them in a lab and locked the door. And this is what they came up with."

"How does it work?"

"Those are lasers," he said, pointing to black boxes atop four tripod towers. "They track body position. The patient stands on this platform," he gestured, "and the lasers capture his or her size and shape in a twelve-second pass. They scan a cylindrical volume two meters high—1.2 meters wide. The result is a 3-D, remarkably accurate model of the human body."

Bayers turned to a hook on the wall and lifted what looked like a wet suit. "The patient wears this full-body peripheral." He presented it to her. Susan gave the rubbery fabric a squeeze and was surprised to find it stiff and cold. "The suit serves two purposes. First, it acts as a sensory deprivation device, shutting off all outside stimuli. Second, it contains a network of electrodes that trigger various acupressure points along the musculo/skeletal system." He replaced the suit and picked up a polished helmet with a black visor—something a motorcycle rider might wear. "This is called the crown." He flipped it to display the inside. It was riddled with wires. A thick, round plug was attached to the center of the lining. "Basically, the halo." Here he tapped the ringed edge of the helmet. "It's . . . well . . . something akin to a functional MRI."

"MRI?"

"Memory Resonance Imaging," Bayers explained. "It measures blood flow and oxygen concentration. Both change with neural activity. For instance, in vision, the neurons fire very rapidly, requiring a great deal of oxygenated blood."

"Uh-huh," Susan said, nodding, pretending to understand.

"This," Bayers said, fingering a long tube, "is a nasal thermistor. It monitors breathing. By keeping track of breath rates, therapists can assist patients in achieving and maintaining a lucid, dreamlike state that enhances the therapy experience.

"The visor is, of course, a screen that displays the virtual environment."

"Of course."

"You've got headphones. And this little knob here," Bayers
said proudly, tilting the helmet to show her the plug, "this is what
sets the MRT apart from other VR toys."

"What's it do?"

"It's an ultrasound cannon." Bayers smiled, obviously pleased by
the puzzled expression on Susan's face. "It shoots ultrasonic waves
into the brain, bombarding the cerebral cortex with—well, false
information. It tricks the brain into sending signals to the nervous
system, thereby causing ghost impressions: joy, sorrow, pleasure, pain,
and so on. The electrodes in the suit compound the illusion.

"The entire peripheral is linked by radio wave to these," he
announced, aiming a thumb at the electronic components. "They
read, respond to, predict, and create the virtual landscape. Full
color, surround sound, with the full gamut of emotions and physical sensations. It's wild."

"What's the purpose?" she wondered, already knowing the
answer.

"The MRT generates a safe, controllable environment that
enables patients to deal with phobias, traumas, and repressed memories. Say a person suffers from acrophobia—fear of heights. In a
series of progressive treatments, the patient can slowly
overcome—"

"Dr. Hanson told me about phobia treatment," Susan broke
in. "You mentioned memories. What's that all about?"

Bayers rubbed his chin, thinking. "By processing the information supplied by the patient, the computer can reconstruct a
memory, producing a scene that bears at least some resemblance
to the original trauma. In this way, the patient can re-experience
it, and, in theory, overcome it. The unit is also useful in rediscov-
ering and recovering repressed memories."

"Repressed memories?" Susan asked, feigning ignorance.

"Experiences that are so extreme or terrifying that the conscious mind refuses to face them. As a survival mechanism, it hides them away, burying them in the subconscious. These lost memories can act like wounds, festering until they incapacitate an individual. Yet the patient may not even be aware of their presence."

"SRA is basically the same story?"

Bayers reappraised Susan with his eyes. "You've obviously done your research, Ms. Gant." Nodding thoughtfully, he explained, "Satanic ritual abuse is similar, yes. But usually much more complex and severe. Unlike sexual and violent abuse, SRA involves acts that even the subconscious has difficulty accepting. Symptoms in these patients are more profound, their codependencies more pronounced. These patients are deeply troubled and often drift helplessly into psychosis."

"And the MRT helps bring them back?"

"Not in every case. But it does have a high success rate."

Susan paused, contemplating her next question. "Dr. Hanson believes that the MRT is overused. He claims that one of the main abuses is in the area of SRA. Would you agree?"

Bayers shook his head. "No, I would not. And I might add that Dr. Hanson is in no position to throw stones."

"Do the doctors at the Institute overdiagnose SRA?" She smiled at him timidly, waiting for an answer.

"Of course not." He chuckled at the suggestion, ushering her out of the room. "As I said, the staff here is arguably the finest in the world. I think if you checked our files—"

"I can't do that because of patient/doctor confidentiality," Susan pointed out.

"Obviously. But if you could, you would find that SRA is not a common diagnosis."

Susan followed Bayers back to his office, the tour clearly over. When they were both seated, she withdrew a pad and looked at her host. He seemed older now, late fifties with crow's-feet around the eyes. His eyes seemed more gray than blue.

"Craig is convinced that someone is offering MRT session files over the Internet as pornography."

Bayers winced at this, as if she had just struck him with her fist.

Maybe the direct approach wasn't the best choice, she decided. But it was too late to turn back now. "Could someone do that? Without you knowing?"

The doctor's face flushed slightly. At first, Susan wasn't sure if it was because Bayers was embarrassed by the subject or offended by what he considered a veiled accusation. When he spoke, the answer became plain.

"How dare you come into my office and accuse me of illegal, unethical activity!" he growled, his deep voice filled with anger. "How dare you!"

"I'm sorry, Doctor. I didn't mean to imply that—"

"My attorney advised me not to meet with you. He said that you would try to turn this mess around and implicate the Institute. Just like the media did when it first came out. But I have news for you, Ms. Gant. Dr. Craig Hanson is guilty. *He* killed a boy. *He* abused his family. *He* mutilated animals. We had nothing to do with any of that."

"But he was your employee, and—," Susan tried to say.

"Yes, Hanson worked here," Bayers interrupted. "And yes, his crimes did reflect poorly on the Institute. Our reputation was sullied. It was a PR nightmare. But we've moved beyond it. We are recovering our dignity and doing our best to forget the entire debacle."

"Dr. Bayers, I understand how you must feel," Susan offered. "But my client is on death row. And this is his only chance for—"

He waved her off, rising from behind the desk. "Craig Hanson is a confessed murderer. He deserves to be punished accordingly."

"But he has retracted his confession, and all I'm trying to do is confirm—"

Another wave of his hand silenced her. "This meeting is over, Ms. Gant. Good luck with your case."

Susan sighed and repacked her satchel. As she was leaving Bayers's office she heard him mutter, "I should have listened to my attorney."

When she reached the ground-floor entry area, she asked the receptionist if Dr. Singer was in.

"No, I'm afraid he's out of the building."

No surprise there, she thought.

On the way back to the freeway, she checked in with the office. There were two messages. The DA's office had called to inform her that Judge Humphries had turned down her request for a continuance. And someone else had called. No name. Just a number and a one-word message: urgent.

She dialed the number as she accelerated onto the freeway. A glance into the rearview mirror rewarded her with a glimpse of a white Dodge pulling into the stream of traffic behind her.

The line rang twice, then a male voice answered.

"Hello, Susan."

She swore softly. This was getting old.

"What is your problem?" she asked.

"On the contrary, Susan. I don't have one. But you do."

She hung up and dialed Campbell.

"Campbell here."

"This is Susan. The nut called the office and left a number." She read it to him. "Can you trace it or something?"

"I'll get on it."

She replaced the phone and flipped on the radio, searching for a decent station. What an ordeal this was turning out to be. Her first real case, her first chance to stand in a courtroom, parry with a prosecutor, regale a judge with argument after convincing argument concerning her client's innocence. But instead of preparing an opening statement, she was running around like a chicken with its head cut off, unable to uncover any new evidence, unable to get in touch with potential witnesses—and on top of that, some lunatic was giving her a hard time, harassing her over the phone and via videotape, apparently watching her disrobe and shower, and generally doing his best to intimidate her into backing off. It was not exactly the dream shot she had been longing for since law school.

The phone buzzed and she picked it up. "Any luck?"

"Luck? I don't believe in it. I believe in evil. That's the ultimate power. When I get you alone, I intend to draw upon it as I ..." And the voice went on to describe a despicable act.

She slammed the phone down, then hit the brakes, nearly rear-ending a van.

The phone buzzed again. She glared at it, silently vowing not to answer. Then, in a fit of rage, she picked it up.

"Listen, you—," she began angrily, then swore at him.

"Ms. Gant?"

"John?"

He chuckled. "I thought for a minute I'd dialed 1–900–SAILOR."

"Sorry about that," she sighed.

"Did he call again?"

"Yeah. The pervert."

"We need to get you caller ID—and bug your phone lines."

"I think he already did. Bug them, I mean."

"We'll have the boys from the lab sweep your place tonight. And that number you gave me ..."

"Turned out to be the Governor's Mansion?" she asked sarcastically.

"No. A pay phone in Colorado Springs. I gave it a jingle, but there was no answer."

210 APPEARANCE OF EVIL

"Figures."

"Drive carefully back to Denver. I'll stay close."

"Thanks, John."

Susan hung up, then unplugged the phone. After two scans of the radio dial, she found a station playing a soothing classical piece. Taking a deep breath, she leaned back in the seat and concentrated on the music. There was no reason the hour-plus trip had to be stressful, no reason she couldn't make it into a mini-vacation, an opportunity to relax and forget about the craziness her life had become over the past few days.

Unless, of course, some nut in a sports car tried to kill her again.

TWENTY-ONE

IT WAS ALMOST FOUR WHEN SUSAN ARRIVED AT the office and checked for messages. There weren't any. Singer hadn't called. Neither had Satan. All was quiet.

She decided to gave the Institute another try, certain that Dr. Singer would not be available. He wasn't. She left yet another message.

She pulled a Diet Coke from the vending machine down the hall, settled in behind her desk, and opened Ruth Sanders's diary.

She flipped along, scanning. The entries continued with the same main themes—depression and grief—the thoughts growing deeper, more insightful, darker on occasion. Some of them dealt with Ruth's husband and his bout with cancer.

The entry dated July 2 seemed to signal the end of a long tunnel.

I feel like a zombie waking from a hypnotic daze, stumbling out of a tomb, looking upon a sunrise for the first time. I know that it was real. I know that I lost the two greatest loves of my life. But I also know that I am alive. I have breath and blood in me. I have a future. I can remember the past. I can mourn it. I can celebrate today. I can cry. I can laugh. I am free to drink in the sweetness as well as the bitterness of life. I embrace both. They continue to instruct me. They are tutors, each with many lessons to impart. Victory without adversity would be empty. One without the other is hopelessly incomplete.

I realize now that I have been asking the wrong question. Instead of shouting at God, demanding to know "why," I should have been crying out to him, begging to know "how." How does one make the journey from birth to death without regret, without bitterness? How does one accept and overcome tragedy, allowing it to build character? How does one find joy in the midst of sorrow? I don't pretend to have found the answers. But I believe that the first step involves taking God's hand and walking quietly, without struggle, in his shadow. That is what I have chosen to do. And it has brought me peace.

The next few entries reflected her change of heart, speaking of joy and God and peace. Ruth Sanders had emerged from her depression. Or so it seemed.

Six entries later, there was an abrupt shift.

Dr. Binker believes there may be more issues involved in my recovery than simply Zach and Richard. I think he's wrong. I think my healing is nearly complete. But I have agreed to let him "probe" my unconscious with a new type of therapy. I don't understand it, but he says that he wants me to be well again. So do I.

The date skipped from July 25 to August 13. This puzzled Susan until she read the next entry.

They've started. Dr. Binker says it's natural. I think it's hellish. I never did any drugs back in the sixties. But I have to wonder if this isn't what it would be like to be on a hallucinogen. I see things. I dream things. Bad things. Dark things. Blacks. Reds. Monsters. Demons. It's hideous. I wish it would stop.

Two entries later, Ruth described a vivid dream.

I was walking down a corridor. It was dark, but I could see that the walls were gray stone with patches of green moss. I came to a wooden door. There was a design drawn on it. The paint was a glossy red. I reached up and touched it and found that it was still wet. I smelled it. It wasn't ink or paint. It was blood.

I remember staggering. I felt like throwing up. Then the door swung open. There was someone standing there. I couldn't see his face. He was wearing a black robe with a hood. He was tall. He grabbed my wrists and pulled me inside.

I fell to the floor. It was concrete and it bruised my knees. The entire room was concrete. Like a basement, or a dungeon. There were candles everywhere. They were arranged in circles. There were people there too, people wearing robes.

When I stood up and turned around, I saw that the man who had pulled me through the door was holding a knife. I still couldn't see his eyes, but I could see that he was smiling. He said, "The Master demands a sacrifice." Then he lifted the knife and moved toward me. I covered my head with my hands and started screaming.

I woke up screaming. The bedsheets were drenched. Not just from sweat. I had wet the bed.

It was the same basic "memory" I experienced in the MRT yesterday. The robes, the candles, the darkness . . . I don't understand. What's going on?

The diary went on in the same vein: visions of robe-clad celebrants engaging in secret rituals, knives, blood, sacrifices . . . They were gory accounts. And Sanders continued to question them, noting that they seemed to be related to her MRT sessions. In one entry, she even wondered if the MRT had induced them. Susan continued paging through the material.

August 25

Today Dr. Binker told me that he thinks I may have been abused as a child. Not just sexually or physically. It's something he calls SRA— satanic ritual abuse. Even the sound of it gives me shivers. Dr. Binker suspects that I was victimized by a satanic cult. I told him that I don't remember anything like that. And if Satanists had abused me, I'd think I would remember it clearly. But he says sometimes when people experience trauma, especially when children experience severe trauma that they are unable to deal with, they hide it or "repress" it somewhere in the subconscious. Kind of like post-traumatic stress syndrome. They stuff the experience deep into their subconscious and then they don't have to face it. Later, say when the child becomes an adult and is in a safe place emotionally, then the memory can be dredged out and processed. He thinks that

these dreams and hallucinations and voices I've been experiencing are actu-
ally flashbacks—repressed memories resurfacing. He thinks it's my sub-
conscious trying to tell me about the abuse.

I don't know what to think. Maybe I'm psychotic.

August 28

As if my emotional state wasn't bad enough, now Binker says I have
MPD—multiple personality disorder. He says it's a condition common to
people who have experienced extreme trauma. Apparently, the mind cre-
ates alternative personalities— "alters"—when it can't handle something,
such as being the guest of honor at a virgin sacrifice. These alters can be
nice, mean, male, female, old, young, whatever. But the idea is that they
assist the primary personality—the inner child—in surviving inhuman
torture.

I've never heard of such a thing. But there has to be a logical explana-
tion for the things I see and hear. I'm afraid all the time. I've contemplated
suicide. There has to be a reason. I hope Binker is right. I hope it's MPD.

The phone rang. Susan placed a marker in the journal before
answering.

"Susan Gant."

"This is Dr. Singer. I'm returning your call."

Calls plural, she felt like saying. "Dr. Singer. I believe I mentioned to your secretary that I am the defense attorney in the
Hanson case."

"Yes."

"Well, I was hoping that we could meet to discuss—"

"I've been advised by the attorneys here at the Institute not
to speak with you."

"I just have a few quick questions."

He sighed. "I have two minutes before my next patient."

Susan paused, trying to organize her thoughts. "You're friends
with Dr. Hanson, aren't you?"

"I was. Before I found out who he really was and what he had
done."

"So you think he's guilty?"

Singer scoffed at this. "He was tried and convicted. Besides that, he confessed. Yeah, I think he's guilty as sin."

"Did you know that he has recanted the confession?"

"I'm not surprised. If I was about to receive a lethal injection, I'd recant too. And pray like mad that my ploy was successful."

"What would you say if I told you Dr. Hanson was framed, that the whole thing was a setup?"

"I'd say you're making up fairy tales in a desperate attempt to save your client's skin. My patient just arrived."

"What's your opinion of Memory Reconstruction Therapy?" she blurted out. "Does it lead patients to preordained diagnoses? Did Dr. Binker use it to *move* Ruth Sanders to SRA victimhood?"

Singer's voice hardened. "If you wish to discuss the Trinity Psychiatric Institute, its employees, or its therapy methods, contact our attorneys."

So much for Dr. Singer, she thought, hanging up. He would clearly be no help in establishing that the Institute had misused the MRT unit or that Ruth Sanders had been "encouraged" to become a ritual abuse survivor.

She had just returned to Sanders's journal when her watch began to beep. Turning off the alarm, she checked the time: 4:30. Picking the phone back up, she placed a call to Super Max for her scheduled powwow with Dr. Hanson.

After arguing her way past three phone dispatchers, she was finally told to wait while Hanson was brought to the phone.

"Susan?" a voice asked several minutes later.

"Craig. How are you doing?"

"Better. Sorry about yesterday."

"No need to apologize."

"It was a bad day. But today I'm—I'm better."

"I'm glad."

"How are things coming? Any luck with those leads?"

"A little. I met with Ruth Sanders."

"And?"

"The woman's still in a lot of pain."

"For good reason."

"Anyway, I got hold of her diary. It reads just like you said it did. And I also met with Dr. Bayers this afternoon."

"Really? I'm surprised he agreed to speak with you."

"We didn't talk long. He gave me a tour of the place, talked about how prestigious it was. As soon as I started asking tough questions, he balked, ranted something about bad PR, and gave me the bum's rush."

"That sounds like Bayers."

"I'm meeting with your wife tomorrow."

There was no response.

"Any message?"

Even long distance, Susan could tell that Hanson was fighting to hold back the tears.

"Tell her . . . tell *them* I love them. The girls too."

"Will do. Oh, I also talked with Roger. We're getting together Sunday."

"Good. What about Grant?"

"I finally got through to him, but he wasn't exactly cooperative."

A breath of air whistled through the receiver at the other end of the line. "Nobody believes me. Sam left me. My girls think I abused them. Now Grant's deserting me."

"Singer testified against you at your original trial," Susan pointed out.

"He was called only to show that Sam and the girls had been ritually abused. Even if his diagnosis was wrong, I can't fault him for his professional integrity. He stated what he thought was true. But he never spoke a word against me. Not directly."

"Yeah, well—let's put it this way. I don't think he's going to be a witness for the defense."

"How did your bid for a continuance go?"

"Thumbs down. The judge—Humphries—he's a bear. The guy has this personal grudge against death-row inmates."

"That's comforting to hear."

"We've still got a shot, Craig," she said, trying to sound convincing.

"I hope so."

Susan referred to her notepad. "I've got a question for you. What happened to your last attorney?"

"Evans? I told you. He didn't believe me. Thought I was guilty, that I was a pathological liar, and that I made the whole frame story up from scratch. Besides, he was a publicity hound. He only agreed to represent me for the news value."

"So you fired him?"

"Right."

"He didn't quit?"

There was a pause. "He didn't want to represent me any longer, if that's what you're getting at."

"Was he threatened?"

"What do you mean?"

"Come on, Craig. Don't play dumb with me. Did someone harass him?"

"Have you gotten more calls from our friend 'Satan'?"

"A few. But what about Evans? Were they using scare tactics against him too?"

Hanson hesitated.

"Craig? Were they?"

"Yeah," he sighed.

"Is that why he quit?"

Silence.

"Craig! You've got to be honest with me or this thing isn't going to fly."

"Yes. He wanted to resign because they said they would come after his kids, his wife—they even tried to run him off the road once. The guy panicked and considered dropping the case. But I fired him before he could quit."

"I wish you'd told me this earlier."

"Why do you think they assigned you those federal marshals, Susan?"

She paused, considering this. "I thought . . . I just thought it was because of the nature of this case—the crimes you were accused of."

"The court knew from past experience that my lawyer would need protection."

Susan suppressed a curse. "Why, if everyone knew, did no one tell me this?"

"Have they done anything . . . serious?" Hanson asked.

"Depends on how you define 'serious.' I've gotten phone calls, videotapes, answering machine messages—and this morning on I–25 I was nearly run over by a semi."

"Are the marshals on it? Did they catch the truck?"

"The truck wasn't to blame as much as this little black sports car. But no, they didn't catch anyone. And now they're taking additional steps to insure my safety."

"What sort of steps?"

"Appropriate steps."

"Susan, I'm worried about you. I—"

"This call will be terminated in exactly one minute," a low voice interrupted.

"We're out of time, Craig. Listen, I'll be in St. Louis tomorrow, but I'll call you Sunday."

"That's a long time from now."

"I know. But you'll make it, Craig. Think positive. We've got until Tuesday to come up with something. Keep your fingers crossed. And while you're at it, pray."

"Believe me, I will."

She hung up and surveyed the office: court records and case documents scattered on the floor, a desk consumed by legal pads, sticky notes, and Sanders's journal. It was the proverbial haystack. And there was still no sign of the ever-elusive needle. Despite her encouraging words to Hanson, there seemed to be little or no chance of discovering the key that would turn the case around. Not in just a few days. If she had six weeks, even a month—then maybe. But by Tuesday? The vultures were beginning to circle above her soon-to-be-executed client.

TWENTY-TWO

THERE WERE TWO WHITE DODGES AND A GRAY, unmarked Ford van parked along the street in front of Susan's apartment when she got home. As she shut off her Subaru, doors on the Dodges popped open and men began climbing out. She spotted John Campbell and Tony Rosselli. They were accompanied by two other large, muscular men—probably fellow marshals. The back of the van swung open, and men and women wearing blue windbreakers piled out carrying aluminum crates of varying sizes. Their jackets bore the letters F-B-I.

"Looks like I'm late for the party," she smirked at Campbell. "What's going on?"

"They're here for the electronic sweep," he told her, nodding to the FBI team.

Susan unlocked the door and gestured for them to enter. The marshals stepped inside, studying the ceiling and walls suspiciously. The others paused outside to open their boxes and assemble the equipment. A minute later they came in, some wearing headphones and wielding long tubes that trailed wires. Others bore monitors—PC-style devices with screens composed of grids and blinking lights. They all wore gloves.

"The problem with this is that it'll tip the guy off," Campbell observed, watching the Fibbies do their work. "He'll know that you know he's been watching and listening."

"I get the feeling he's not too concerned with that," Susan said, frowning. "He was gloating over the fact that he knew I was about to step into the shower. Even described my body—in detail."

Tony perked up at this. "Really? Well, he may be a pervert, but at least he has good taste."

Campbell gave Tony a firm shot to the ribs with his elbow.

"What!" He rubbed his injury. "It was a compliment. I was complimenting Ms. Gant on—"

"I know exactly what you were doing, partner. You were engaging in sexual harassment. She could sue you from here to Ft. Collins. Isn't that right, Ms. Gant?"

Susan nodded, giving Tony her best courtroom glare—the one she'd been practicing in the mirror for months. Tony wasn't a bad guy. He was just suffering from an overdose of testosterone. Purely hormone driven. That was probably why he'd become a marshal—for the adrenaline rush he got from tangling with dangerous criminals.

"Anyway," Campbell said, still admonishing Tony with his eyes, "this loon will know he's been found out. So I advise a couple of courses of action."

"I'm listening."

"First, we get you out of here. Put you in a safe house somewhere until the trial."

Susan shook her head. "I can't hide out. I have too much preparation to do."

"That's what I expected you to say," Campbell replied, nodding. "So what about this—we put in a surveillance system and a security system. That way we can keep an eye on you and keep the scumbag out."

Susan could see the wheels inside Tony's head turning. "Instead of being watched by a crazed lunatic who calls himself 'Satan,' I can let Mr. Hormones here gawk at me. Wonderful."

"We'd be discreet, Ms. Gant. No eyes in the bathroom or the bedroom."

Tony seemed disappointed.

"Whaddaya say?"

Susan shrugged. "I guess."

Campbell said something to one of the FBI agents, and two of the team members were dispatched to the van for more equipment.

"John!" one of the other agents called. "Got something here." He waved Campbell and Rosselli over. Susan followed.

The agent pointed to a tiny hole in the wall. It was no bigger than a pinprick and couldn't be seen from more than a foot away.

"What is it?" Susan asked.

The agent stepped aside and a woman with an undersized crowbar went to work on the hole, chipping away the Sheetrock. Thirty seconds later they could see a shiny lens, then a flexible tube. The woman wiggled the device free and handed it to the agent.

"Fiber optic camera. Nice one too." He offered it to Campbell.

"You're not going to dust it?" Campbell asked.

"We could. But trust me, there won't be any prints."

"Why not?" Susan asked.

"If you spend the money and time to put one of these babies into somebody's wall—and by the way, this was a slick installation—you're not going to get your grubby hands all over it. These folks are pros."

"Got another one in here," a voice called. It came from the bathroom.

"What about the phone?" Campbell wondered.

A young lady was in the process of disassembling it. "Let's have a look," she answered, twisting a screwdriver. "Here we go." She set the pieces aside and displayed a thin buttonlike object the size of a dime. "Latest generation counterintelligence."

Campbell gave the bug a quick look, then shook his head. "If I didn't know better, I'd say Langley rigged the place."

"Except the spooks at the Agency aren't usually this neat," one of the agents shot back. "They don't spit-polish their ops like this."

After another hour of poking, prodding, stringing wire, and cleanup, the place looked as good as new. The security system was up and running, and the array of hidden video cameras and microphones had been tested and approved.

"We're out of here," the leader of the FBI team announced, ushering his people toward the van.

"Thanks, Tom." Campbell gave him a thumbs-up. He turned to Susan. "I'm gone too. Told my wife I wouldn't be home late." He glanced at his watch, then rolled his eyes. "Oops." Campbell started for the door, stopped, and dug something out of his pocket: a small pistol. He held it out to her, butt first. "Here."

Susan stared at it with wide eyes.

"Go on, take it," Campbell insisted, forcing the gun into her hand. "If this nut somehow gets past Tony and me, it may come in handy."

"Know how to use it?" Tony asked.

She shook her head. "No. And I don't want to learn." The pistol was cold and even heavier than it looked. She turned it over, examining the barrel and the trigger with an expression of distaste.

"This is the safety," Tony said, pointing. "Check the clip first. See—the chamber's empty, but you've got rounds ready to rock and roll. You cock it like this." He pulled back the hammer, and the gun elicited a smooth click. "Don't point it at anyone unless you mean business. That's really all there is to it."

"Carry it in your purse," Campbell told her. "I'll take you by the range and give you a crash course in gun safety and marksmanship when you two get back from St. Louis."

"You two?" Susan gasped. "Tony's going? But I thought—"

"We flipped for it. He won." Campbell grinned. "Lucky for me. If I'd missed my daughter's birthday, my wife would have had a conniption fit. Talk to you when you get back."

Susan watched Campbell leave. "Are you on night duty, too?" she asked Tony.

He nodded. "I'll take the couch." He sat down and tried it out, bouncing on the cushion.

"You'll what?"

"You take the bed. I'll sleep right here. I don't mind."

"You're *staying* here?"

"Didn't John tell you? Since you won't let us take you to a safe house, he thought it would be a good idea to—"

Susan hurried through the front door into the street, waving at Campbell's car. "John! John!" He drove on, never seeing her.

"What's the matter?" Tony asked, trotting to her side.

Everything, she wanted to say. It was bad enough having to travel across the country with an oversexed bodyguard. But having him sleep in her apartment?

"Nothing," she muttered, returning to her apartment. "I'll get you a pillow and a blanket."

When Tony was comfortable on the couch, Susan took an armload of books and retreated to the bedroom. "Goodnight, Tony."

"Goodnight, Susan. Remember, our plane leaves at 7:15. We should probably leave for DIA by 5:30. Maybe even 5:15."

"I'll be ready," she groaned.

As she settled into her bed for the first time in days, she decided that having Tony around wasn't all bad. At least she felt safe, secure in her own home.

Propped up against two pillows, she took the *Spiritual Warfare Manual* and a pad, and began reading and making notes. She managed to trudge through a chapter that outlined the basic conflict between God's kingdom and Satan's kingdom before the phone rang. The shrill pulse caused her to flinch.

"Want me to get that?" she heard Tony call.

"No, I've got it. If it's you-know-who, I'll yell."

She took a deep breath and picked it up.

"Ms. Gant?"

"Yes."

"This is Grant Singer."

"Dr. Singer?"

"Sorry about this afternoon. I just—I couldn't talk. Things at the Institute are pretty tense right now."

"Because of Dr. Hanson's hearing?"

"Yeah. Dr. Bayers and his legal consultants have really buckled down. They held an in-service last week and basically ordered us not to comment on the case."

"Bayers was tense when I met with him," Susan told him. "But I'm still not sure what he has to be worried about. The Institute isn't being charged with anything."

"But it's terrible PR. One of our docs—a practicing Satanist, convicted of murder. Not exactly something that instills confidence in patients. And if Craig gets off—I think that's Bayers's worst fear."

"It shouldn't be. He should be crossing his fingers, hoping I pull a rabbit out of my hat. If I can get Hanson acquitted, the Institute's reputation will be cleared."

"I agree. But Bayers sees it differently. He's thinking 'once accused, always guilty.' Even if Craig's exonerated, people will continue to wonder if he did it, you know. He'll wear that around for the rest of his life. And the same is true of the Institute. They get a bad rap and it sticks with them, especially if Craig is walking around free. So the idea is to make sure he isn't."

"You're not saying Bayers would do anything—"

"Let's just say that Bayers and the rest of the upper management at the Institute are shaking in their boots over this thing. They're envisioning their little kingdom crumbling to the ground. And apparently the going line is that desperate times warrant desperate measures."

"Why are you telling me this?" Susan thought to ask.

"You said something when we talked earlier about Craig being sandbagged. It made sense. I never did think he was guilty.

I couldn't imagine Craig doing those terrible things. But he confessed. So that seemed like the end of it."

"What about his kids? You said yourself they were SRA victims."

"I still think they may have been. But that doesn't mean Craig
was the abuser."

"But they said—"

"I know. They named him. But that's not always dependable.
Especially where kids are concerned. They could have been
coached to say that. Or they could have been acting out their
anger, punishing their father for his absence. Maybe they considered his imprisonment a form of abandonment."

"I never thought about that," Susan admitted.

"Anyway, now that he's retracting his confession . . ."

"Do you suppose that's what spooked the Institute? They're
afraid he's going to start pointing fingers?"

"That would be my guess. And I get the feeling it's more than
just a matter of bad PR. I think Bayers is worried about being
incriminated."

"Incriminated? In what?"

Singer paused, then asked in a voice just above a whisper, "Did
Craig say anything about the MRT unit?"

"Yes."

"Did he tell you that patient sessions in the unit were
recorded? And that . . ."

"And that what?"

"Maybe we shouldn't be talking about this over the phone."

Susan started to argue, then remembered that her own lines
had been bugged.

"You're probably right. Can we meet?"

"When?"

"Well, it's already late," she thought aloud. "And I have an early
flight. I'll be in St. Louis all day. What about tomorrow night?

We're scheduled to be back around seven. Could we get together at, say, nine?"

"Fine. Where? I don't mind driving up."

"Okay, then. You know where Bennett's is?"

"The barbecue place? Sure."

"How about if we meet in the bar?"

"Okay."

"Listen, I may need you to testify at the hearing."

Singer sighed at this. "I'll have to think that over. I'd do anything to help Craig. But ... well, testifying—that could get me fired."

"I don't suppose you have any hard evidence about the way the MRT is being used—or misused."

"I've got a disc. Thought it might be good insurance, just in case things got dicey."

"Bring it."

"Okay. See you at nine, in the bar at Bennett's."

Susan laid the phone on the bedside table and rose to start packing. Shoving books and notepads into a day bag, she couldn't help feeling optimistic. Maybe, just maybe, there was hope for Craig Hanson yet.

TWENTY-THREE

THE SPRAWLING DIA TERMINAL WAS DESERTED WHEN SUSAN and Tony checked in at 6:45. With no bags, just carry-ons, they went straight to the gate, handed the attendant their tickets, and waited to board. Susan took up one of her spiritual warfare books and began reading. Tony paged through the swimsuit edition of *Sports Illustrated*.

When they filed into the loading corridor thirty minutes later, it was clear that the flight would not be full. Not even close. Apparently there weren't many people—not even business-people—willing to get up at the crack of dawn to fly from Denver to St. Louis.

Reaching the plane, Susan nodded to her traveling companion and turned left, toward first class. Tony lumbered down the aisle to the right, to a seat just two rows in front of the rear galley.

After settling in, Susan returned to her book, contented. She was happy to be riding in style, in a comfortable seat with adequate legroom. Paul deserved a big thank-you for this one. And she was happy to be flying a plane-length apart from Tony the sex-machine. He wasn't such a terrible guy, really. Just overly amorous.

She had reached a chapter that focused on Satan and was surprised to find that she was fascinated by it. According to this author, the devil was not some omnipotent evil power, equal to God. He was a created being with limited authority and venue. The subjugation of humankind was his principle goal, and to that end, he and his demonic cohorts lied to, deceived, tempted, afflicted, and blinded the people of the earth. Destined for hell, he was intent upon taking a sizable portion of the human race with him. To that end, Satan openly opposed God's children.

The next section discussed the clash between the two opposing camps: the kingdom of heaven versus the kingdom of hell. The "warfare."

Susan read three more sections and was about to launch into a chapter discussing the cross of Christ and the blow the crucifixion had dealt to "the enemy" when someone slumped into the seat next to her. She looked up, then sighed.

"What's the matter?"

"Nothing, Tony," she said. "What are you doing up here? You'd better get back to your seat."

Tony gave her a big grin. "The stewardess said it would be okay. I explained who I was and what we were doing, that it was 'imperative' that I keep an eye on you. And since the flight wasn't full—here I am."

Susan fought the urge to groan. So much for getting anything done.

Tony nodded his head toward the helpful stewardess. The woman smiled back and disappeared into the forward kitchen compartment.

"She's a looker," Tony said, wiggling his eyebrows. "Wonder if she's married."

"What happened to Bambi?"

His face fell. "She dumped me. I stood her up twice—well, as of tonight it would have been twice. Anyway, she told me not to call anymore. Said I was too undependable."

"Are you?"

"What?"

"Undependable?"

"No. It's just the job. Being a marshal isn't nine-to-five. I'm never really off duty."

"So you're married to it, to your job?"

Tony thought about this, his brow crinkling. "Sort of. Devoted to it, at least. I'll have to find a very special lady who understands that and can handle the hours and the demands."

"Good luck."

"Listen, maybe tonight, when we get back—maybe we could—"

She shook her head. "No."

"You didn't let me finish. That's rude, you know."

"Okay, what were you going to say?"

"I thought maybe we could go grab a bite to eat."

"No." She smiled at his persistence. "Now, I have some work to do. So why don't you just sit back, relax, and ogle those bikini babes of yours."

Tony sniffed at this, pretended to be offended, then dug out his magazine.

The engines began to rumble and the plane lurched forward, accelerating down the runway.

Returning to her book, Susan read the section concerning the cross of Christ. As the author told it, Jesus had defeated Satan, effectively winning the war between the kingdoms—yet the battle continued to rage. She had just begun a chapter detailing the inherent power of the name of Jesus when Tony gave a melodramatic sigh.

"What's the matter?"

"I'm bored. Should have brought a book."

You read? she almost asked. "I've got several, but they're all research oriented. Nothing interesting."

"No Michael Crichton or Dean Koontz?"

"No. Why don't you watch the show?" She gestured toward the small screen at the front of the compartment. Police had a 7-11 barricaded on a segment of *Cops*: cars parked at odd angles, doors open, guns drawn and aimed at the convenience store.

Tony studied it for a moment. "I've seen it. That's from last season."

Susan watched as the officers converged on the main entrance. Three men wearing black body armor and carrying rifles rushed the door. The picture jumped as the cameraman moved forward to catch the action. Someone shouted, "Put it down!" Seconds later there was a shot, and the front window shattered. More shouting. Another shot. She wasn't surprised Tony had already seen it. It looked like his kind of program.

Tony eyed her book. "What's that one about?"

"This? Oh, it's . . ." She hesitated, not sure she wanted to get into a theological discussion—with Tony, of all people. "It's background. For the Hanson case."

He frowned at her. "You think I'm stupid, don't you?"

"No. I'm sorry, I just supposed you wouldn't be interested."

"I know I look like a big jock. But I'm not stupid."

"I believe you, Tony."

"I played football in school, sure. Pushed a lot of weights. I still push weights six times a week."

That much was evident. His neck had ceased to exist, two massive shoulders connecting directly to his head.

"But I studied hard. Graduated with honors."

"Really? What was your major?"

"Political science."

Susan looked at him, surprised. Not phys ed? "Where'd you go to school?"

"Air Force Academy."

Now she was truly impressed.

"After graduation I did a twenty-four-month stint at Edwards. Then I joined the U.S. Marshals. Almost two years ago."

Susan made the mental calculations, amazed that this fresh-faced "kid" could have managed all this. It had to make him—at least twenty-six? Just three years her junior?

"Probably stick with the marshals another five or so," Tony was saying.

"Then what?"

"I'm not sure. Secret Service? Or who knows, I might run for office."

"Really?"

"Eventually, I plan to be in Congress. U.S., that is."

"Wow, Tony. I didn't know you were so ambitious."

"Yeah. Most people don't. They take one look at me and decide I'm a brain-dead linebacker. They don't take the time to—"

Susan's cellular line rang. "Excuse me." She dug it out of her bag and punched the button. "Susan Gant."

"Having a nice flight, Susan?" the caller asked.

"Who is this?"

"I'm hurt, Susan. To think that after all we've been through, you still don't recognize my voice. Maybe, even though I've seen you without the towel, we still need to get better acquainted."

Susan made a sour face at the phone.

"Who is it?" Tony asked. "Is it him? Is it Satan?"

Susan nodded and handed him the phone.

"Listen, you little—," Tony began. But he was speaking to a dial tone. "Hung up. The coward." He flipped the phone shut and stuffed it back into her bag.

"Who's doing this?" Susan wondered aloud, her face still twisted into an expression of horror.

"Describe the voice."

"What do you mean? How do you describe—"

"Is it male or female?"

"Male."

"High, low, medium?"

"Medium . . . medium low."

"Any accent?"

"I don't think so."

"What about a speech pattern? Does he stutter? Lisp?"

"No."

"Does he use any phrases repeatedly?"

"I don't know," she said, shrugging. "He says my name a lot. And sometimes he says, 'See you in hell.'"

Tony considered this. "Once we get it on tape, we can have the FBI run some tests, run it against the audio file. Of course . . ." His voice trailed off.

"Of course, what?"

"If this guy is as smart as we think he is, he's probably using a modulator."

"What's that?"

"It's a device that masks your voice—disguises it. The new generation of modulators can turn a man's voice into a woman's and vice versa."

"You're kidding."

"They're pretty slick. Makes it that much tougher to come up with a match in the lab."

"Great," she muttered.

"Don't worry. We'll catch him sooner or later. He's bound to make a mistake."

Susan grunted at this.

"Now back to my original question. What's your book about?"

She began to explain—why she had purchased the books and the subject they focused on.

When she finished, Tony asked, "What's Hanson trying to do? Say the devil made him do it?"

"No. First of all, he claims he's innocent."

Tony gave this a raspberry.

"It's not like he's trying to explain it away as otherworldly. But he believes there's a spiritual component to it. Apparently it's not uncommon among Christians. At least, not according to this literature survey I'm doing."

"You a Christian?"

The question caught her off guard. On most occasions, when facing the issue of religious affiliation, she would nod and agree, explaining that she had been raised going to church. But in this context, when discussing spiritual warfare, the word "Christian" seemed to take on a more serious connotation. Was she a believer in the born-again sense—saved, going to heaven, and waging warfare against the devil?

Tony smiled at her hesitation. "It's not a tough question, is it?"

"I don't know, Tony. I used to go to church when I was a kid. My parents made me. And I even went forward at an altar call once. But now—I'm just not very religious anymore. I don't belong to a church, if that's what you mean."

"Do you believe in God?"

"Yeah. Of course. Don't you?"

"Sure."

"When was the last time you darkened the door of a church?" she asked.

"Hey, I go every week."

"Right," she scoffed.

"I'm serious. I'm a Presby. Born and bred. Fourth generation."

"You go to church?"

"What's wrong with that?"

Susan looked him over. "You just don't strike me as the type of guy who—"

"That's the trouble with judging people by their outward appearance."

"What about your female companions?"

"What about them?"

"The playboy lifestyle doesn't exactly jibe with the Bible, does it?"

"Who said I was a playboy? I date, sure. And I'll admit I'm attracted to beautiful women."

"Like Bambi," she teased in a dreamy voice.

Tony glared at her. "I'm looking for a good wife. Not a playmate."

Susan examined his face, wondering if he was sincere. Time to change the subject, she decided. "So, Mr. Churchgoer, what do you know about spiritual warfare?"

He shrugged. "Not much. I read *This Present Darkness*. That's about it."

She dug it out of her bag and presented it to him.

"Good book. Fun read. Very exciting."

"You sound like a literary critic," she joked.

"But it's fiction," he told her, handing back the book.

"Don't you think there could be something to it—the whole kingdom warfare business? Isn't it possible that there's some sort of . . . I don't know. Spiritual connection? A demonic conspiracy at work in the Hanson case?"

"Maybe. But if there is, Hanson is the head demon. The guy is a confessed Satanist—a murderer. If there's a 'spiritual connection,' he's it. The man is evil."

"What about the calls I've been getting?" she asked.

"What about them? There's a wacko running loose out there. But he's no spirit. He's a man with a demented sense of humor. A prankster."

"I think trying to run me off the road qualifies as more than a prank," Susan argued.

"Okay. Call him a dangerous prankster—even a hit man if you want to. But he's still just that: a man. Not a ghoul or a ghosty. A man."

Susan suddenly recalled something she had read that morning. The "warfare" Christians were supposed to be engaged in was not against other humans but against spiritual beings—demonic hosts in league with and orchestrated by Satan. In this case, however, the battle seemed to have a flesh-and-blood component. Tony was right. The Satan stalking her was no principality or power.

He was a man.

TWENTY-FOUR

SAMANTHA HANSON AND HER TWO DAUGHTERS LIVED WITH Betty Mitchell, Samantha's mother, in a modest, three-bedroom ranch located on the southwest side of St. Louis. It was a fifty-minute drive from the airport on the congested, eight-lane 270 interstate.

When Susan and Tony finally found the address, Tony parked the rental car directly in front of the house and started to get out.

"Stay here," Susan ordered.

He muttered something under his breath and picked up a newspaper. "Holler if you need me."

Susan didn't expect to. Samantha Hanson was not dangerous. Neither were her children. Mrs. Mitchell was another matter altogether. She seemed antagonistic, at least over the phone—protective of her daughter, bitter, and with a real ax to grind against Craig Hanson. Susan was glad that the mother-in-law would not be taking the stand at the hearing.

Mrs. Mitchell answered the door with a deep scowl on her aging face. The woman was probably no more than sixty, maybe sixty-five years old. Yet her expression caused her to appear much older.

"Hello. My name is Susan Gant. I'm here to see—" That was all Susan got out.

"I know why you're here," the woman said, her eyes flashing with animosity. She moved aside to let Susan in, then shut the door with authority. "Sam is in the kitchen. Down the hall. You can't miss it." There was still no hint of cordiality.

Susan took a step and then felt Mrs. Mitchell's hand on her shoulder. The woman had a surprisingly strong grip.

"You be careful with my daughter," she warned. "She's been through a lot. I don't want her hurt like that again."

"Mrs. Mitchell, I just need to ask her a few questions. I assure you that I don't intend to——"

"It's time that this nightmare was over and done with," she said. "Craig Hanson is a monster. He victimized my daughter and her girls. He deserves to be in prison. He deserves to be on death row. We'll all be better off when he's dead."

Mrs. Mitchell released her grip and disappeared down the hall.

On the other hand, Susan thought, massaging her shoulder, maybe she should have let Tony tag along.

She found Samantha sitting at a table in the breakfast nook. An attractive woman with short, dark hair, her face was lined with premature wrinkles. She looked tired or troubled or both. Hunched over a coffee mug, Sam was staring out the window, seemingly lost in thought.

Susan was about to introduce herself when the girls came running through, giggling. They were just as Craig had described them: Emily was cute, Rachel pretty, but gangly, both had dark locks that fell halfway down their backs.

They paused and surveyed the visitor. "Mommy's having a bad day," Emily offered. Then they raced off in a flurry of screeches and shouts.

"Mrs. Hanson?"

Sam continued to gaze out the window.

Susan sat down and pulled out her pad. "Mrs. Hanson, I'm Susan Gant. I'm representing your husband."

Sad eyes looked in her direction. Samantha's face was blank.

"Do you remember? We spoke on the phone?"

She nodded, slowly.

"Are you feeling all right, Mrs. Hanson?"

She responded with a slow-motion shake of her head.

"Can I get you something?"

Another shake.

"Are you ill?"

"I'm having a bad day," she replied in a soft, wavering voice.

"I'm sorry to hear that. I would offer to come back at a different time, but as you know, I flew in from Denver, and the hearing is set for Tuesday."

"Go ahead. Ask your questions."

With Sam's hound-dog eyes staring at her, Susan found it hard to concentrate. "Well—let's see. I guess we could start by talking about the murder."

Sam blinked at half-speed.

"Your husband was at a conference when it occurred. Did he say or do anything when he returned from that conference that led you to believe that he had engaged in any illegal activity?"

"No."

"What about when he was arrested? What did he tell you then? Did he claim to be innocent?"

"At first."

"Then what happened?"

She took a long, deep breath, as if the explanation would require extra energy. "The second day, he changed his story. He confessed."

"What did you think about that?" Susan asked, scribbling a note.

Sam gave a miniature shrug. "I didn't know what to think. I was shocked."

"But you believed him? You believed he committed the crime?"

"Eventually."

Sam's blunt answers were making short work of this interrogation session. They had only been at it for a few short minutes and already Susan was about to breach the touchy subject of ritual abuse.

"When did you learn that Craig had abused the girls?"

"Just before the trial."

"How did you discover this?"

"In therapy," she said through half-closed eyes. "I was being treated for depression, the girls were going through grief counseling . . . at the Institute."

"Before this therapy, did they ever have memories of abuse?"

"No."

"Did the memories begin surfacing in their sessions with Dr. Singer?"

She nodded. "But not in earnest until they started in the MRT unit. It's a type of therapy that reconstructs—"

"I'm familiar with it," Susan told her. "And after they underwent Memory Reconstruction Therapy, that's when they began to remember?"

"Flashbacks at first. Then nightmares. Then open-eye visions. They still have them, sometimes."

"What about you, Samantha? How are you holding up?"

"I'm still in therapy. I've been diagnosed as suffering from severe, chronic depression." She paused and exhaled. "I'm taking all sorts of drugs. Even Prozac. Some days they work. Some days I feel okay; I'm functional. Other days . . . I'm like this. It's rough on the girls."

"Did the girls have memories of actual ceremonies?"

"Yes."

"And they're certain the abuser was your husband?"

Sam hesitated. "Yes."

"You're certain of it too? That Craig was the one who abused them?"

The sad eyes grew wet with tears. "I . . . I think so."

"You don't sound sure."

"Well, I . . . he was my husband. And Craig never . . . he loved the girls. He didn't seem . . ." Her breaths came in quick, weepy gasps. She was losing control.

"The girls didn't remember anything about this until they underwent Memory Reconstruction Therapy," Susan pressed. "Didn't that seem suspicious to you? A rather unlikely coincidence, wouldn't you say?"

"I . . . I don't know!" she said, openly sobbing now. "It's all such a nightmare."

"That's enough!" Mrs. Mitchell growled as she entered the kitchen. "I'll have to ask you to leave."

"Thank you, Mrs. Hanson," Susan said, gathering her notes. "You've been a big help."

Sam was still crying. She made no effort to reply or say goodbye.

Retracing her steps to the front door, Susan decided that her parting comment hadn't been just a polite thing to say. Sam really had been a help. It was clear that Sam was depressed and that the girls had experienced a serious trauma of some variety. Maybe, as Dr. Singer had said, it had been ritual abuse. But the issue of who had done the abusing seemed murky. If the only evidence concerning the perpetrator had been gleaned from the MRT unit, and Susan could prove that the MRT itself was suspect—there was a glimmer of hope.

"You done already?" Tony asked when she reached the car. "That was quick."

"It certainly was."

"What now? Our flight doesn't leave till four." He checked his watch. "It's only noon."

"I guess we hang around the airport."

"Why don't we go to lunch?" Tony offered as they pulled away from the curb. "My treat."

Susan sneered at this. "We can grab something at the airport."

"Ugh! The food's terrible."

"How do you know? When's the last time you ate at the St. Louis airport?"

"I never have. But all airport food is bad. It's a rule of life."

"Is that right?"

"Yeah. Never spit into the wind, and never eat at the airport." Susan shook her head. What an operator.

"Come on. It's just lunch. My treat."

"I guess."

They wound up at a moderately priced Italian restaurant near the airport. Both ordered pasta, and both were pleased with the quality.

"Not too shabby," Tony said, cleaning his plate. "Not as good as Gramma's. But not shabby."

"Did your gramma come over from the old country?"

Tony nodded, smiling. "From Sicily. Boy, could she cook. Whew!"

"Where are you from? New York?"

"Pittsburgh. My family's still there. I visit every so often. But they're not too keen on me."

"Why's that?" Susan put her fork down, stuffed, and pointed to her plate. It was still half-full of noodles. "Want this?"

Tony nodded and reached for it. "Well, Mama thinks I deserted. I left for the Air Force Academy and never came back. The Rosselli family frowns on that." A fork laden with pasta strands traveled to his mouth. "What about you?" he asked, as he dug out his wallet and covered the check with a credit card. "You said something about Portland. That where you're from?"

"No. I'm originally from Idaho. My dad still lives there. My mother died when I was a teenager. I went to the University of Colorado, then did grunt work for the public defender's office in Portland. Something opened up back in Denver, and I jumped at it. I love Colorado. It's a lot like Idaho, except with fewer rednecks."

"Colorado has its share, believe me."

"We'd better get going," Susan announced. "We have to turn in the car and everything."

The waitress returned with the receipt and Tony signed. He shoveled into a half-dozen loads of noodles before wiping his mouth and abandoning the empty plate.

"Thanks for lunch, Tony," Susan said when they were outside.

"You're welcome. Not a bad first date."

"Hey, this wasn't a—" Susan stopped when she realized that he was joking.

"You're easy to rile, you know that?"

Susan stepped off the curb, her mind struggling to come up with a witty retort. She was too distracted to even notice the gray sedan.

"Susan!" Tony shouted.

She looked up and saw the car hurtling toward her. There was no time to react. The instant before it reached her, she experienced something that, until that very moment, she had assumed was only a myth: her life flashed before her eyes. It didn't do so in scenes, like a video summary or a collection of clips from beloved home movies. Instead, she *felt* her life—the joys, sorrows, mistakes, accomplishments, regrets. It was a montage of emotions so powerful that they eclipsed the dreadful certainty that she was about to die, and she forgot to be afraid.

Out of the corner of her eye, she saw Tony leave his feet, launching himself through the air like a linebacker intent upon leveling an approaching running back. In this case, the object of his tackle was Susan.

He hit her with as much force as, she imagined, any car could have, and then they slammed into the asphalt, tumbling across it and rolling under a parked pickup. The sedan continued on its way, never even slowing down as it screeched around the corner and down an alleyway. Tony jumped up and pursued it—on foot.

Susan crawled out and, still sitting, leaned against the tire of the truck that had served as her refuge. Her hands were skinned, one elbow bleeding. She was still dabbing her wounds with a tissue when Tony came back.

"Did you hit your head?" Tony panted, crouching to examine her.

"I don't think so." She rubbed her shoulder. "I bet you were first string."

"Sorry."

"Don't be sorry. I'd rather be tackled by an All-American than run over by a Buick."

"All-Conference," Tony corrected. "And it wasn't a Buick. It was a Mercury Sable. This year's model. Rental. I couldn't get close enough for a plate."

"It probably said 'Satan,'" Susan suggested, trying to get up.

"I need to contact the St. Louis PD," he said, helping her to her feet. "Give them a description of the vehicle."

"What's the point? It's long gone by now."

"Probably," he agreed, helping her up. "But it's procedure."

She waited in the car while Tony went back inside the restaurant to phone in the incident.

"Are you sure you're okay?" he asked when he returned. "I could run you over to the hospital."

"I'm fine."

He started the car, then frowned at her. "Let's hope the rest of the trip is less eventful."

"Yeah, let's."

They spent the next two hours wandering around the St. Louis airport, waiting. When their plane finally left, it did so a full forty-five minutes late. The flight was nowhere close to capacity, so they were seated together again. Thankfully, Tony had bought Michael Crichton's latest offering at a newsstand, ensuring a quiet return trip. He cracked the cover and made it through a half-dozen pages before dozing off.

Susan opened her *Spiritual Warfare Manual* to the bookmark, suddenly keenly interested in God, his kingdom, Jesus, the cross, salvation. As she began to read, she was reminded of the old adage: there are no atheists in foxholes. After almost meeting her fate on the grill of a Mercury, she could appreciate that. Near-death experiences had a way of sending you running, right into God's arms.

Susan consumed the material ravenously, a seeker hungry for the truth. In the seat next to her, Tony began to snore.

TWENTY-FIVE

BUY YOU A DRINK?"

"No thanks. I'm waiting for someone."

Susan glared at the guy, hoping this would deter him. He was relatively good-looking. About her age. But he had that singles bar look: shirt a little too tight, hair a little too perfect, and a gold chain dangling from his neck. And it was clear from his smug grin and the sparkle in his eyes that her cold-shoulder routine was not deterring Mr. Charm.

"Just a short one, then?" he said, sliding onto the stool next to her.

"No."

"What'll it be?" the bartender asked the man.

"Whatever the lady's having," he replied smoothly.

The bartender looked at her, trying to remember the drink.

"Diet Coke," she muttered.

Mr. Charm raised his eyebrows. "On the wagon, huh? Make mine the same," he told the bartender. "With a double shot of Bacardi."

Susan groaned at this and examined her watch for the tenth time in the past two minutes. Singer was late. Nearly half an hour late. She and Tony had rushed directly from DIA to Bennett's, going twenty miles per hour over the speed limit. Now Tony was seated across the room at a booth, gorging on barbecued beef, while she sat at the bar, fending off wolves.

"Lived in Denver long?" the man asked, grinning again.

"No," Susan sighed. She shifted toward the television, away from Mr. Charm. Gazing up at a basketball game, country music blaring in the background, she tried to think. Should she wait for Singer to show? How long? What if he didn't come? Maybe she should give him a call. Or maybe she should just go home, get a good night's rest, and worry about Singer in the morning.

Pulling out her cellular phone, she hit the speed-dial button. Seconds later she heard her own voice: "I'm not in. Please leave a message at the tone."

She punched in the security number and waited for the tape to rewind.

"Handy little gadgets, aren't they?"

She glanced back over her shoulder. Mr. Charm was still in the hunt.

"Don't know what I'd do without mine. I'm a lawyer. What do you do? Wait. Let me guess . . . an executive secretary. Or—or a real-estate agent, right?"

Susan gritted her teeth, resisting the urge to lay into the guy, to explain to him in no uncertain terms that she was neither an executive secretary nor a real-estate agent, but a lawyer who in all likelihood was far more competent than he was.

"Three messages," the computerized voice announced.

The first was from a charity. They would have a truck in her area next week and . . .

She wished she could fast-forward. Instead, she listened to the spiel in one ear, Mr. Charm in the other.

"I know a nice little spot not too far down the road," he was saying. "Good band. We could dance, have a few drinks, then maybe go back to my . . ."

The second message was from Paul. He had spoken with a clerk at the DA's office and been informed that there were no copies of Ruth Sanders's journal available. Paul didn't know, of course, that this didn't matter anymore, since Susan had already obtained the original. Paul droned on, talking to her machine as if it were his best friend.

"I've got a hot tub, too," Mr. Charm continued. "I tell you, after a long day at the office, slipping into that baby is paradise. You could join me. There's plenty of room."

The third message finally played: "Hope you had a nice trip, Susan. Wish I could have gone with you. Oh, that's right! (laughter) I did. Listen, from now on, make sure you look both ways before you cross the street. Wouldn't want anything to happen to you. (more laughter) You might want to look over your shoulder now and then, too. 'Cause I'll be there, watching, waiting for an opportunity to . . ." And 'Satan's' description of what he would do next took a decidedly raunchy turn.

"Bathing suits are optional," Mr. Charm said with a wiggle of his eyebrows. "Just you . . . me . . . hot water . . . bubbles . . . a bottle of wine . . . How's that sound?"

Susan chuckled at this, wondering which was worse—a phone call from Beelzebub incarnate, or being stranded at the bar with this bozo.

She was about to signal Tony to tell him that Satan had left another message—a message that probably wouldn't be there when she got home—and to enlist his help in turning Mr. Charm's amorous intentions in another direction, when she heard her name being called.

"Susan Gant?"

She signaled the bartender, and he brought her a phone. "Call for you."

"Me?"

He shrugged. "If you're Susan Gant."

Singer, she decided. Calling to say he can't make it.

"Hello?"

"So you got my message."

"Who is this?"

"Let's not go through that again, Susan."

She cursed into the phone. "Listen, *Satan*—whoever you are—I've had it with your trash talk, your taunts, your threats—you are *sick*. You're a pervert. You need professional help."

Mr. Charm's eyes grew wide and he slid two seats down the bar, next to an attractive redhead.

"Actually, I wasn't calling to incite you, Susan," the caller said.

"How did you know where I—"

"Susan. Surely you realize by now that I am omniscient. I know all things. I know where you are and what you're doing at every moment of the day and night."

Susan closed her eyes. "Why are you doing this?" she asked in a small, desperate voice.

"I'm just doing you a favor. Thought you might want to know that Dr. Singer won't be able to make your little meeting."

There was a long pause. "Why not?" Susan asked warily, not sure she wanted to hear the answer.

"He has been . . . unexpectedly detained."

"What happened? What did you do to him?"

"You have to realize, Susan, that he didn't have a bodyguard following him around, pushing him out of the path of careless drivers like you do."

"You didn't—"

"But of course I did. Adios, Dr. Singer." The caller laughed wickedly. "Oh, and I should probably remind you that you are destined for the same fate, Susan. After all, Mr. Rosselli may be a strapping young law enforcement officer, but he is not Superman. All it takes is a moment's distraction, a slight preoccupation, even a catnap—like the one he caught on the plane. The next time he leaves an opening—well, consider this your final warning, Susan. I won't bore you with the details of the use my colleagues and I will make of your body after your soul has departed. The bottom line is: Drop the case or die. See you in hell."

Susan sat there, dazed, listening to the dial tone. Across the dining area, Tony was wolfing down an ice-cream dessert. Down the bar, she could hear Mr. Charm repeating his patter to the redhead: "Then we could go back to my place. I have a hot tub . . ."

Replacing the receiver, she stared into her pop. As she watched the bubbles rise to the top of the dark liquid, she wondered where it would all end. "Satan & Company" had forced a well-respected psychiatrist to confess to murder—or so Dr. Hanson claimed. This same person—or group—had bugged her apartment, run her off the road, nearly killed her outside a restaurant, and had apparently done something terrible to Dr. Singer. The caller was right. It was only a matter of time until they got her. Even a bruiser like Tony wasn't enough to stop a determined, well-planned campaign of violent coercion.

How on earth did they always know where she was? Only she and Singer had known about this meeting. And the marshals. Maybe Singer's phone was bugged. Or maybe—

She stopped herself. No. Not the marshals. That was way too paranoid. She had to trust someone. Not everyone was part of the Satan squad. Despite what she had read about transgenerational cults, how they supposedly managed to maintain a code of silence, their members creating facades of normalcy by holding respectable positions in the community—doctors, accountants, PTA members, church elders—it was still too much to suspect a federal marshal of Satanism. Way too much. A signal that she needed rest. A sign that Satan's scare tactics were accomplishing their goal.

She paid for her soft drink and joined Tony. He had finished his feast and was waiting for the waitress to return with his credit card.

"No show?" he asked, wiping his mouth with a frayed paper napkin.

Susan shrugged.

He took a long draw from his iced tea. "Hungry? The food's great. Especially the mesquite-grilled beef." He let out a thundering belch, and heads from the surrounding tables turned in his direction. "Excuse me," he smiled, apologetically. "Hate it when that happens."

She shook her head, disgusted by his table manners—or lack thereof. "I think something may have happened to Dr. Singer."

"What do you mean?"

"I mean I got another call. At the bar."

Tony squinted at this. "What did he do, tail us from DIA?"

"I have no idea. Maybe he really is omnipresent. Anyway, he implied—no, it was more than that. He basically admitted to doing something to Singer."

"Sheesh." The pleasure of his meal seemed to disappear and a serious expression returned to Tony's face. He was back on duty.

The waitress dropped off Tony's card, and a minute later he and Susan were sitting in the Dodge.

"Denver PD doesn't have anything?" he asked the radio.

"Nope," a faraway voice replied through the static.

"What about the hospitals?"

"That'll take some checking," the voice answered.

"Then check and get back to me—ASAP." He set the radio mike on the seat and reached for the phone. "Better call John."

Susan looked out the window anxiously. Cars were gliding by in the darkness. A pale, oval moon peaked out from behind a ridge of windblown cirrus clouds. It looked like it would be full in another two or three days. In the distance, the Front Range of the Rockies stood tall and black, a steep, featureless wall behind a sprawling field of city lights.

"Yeah," Tony grunted into the phone. "No, John, I don't." He paused, listening. "Oh, I wouldn't say it was without problems." Another pause. "We had a little—incident."

The radio cackled at them.

"Hang on, John." Tony picked up the mike and mashed the button with his thumb. "Rosselli."

"We got a Singer over at Swedish."

"Dr. Grant Singer?"

"Let me check." Static. "Right. Dr. Grant Singer."

"What's he in there for?"

"Auto accident. Hit an embankment on I–25."

"How bad is he?"

"Pretty bad. The EMTs had to cut him out of the car. He's in critical condition in ICU. The hospital said something about an operation."

"What time was he admitted?"

The static rose in intensity, then, "9:20."

"That puts the accident back to . . ." Tony paused, calculating the time it would take the emergency team to reach the scene and pry the guy out. "8:30? 8:45?"

"Sounds like a good estimate," the radio said.

"All right, thanks." He picked up the phone. "John, Singer's down. Car wreck."

"Maybe we should—," Susan started to say. But Tony waved her off.

"Okay. Talk to you then." He hung up and started the engine.

"Where are we going?"

"You're going home. Then I'm going to Swedish Hospital."

"And who's going to be watching me?"

Tony swore. Apparently he hadn't thought of that.

"I need to speak with Singer anyway," Susan told him. "Take me with you."

He vacillated for a moment, then caved in. "Okay. I don't know any other way to do it."

Traffic was heavy, despite the hour, and it took them nearly twenty minutes to make the drive to Swedish. After walking the mazelike corridors of the hospital for another five minutes, they located the admittance desk outside the intensive care unit.

"We're here to see Dr. Grant Singer," Susan told the nurse.

The short, heavyset black woman didn't even bother to check her list. She simply scowled up at them. "Visiting hours are over. Come back tomorrow between nine and three."

Tony flashed his badge at her. "Rosselli. U.S. Marshal. We need to speak with Dr. Singer."

She gave the ID a hard, critical glare, then referred to her clipboard. "Room 123. But it'll be a short talk."

"How's that?" Tony grumbled.

"He's unresponsive. Level One coma."

"He's a vegetable?" Tony asked.

"We don't like to use that term," a deep voice said.

They turned and faced a tall, thin man in a white clinician's coat.

"I'm Dr. Zimmerman. Singer is my patient."

"These folks are federal marshals," the nurse told him, still frowning. "They want to talk with Dr. Singer."

"I'm afraid that's impossible. We managed to stabilize him. The EMT did a great job on-site. But his injuries are simply too numerous and too serious. He needs surgery, but isn't able to tolerate it right now. He may never."

"You mean he won't make it?" Susan asked.

The doctor shrugged. "I'd say his chance of survival is hovering somewhere around twenty percent right now. It'll improve the longer he hangs on, but—"

"Can we see him?" Susan asked.

"I suppose. Not much point, really, but sure. You can see him."

He led them through a set of double doors and down a long corridor. Halfway down the hall a buzzer sounded. "Crash team to 123," a speaker demanded from the ceiling. "Code red."

What's that mean? Susan wondered. But Zimmerman had already sprinted off. They followed, jogging to keep up.

Singer's room was a confusing melee of noise and movement. In the corner, an array of monitors emitted an odd chorus of pulses, beeps, and warning alarms. A team of nurses and doctors had encircled the bed, each member focused on his or her task—preparing an IV, filling a syringe, checking the pupils, charging the crash-cart paddles—each announcing aloud his or her progress, as well as the status of the patient. In the middle of it all, Singer lay perfectly still.

The team worked frantically, heroically pumping, shocking, and thumping Singer's body. Yet the alarms continued to sound. Zimmerman swore at his patient, commanding him to live. Five minutes later, the frenzy ended. Zimmerman ripped off his gloves and swore again.

"That's it," he mumbled.

"Time of death—10:37," another voice noted. "Notify the morgue."

A nurse covered Singer's face with the sheet. Another shut off the monitors, and the team filed out in silence, their shoulders drooping.

Zimmerman was still breathing hard, his shirt wet with perspiration. He cursed quietly and shook his head at the corpse before leaving.

"Poor guy," Tony said. "That's too bad."

Susan stared in horror at the lifeless, cloth-draped form—the empty body that only minutes earlier had been Dr. Grant Singer. Was "Satan" really responsible? she wondered. Had the crank on the phone really brought about this man's death? If so, how long would it be before she was the one beneath that sheet? Would she too meet with an "unexpected delay" and be deposited, like a broken doll, in an ER somewhere? Would she be kept alive by electronic devices? Would a medical team fight in vain to save her when her organs ceased to function? How long would it be before Tony stood at the foot of *her* bed, lamenting *her* untimely death?

TWENTY-SIX

LOOKS LIKE SOMEONE BEAT US TO THE PUNCH," Tony said, pointing through the windshield. They had just pulled up in front of Grant Singer's home. Another Dodge was parked out front already and a large figure was standing on the porch, revolver in one hand, shining a high-beam flashlight into the darkened house with the other.

"Door was open when I got here," Campbell told them when they joined him.

"Have you been inside?" Tony asked.

He shook his head. "Not yet. I was waiting for backup."

"Stay here," Tony told Susan.

"Oh, no. I'm going with you," she replied.

"Whoever broke in could still be around somewhere," Tony explained.

"Exactly," Susan nodded. "So I'm not going to stand on the lawn and give them something to shoot at."

"Who said anything about shooting?" Tony asked, frowning.

"Denver PD should show up any time now," Campbell said.

"Wonderful. But until then, I'm sticking with you two."

The marshals shared a look of disapproval. "Stay behind me," Tony finally muttered. "If you hear something—a footstep, a door, a hiccup—hit the deck and stay there."

"Yes, sir," she responded, offering a mock salute. Her hand trembled as she made the gesture, and the meager attempt at humor had no effect on her heart, which seemed intent upon pounding its way out of her chest. For some odd reason, the idea of traipsing into the home of a man who had just been assassinated, at night, when it was apparent that someone had burglarized it and might still be in there, lurking in the shadows, waiting to do them bodily harm, made her ever-so-slightly nervous.

Susan took a deep breath, ordered herself to stop thinking about the utter recklessness of this undertaking, and followed Tony through the doorway.

The marshals sprung across the entryway and down the hall like nimble cats: heads darting back and forth, guns raised toward the ceiling, muscles tensed as they hugged the walls, silently signaling each other forward.

Susan was careful to remain well behind them, proceeding only when Tony waved her forward. The house was a trilevel. After prowling through the main living area, they moved quickly, quietly up the stairs. The three bedrooms were empty. Not only were they void of occupants, but they contained no furniture. The marshals shrugged at each other and slipped back downstairs.

The basement was unfinished with a concrete floor. Area rugs had been spread out on it. Boxes were stacked in one corner. There was a desk in the other corner bearing a computer terminal. The drawers of the desk had been emptied onto the floor. Next to the workstation was a futon with disheveled blankets and a pillow.

Campbell harnessed his gun and flipped on the light. "Looks like Dr. Singer was living alone."

Susan examined a picture sitting on the desk, reaching to pick it up.

"Don't touch anything!" Campbell ordered.

"Okay," she said, flinching. The photo showed a man, a woman, and two children—a boy about five and a girl about seven. "He had a family. But those bedrooms upstairs . . ."

"Divorced?" Campbell thought aloud, eyeing the futon.

"Maybe she left him recently," Tony offered, "took the kids."

"Maybe," Susan said. "Or maybe things at the Institute got too intense."

"What do you mean?" Campbell asked.

"When I talked to Singer he was pretty agitated. He said the phones at the Institute might be bugged. And he mentioned that he had some sort of evidence—something he considered insurance."

"What do you think it might have been?" Campbell asked.

Susan shrugged. "I got the feeling it had something to do with the MRT unit."

"The what?" Tony wondered.

"It's—," Susan started, then shook her head. "Too complicated to explain. But if he had something, it would have been on a computer disk or a CD, I think."

"You suppose that's what they were looking for?" Campbell said.

"Who?"

"Whoever broke in."

"Maybe. Let's say the nutcase was telling the truth," Susan said. "Say Satan had something to do with Singer's 'accident.' Then he comes over and goes through Singer's house, looking for the evidence, afraid that it might implicate him. Or someone." Susan sighed. "I feel like I'm working a jigsaw with my eyes closed—and a bunch of the pieces are missing."

"You're saying Singer had some dirt on the Institute," Campbell tried. "He got scared. Maybe sent his family away—to Gramma's. Satan finds out, ices him, snatches the incriminating disk—or whatever it was."

"Which means Satan works for the Institute," Tony added.

Susan considered this. "Mmm. I don't know. Something's not quite right."

"Something's screwy," Campbell threw in. "Downright wacko. What if Singer had nothing? What if his wife got tired of telling him to put the cap back on the toothpaste and walked? Packed up the kiddos and left. What if Singer was killed in a bona fide accident? The guy could have been drunk, for all we know. Did anybody check his blood alcohol level?"

Tony shrugged. "I didn't ask."

"Ask," Campbell told him.

"What about this mess?" Susan gestured toward the debris on the floor. "Singer's home is burglarized the same night he dies in a car wreck? The same night I'm supposed to meet with him? The same night he's going to show me his evidence? You wanna tell me that's just a string of unrelated coincidences?"

"Could be," Campbell offered.

Susan rolled her eyes at this.

"Denver PD!"

The shout came from upstairs.

"About time," Tony muttered.

"We're down here!" Campbell called.

There was a rumble of feet and then three officers, guns drawn, appeared at the top of the stairwell.

"Freeze!"

"Federal marshals," Campbell told them calmly, displaying his badge. "The house is clear."

"All clear!" came a shout from upstairs.

The officers visibly relaxed, holstering their weapons as they walked down the steps.

"Whattya got?"

"Burglary," Campbell answered. "Print the place. Have the investigating team look for computer materials—disks, CDs—"

"Maybe printouts or a video," Susan threw in.

"Anybody know the owner?" one of the officers asked. "He'll need to make a list of the missing items and file a report."

"Name's Dr. Grant Singer. But he's not . . . available," Tony answered.

"Where is he?" the officer wanted to know.

"Swedish Hospital," Campbell said.

The officer fingered the radio on his shoulder. "Contact Swedish—"

"In the morgue," Tony added.

The officer gave them a quizzical look, then used his radio to call in the detectives.

When they were back outside, in the cool night air, Campbell told Susan, "I'm bunking at your place."

"What about Singer and the break-in?" she asked. "Aren't you going to stick around and see what you can turn up?"

Tony shook his head. "Not our jurisdiction. Burglaries aren't federal offenses."

"Neither are vehicular deaths—homicide or not," Campbell explained. "We'll have to wait and see what DPD comes up with."

"I'm out of here," Tony told them. "See you in the morning."

"Night, Tony," Susan waved. "Thanks."

She and Campbell climbed into his Dodge and drove back toward her apartment.

"How was the party, John?"

Campbell made the corner, then looked at her, puzzled. "Huh?"

"The birthday party. For your daughter."

"Oh, that. Loads of fun," he said sarcastically. "We survived."

"How old was she?"

"Twelve. One more year and she'll be a teenager." He made a face, shaking his head. "Sounds like you and Tony had an interesting time in St. Louis."

"Yeah," she scoffed. "Interesting."

At Susan's place, she pointed to the couch. "Hope it's not too lumpy." She threw him a pillow.

"If Tony can do it," he responded, "I can do it."

"Goodnight, John."

"Goodnight."

Inside her bedroom, she slipped into a nightshirt and collapsed onto the bed with a groan. It had been a long, taxing day. And unfortunately it wasn't over. She still had reading to do. With only one day until the prehearing meeting, two days until the hearing itself, it was time for her kick—that last burst of energy that would enable her to out-distance the competition. There was no way around it. She would have to pull a couple of all-nighters if she expected to have any chance of rescuing Dr. Craig Hanson from execution.

"Just do it," she told herself, rising slowly to a sitting position. She grabbed Ruth Sanders's diary, the *Spiritual Warfare Manual,* and her new Bible. Fifteen minutes later, just as she was starting a particularly disturbing entry involving a memory of severe sexual abuse, there was a light tap on the door.

"Susan?" a deep voice whispered.

She rose and opened the door. Campbell was standing there, bearing a platter. It held a can of pop and a bowl of popcorn.

"I got hungry," he told her. "Raided your pantry. Hope you don't mind."

"No. That's fine. Eat whatever you want, John."

He offered her the tray. "I saw your light was on. Thought you might like a snack."

She smiled at this gesture, reminded once again of her father. "Thanks," she said, accepting the tray. "To tell you the truth, I'm starving. And it's going to be a long night."

"Well, I'll let you get back to your work. If you need any-thing, just holler."

Back on the bed, munching handfuls of Orville Redenbacher, sipping Diet Coke, she paged forward in Sanders's journal.

TWENTY-SEVEN

SUSAN?" A VOICE WHISPERED.

She shook her head and sighed. John again. What was it this time? Had he baked cookies?

Setting the diary aside, she rolled across the bed and opened the door. There he was. No goodies this time. He wore an expression of concern. Then she noticed the revolver in his hand.

"What's the matter?" she asked, immediately frightened.

"I'm not sure, but I think we have a problem," he replied gravely. He stepped into her bedroom and shut the door. "I heard something."

"What was it?"

He shrugged, reaching for the phone. "I'm not sure, but—" He paused to curse. "It's dead." He rubbed his face with a large hand, then looked up at the window thoughtfully. "Where's that go?"

"Parking lot."

"Good. We'll get to my car. I can radio for help." He opened the chamber of his pistol and checked the ammunition. "Unlock it."

She complied, fumbling with the window latch.

In the next instant, she was falling backwards, pulled by a powerful hand that clutched at her neck. Her head thudded against the hardwood floor. Dazed, she looked up. John was standing over her. Smiling.

She stared at him, confused. "What are you doing?"

The smile disappeared. His features grew hard, his eyes cold. "I'm keeping my promise."

"What?"

He reached down and yanked her up by her hair. "Don't tell me you've forgotten. I told you exactly what I would do to you if you didn't drop this case. And now, I plan to make good on that."

"But—you're not—you can't be . . ." Her voice trailed off as he twisted her hair, causing her to grimace. Then he shoved her onto the bed. A wicked grin spread across his face.

Susan couldn't breathe. She couldn't think. She couldn't move. She tried to scream, but it came out as an impotent sigh. She clutched at her clothing and began to sob. "Please. Please, John, don't. Please . . ."

He laughed at her. "Stop whimpering." Grabbing at her night-shirt, he . . .

The books slipped from the bed, slapping against the floor, and Susan awoke with a start. Groggy and disoriented, she took a deep breath. Her nightshirt was wet, her hair stuck to her cheeks in clumps. She squinted at the clock: 3:17.

Gradually, she realized that it had been a dream. A bad one. A nightmare. But still, only a dream.

The main elements of her dream's twisted plot continued to swirl around in her head: John . . . the sudden revelation that he was "Satan" . . . the assault . . . It had all seemed so real. Terrifyingly real. But like most dreams, the story line was preposterous to the wakened mind. That a federal marshal could be her mysterious enemy, that John Campbell was the man who had been harassing her, threatening her, even trying to kill her—it was outlandish. Ludicrous. Totally implausible.

Except . . .

Before she could stop herself, Susan's tired mind reeled, leaping like a frightened rabbit from one unlikely conclusion to the next.

The first phone call from Satan had come in Florence—at a time when only two people knew where she would be staying:

Rosselli and Campbell. Then there had been the disappearing phone message and the videotape. She had handed them over to Campbell. And the near-accident on the way to the Springs? Who was the first person on the scene afterward? John Campbell. He claimed to have been hemmed in by trucks, unable to keep her Subaru in view. And what about St. Louis? Tony was with her. But Campbell . . . What if he had rented a Sable and—no, he couldn't have, because he was attending his twelve-year-old's birthday party.

Instead of dissipating, the storm of crazed suppositions picked up speed and power.

Campbell had told her about his family on the way back from Florence. He had said his daughter was ten. Yet when she asked him about the party earlier that evening, he had said she was twelve. And at first, he had blanked. As if he had no memory of the party. As if it had never happened. What if he hadn't gone to the party? What if there had been no party—no daughter—no family?

At Singer's house, Campbell had pooh-poohed her theory about a connection between Singer's death, the burglary, and the evidence Singer claimed he had. Maybe Campbell didn't want a link to be found. Maybe he didn't want the theory entertained because it was true. Maybe he knew that it was true because—

Now it all made perfect sense. It was the ideal setup. Who better to stalk her than a federal marshal assigned to "protect" her? Campbell knew where she was every hour of the day and night. He knew when she would be at the office, in the car, in St. Louis, waiting at the bar at Bennett's.

Where was Campbell when Singer was traveling up I–25 to meet with her? Where was he when the doctor's car met with that embankment? And what if after he took care of Singer, he went by Singer's home, broke in—

There was a knock at her door. "Susan?"

She shuddered, then swore. Swallowing hard, she tried to get hold of herself.

"Susan, you all right?"

"I'm fine, John," she replied, fighting to stay cool.

"I heard something."

"I'm fine, John. Just some books. Go back to sleep."

He paused. "Okay."

She got up, tiptoed to the door, and carefully locked it. Then she went into the bathroom and began splashing cold water on her face. Then she looked up into the mirror—and chuckled. What she saw there was the face of a woman who had obviously not gotten enough sleep, a woman who was overly stressed, who was running scared, afraid that a faceless maniac was after her, who was fighting like mad to win her first bona fide case. In other words, what she saw was a paranoid nut: dark rings beneath blood-shot eyes, wrinkles that weren't usually there. She was a mess—physically as well as emotionally. Accusing John Campbell, her guardian angel, a man who had taken a fatherly interest in ensuring her safety, of being "Satan"? It was laughable! Clearly the demented mental ravings of a woman on the edge.

Changing into a fresh nightshirt, she mentally outlined a logical, decidedly more sane interpretation of her night terror. This "Satan" had gotten to her. Her conscious mind tried to deny that, to put up a brave front. But unconsciously, this maniac—now, apparently, a homicidal maniac—had accomplished his goal. She was genuinely frightened. And now, that fear was evidencing itself in her dreams. In the past few days she had been harassed, nearly killed, had witnessed a man flatlining at the hospital, investigated a burglary—all in the context of defending a death-row inmate accused of murder, Satanism, and ritual abuse. Now if those weren't the ingredients for one whopper of a nightmare, what was?

And poor John Campbell just happened to be a handy fall guy—sleeping over, bringing her that tray of snacks just before she fell asleep.

No. John was not the bogeyman. He was her friend.

That conclusion should have provided Susan a sense of relief. Yet somehow, in the middle of the night, with a wacko still out there promising to do her in, affirming John's innocence didn't offer much consolation. She was still trembling, still terror-stricken.

Though thoroughly exhausted, she knew that sleep would not come easily. So she browsed through her small library of materials. Might as well read, she decided. She wasn't up to Ruth's diary. Not at this hour. Not after that disturbing dream. In fact, in all likelihood, the journal had played a role in creating the dream. The *Spiritual Warfare Manual* didn't interest her either. Too heavy. Too much emphasis on Satan and demons. Therefore, too creepy. Discarding two similar books, she finally came to the new Bible she had just purchased. Too boring, she thought. But she opened it anyway. At this time of night, in her mental condition, boring might be just what she needed. Maybe it would cure her insomnia.

Opening to the table of contents, she scanned the list: Genesis, Exodus, Leviticus, Numbers . . . She yawned. Her plan was working already. Just reading the names was making her sleepy. After giving the rest of the titles a cursory glance, she decided on Psalms. That seemed like a nonthreatening choice. The Psalms were poetry, she recalled from her Sunday school days.

Psalm 1 turned out to be more harsh than she had remembered. It spoke of sinners, law, the wicked, judgment . . . Psalm 2 looked like more of the same: "Why do the nations rage . . ." She flipped pages, in no mood for fire and brimstone.

Psalm 23 caught her eye. She had memorized it as a girl. Reading it again, for the first time in years, the words seemed familiar and comforting.

The LORD is my shepherd, I shall lack nothing. He makes me lie down in green pastures, he leads me beside quiet waters, he restores my soul.

Now that was poetic. Lacking nothing . . . Lying down in a soft, green meadow somewhere, next to a little pond . . . She could feel her tense nerves relax slightly.

He guides me in paths of righteousness for his name's sake.

It sounded so serene, so tranquil. But the "he"—she wasn't sure what to make of that. Obviously it referred to God. But what was required in order for God to lead you "beside quiet waters"? What did a person have to do to enjoy the nirvana-like peace described here? She felt as though she should know the answer—as if, perhaps, she *did* know the answer, but it was just beyond her ability to verbalize it.

Even though I walk through the valley of the shadow of death, I will fear no evil, for you are with me; your rod and your staff, they comfort me.

No wonder this was such a popular psalm, always read at funerals. Who, in their right mind, wouldn't want the courage to face evil and not be afraid? Who wouldn't want someone—in this case, God—by their side, walking them through death, comforting them with his presence? Susan knew that she wanted that. Now more than ever, she wanted that. She was facing evil, possibly even death. And she was dreadfully fearful of both.

Her thoughts returned to the hospital room, to the motionless form of Grant Singer. She could still see the lifeless look on his face, the emptiness in his eyes, the pallor of his skin. One moment he had been alive—barely, his breathing made possible by a respirator, his heart pumping only because a machine forced it to. Then the next instant—gone. His spirit, or his soul, or whatever it was, had exited his body in flight to . . . heaven? Hell? Purgatory?

Susan wondered if there really was an afterlife. She hoped so. Most people hoped so. Especially when they faced the end of their physical, earthly existence. It would be a cruel, cruel thing to end life and vanish into blackness, knowing nothing, thinking nothing, ceasing to be. Of course, it would also be terrible to wake from death and find yourself in a pit of fire, with Satan by your side.

She shook off these morbid thoughts, her eyes returning to the psalm. She finished it, then read it again, and again, and again. Ten minutes later, as she drifted off to sleep, her mind issued a simple but desperate prayer: *I will fear no evil, for you are with me. Please be with me . . . Please be with me . . .*

TWENTY-EIGHT

Susan opened her eyes, blinked at the brilliant morning sunlight streaming into her bedroom, and was struck by a strange thought: *I'm going to church this morning.*

She laughed at the idea. *Church?* She hadn't been to church since early high school, back when her parents had forced her to go. Aside from an occasional wedding, she hadn't stepped inside a stained-glass sanctuary in more than a decade.

Church? She did need to do some digging into Trinity Fellowship. But its therapeutic arm—the Institute—was the focus, not their Sunday morning service. What good would it do to sit in a pew for an hour, listening to a sermon? Then again, what harm would it do?

Susan staggered into the bathroom, surprised by her own attitude. *Church?* She shook her head in amazement. Last night she had read the Bible, something she would never have imagined herself doing again in this lifetime. Now she was going to church? Had she suddenly found religion or something?

Convinced that a shower would wash the nutty notion away, she cranked the nozzles and let the hot water work its magic on her skin.

Seven minutes later, clean, invigorated, and dripping wet, she reached for a towel and realized that she was still intent upon going. Why? She had no clue. Something inside seemed to be drawing her, impelling her to go. It didn't make any sense. But there was an acute, albeit irrational, longing to return to the institution of her youth. Maybe it was the safe feeling it had offered her as a child, attending each week with her parents and brothers. Of course. That was it. Now, at a time of crisis, she was unconsciously seeking refuge. First the dream, then the psalm—church seemed like the logical next step in the progression.

Having rationalized her motives, she readied herself quickly: dabbing on makeup, wiggling into a skirt and blouse, choosing a pair of shoes. When she opened the door of the bedroom, she found John Campbell on the couch under an afghan—snoring with a vengeance.

She considered waking him, then thought better of it. Let the guy sleep. She fished the yellow pages out of the bottom drawer of the kitchen cabinet and began paging through it rapidly. Churches . . . Churches . . .

She was surprised at how many church listings there were. Hundreds, possibly thousands of them, all categorized by denomination. She paused, trying to remember what Trinity Fellowship was affiliated with. Unable to come up with an answer, she resorted to the white pages. Trinity Benevolence Ministries . . . Trinity Bus Service . . . No Trinity Fellowship. But then, why would a Springs church be listed in the Denver phone book?

Dialing directory assistance, she got the number and placed the call. It was long distance. After two rings a recorded message clicked in. The church held worship services at 8:00, 9:30, 11:00 and 6:30 on Sundays. She hung up as the recording launched into a rundown of weekly activities.

Checking her watch, she considered her options. It was already almost 8:30. Too late for the early-bird special. And by the time she made the drive to the Springs, she might be too late for the 9:30 service. But it was worth a try.

After scribbling a note to John and attaching it to the refrigerator—where she was certain he would see it—she left quietly.

Not usually out and about before noon on Sunday, Susan was amazed by the streets. They were nearly deserted, vacant asphalt as far as the eye could see. Even I–25 was quiet. Apparently the twenty-four-hour stream of traffic on Denver's overly congested system of roadways took a brief respite on what was traditionally considered a day of rest. Consequently, she arrived at Trinity five minutes before the service was scheduled to begin.

Sitting in her car, she surveyed the building. It was an attractive design: a large glass structure bordered by trees and a network of grass and concrete paths. It reminded her of a business park or the campus of a city college, except that on the side of the building stood an enormous cross. Next to it, stylish letters declared: Trinity Christian Fellowship. People were filing into the church from every direction—men, women, children, seemingly all ages and races. She watched as cars filled the shopping-mall-sized parking lot.

At home, in bed, coming here had seemed like the appropriate, even the noble thing to do. But now, watching the faithful stream into their house of worship, she felt out of place, like someone about to crash a private party.

Go anyway, she told herself. *At least it will give you a feel for this place. That could be helpful for Hanson's hearing. And he needs all the help he can get. It's your duty to go.*

Armed with this mandate, she locked her car and walked self-consciously toward the door. Several people smiled and spoke to her en route to the entrance. A man in a navy blazer nodded and opened the door for her; inside, two smiling women extended their hands in greeting. One of them handed her a program.

The sanctuary was larger than most civic auditoriums. Susan estimated that it would seat at least five thousand, maybe more. It was built at a steep incline, ranks of balconies hovering overhead, scores of rows below, falling away toward a wide, brightly lit platform containing a podium and a variety of musical instruments. The auditorium was nearly half full, alive with voices. A few people were seated quietly. Most were engaged in energetic, even boisterous discussions. Determined not to stick out, Susan snuck up the stairs to the first balcony area and slid into an aisle seat.

She had just begun to examine the program when a half-dozen people ascended the platform. Moments later, the music began: drums, bass, piano, electric keyboard, even a saxophone. The beat was contemporary—a pleasant pop/rock blend. A young man with an acoustic guitar strapped to his chest approached the microphone and invited everyone to stand.

The congregation rose, conversation and laughter quickly dissipating. A surge of last-minute arrivals poured through the doors, hundreds of people seeking out seats. People began to clap. Some raised their arms. Others started swaying back and forth. Everyone seemed to be singing, except Susan. And she didn't know the words.

She checked her row for hymnals. Nothing, not even a slot in the seat back. How were they supposed to—

Big-screen monitors above the platform blinked on, displaying the lyrics to the song.

High-tech church, she thought, suppressing a grin. She followed the words, trying to hum along without being noticed.

Song followed song. The first "set" was upbeat, the songs real foot-tappers. The next "set" was a little more subdued, the "set" after that calmer still. This had a curious effect. The first few raucous numbers created a sense of energy, even excitement. Then, as the pace slowed, the congregation seemed to settle in, the atmosphere growing peaceful and contemplative.

Susan watched, an impartial observer, interested in what was taking place but unwilling to fully participate. She didn't feel that she could. The people around her seemed at ease with this physical, outward style of worship—closing their eyes, lifting their hands, some sinking to their knees. But it made her uncomfortable. Furthermore, she wasn't clear on the object of this behavior. What was the focus? Maybe a better question: *Who* was the focus? That was the problem. They were communing with a God she didn't know. Or at least, had grown distant from.

As a child, she remembered, she had considered God a close friend. She had been taught to appreciate his existence and to anticipate his involvement in her life. At the insistence of her parents, she had "given her heart to Jesus" at the age of ten. This act had solidified and enriched the bond between her and the unseen Creator of the Universe.

In the years since, that bond had eroded, the gulf between her and her Creator growing. As a teenager, she had maintained a polite but shallow relationship with Christ—for a while. In college, even that fell away, replaced by a mere familiarity with the general concept of spirituality. Ultimately, she had adopted an ambivalent attitude, disinterested in all things religious.

How does one return to God? she wondered, gazing across the auditorium.

After more than a half hour of singing, the music ended, and her question remained. The band left the stage and a woman took the microphone. She sang a ballad to a recorded accompaniment while a team of ushers passed offering plates.

Announcements were made. A missionary couple was brought forward for prayer. Several dozen babies were dedicated in a brief, mass ceremony. Finally there appeared on the stage a man who introduced himself as the senior pastor: James Riley.

He spoke for twenty minutes, delivering a teaching from the Bible in a conversational tone of voice. Susan listened, not getting much out of it. The doubts were back. Why had she come? She didn't belong in church. Not anymore.

When he finished, the band hurried back to the stage, took up their instruments, and waited for his signal.

"Let's listen to God," Riley said. "Let's see what he has for us this morning."

Heads bowed. The room grew quiet. The silence stretched.

Susan glanced around, wondering what would happen next. After what seemed like several minutes, the pastor finally nodded to the band. They started playing one of the more memorable songs that had been sung earlier—softly, the leader gently strumming his guitar.

A woman rose from her seat in the front section and climbed the steps of the stage. After conferring with the pastor, she was handed a microphone.

"I feel impressed that the Lord is here in power this morning," she began. "His Spirit is present, right now." She paused. "He's moving through the auditorium with an open hand, extending gifts to all who are willing to receive. To the sick, he offers healing. To the depressed, he offers joy. To those in bondage to addictions, he offers freedom. To those who are spiritually hungry, he offers food—the Bread of Life. And to those who are suffering under the heavy burden of self-condemnation and sin, he offers forgiveness."

She paused and surveyed the crowd. "I think there is an unusual anointing today. And the Lord's invitation to you is this: You have many needs, but I am greater than your needs. You have many hurts, but I am the healer of hurts. You have many regrets and sorrows and infirmities, but I am sovereign over them all. My power is greater. Come and receive." The woman gave the mike back and returned to her seat.

"Do you feel it?" the pastor asked. "Do you feel the Spirit's presence? I do. Isn't it wonderful?" He smiled. "If that word spoke to any of you—and I know that it spoke to many of you—why don't you come down." He gestured to the area in front of the stage. "We'll have people to counsel and pray with you." Even as he said this, bodies all over the auditorium rose and made their way toward the front.

The band continued to play, the congregation singing reverently. Susan could hear people sobbing. Down front, hands were being placed on the heads and backs of those who had gone to seek healing. The crowd of respondents grew, clogging the aisles in the first section of seats.

Suddenly there was a gasp and someone fell over. At the other end of the row of supplicants, someone else tumbled backward. Susan expected to see someone rush to their aid—but instead, they were allowed to lie on the floor undisturbed, and those around them acted as if nothing had happened.

Just a few rows up from Susan, a man began to chuckle softly. The volume rose until laughter seemed to be welling up from the depths of his belly. He was laughing so hard that tears were streaming down his cheeks. Sinking into his seat, he kept at it, his voice echoing across the auditorium.

Then another person started laughing. Then another and another. It swept across the congregation in contagious waves until the entire church was rocking with it.

Susan picked up her purse and looked for an exit. This was too weird. Time to get out. But the pastor's voice stopped her.

"I can tell that some of you are uneasy about what's happening," he said, raising his voice above the din. "Don't be alarmed. The people laughing around you are not out of their minds. They haven't gone crazy. They're not drunk. What they are experiencing is a manifestation of God's presence resting on them.

"When the Spirit comes in power, he often chooses to do strange things: people cry, shake, fall down, laugh . . . Read through this book," he said, holding up a Bible, "and you'll find all manner of odd and inventive ways in which God reveals himself: a whirlwind, tongues of fire, a cloud of glory, earthquakes. Trust me, what we're seeing here today is mild in comparison.

"But for some reason, laughter is particularly disturbing to some parts of the body of Christ. I'm not sure why. I suppose that it just goes against what most of us have been taught to expect in church. We're supposed to be solemn and glum." Here he made a face, frowning. "But as C. S. Lewis once said, the serious business of heaven is joy. Though I don't pretend to understand God's ways, I do know that laughter can be quite therapeutic. I think the Spirit sometimes makes us laugh in order to free us from the bonds of our own religiosity. He also does it to deliver us from depression, stress, and various other ailments, including demonization.

"Some of you are looking at me like, 'You've got to be kidding. God would never do something so bizarre.' I'd wager that others of you are ready to walk out and write this experience off as a work of the devil—to classify Trinity Christian Fellowship as a fringe cult."

The smile on his face widened. "If you want to leave, be my guest. But I have to warn you, you'll be missing something good—a good and perfect gift from the Father of lights."

The laughter began to subside, waves slowly sinking away like the tide. In the background the musicians continued their song. The crowd at the front was engrossed in prayer, hands laid on those in need.

"Anybody ever read The Chronicles of Narnia?" Riley asked the congregation. "Great books. In one of them, a character asks about Aslan—the lion who's the Christ figure. The little girl wants to know if Aslan is safe. The creature she's talking to scoffs at this. 'Of course he isn't safe,' he says. 'But he's good. He's the King, I tell you.'

"I'm here to tell you that God isn't safe. He's powerful and wild. Like a lion. His Spirit is like the wind. But he's good. And he's the King."

The pastor signaled the band, and they launched into one of their rowdier songs. "If you don't know the King, we invite you to come and meet him. Here. Now. Maybe you knew him once, but you've drifted away. Come on. He's waiting for you with open arms."

Susan had listened to the short dissertation with a grimace, offended by the emotionalism, put off by the spiritual ecstasy some of the members seemed to be experiencing. She had cringed at the hysterical laughter, at the people falling down in front, aghast at what she was seeing, wondering if they would soon pass out snakes like the hillbilly churches of the Appalachians.

But when the pastor mentioned meeting the King—when he spoke of those who'd known him once but had drifted away— the unusual, disturbing behavior she had witnessed was quickly forgotten. It didn't matter anymore. Something within spoke to her. It called to her, like a long-lost love. Before she could think about what she was doing, before she could stop, she found herself out of her seat, headed for the front of the auditorium.

After wading through the throng, she reached a smiling couple.

"My name's Tom and this is my wife, Evette," the man told her, touching the arm of the attractive woman next to him.

"I'm Susan," she smiled back, suddenly feeling incredibly stupid and wishing she hadn't come down.

"Are you sick, or . . . ," Tom asked.

"How can we pray for you?" Evette added.

Susan glanced to her right. A sign above a nearby door read EXIT. This was her chance. A short sprint and she would be in the parking lot. Away from the "workings of the Spirit." Away from the music. Away from the pastor. Away from Tom and Evette. Away from this threatening situation. It was tempting.

"Uh . . . well . . . I . . . I accepted Jesus . . . when I was ten," she told them, haltingly. Her voice sounded weak and tiny. She swallowed hard. "And since then . . . I . . . well . . . I don't know . . . I'm not sure what happened, or where I am with that."

Evette nodded sympathetically.

"I . . . don't know what I want. I just feel like . . . well . . . I guess I just want to come back. I want to come back to God. And I don't know how."

TWENTY-NINE

Driving back to Denver, Susan reflected on what she had just experienced. She had gone to church. Why? A sense of guilt at having forsaken her religious roots? Hoping to find some modicum of spiritual security in the face of physical peril? Simple curiosity? A combination of the three? Whatever the reason, she had come away with much more than she had bargained for: a renewed relationship with her Creator—new life in Christ.

But her naturally cynical mind couldn't help questioning the validity of it all. Had she gone forward merely to obtain a theological insurance policy against death—to gain heaven and avoid hell? Was it Satan's harassing phone calls that had nudged her toward the God of her youth? Had fear been the primary factor? If so, was the "conversion," the "salvation," her "rededication"— whatever it was called—was it genuine?

Tom and Evette had prayed the sinner's prayer with her, leading her in the confession of her sins and the acceptance of God's grace and forgiveness. And they had counseled her concerning the major tenets of the faith. According to their explanation, God's love was unconditional, lavished on anyone and everyone willing to receive it—no matter their motivation.

She was still mulling this over, weighing God's generosity against her mixed intentions, when she reached Castle Rock. The phone rang just as she was passing the looming stone monolith.

"Hello?"

"Made a decision for Christ, did we, Susan?"

"Who is—"

"Rejoice and be glad, Susan," the caller mocked. "For your name has been added to the Lamb's Book of Life." Each word was drenched in sarcasm.

"I am so tired of your—"

"I realize that you're tired, Susan," he said in a pretense of concern. "Not sleeping, having nightmares when you do manage to nod off—it's tough. So I'll keep this short. I just wanted to let you know that I am aware that you have sided with the enemy. And I'm shaking in my boots." He paused, cackling. "If you think a Jew executed two thousand years ago is going to keep me from—"

Susan hung up before the lunatic could complete the statement. Seconds later, the phone buzzed again. She glared at it, the positive, hopeful mood she had left Trinity with quickly dissipating. Nothing had changed. Before responding to the altar call, Satan had been after her. Afterward, he was still out there, as determined as ever to intimidate her.

On the third ring she picked it up. "I'm not dropping the case," she said. "So if you're going to kill me, quit talking about it and get it over with."

"Susan? Where are you?" It was Campbell. He sounded upset. "I've been trying to call you all morning."

"John. I thought it was—you know who."

"Obviously. Where are you?"

"On my way back to Denver."

"Back? From where?"

"I wrote you a note. It's on the fridge."

There was a pause. "Trinity Fellowship. In the *Springs?*" He cursed. "Why didn't you tell me?" The concern in his voice had changed to irritation.

"You were asleep. Besides, I didn't think you'd want to go."

He swore softly at this. "It's my job to go everywhere you go, Susan. Next time wake me up!"

"Okay. Boy, what a grump. What happened? Did you get up on the wrong side of the couch?"

Campbell ignored this. "Where are you headed now?"

"I have a meeting with Roger Thompson—at Chevy's in—" She looked up at the clock on the dash. "Well, I'm already late."

"The one on Arapaho?"

"Yeah."

"I'll see you there."

"Okay, John. Sorry."

Hanging up, she was struck by two thoughts. First, John Campbell was worried about her. He was acting like an overly protective father. It was touching, really. The second thought was in direct opposition to the first: Hadn't Campbell called just after Satan on at least one other occasion? Coincidence? What if it weren't? What if there were a connection . . .

No. It didn't make sense. If an intelligent federal law enforcement agent was covertly engaged in a scare campaign, he wouldn't be so careless as to leave such obvious clues. More to the point, an intelligent federal law enforcement agent wouldn't do such a thing in the first place. Especially not Marshal John Campbell.

And a rational female lawyer would reject such ideas for what they were: zany.

John's not Satan, she told herself. But even as she did, she decided that she would place a few discreet calls on Monday morning—one to Campbell's wife, another to his supervisor. Just to make sure. It was conspiracy-minded thinking at its finest. But better safe and paranoid than sorry and dead.

The lot at Chevy's held no empty spaces, evidence that the Sunday afternoon crowd was out in force. Susan made two passes, then gave up and parallel parked her Subaru on the street two blocks away. As she climbed out of the car, she wondered if there was any point in pursuing this meeting. Getting a table would be impossible—a good forty-five-minute wait. And since she was nearly thirty minutes late already, there was a strong chance that Thompson had given up and left.

Or been killed en route, she thought grimly, reminded of her last meeting—with the late Dr. Singer.

Fifteen or twenty people were milling around outside the entrance to the restaurant, hands in pockets, frowning, talking, checking their watches. Susan decided that the wait would be more like an hour—plus. She could smell tortillas being baked as she waded through the throng outside, then through the crowded entry area, trying to reach the hostess's station. Screaming children and perturbed adults glared at her as she fought her way past.

"How many?" a woman in a brightly colored skirt asked. She looked tired and overwrought, her long black hair snaking away from her head in a half-dozen different directions.

"Two," Susan answered in something of a shout in order to be heard above the din of dishes, music, and hungry guests. "I'm meeting someone."

The woman scribbled on a pad. "Name?"

"Susan Gant."

She looked up at her, smiling for the first time. "Your party is already seated. Right this way."

Susan followed her through the tables, dodging waiters and waitresses bearing wide trays of food. They arrived unscathed at a window table occupied by a man around forty, slightly overweight, with a gray ring of hair surrounding a shiny bald head. In front of him were four empty bottles of Corona and a half-eaten basket of chips.

"Roger?" Susan tried.

The man looked up sleepily. "Huh?"

"I'm Susan Gant." She extended her hand.

Roger reached to shake it, nearly toppling two of the beer bottles.

Great, Susan thought, sliding into the seat across from him. *The guy's baked.*

"I'm sorry I'm late," she apologized. "I went to Trinity Fellowship this morning."

His pudgy face remained placid, like a tired hound dog.

"Do you go there?" she asked.

He shook his head and took a swig from one of the bottles, sucking up the last drops. "Another Corona over here!" he yelled.

"I just assumed that since you and Craig Hanson were friends—"

"I'm not much of a churchgoer," Roger admitted.

"Then how do you know Craig?"

"We're old friends," he sighed, looking expectantly toward the bar. "Played ball together in high school."

"Really?"

"Where's that beer?" he shouted. Frowning at Susan, he asked, "What do you want to talk to me about?"

Susan looked at him, taking in the red nose and bloodshot eyes. Was he going to remember any of this? Why hadn't Craig warned her that Roger was a drunk?

A short, pretty waitress arrived with Roger's beer and a fresh basket of hot chips, vanishing before Susan could order anything.

Roger took a long draw from his brew. "Ah . . ." He seemed to anticipate her question. "I don't usually drink. Maybe a beer on occasion. I'm not an alky."

Susan shrugged, not sure how to respond to this disclosure.

"But ever since I helped that Singer guy—"

"You did what?"

He peered left, right, surveying the patrons, then leaned into the table. "I assume Craig told you about our little hack job into the Institute's system."

Susan nodded.

"Well, this Dr. Singer wanted to do the same thing. He said it was to help Craig. So I said sure." He shook his head. "Big mistake. *Big* mistake."

"Why?"

"First off, the Institute had constructed a new set of security barriers. Took me a couple of days to make the codes, then another day to keep from setting off the alarms."

"But you got in?"

He flashed a smug grin. "Of course. I always get in. And Singer got whatever it was he was looking for. End of story. Until I start getting these phone calls."

"What kind of phone calls?"

"Hang-ups, at first. Then obscene stuff—you know, a heavy-breather getting his kicks. I didn't like it, but I figured it was just some kid or maybe a dirty old man. Nothing serious. Annoying, but innocuous. But it kept getting worse. Pretty soon this nut starts calling me by name, threatening me, telling me he's going to get me if I don't quit nosing around the Institute. Scary stuff." He paused to gulp down half of the new Corona.

"Did you call the police?"

"Yeah. They said they'd check it out." He followed this with a raspberry. "I don't know what, if anything, they ever did. Basically their advice was to grin and bear it. They said weirdos like that don't usually act on their threats. It's just talk. So I should blow it off." Another long swig. "Then I'm driving along I–25— couple weeks ago—and this semi nearly runs me off the road." He cursed. "I wasn't hurt. But I could have been. I could have been killed."

"And you think there may be some connection between the calls and the accident?"

"You bet I do."

"What did the police say?"

"Nothing. Without any hard evidence, they can't do squat. Or won't. I'm on my own. That's when I started chuggin' down the brew." He raised the bottle and tipped it toward her. "It's the only thing that's kept me sane."

Susan tried a chip, dipping it in a small bowl of green salsa.

"What is it you want from me, Ms. Gant? You want me to testify for Craig?" He rubbed his broad, hairless forehead. "I can't. Call me a coward, but I don't want anything to do with him— friend or no friend. Who knows? They may decide to ice me just for meeting with you." He finished the beer and lined it up with the other empties.

The waitress returned and took their order. Susan wanted a chimichanga and iced tea. Roger wanted another Corona.

"You can't drive," the waitress told him with a cross look.

"I don't want to drive," he muttered. "I want a beer."

The waitress sniffed at him and left.

Susan tried to decide how to word her request. Roger wasn't in a favor-giving mood, and if she didn't convince him to help her in the next couple of minutes, the window would close, and he would be falling down drunk.

"I need to get into the Institute files."

"Go down there tomorrow morning and talk to them," Roger replied. He picked up a chip, examined it closely, and tossed it back into the basket.

"No. I need to get into the MRT files."

Roger swore at this and told her where to go. He obviously got mean when he drank too much.

"I'm not asking you to testify, Roger. Your name won't be mentioned in court. If we turn up any evidence, I'll say that it came from a confidential source."

"Confidential source," he repeated with a sneer.

"Right. I'll go to jail before I reveal your name."

He belched at this.

"I need to get in there, Roger," she pled. "And you're the only person who can do it. Besides, they can't tell who hacked their way in, can they?"

"If you're sloppy they can." His eyes were no longer focusing.

"But you're not sloppy, Roger. You're careful. And you're the best. That's what Craig said."

"Yeah."

"It can mean the difference between life and death for Craig."

"Same for me," he said, peering into one of the bottles. "It could get me killed."

"It could get *us* killed," she told him. "But I'm willing to risk it."

He sighed deeply and propped his sagging head up on his hand. "It won't be easy. They've probably scrambled the codes again by now."

"It'll be a challenge. You're up to a challenge, aren't you, Roger?"

"Won't be able to do it with my system," he said, thinking aloud. His eyes were closed now. "Have to use the new accelerator chip . . . And the triple 8, at Phoenix . . ."

"When can we do it?" She started to suggest that afternoon, but Roger was in no condition to perform any task requiring mental concentration.

"I don't know." He rubbed his eyes and hiccuped.

"What about tomorrow?"

Roger was silent for a long moment. His head wavered from side to side. Susan wondered if he were about to pass out. "After work," he finally muttered. "Meet me at my office at . . . seven." He belched again, groaned, and laid his head on the table.

The waitress showed up with Susan's food and Roger's beer.

"Could you call him a taxi, please?" Susan asked, digging into her entree. "Someone who can take him back to the Springs."

The young lady nodded and disappeared.

"I could probably drive," Roger slurred without lifting his head.

"But you're not going to," Susan told him between bites.

"What about my car?"

"I'll figure something out. Give me your keys."

Roger did, describing his car in two simple words: "Blue Cressida."

When she finished her meal, Susan paid the bill—cringing at the cost of Roger's little binge—then woke her dining companion and assisted him to the door. Outside, the cab was waiting.

"Take him to . . ." Susan paused and withdrew Roger's wallet from his jacket pocket, then read the cabby the address. "Will this cover it?" she asked, handing him a wad of bills.

The cabby counted it, then nodded, smiling. Together they loaded the inebriated passenger, propping Roger into a sitting position. He immediately leaned and fell sideways onto the seat. The cabby shrugged and returned to his place behind the wheel.

Susan stood watching the cab speed away, hoping Roger Thompson was the talented computer hacker he claimed to be—and not the hopeless lush he appeared to be. Her client's life might well depend on it.

THIRTY

I MET WITH YOUR BUDDY."

"Who's that?"

"Roger."

"Oh, yeah? Is he going to help you? He is, isn't he?"

"I guess," Susan said. She propped her feet up on the coffee table and fingered the remote, rendering the old movie mute. "If he isn't too drunk."

"Roger?" Hanson scoffed. "He doesn't drink."

"He does now. Apparently whoever it was that was pressuring you, and is now pressuring me—well, they're after Roger too. He says he was nearly killed on I–25 recently. Which makes him part of a growing club."

"Huh?"

"I told you about my little problem on the way to the Springs, how I was run off the road." She paused and took a deep breath. "Grant Singer wasn't so lucky."

"What do you mean? What happened? Is he okay?"

"No. He's dead."

The line was silent.

"His car hit an embankment last night—the night I was supposed to meet with him. He said he had something to show me."

"What was it? Did he tell you what it was?"

"No. He never got a chance to."

"This is . . ." Hanson sighed into the phone. "This is . . . this is . . . Maybe I should just . . ."

"Maybe you should what?"

"Give up. Too many people are getting hurt and being put in danger on my behalf. Maybe I should just drop my defense, like *they* want me to. Let the judge set my execution date on Tuesday. The whole nightmare will be over in no time."

"Forget it, Craig. I'm not giving up. And neither are you. We can't let them have the satisfaction. This fight is not over."

He didn't respond.

"Remember, you said this was *spiritual* warfare. And I think you may be right. There's some strange stuff going on. And we need God's help to put an end to it, to get you out of that prison and back where you belong—with your family. With Sam and the girls."

"Sam and the girls," he snorted. "Sam's divorcing me, and the girls—I'm their abuser. I may never see them again—lethal injection or no lethal injection."

"Craig—come on. Don't lose faith. Anything can happen when God's in the mix."

Hanson chuckled wryly at this. "You sound like I used to sound: upbeat, optimistic. Determined. In fact, you sound like a believer."

"I am." Susan considered telling Hanson about her experience at Trinity, then thought better of it. Later. After the hearing, maybe. "Don't lose hope, Craig."

He paused. "So what's the next step?" he finally asked. "Are we out of options?"

"We have two wild cards left," she explained. "I have a friend who's posing as a patient at the Institute. She may or may not turn up anything. But it's a shot. And then there's Roger. If he can sober up and get us into the MRT files, we may get our hands on some hard evidence. If we can show the judge that your girls and Ruth Sanders were moved, or at the very least hurried, toward an SRA diagnosis—and if we can show that the Institute misused the

MRT files—and if we can prove that you uncovered their cyber-sex operation, giving them a clear motive to frame you—and if we can prove that Zach Sanders was killed for the same reason—then we stand a decent chance. The judge might issue a stay."

"That's an awful lot of 'ifs.'"

"Yeah. I know."

"Thanks for hanging in there, Susan. I don't know what I'd do without you."

Hanson sounded so forlorn. So alone. So in need of comfort and support. Susan felt the sudden urge to hold him in her arms, stroke his brow, and assure him that everything would be all right. There were two serious problems with that idea. First, it was totally unprofessional. Hanson was her client, not her boyfriend. Second, she was not at all certain that everything would, indeed, be all right.

"I'm with you, Craig," she encouraged. "I'm with you. Talk to you tomorrow. Keep praying."

"I will. You too."

She hung up and gazed at the movie without seeing it. It was black and white, an ancient B-movie. She didn't even know the title. The television was simply providing her with an interesting visual distraction, something to focus on while she thought.

As the characters carried on their silent drama, her mind continued to gnaw away at the case. Hanson was right. There were an awful lot of "ifs." And if just one of them failed to pan out, she felt sure that the judge would assign Hanson an execution date. And even if they all fell into place—if, say, Cindy did glean something useful, despite the untimely death of the man who was to have been her therapist, and if Roger did turn up a firm link between the Institute and the cybersex business—and even if she was able to convince the judge that the Institute had misused files and manipulated patients—that still might not be enough to rescue a convicted murderer from death row.

She paused, her attention captured by the action on the screen. It was a horror flick, she realized. Boosting the volume, she watched as a pale, very attractive young woman fled from a dark-haired man in a tuxedo. Susan couldn't place the actress. But the actor was either Bela Lugosi or Boris Karloff. She always got those two confused. The man caught the woman. The woman screamed, her eyes filled with terror. Then the man opened his mouth to reveal a set of long, sharp fangs. A vampire. This was *Dracula* or some derivative on the bloodsucking theme.

Susan had never noticed the blatant sexual overtones of the vampire genre before. Even this old flick seemed obvious in its innuendo: the woman's exposed cleavage, her youthfulness and attractive figure, the man's power over her, his ability to capture her and have his way with her, sucking away her life. She was considering this, thinking first of sexual harassment in the workplace, an issue clogging the justice system at present, and then of her own predicament—how a man she had never met was exerting power over her, causing her to change her routine, to "run scared," like the woman in the movie, fearing for her life—when there was a knock at the door.

She flinched, dropping the remote, suddenly aware that Campbell and Rosselli weren't around. She was alone. Shivers were still racing up and down her spine when she rose to answer it.

"Who is it?" she asked.

"Tony."

She confirmed this by squinting through the peephole. Satisfied, she opened the door and smiled at him.

"What's the matter?" he asked. "You look pale."

"I thought it might be someone else."

"Satan?"

"Or Dracula. Come on in. Where's John?"

Tony removed his bomber jacket before answering. "I just relieved him."

"I didn't see him at the restaurant."

"He was there. Told me it was torture—sitting out in his car, smelling all the Tex-Mex food while he choked down a lukewarm Whopper."

"Have you eaten?"

"Yeah. But I could go for a Coke or something."

"Help yourself," she said, aiming a thumb at the fridge. Tony did, returning in a moment with a can of pop.

"What's the plan?"

"Plan?" Susan asked from the couch.

"Are we hanging out here this evening? Or do we have a meeting or something?"

Susan shrugged, feeling slightly guilty for her boring existence. "Hanging out, I guess."

"I could take you to dinner later, if you want."

She groaned at this, not interested. Tony was a nice guy and all that, but . . .

"I have some calls to make," she told him, picking up the cordless.

He was already entranced by the television, clutching the remote, surfing through the circuit of channels: golf, bowling, infomercials, public forums, syndicated sitcoms. Programs sped by at lightning speed.

Susan punched the speed-dial button and waited as the line rang. Four rings later an answering machine picked up.

"Cindy, this is Susan. I, uh . . . well, there's been a . . . a development. I thought you should know—"

"Susan?"

"Cindy?"

"I just walked in the door," she said, slightly out of breath. "What's up?"

"About the Institute."

"Oh, that. The entrance interview was great. Dr. Singer asked me some general questions. We talked for—I don't know—maybe twenty minutes. He seemed to buy it. He said he agreed with my last therapist, that I fit the SRA victim profile. At the end of the meeting, he said he'd be glad to take me on as a new patient. So I'm scheduled to see him tomorrow morning at nine for my first session. And get this: He told me about a new treatment he wanted me to try: Memory Reconstruction Therapy."

Susan didn't respond.

"That's what you wanted, isn't it?"

"Yeah . . ."

"Then why so glum?"

"Dr. Singer. He had an accident. He's . . . dead."

"Dead? You're kidding!"

"So at the risk of sounding callous, I'd say that a wrench has been thrown into our strategy."

"Dead? I can't believe it. Are you sure?"

"Very."

"That's weird. I just talked to him Friday. And he's dead? What should I do? Should I call in and cancel? Or just skip the appointment?"

"No," Susan muttered. "That would leave me without proof that the Institute overdiagnoses SRA. Which is precisely what they want."

"*They?* They who?"

"Whoever it was that killed Singer."

"Killed! I thought you said he had an accident."

"A very convenient accident, Cindy. He was on his way to meet with me, apparently with evidence in hand."

"Good grief!"

"Exactly."

They were silent, both thinking. Finally Cindy said, "I guess I could go in anyway. Pretend like I don't know anything. Maybe they would have me see someone else."

"Maybe."

"It's worth a try. Especially if it's that important."

"It is."

"Okay. I'll play dumb and see what happens."

"Be careful."

"What do you mean by that?" Cindy asked.

"Just watch yourself," Susan warned. "Talk to you tomorrow." She punched another speed-dial code.

"Hello, Paul?"

"Yes?"

"This is Susan. I've got a favor to ask."

"Anything for you, Susan—as long as it's not today."

"Why? You busy?"

"I certainly am. I'm holding a barbecue at this very moment."

"And why wasn't I invited?" she asked, pretending to be offended.

"Because you're not on my softball team."

"Fair enough. So I suppose you couldn't return a car to the Springs for me?"

"Sounds like a whole lot of fun, but no, I can't. Sorry."

"Thanks anyway," she muttered.

"See you at the office."

"Great," she moaned, setting down the phone.

"What? What's the matter?" Tony asked, never looking away from the television. Channels continued to flash by, creating a strobe light effect in the living room.

"I told Roger I'd get his car back to the Springs. And Paul can't do it."

"Why don't we run it down?" he suggested, still hypnotized by the parade of images. "I'll follow you. We can grab a bite to eat on the way back."

Susan thought this over. Not a bad idea, actually. She still had plenty of preparation to do for the pretrial in the morning, but it could wait a few hours. The break might do her good.

Tony rose and set the remote aside. "Let's go. There's nothing else to do around here. I can only surf for so long before my eyes go buggy."

"Ever try reading?" she joked, getting her coat.

"We've been over that, haven't we." He frowned at her as he slipped on his jacket. "Besides, who had the TV on when I got here? And who told me that she left it on all night a couple of times recently?" He flipped off the set and opened the front door.

"I was scared. It kept me company."

He shook his head. "I bet you watch way more television than I do."

"Hardly." She locked the door and they walked to Tony's Dodge.

"On the nights when I'm home," Tony told her as they climbed in, "when I'm not out with a lady friend—"

"Like Bambi?" she smirked, fastening her seat belt.

Tony glared at her. "When I'm home, I read."

"Right. *Sports Illustrated,* swimsuit edition. Oh, and Michael Crichton."

"And what exactly do you read in your spare time?" He started the engine.

"I read all day at work. When I get home, I'm tired—"

"And you flip on the TV the minute you walk in the door." He shook his head and pulled away from the curb. "Face it, you're addicted."

"Get out of here!"

"I'm serious. One of the first signs of addiction is denial."

She made a face. "*Please* . . ."

"The guy's car is at Chevy's, I'm assuming."

Susan nodded. "Make a right here."

"Huh? Why don't I take Broadway?"

"Because that's the long way around."

Twenty minutes later—after a lengthy argument over which route was, in fact, the shortest and fastest—they pulled into the lot behind Chevy's. It was still two-thirds full even though it was after five—past the lunch frenzy, and a good half hour before the dinner crowd started showing up in force. Susan spotted a car that fit Roger's brief description.

"Let's try this one," she said, pointing to a navy Toyota sedan.

"Try?" Tony asked. "You don't know which car is his?"

"I'm pretty sure that's it."

"Well, if the car alarm goes off, don't look at me."

She got out and fiddled with the security device on the key chain, and the car issued a beep-beep: all clear.

"Shoot."

"What?" Tony asked.

"I don't know Roger's home address. I saw it on his license— he lives in Fountain. But the street address . . ."

"We could try the phone book."

Susan shrugged. "Let's just take it to the Phoenix complex. Know where that is?"

He shook his head. "I'll follow you."

Susan slid behind the wheel and started the Cressida. It purred smoothly. Then she fished the address of Phoenix Computer out of her Daytimer. She wasn't sure where it was either, but the Springs wasn't that big. How hard could it be to find?

She left the lot, turned right on Arapahoe, and accelerated up the I–25 on-ramp a block later. Tony stayed directly behind her.

Southbound traffic was light and they made good time, passing Castle Pines and Castle Rock in the first thirty minutes. They were approaching the exit at County Line, the same spot where Susan had almost been flattened by a big rig, when she noticed her speed: 82. Even with a federal marshal in tow, this section of road was not a good place to speed. She tapped the brakes, intending to slow to a safer, less ticketable 75—but nothing happened. Pumping the pedal with greater force, she felt it sink to the floor. The gauge on the dash now read 84.

Fighting to remain calm, she examined the display console, looking for warning lights. There were none. All systems were go—supposedly. She tried the brakes again. Still nothing. She fiddled with the cruise control; maybe it was stuck. The speedometer now told her that the Cressida was moving at 87 miles per hour.

Behind her, Tony flashed his lights on, then off. She lifted one hand off the steering wheel in a gesture of frustration, then flicked the hazard light switch. Pumping the brakes, she watched the car speed up to 89, 92, 94—every time she mashed on the brake pedal, it seemed to accelerate.

Tony came streaking up in the passing lane. He matched her speed and asked a question without using any words. What's going on? his expression demanded.

Susan shook her head, the panic rising. "No brakes!" she said, overenunciating the message.

She was able to lip-read Tony's response. It was a curse. He leaned over and rolled down the window. Susan did the same, air rushing into the car at nearly 100 miles per hour.

"Try—," Tony shouted. But it was all he got out. He hit his own brakes, the tires on the Dodge smoking. Susan looked ahead and saw why. There was an eighteen-wheeler in her lane. It was barely moving, struggling to climb Monument Pass.

She swerved wildly, just missing the hind end of the tractor trailer on one side, narrowly avoiding the hood of the Dodge on the other. The Cressida leaned back and forth, skidding along the inside shoulder, then back toward the truck for a long, terrifying moment. Regaining control, she pulled into the right lane again, in front of the slow truck.

Tony reappeared on her left. His face was pale. "Shift into neutral and turn the engine off!" he screamed over the roar of the wind.

Susan nodded. "Okay!" The transmission groaned at her as she pushed the stick to the "N" slot, then switched off the key. Nothing seemed to happen at first. Then her speed began a slow descent: 96, 93, 89 . . .

When they reached the crest of Monument, the two cars were rocketing in parallel paths, still doing 85 miles per hour. Up ahead cars and trucks were streaming in and out of a busy weight scale/fast-food interchange.

The speedometer recorded the deceleration: 82 . . . 78 . . . 74 . . . It was a long, downhill stretch, and the Cressida seemed reluctant to bleed off much speed.

As they neared the heavily trafficked area, Tony pulled in front of her, his lights blinking, and started honking his horn. A red, flashing light dome appeared on the roof of his car. Susan followed, watching the numbers: 66 . . . 62 . . . 59 . . .

She was doing 52 miles per hour when they reached the interchange. She might have made it past the area—if it hadn't been for the pickup entering the interstate. The driver seemed intent on forcing Susan to let him merge. He matched her speed, then attempted to slip in between the Cressida and the Dodge as the on-ramp lane ended.

Susan screamed and twisted the wheel. But it wasn't in time. The Cressida clipped the pickup's bumper and spun, careening into the fence that bordered the right-hand shoulder. The chain link crumpled beneath the weight of the Toyota, and she continued, out of control, the car shuddering across a parking lot and hitting, head on, a metal dumpster.

Just before she lost consciousness, Susan noted three things. First, the steering wheel was infinitely hard and had caused great pain to her head. Second, if the car was equipped with an air bag, the bag had failed to deploy. Third, the battle between the industrial-sized trash container and the Japanese automobile had been won decisively by the former: Roger's car was totaled.

THIRTY-ONE

Pain: INTENSE, RELENTLESS, WHITE-HOT. IT THROBBED ACROSS HER brow in electric waves, reaching deeper and deeper into her skull, pounding against her brain with explosive force.

Without opening her eyes, Susan reached up to touch the part of her head where the pain seemed to be originating; her fingers were met by gauze. A thick, pillowy array of bandages had been affixed to her forehead. Why? she wondered groggily. Why did her temples ache? Why did the space behind her eyes hurt? Why was her entire head on fire?

"Susan?"

Her eyelids flickered open and she squinted against the bright light. A wide, dark form was standing over her. But the light—it made the pain even worse. Before she could focus on the figure or discern the features of the person's face, her eyes blinked shut again.

"Susan? Can you hear me?"

"Uh-huh," she groaned. Even talking hurt. "Tony? Is that you?"

"Yeah. It's me. I'm right here."

She felt him take her hand. "What happened?"

"You had a little accident."

The word "accident" triggered her memory. "Oh. Roger's car. I ruined it."

"You didn't ruin it," Tony corrected, squeezing her hand. "Someone else did. You just went along for the ride."

"Am I okay? Do I have brain damage or anything?"

"No," Tony chuckled. "The doctor says you bruised your orbital septum—whatever that is. And you have a gash on your forehead. Took a few stitches. But apparently it's not fatal. You may also have a mild concussion."

"Neato." She forced her eyes open and gazed up at Tony. "That was scary."

"Yeah. It was. I never felt so helpless in my whole life— watching you ride that runaway Cressida." He shook his head, then swore softly.

"It wasn't an accident," she told him, struggling to sit up. The pounding subsided momentarily, then returned with a vengeance.

"No. It wasn't. Someone wants you out of the way."

"Or they want Roger out of the way."

"Roger?"

"Roger Thompson. It was his car," she reminded him. Gritting her teeth, she tried to think through the pain. "Did you check the brakes?"

Tony nodded. "No surprise—someone had tampered with them. And the air bag had been deactivated."

"The car was sitting in that lot all afternoon," Susan pointed out. "Anybody could have done it." But even as she said it, she realized that one person in particular had had the opportunity. One specific individual had been present in that lot—supposedly sitting in his own car, gulping down a Whopper.

"How well do you know John?"

The question caught Tony off guard. "Campbell?" He shrugged. "We've been partners for over a year—ever since I became a marshal. He taught me the ropes. Broke me in."

"Hmm."

"What are you getting at?" Tony asked. Then his expression changed as the implication dawned on him. "You're not trying to say that John . . . no . . . you can't be serious. Not John."

"Why not?"

Tony opened his mouth, but nothing came out.

"He was in the lot. There was plenty of time."

"But—but he wouldn't . . . John, wouldn't . . . he would never . . . ," he stuttered. "That's preposterous!"

"Think about it. John's been conspicuously absent on several occasions when I was threatened and/or nearly killed."

"So what! The governor was conspicuously absent too. That doesn't make him a psycho."

"What about back in Florence? Who knew that I was staying at that hotel?"

Tony shrugged, thinking. "I don't know."

"You and John. That's it. Nobody else."

"So what? What's your point?"

"I got my first call from Satan that night. Now you tell me how he knew where to get hold of me."

"I think that bump on the head scrambled your brains," Tony said, frowning. "John Campbell is the best marshal I've ever been associated with. He's a great partner, a great husband and father. We're talking a real upstanding guy. Don't go trying to tell me—"

"How old are his kids?" Susan thought to ask.

"His kids? I don't know. Uh, let's see . . . Caitlin is . . . she must be sixteen. LaRae is . . . well, she just turned twelve on Saturday. And Halle's ten, I think. Why?"

She considered this. So much for the "no daughters" theory. So much for thinking Campbell had misquoted their ages. There was a twelve-year-old *and* a ten-year-old.

"I realize that you're a little mixed up right now, what with the head banging and all," Tony told her, "but don't go accusing my partner of being a maniac, okay?"

Susan nodded. She would let it slide for the time being.

"What time is it?" she asked. "For that matter, what day is it?"

"Sunday night. About 6:30. You weren't out very long."

"What hospital is this?"

"Memorial." When this brought a puzzled look, Tony added, "in the Springs."

"Did you tell Roger about his car?"

"Not yet. Thought you might want to," he smirked.

She looked around the small room. "Do I have to stay here tonight?"

"The doctor said that he wanted to run a few tests. He recommended spending the night."

Susan was up, grimacing against the pain, putting on her coat in slow motion.

"Hey, I think you should give it a rest. Stay the night at least."

"I have work to do."

Tony laughed at this. "You look pathetic, you know that? That turban you're wearing . . . Your eyes are already turning black . . . Just how much work do you think you'll get done with that headache of yours?"

"Enough to help save Craig Hanson."

"Messiah complex," Tony said, rolling his eyes. "What about the tests?"

"I'll come back later."

"Yeah, I'll just bet you will," Tony grumbled. "And I thought *I* was bad about doctors and hospitals." He helped her out the door and down the hall to the nurse's station. After checking out and waiting for a prescription to be filled by the hospital pharmacy, he led her to the Dodge and gingerly loaded her.

Susan took a painkiller, commented that her head felt slightly better, then quickly dozed off as they raced north on the freeway.

———————————

Tony pulled the Dodge into the parking lot for Susan's apartment. "Susan?" He nudged her. "Susan? Wake up. We're home."

Her eyes became narrow slits, but didn't move. After three more attempts to rouse her, Tony resorted to force—taking her keys and carrying her from the car to the front door. Awkwardly unlocking it, he carted her to the bedroom, placed her on the bed, and covered her with a comforter.

Susan lifted her head, eyes still closed. "I have a prehearing in the morning. I can't go to bed. There's too much to do."

"Right," Tony muttered. "Goodnight."

A half hour later, during a commercial break from the *Sunday Night Movie*, Tony put his ear against the bedroom door to see whether she was still asleep. He heard a strange noise. Straining, he realized what it was: Susan was snoring like an old man.

THIRTY-TWO

S USAN'S FIRST WAKING SENSATION WAS THE DISTINCT, DELICIOUS aroma of bacon frying. Lying still, one arm over her face, she listened as it popped and sizzled in the pan. It was accompanied by the rattle of silverware and the clunks of cabinet doors and drawers shutting.

Her mind came alive with memories: the way her mother used to fix big "country-style" breakfasts—eggs, pancakes, bacon, biscuits, juice, coffee—how her three brothers would roll out of bed and stumble into the kitchen, still half asleep, to down obscene amounts of food, her father sitting at the head of the table, lording over his hungry brood with a smile of approval . . .

"Susan?"

"Yeah," she groaned, unwilling to move. Her head felt fat and sore.

"It's eight o'clock. You better get up if you plan on making that meeting."

"Okay . . ."

"I've got breakfast going in here—it'll be ready when you are."

She wondered if this was what it was like to be married. No. Probably not. Husbands didn't generally jump up and fix breakfast. Maybe on the honeymoon. In the next instant, her hazy thoughts turned to Tony. What kind of husband would he make? Loyal, faithful, jealous . . .

But he's too young for you, she told herself, struggling to rise from the mattress. Even if he was older than she had first assumed, he still had to be at least four, maybe five years her junior. Too young. She managed to sit up, and was immediately rewarded with a pulsing headache. She hobbled into the bathroom, swallowed a pair of painkillers, and set about the arduous task of cleaning herself up—without getting the bandages wet.

After showering, she slipped on one of her best navy skirt suits, stood in front of the mirror, and frowned. Not the look she had been hoping to take into her first prehearing appearance. One eye was bloodshot, the other encircled by a ring of deep purple. As for the bands of gauze stretched around her head—no wonder turbans had never caught on as a fashion trend. She unwrapped the bandages and assessed the damage: a short, jagged line fastened shut with a half-dozen sutures. Nothing a large Band-Aid couldn't cover. She dug one out of the medicine cabinet and pasted it to her forehead. Better. She no longer resembled a survivor from a plane crash. Now she simply looked like she had been in a barroom brawl—and lost. She headed toward the smell of breakfast.

The kitchen table was a picture out of a Martha Stewart article: plates laden with omelets, croissants, and strips of bacon, bordered by silverware, napkins, cups of juice, flowers . . . Tony was either wooing her with his domestic skills, or he was one of the last truly nice guys on the planet. Maybe both.

"Where'd all this come from?" she asked, staring at the meal. She leaned in to sniff the beautiful centerpiece.

"I made a run to the market," he told her. "You look great. Ready to knock 'em dead?"

"Right," she scoffed. "I'm a walking advertisement for life insurance. I'm hardly ready to handle a fork, much less a meeting with Judge Humphries."

She sat down and began consuming Tony's creation. "You could have been a cook," she told him between bites.

He shrugged. "Worked short-order in high school."

"What did you put in these eggs? They're wonderful."

Tony blushed slightly. "Cheese, oregano, a dash of cilantro . . . Try them with a little salsa," he suggested, pushing a bowl of picante sauce toward her.

"If I could cook like this," Susan said, draining her juice, "I'd be as big as a barge."

There was a knock at the door, and Tony rose to answer it.

"Morning, John."

Campbell started to say something, then lifted his nose into the air, inhaling. "Man! What smells so good?"

"Breakfast," Tony announced with the crisp, dry accent of a British butler. "Right this way, sir." He led Campbell to the table.

"Geez Louise! Looks like brunch at the Scanticon."

"Have a seat. There's plenty of grub for everyone." Tony retook his chair and began wolfing down a croissant.

Campbell sneered at the feast, rubbing his bulging stomach. "I wish you'd told me. I wouldn't have wasted my appetite choking down three breakfast burritos and an Egg McMuffin at Mickey D's."

When he saw Susan's face, he swore. "Ms. Gant," he said, shaking his head, sympathetically. "Why, that—listen, we're gonna catch him. And when we do . . ." He grimaced and made a fist, waving it in the air. "How do you feel?"

"Not bad, considering."

Campbell muttered something under his breath.

"What's the plan?" Tony asked, his mouth full of eggs and salsa. He looked first at Campbell, then Susan. "Who's up? When and where?"

"I've got the prehearing," she told them. "Then I've got a meeting with Cindy. This evening I'm supposed to go back to the Springs to see Roger."

Campbell considered this. "Okay. I'll run you to court and to your next meeting. Tony can take a break for a while. Then we'll both go down with you to the Springs. The hearing's tomorrow, right?"

Susan nodded, finishing her bacon.

"We'll all go to Florence together. I'll see what I can do about arranging a safe place to stay. How long of a hearing are we talking about? Hours? Days? Weeks?"

"Depends," she said, wiping her mouth. "If I bomb, it could be a matter of a few minutes." She frowned at them both. Rising, she told Campbell, "I'm ready. Let's go."

They were halfway downtown before either of them spoke again.

"Tony's got a thing for you," Campbell announced out of the blue.

"You think so?"

"Yep. He's smitten. I told him to back off. I told him not to get all lovey-dovey with someone we're supposed to be protecting. And I thought maybe he listened to me, but when I walked into your apartment this morning . . ." He paused, shaking his head. "I hope you realize that was his very best song and dance."

"I'm flattered. But he's just a kid. Twenty-four?"

"Twenty-five," Campbell corrected.

"I'm four years older than he is."

"Doesn't make any difference to Tony. Younger, older—no big deal. He has a one-track mind. The guy thinks about women around the clock."

"In that case, maybe his infatuation will pass quickly."

"Let's hope so."

They made the remainder of the drive in silence—Campbell concerning himself with the heavy flow of traffic, Susan paging through her notes. She felt like a student engaging in a last-minute cram session on the way to a final exam. And like a student, she knew that if she didn't already know her stuff, it was now too late.

"Here we are," Campbell said, pulling into a reserved parking spot. "Nervous?"

"A squadron of butterflies is performing an air show in my stomach."

"Don't worry, you'll do fine," he consoled.

She sighed at this and stepped out of the car. "Wish me luck."

"Good luck!" Campbell called.

It would take much more than luck to win this appeal, she realized as she hurried across the lot toward the courthouse. Even an avalanche of serendipitous "breaks" would not change the circumstances. Dr. Craig Hanson was a convicted murderer. A jury of his peers had listened to his confession, examined the evidence, heard testimony, and deemed him guilty of killing a teenager with cold-blooded premeditation. He had also confessed to the crimes of child abuse and cruelty to animals. Hanson had admitted that he was a closet Satanist. Convincing the judge otherwise—even if she had strong evidence in hand, which she did not—would be extremely difficult. Convincing His Honor that Hanson had been framed, that his confession had been coerced, and that he was neither a killer nor an abuser nor a cult practitioner would be—well, the word *impossible* came readily to mind.

Anxious and unfocused, she mounted the steps and followed the trail of people moving into the large stone building. What she needed was a miracle—a sudden, unmistakable visitation from the heavenly realm. More to the point, that was what Hanson needed. Divine intervention. If God himself didn't reach down and pluck him from death row . . .

Pushing her way through the circular door, Susan found herself lifting up a silent prayer to the Deity she had reacquainted herself with just twenty-four hours earlier.

God, I'm in over my head. This case is . . . it's a farce. I haven't had the time or the resources to put it together. I'm not prepared. I'm inexperienced. Craig Hanson deserves better. He deserves justice. And then there's the DA; McDermott's out for blood. And Humphries, who thinks the death penalty is the best thing since sliced bread. I guess what I'm asking for is the truth. Let the truth win out over human ambitions and lies and appearances of evil and harassing phone calls and pompous judges and arrogant prosecutors and inadequate public defenders.

Enlisting the help of her Creator had the curious effect of making things seem less desperate. The situation hadn't changed. She was still the underdog: Wyatt Earp approaching the O.K. Corral for a showdown with the dreaded Clanton gang. But she had the distinct impression that she was not alone, that someone else was on her side—a very big Someone. Her newly revived faith seemed to draw courage from this, instilling within her a calm, growing sense of hope.

She was still reveling in this unique emotional/spiritual state—something between mere optimism and the giddy assurance that something good was about to happen—when she located Judge Humphries' office. The rising attitude of positivism leveled off abruptly when she entered the reception area and saw her opponent: District Attorney McDermott.

The ruggedly handsome, impeccably dressed attorney was surrounded by a half-dozen colleagues, aides, and understudies, all engrossed in what Susan supposed was a last-minute strategy session. McDermott glanced in her direction, saw her, but continued issuing orders in hushed tones, never acknowledging her presence with so much as a nod. Apparently junior members of the public defender's office were unworthy of his attention.

Susan tried to ignore this. After introducing herself to the receptionist, she took a seat on the opposite side of the room and began leafing through a law journal. Ten uncomfortable minutes later, both sides of the battle were summoned into the judge's office.

It was a large, impressive room dressed in oak with a hardwood floor that had been waxed to a healthy shine. Shelves laden with law books consumed two walls. Dark leather chairs and a leather couch were positioned in a semicircle around a heavy oak desk. Behind it sat Humphries, a lanky, middle-aged black man with a graying beard.

As the legal representatives entered, the judge removed his reading glasses and glared up from the folders that were spread on his desk.

Before Susan had even taken her seat, the DA launched into a well-polished spiel. "Your Honor, if I might speak—the office of the District Attorney would like to submit a motion to—"

Humphries cut him off with a look. "This is my office, Mr. McDermott," he admonished, shaking his glasses at the DA. "I do the talking here. Unless I ask you a question, it would be in your best interest to keep your trap shut."

An odd look—a mixture of fear and respect—flashed across the DA's face. An instant later it was replaced by the usual cool, smug countenance. "Yes, sir."

"I have reviewed this case at length," the judge said. "The hearing begins tomorrow. This meeting is merely to determine if that hearing is, in fact, necessary. Therefore, it will be short and sweet." He set his glasses back on his nose and examined the folders. "Ms. Gant."

"Yes, Your Honor?" Susan sat forward, trying to swallow but finding her throat blocked by an immovable lump.

The judge looked up at her, started to say something, then noticed her wounds. His grumpy expression softened. "Are you all right, Ms. Gant?"

"Yes, Your Honor."

"What happened?" he wondered, his eyes moving from her black eye to her Band-Aid and back again.

"I had an accident. But I'm fine, really."

He shook his head at her, puzzled, then returned his gaze to the files. "You requested a continuance, is that right?"

"Yes, Your Honor."

"Why?"

"I believe it was explained in the request."

"Humor me, Ms. Gant." He looked at her, expectantly.

She took a deep breath, hoping she could form words into cohesive, meaningful sentences rather than the gibberish that was flying through her mind. "I based my request on three points, Your Honor. First, that my client, Dr. Craig Hanson, has retracted his confession. My client now claims innocence."

Humphries nodded sleepily. "Point two?"

"Dr. Hanson fired his attorney last week."

"Point three?"

"I needed time to collect new evidence that would prove my client's innocence."

The judge frowned at the desktop. "Those would seem to be convincing circumstances, Ms. Gant."

"Your Honor, I object!" McDermott said, springing from his seat and approaching the judge's desk. "In my opinion—"

"Sit down!" Humphries barked. "This is not a court of law, Mr. McDermott. It is my office. I don't give a hoot if you object or not. Keep your opinions to yourself."

The DA skulked back to his seat.

"As I was saying before I was so rudely interrupted," the judge said, still eyeing McDermott, "those would seem to be convincing circumstances for a continuance."

Susan fought off a smile. Maybe Humphries wasn't such a bad old guy after all. He had already put the DA in his place and was now on the verge of handing her a continuance that had already been declined. She was watching the miracle she'd been calling for transpire right before her eyes.

"But in this case, since it concerns a death-row inmate," the judge continued, "I was not, nor am I now, inclined to grant it."

The DA breathed a sigh of relief, and two of the younger members of his team exchanged an energetic high five.

"Another end-zone celebration and your entourage will be made to wait in the reception area," the judge warned McDermott. "My views on the death penalty are well documented," he continued. "It is my feeling that the appeals process is commonly abused in such cases, misused as an effort to delay the inevitable—at the expense of federal taxpayers. Therefore, though I can empathize with you, Ms. Gant, I cannot in good conscience allow a continuance."

Susan watched the gleam in McDermott's eye grow, as if the judge had just stoked the DA's internal fire.

"I will, however, allow you to introduce new evidence with the intent of establishing that Dr. Hanson deserves a new trial."

"Objection!" one of McDermott's aides threw in.

"Out!" Humphries pointed to the door. "Everyone but the prosecutor and the public defender, please leave my office."

The new grads and DA wannabes filed through the door. When it was shut behind them, the judge continued.

"The good news for you, Ms. Gant, is that I will allow the introduction of new evidence. New testimony may also be entered into the record.

"The bad news is that the hearing is principally a formality. I expect to set a date of execution. And the hearing will be held tomorrow—as scheduled. Will you be ready, Ms. Gant?"

Do I have a choice? she thought but didn't dare ask. "Yes, Your Honor. The defense will be ready."

"Mr. McDermott? Will the prosecution be ready?"

"Of course, Your Honor," the DA said, shooting Susan a dirty look.

"Very well then. I'll see you both in the morning—10:30, courtroom 3, Super Max." Humphries returned to his folders, closing one and opening another.

The two attorneys rose to leave. "Oh, Mr. McDermott," Humphries said, his expression one of distaste. "Please refrain from bringing the entire class from Torts 101. I will allow no fraternity antics in my courtroom. High fives will be punishable by contempt charges."

As Susan left the building, she passed the DA team. They were huddled in the entryway holding another confidential discussion.

"Counselor," McDermott called. He stepped away from the group of serious-faced young lawyers.

Susan paused, wondering what was up. Would McDermott make a snide remark about her lack of courtroom experience, or would he resort to rude insults about the "weaker" sex?

"Ms. Gant—can I call you Susan?" He smiled, attempting to be cordial. "If you have a minute, I'd like to have a word with you."

The man *was* rather charming, Susan had to admit, when he wanted to be. He reminded her of a hungry lion toying with its prey just before the kill. There was a ruthlessness in those cold, gray eyes.

"Listen, Susan. If you're going through the motions here, pulling out all the stops for this hearing, hoping that we'll wear down and go for a stay, forget it. We can't. The public would go berserk if we let a murdering Satanist off death row."

"What if he's innocent?"

He laughed at this, a deep, attention-attracting belly laugh. "Why don't you save us both a great deal of time and effort by foregoing this last-minute defense? Drop the case and leave Hanson to the needle. He's going to wind up there eventually."

Susan looked at him, taking in the arrogant air, the know-it-all expression, the lady-killer looks and thought: *What a jerk! It would almost be worth dealing a surprise blow at the hearing just to teach this conceited, self-centered pig a lesson.*

"See you at Super Max," she said.

He muttered something under his breath—definitely not a compliment, it classified Susan among the poodles and spaniels—and returned to his groupies.

Susan stood there, enraged by the insult, yet unwilling to sink to McDermott's level of childish name-calling. She took a deep breath, vowing to vent her anger constructively by presenting a winning case in the courtroom, and marched out of the building.

THIRTY-THREE

"MISSED. THAT'S THE TENTH TIME."

"Try again. Relax. Focus."

"John, I have to get to the office."

"Just once more. You need to feel confident with it. Take a deep breath. Concentrate. Don't go for the head. Go for the body. When you're ready, give it a squeeze."

Susan followed his instructions. She made a conscious effort to relax and then focused her attention on the black cutout of a man hanging at the end of the range. Holding the revolver in two hands, her arms rigid, she closed one eye and carefully aimed. After a deep breath, she gave a gentle tug on the trigger.

There was a pop, the gun jerked up slightly, and the target rippled. Campbell pushed a button and the cardboard bad guy rushed toward them. When it arrived, he stuck his finger into a neat hole in the silhouette's upper abdomen.

"Nice shootin'," he said, smiling. "Dirty Harry would be envious."

Susan chuckled at this, removing her goggles. "I can't believe it. I finally hit something."

"If this Satan knows what's good for him, he'll leave you alone. Otherwise—*blam!*"

She nodded, wondering if she would have the presence of mind to draw the gun if she were confronted by whomever it was that was harassing her. And if she managed to get it out of her purse, she would probably be too nervous to shoot straight. Did she have what it took to gun down another human being? She hoped she would never find out.

After Campbell cleaned and reloaded the gun, they left the range and headed for her office. It was almost eleven when they pulled into the parking lot. The sun had just broken out of a swiftly moving ridge of silver, wind-sculpted clouds, and the temperature was climbing.

"You want to come in, John?" Susan asked.

He shook his head and rolled down the window. "Nah. I'll hang out here, read the paper, maybe take a little walk. Beautiful spring day. I hate to spend it inside. Let me know if you want to go anywhere or need anything." He tapped his cellular phone unit.

"Okay." She started across the lot, satchel in hand, her mind racing. Had Paul gotten a copy of Hanson's business itinerary from his last employer? What about the membership roll for Trinity? How had Cindy's therapy session gone? Had she been inside the MRT? If so, would that experience lend support to the premise that the Institute was SRA happy?

As she entered the building and waited for the elevator, the weaknesses of her case paraded through her head. First, with Dr. Singer dead, she had no expert to put on the stand. Singer and Hanson had been friends. And Singer seemed to be at least somewhat sympathetic to the notion that the abuse of Hanson's family may well have come from someone other than Hanson. *Had*, she corrected herself. Singer *had* seemed sympathetic. He was no longer around and, consequently, she was minus one valuable witness.

Second problem: Judge Humphries. Even if she came up with a wheelbarrow full of startling new evidence, it seemed unlikely that the judge would issue a stay. The fact that Hanson was retracting his confession obviously did not impress Humphries. It was to be expected. Everyone in prison claimed to be innocent. And death-row inmates often changed their stories at the last minute— anything to avoid the business end of a lethal injection. To

Humphries, the one-eighty Hanson was performing was a natural instinct, a survival mechanism. The man wanted to live.

Problem number three: District Attorney McDermott. He and his legion of lawyers had been on this case since the beginning. They held all the cards. And with McDermott rumored to be making a bid for mayor in the next election, there was no chance he would allow a dangerous felon—especially a teen-murdering Satanist—to walk. If he did, the press would crucify him. The voters would abandon him. It would be political suicide to allow a stay, much less a retrial.

Last but not least: Satan. That lunatic was still out there somewhere. Possibly out in the parking lot reading a paper, she thought half seriously as she headed down the hallway toward her office. No. Campbell couldn't be the culprit. Could he? Dismissing the obvious reasons, there was still the problem of motive. Why would Campbell harass her? Maybe he had been bought off. But by whom? By the Institute? By whomever didn't want Hanson to go free? Doubtful. She didn't really know John Campbell, but he appeared to be a kindhearted family man and skilled marshal. Either that or one heck of a great actor.

Her mind suddenly returned to McDermott. Could he be Satan? He was an evil man. Scheming, selfishly ambitious, probably willing to do whatever it took—lie, cheat, steal—to win cases. No doubt corrupt. In other words, he was perfect for politics. And back at the courthouse, what was that all about? Pretending to be Mr. Nice Guy, asking her to forgo the hearing. When she refused, he transformed back into his usual, unlikable self, putting pressure on her to drop the case. Maybe he was so obsessed with winning, with using Hanson as a springboard to the mayor's office that . . . No. She couldn't visualize McDermott making obscene phone calls. He might order one of his underlings to do the job, but the DA was far too important and much too busy to bother with such trivial matters.

When she reached her office, the door was standing open. Setting her satchel down, she sank into her chair and picked up the phone to buzz the front desk and find out who had unlocked her door. Then she saw the folder. There was a Post-it attached to the cover. It said: "No luck on the itinerary yet. I told them we need it by tomorrow. They said they'll FedEx it, but don't hold your breath. Hope the church membership is useful. Accessing it was a real pain in the neck. Paul."

She smiled at Paul's note and began examining the contents of the folder. It held a two-inch-thick sheaf of paper. The top of the first page said simply: Trinity Fellowship Membership Roster. There was no date. Below the heading came line after line of tiny type: names, addresses, phone numbers.

Obtaining the list must have been tough, she decided, scanning the names. A church, especially a megachurch the size of Trinity, would probably guard their roll like a coveted prize. These people were, after all, the financial backbone of the church. Their "tithes and offerings" accounted for the benevolence programs, the educational programs, and the staff salaries. Without the names on these pages, Trinity would cease to function.

How had Paul obtained this? Illegally? Maybe. Maybe that was why he hadn't told her. If she wasn't aware that it had been "stolen," then she could submit the material in court with a clear conscience. A relatively clear conscience. She decided to ask Paul how he got it.

That didn't matter, of course, unless the list held something of value. What was it she hoped to find? A familiar name. The names of individuals involved in the case, thereby supplying them with at least a hint of motive. If she could establish misuse of the MRT and a cybersex operation and a cover-up of both, then an interested party might have cause to bend the facts or engage in a frame.

She turned to the list. Nope—no McDermott. What about Humphries? A minute later she had confirmed it: Judge

Humphries was not a member of Trinity. No surprise. Campbell? She felt a tinge of guilt as she found the Cs and ran her finger down the list. There were four Campbells. But no John. Good. Grant Singer? Sure. He would be on there. She found his name and marked it with a highlighter. There was a D next to his name. "Dead"? More likely it stood for "deceased." Trinity had apparently already updated Singer's status.

Craig Hanson? Yep. Another mark. Next to his name was N/A. "Not applicable"? "Not available"? That fit, since Hanson was in Super Max. How about "nonactive"? Looking down the page she saw a number of "nonactive" members.

Ruth Sanders? Sampson . . . Sand . . . Sanders. A capital A stood beside her name: Active. Susan marked it.

Roger Thompson? He claimed he wasn't a churchgoer. There were half a dozen Thompsons. No Roger.

Clint O'Connor? There he was. Another A—active. She drew through the name with the highlighter.

So far this little fishing expedition was less than enlightening. Grant Singer, Craig Hanson, Ruth Sanders, and O'Connor were all members of Trinity. One D, one N/A, two As. Big deal. She had known that much going in. John Campbell, McDermott, and Judge Humphries were not on the roster. Not exactly earth-shattering news. And it didn't put to rest her nagging—albeit paranoia-driven—suspicions about Campbell. Just because he wasn't a card-carrying member of Trinity didn't mean he hadn't been stalking her.

A comical idea hit her. What about Tony? She scanned the Rs, just for the fun of it. Rose . . . Rosen . . . Rosselli. A. Rosselli. Susan stared at the name. Could that be Tony? A—as in Anthony? No. It couldn't be Tony. Could it? Tony the big horse of a guy? Tony the twenty-five-year-old with a crush on her? Tony the Presbyterian? Tony involved in the Trinity cover-up?

It made about as much sense as thinking Campbell was Satan, but her mind immediately went to work on it. Tony knew where she was that night in Florence. He was absent when Satan showed up on I–25 driving a black sports car. He was with her in St. Louis when she was nearly run down, saving her life in the nick of time. How convenient. And it had been his suggestion that they return Roger's car to the Springs, and that she drive it.

It was the perfect cover, really. Who would suspect a strapping young federal agent of stalking her? Especially if he pretended to like her—to be romantically interested in her. The nerve.

What did she know about Tony Rosselli? He was from the Springs. He had attended the Air Academy. It wasn't beyond reason that he had been a member of Trinity—the largest church in the area. Except that he claimed to be a dyed-in-the-wool Presbyterian. Rechecking the list, she found the letters "N/A" next to his name. Hmm . . . probably a different Rosselli. And even if he was a former member, that didn't exactly prove he was a mass murderer. Not any more than certain strange circumstances made his partner, John Campbell, a serial murderer. What if they were in this together? What if they had been dispatched by some higher power at the church to silence a curious teenager, a boy who had accidentally uncovered an illegal porn business? What if they were *both* Satan, both out to ensure that she didn't win Hanson's case?

Susan shook off the wild train of thought. Whether her bodyguards were angels or demons didn't change the fact that she had a hearing to prepare for. And conjuring up conspiracy theories distracted her from that purpose.

Setting the list—and the demented brainstorming session it had produced—aside, she was reaching for a pad, intent upon outlining a strategy for court, when the phone rang.

"Susan Gant," she answered.

"Susan? This is Cindy."

"Hey, how'd it go?" Even as she asked the question, a voice inside told her that Cindy had struck out, that yet another door had closed on her client.

"It was weird."

"What do you mean?"

"I saw a Dr. Bayers. He's the chairman of the Institute."

"Yeah, I know who he is. What happened?"

"Well, he let me talk about my emotional state for the first half of the session: the dreams I've supposedly been having, the disturbing flashbacks, the trouble with alcohol, the fear of social interaction. Then he took me into the MRT unit."

"Great. And?"

"I'm telling you, that thing is—it's weird. The physical sensations alone are enough to bring up your lunch. It reminded me of one of those huge-screen movies."

"IMAX?"

"Yeah. You know how those make you kind of queasy after a while? Well, this is worse. You're walking around, looking around, seeing all sorts of images. Except you're not really. Actually you're just standing there with this suit on."

"Did you have any memories?"

"Not at first. At first I just stumbled around in this hallway and this talking head gave me a tutorial on how to run the equipment. I opened doors to these rooms, but they were empty. Then the doctor started helping me."

"What do you mean *helping?*" Susan asked, scribbling notes.

"He called it 'prayer therapy.' First he had me relax and visualize a quiet, peaceful place. As I did, the place—a meadow by a stream with a mountain in the background—it just appeared out of nowhere. Then after I was relaxed, he had me go back to the hallway and open one of the doors. Except this time there was something in there."

"What was it?"

Cindy hesitated. "It was . . . it was creepy. It was just like the stuff I read in those books you gave me, the things I described to the doctor: a dark place, candles, people in black robes and hoods . . . This guy, the leader, took a knife and killed a cat."

"You're kidding."

"No. I'm serious. He killed it. I could hear the cat and see the blood. It was gross, utterly grotesque."

"Then what?"

"That was it. I exited the system and had this short 'debriefing' with Bayers. I'm scheduled for another session on Wednesday."

"What did the doctor say about the SRA angle?" Susan asked.

"He seemed to think I was right, that I had been abused as a child in a ritual fashion. But he didn't go so far as to diagnose me SRA. He said I fit the symptoms, but that it was too early to tell."

"Well . . ." Susan considered this. "I think we can use that. The fact that he took you into the MRT, first shot, and that he helped construct a ritual abuse memory—I think we can use it. The hearing starts tomorrow. Can you come to Florence in the morning? 10:30 sharp?"

"Do you really think you'll need me that early? What about opening statements?"

"The impression I got at the meeting today was that Humphries intends to move this thing through. 'Short and sweet'—those were his words. I'm afraid if you aren't available to take the stand right off the bat, the whole business will be over and done with. It may be anyway."

"I've got a full schedule," Cindy protested. She paused. "But I'll rearrange things. See you at 10:30."

"Thanks, Cindy."

Susan hung up and returned to her strategy session, jotting notes on the pad:

I. Murder charge
   a. expose cybersex operation

She hoped that the evidence she needed to do that would be recovered tonight, with Roger's help.

b. show that Zach Sanders discovered it

c. suggest that the Institute engaged in cover-up (i.e. had motive to kill Zach)

II. Abuse charges

a. present evidence that Institute is SRA happy (overdiagnosing)

That meant putting Cindy on the stand. And entering Ruth Sanders's diary into evidence. She made a mental note to obtain Sanders's permission.

b. argue that Hanson's family may have been abused, but not by him

c. prove that the charges are vague and unconfirmed

III. Animal cruelty charges

She could think of no plan for refuting these. They had never been proved in the first place. And they were unimportant. If she could sway the judge in the first two points of her presentation, number three would no doubt be dropped.

She looked at her watch: almost noon. Time was running out. Taking Sanders's diary, she turned through it, scanning the pages she had marked with Post-its. The accounts were graphic, if nothing else, and would put the judge in the mind-set of what SRA was all about.

Satisfied that she had noted the most significant passages, she reminded herself to copy the material, then picked up the phone to call Sanders. Ruth was unavailable. Susan returned the phone to its cradle and shook her head. Then she buzzed Paul.

"Paul? Listen, thanks for the roster. I've got something else for you. I need Ruth Sanders's written permission to use her diary in court tomorrow."

"What's the problem? She doesn't want to give it?" he asked.

"No. I can't reach her. I should have gotten it when I was down there."

"Should I head for the Springs?"

"No. Just keep calling. Have her handwrite something and fax it up, pronto."

"Gotcha."

Precedent, she thought as she hung up. *I need to show precedent in a "repressed memories" case. In several cases.* With all of the litigation concerning this controversial subject, there had to be several that fit her needs.

She glared at her watch again, wishing she could make the hands freeze—to make time stand still. Unable to accomplish this trick, she decided against making the trek to the University's law library. Travel time alone would take a big bite out of the day. Instead, she hurried down the hall, toward the in-house library, hoping that it would have what she was looking for.

THIRTY-FOUR

IT TOOK SUSAN MOST OF THE AFTERNOON TO dig up four cases that loosely resembled Hanson's situation. Each dealt with a father who had been accused of sexually abusing his children. Each case hinged on memories that had arisen suddenly, without warning. Three daughters and one son had grown up loving their respective fathers until one day, with the help of a therapist, they recalled occasions of abuse. All four cases had been overturned, the alleged abusers exonerated. Unfortunately, none of them involved satanic ritual abuse.

Determined to find one that did, Susan was hunched over a long table, a dozen open books stacked in front of her, when Paul came in.

"Susan? Call for you."

"Is it Sanders?"

He shook his head. "And I haven't been able to reach her."

"Keep trying," she told him. She returned to her office and punched the flashing button on the phone.

"Susan?"

"John?"

"Aren't we supposed to head for the Springs this evening?"

She glanced at her watch and frowned. It was twenty-five till six.

"What time are you meeting this Roger guy?"

"Seven."

"Traffic could be a bear. We'd better get out of here pretty soon."

"Right. Oh . . ."

"What?"

"I forgot to call Craig. Be down in a couple of minutes."

"Tony and I'll be waiting."

She reflected on the ominous sound of that announcement as she dialed Super Max.

"Dr. Craig Hanson."

There was a long pause. "I'm sorry but his phone hours are—"

"I know when his phone hours are," she interrupted grumpily. "I'm his attorney and he has a hearing scheduled for tomorrow. Just put him on."

"Ma'am, I—"

"Give us one minute—sixty seconds. That's all I need."

She could hear the sigh over the long-distance connection. "Hang on."

The silence lasted long enough that she began to wonder if the line was dead.

"Susan?"

"Craig. Sorry I didn't call earlier. I've been swamped. Last-minute preparations. Things are a little frantic."

"I bet. How's it coming?"

"Good," she answered confidently, trying not to let her voice betray her. "The pieces are falling together. I'm meeting with Roger tonight. If he can provide us with something solid, I think we've got a chance."

"I trust you, Susan. And Roger's the best when it comes to computers. You guys will pull it off. I know you will."

Susan resisted the urge to laugh at this. Here was a guy on death row, one swing of the gavel away from a lethal injection, and he was giving *her* a pep talk.

"God's on our side," he continued. "I'm praying for you."

"Me too, Craig. Me too. I'll see you tomorrow," she said, hanging up.

Closing her eyes, Susan took a deep breath. Her nerves were ragged, the stress taking its toll on her.

"We need your help, God," she muttered. "And I could use a little peace of mind—to keep me from going off the deep end before this is all said and done."

Two more deep breaths and she was at the door, satchel and coat under her arm. The phone rang, stopping her in her tracks. Since she was already running late, she considered letting the front desk pick it up. But maybe it was important. It might even be Ruth Sanders.

"Hello?"

"Hi, Susan. Satan here. Just wanted to touch base with you, make sure your trip down to the Springs was still on?"

"Take a flying—"

"Now, now. I know you're a little tense what with the hearing tomorrow and all. That accident of yours couldn't have been a pleasant experience either. Nasty cut on your forehead. And your eye." He chuckled. "Looks like you've taken up boxing, Susan. Anyway, I look forward to seeing you tonight."

Susan swallowed hard. *"Tonight?"*

"You didn't really think I'd sit by and let you expose my operation, did you?"

She slammed the phone down and stepped to the window. There was the Dodge in the corner of the lot. She could see the dark outline of two figures inside: Tony and John. And they had access to a phone.

Am I about to take a ride with the Satan Brothers? she wondered.

Shrugging this off, she locked her door and rode the elevator down to the ground floor. She was almost certain that Tony and John weren't responsible for the calls. Almost. Still, she wasn't going to tell them about the threat—about Satan's promise to see her tonight.

"You look tired," Campbell observed as she climbed into the backseat.

"I am."

"Try to catch a nap on the way down," Tony suggested.

Sure. Why not? she thought. *That would make it much easier to kill me and leave my body in a shallow grave along the highway.*

Susan caught herself, ordering her weary mind to stop the nonsense. She was exhausted and her mood had turned ugly. Maybe a nap *was* what she needed. It certainly wouldn't hurt. By the time they reached Castle Rock, she had nodded off, her last thought the question of whether she would ever awaken.

Susan opened her eyes as the Dodge bounced over a speed bump. They had reached the Phoenix Computer Complex, and Campbell was presenting his ID badge through the driver's side window, to a guard. The elderly uniformed man mumbled something, and an iron barrier automatically lifted, allowing them to pass through. It was just after seven and the parking lot was mostly empty.

"Are we taking you to the front door?" Campbell asked.

"I guess so."

Campbell parked in a loading zone and switched off the ignition. "Do you want us to come in with you?"

Susan thought about this for a moment. If these guys weren't involved in the harassment, whoever was might be waiting inside somewhere. Of course, if they *were* involved . . .

"No. I guess not. I've got a phone. I'll call if I need you."

"Okay. Be careful."

"I will."

"What are we gonna eat?" she heard Tony ask his partner just before she slammed the door shut.

There was another guard station just inside the entrance of the main building. Two large black men sat behind a Plexiglas window, surrounded by banks of electronic equipment. Cameras monitored her approach to the window.

"I'm here to see Roger Thompson," she told them through the intercom.

One of them eyed her suspiciously. "I'll page him." The intercom switched off, and she watched him mouth the page into a microphone. The booth seemed to be soundproof.

"Have a seat," he told her, flicking the intercom button.

She complied, the cameras mounted high on the wall whirring to follow her action. *Self-conscious.* That was the word for the way she felt. Not nervous so much as watched.

Five minutes later, the door next to the guard's booth buzzed and Roger's bald head poked out. He held it open for her, waving her inside.

"Sorry about your car," Susan apologized, following him through a maze of administrative offices and cubicles.

"Are you okay?" he asked, turning to examine her face.

"I'm fine. Just a nasty bruise."

"To think that someone was trying to—that my car was—that I could have been—that you were almost—" Roger shook his head, then shuddered at the thought. He paused at the intersection of two hallways. After peering to the right, he set off to the left. "Come on." Susan trailed after him, watching as he zipped his identity card through slots, pressed his thumb against sensors, and entered codes in keypads to satisfy the security devices on a dozen different doors. At the last door he said: "Roger Thompson. Voice recognition ID." The lights next to the lock blinked, then the bolt slid away and the door opened with a whoosh.

"I didn't realize security was so tight here," she observed, following him down a brightly lit but deserted corridor.

"Precautions against industrial espionage," he explained. "Phoenix designs and manufactures the fastest chips and the most powerful mainframes in the world. Everybody wants what we have: Silicon Valley, the Japanese—"

"Everybody except the customers," she said. "I've read about the company's financial woes in the paper."

Roger shrugged at this, walking down yet another empty hall-way. "Our P8 is the finest machine ever made. Problem is, it's too expensive. Or so our clientele keep trying to tell us."

They finally arrived at a door marked "Clean Room 7." Roger stopped in front of it, his expression solemn.

"You sure you want to do this?" he asked.

"If I'm going to get Craig off, I need hard evidence."

"Let me put it this way. To access that evidence, we're going to have to bend a few rules. Are you up for that?"

"That depends. What sort of rules are we talking about?"

"First, I've got to get a chip out of this clean room. That's against policy. No one's allowed inside after hours. But I can work around that. Then I've got to load the chip into our proto main-frame—the one we tinker around with."

"That's a no-no?"

"You bet it is. Of course, if we do it right, no one's going to know. After that, when we hack into the MRT—well, you're a lawyer. You know about privacy laws and the confidentiality of patient records."

She nodded her head. "Ethically, we're on thin ice. But if we can prove that the Institute is playing illegal games with those records, I'm betting the judge will overlook that."

Roger snorted at this, obviously unconvinced. "I just want you to know that when we open this door, we'll be taking the first step in a journey that could cost me my job, get you dis-barred, and land us both in prison."

Susan frowned back at him, weighing this information. "It's risky. But it's also the only hope I have of clearing Craig. I say we do it."

Roger shrugged and turned to the door. He fed the keypad a code, and then, when the door opened, he fed it another. "That'll erase our footsteps."

She looked at him, puzzled.

"Every time you access a secure area, the system monitors it. It goes into the record: time, name of the employee, all that. But some of us know how to delete the record—make it look like the door never opened."

He led her inside, to a small room with a cabinet. Opening the cabinet, he handed her a set of clothes. They looked like surgical scrubs. "Put these on."

They both slipped the sterile garb over their clothes, pulled shoe covers on, then donned white masks.

"Come on," he said.

Three doors later they were in the clean room—a space the size of a small warehouse packed with metal tables. Each table held a set of diagnostic tools. Pieces and parts from electronic circuit boards were scattered everywhere, even on the floor. They snaked their way through the tables to a steel door. It looked like a vault.

Roger fiddled with the security device for a moment, then pulled it open to reveal a closetlike space with racks of shelves. The shelves bore more computer components.

He flipped on a fluorescent light and examined the contents of the shelves, picking through stacks of circuit boards. "No ...," he muttered to himself. "No ... Here we go." He used a gloved hand to remove a small silver square from a row of such squares.

"What is it?" Susan asked.

"Our chip."

"Now what?"

"Now we head for the P8."

They followed a back-door passage to another large room, this one containing nothing except a large black crate, four foot by four foot square with a console panel on the top.

Roger lifted a panel cover and began entering information on a sunken keyboard. Seconds later, the device sprang to life, lights blinking, internal mechanisms activating.

"Oh, I forgot the VR suit," he mumbled. "I'll start this baby working on the codes, then I'll go get it." His fingers flew over the keyboard, clicking in sequences of numbers and letters. "There. Be back in a minute." And he hurried out the door.

Susan found herself alone with the Phoenix 8. As she watched the rows of tiny lights flash on and off, she realized that there was still time to back out. They had broken a few in-house rules. But they hadn't committed on-line burglary yet. She was thinking about this, wondering if obtaining evidence was worth the risk, wondering if saving Craig Hanson was worth the moral com-promise, wondering if maybe she should phone Campbell and get out of there, when Roger returned. Under one arm he had a black foam suit that resembled something a scuba diver might wear. Under the other was a motorcycle helmet with a thick, dark visor.

"What's that for?"

"I can get us inside the MRT," he told her. "But to access patient files, you have to enter the virtual environment. That's the way Craig did it. And that's the way Grant did it."

"Grant was inside?"

Roger nodded. "He'd already seen the inside of the MRT—firsthand. But he had me hack into the cybersex service. So he could compare the files, I guess. I don't know. Anyway, you can do the cybersex service without a suit. It doesn't even require VR technology—though it's a much more 'powerful' experience with it. But the MRT takes a suit. Or at the very least a helmet and a data glove. You have to do interactive/virtual to engage the on-line ghost."

"The what?"

"It's a 'help' function, this floating face guy that—you'll see." He set the suit down and stepped to the computer to check a readout. Numbers were ticking off at high speed. "It has half the codes already."

"I thought you said it would be tough to crack the codes, that they changed them or something."

"They did. I think they probably change them every week—maybe every day. And they've started encrypting. It's a smart setup. With a run-of-the-mill PC, you couldn't break in in a million years."

"But you can."

"Hey, this baby—" He patted the black box affectionately. "There ain't nothing it can't do. It runs codes like nobody's business."

Susan smiled at him. So this was the real Roger, the man Craig had befriended. She could see why Craig liked him. He was a little eccentric, but overall, he was a nice guy. When he was drunk—well, that was a different story.

"Go ahead and put the suit on."

"Over this stuff?" She gestured to the scrubs.

"You don't need that anymore. This room isn't clean."

She removed the mask, booties, and apronlike gown and began squirming into the suit.

"Your street clothes come off too," Roger added nonchalantly.

"Huh?"

He looked up from the readout. "The suit has to touch your skin."

"Why?" she asked suspiciously.

"That's how it positions you." When the look on her face didn't change, he explained, "This is the next generation in VR equipment. No landing pad to stand on, no wires, not even a laser-arrayed positioning system. The suit monitors your movements with sensors embedded in the foam, then relays them—via radio wave—to the computer."

"Like a TV remote control," Susan surmised.

"Kind of. But much more complicated than that."

"Without a treadmill, won't I run into a wall?"

Roger shook his head. "The system is extremely sensitive. Shift your weight and you'll be moving—in the VR environment."

When Susan shot him a puzzled look, he said, "Don't worry. You won't hit anything. You'll hardly move from that spot."

Susan sighed at the getup. "This is wild."

"You should have seen the prototype we were working on before Chapter 11. All you had to do was think and you were going forward, backward—whatever."

"I still don't understand why I have to strip."

"It won't work if you don't," Roger said, frowning. "Trust me." He turned his back. "I promise I won't look."

Susan begrudgingly slipped off her shirt and pants, then wiggled into the suit, zipping it shut. "Okay, now what?"

"Two codes to go. Put on the brain bucket."

She pulled the helmet on and was immediately blind. "I can't see anything."

Roger depressed a button on the rear of the helmet and the visor lit up. She was suddenly staring at a full-color scene of the Grand Canyon.

"Looks flat. I thought virtual reality would be more 3-D."

"That's just the standby mode," Roger told her. "One code left."

She waited, feeling like a ninny in the suit and helmet.

"Bingo!" he shouted. "We're in."

Two seconds later the screen blinked and Susan was looking at a room. It was spatially correct. She reached out her hand and touched the wall. It felt hard. And she could see her own hand. "Wow!"

"Is the face there yet?" Roger asked, all business.

She swung her head slowly to the left, then the right. It made her slightly dizzy, the room moving oddly around her vision. "Wow!"

"Do you see the face?" he repeated. "Come on, Susan. We don't have all night."

"Uh ..." She surveyed the room. Three walls. A door. Even a ceiling. But no face. "Nope."

"Call him."

"What?"

"Ask for help."

"Okay. Help."

A silver face magically appeared. It floated next to the door, eyes wide. "How may I help you?"

"There it is. What should I tell it?" she asked Roger.

"Please restate your question," the face said.

"Tell it you want to access patient records. The general file."

"Can you record what I'm seeing?" she asked.

"Yes," the face answered.

"No, not you. Roger?"

"I'm already downloading to mini-CD."

"You do not wish your journey to be recorded?" the face wanted to know.

"No. I—I want to access patient files."

"Please enter your code and password."

"He wants a code and a password, Roger. What do I do?"

"Hang on a second." She could hear him typing on the keyboard again. Suddenly the door in front of her opened.

"Thank you, Dr. Singer," the face said. "Please proceed."

"It thinks I'm Dr. Singer," Susan said. "What did you do, Roger?"

"Doesn't matter. Did the door open?"

"Yeah."

"Go through it."

Thirty-Five

Susan hesitated. There was nothing beyond the doorway but a void of static. It reminded her of the electronic snow that danced on a TV screen at the end of a videotape.

"Please proceed," the face repeated.

Stepping forward, she grasped the door frame with both hands and stuck a timid foot through the portal. The static flashed and a whirlpool of colors spun out of nowhere. A force, like a gust of wind, sucked her forward. For an instant she had the sensation that she was falling. But as the rest of her body passed through the rectangle, the twirling colors slowed, the wind subsided, and a new scene splashed into existence: an ornate, high-ceilinged atrium.

Looking down, she saw that she was standing on a beautiful marble floor. Pillars ran down the center of the hall, thick, stone fingers reaching up to a clear, glassy roof. Trees and shrubs grew from large, bench-lined marble planters. Birds tweeted and sang, winging playfully from branch to branch. Outside, above the skylight, she could see the sun, planets, and stars in the distance. The sides of the room were lined with wooden doors. Each bore an intricate, inlaid pattern and a bright brass knob.

The face was hovering near one of the pillars, apparently awaiting her next directive.

Susan approached the first door and placed her hand on the knob. It was cold. She tried to turn it.

"I'm locked," the door told her.

"What is this?" she wondered aloud. "*Alice in Wonderland?* How am I supposed to get in? Eat something that makes me small and slide through the keyhole?"

"Do you require help?" the face asked.

"Yeah, how do I get in?"

"To enter a memory file, please provide the patient code."

"Patient code? Roger?"

"I'm working on it," she heard him say.

The face stared blankly at her. She stared back. "Can this thing see me?"

"What thing?" the face and Roger asked simultaneously.

"This face. It gives me the willies."

"Sure, it can see you—after a fashion," Roger explained. "It's artificial intelligence. It can't actually see or think. But the sensors in your suit feed it information on your location and movements. So it knows what you're doing."

"Creepy," Susan muttered.

"Try the knob again," Roger's voice told her from outside the environment.

She twisted it and pushed back the door. It was heavy and swung open with a long creak. The space inside was small and empty. No color, no shape, no static.

"Nothing there."

"You must enter the room in order to access the file," the face explained.

"Thanks," Susan groaned, shooting the face a disapproving look. "Here I go, Roger. If I'm not back in a few minutes, send a search party."

Roger chuckled at this. "Right."

Entering the room turned out to be similar to stepping through the first doorway. Only when she breached the invisible barrier did the scene spring to life. This time she found herself in a long, narrow hallway. The sides were cinder block, the low ceiling covered with a network of pipes and electrical lines. Water seeped down cracks in the walls, pooling on the concrete floor. Overhead, bare bulbs ran the distance of the hall, providing a dim, yellow trail of light.

It was quiet except for the sound of dripping water. The place reeked of mildew. Susan looked behind her. A dead end. The door she had entered was gone. Following the passageway, she stepped over and around the puddles. Twenty paces later, she reached a series of stone steps. They led down, into a black hole. She squinted into the darkness, unable to see what might be waiting there.

The stairs were slick, wet with a slimy film. Bracing herself against one wall, she carefully descended into the pit. Tracing her hand along the cinder blocks, she crept down until the stairs ended and she was standing on level ground again. Taking another step, she kicked something. A wall. Or maybe a door. The surface was metal. And it was very cold. She felt for a knob, but couldn't find one.

"I'm stuck," she observed aloud. "Either that or I need another code." She pushed against the barrier and it gave way, a groan echoing through the darkness as metal slid against concrete.

Through the door she could see a faint light. It was a glow that seemed to rise and fall in intensity. Ten gingerly placed steps later she found herself at a corner. The hallway turned and opened into a large room.

Candles. That accounted for the glow. Hundreds of them had been placed in a series of concentric circles. A slight breeze whispered through the room, sending the tiny flames into a frenzied celebration. Shadows danced on the walls. The stale, moist smell had been replaced by a sickly sweet blend of incense and smoke.

Then she heard something. It was muffled, distant. But as she strained her ears to listen, it came closer. And closer. And closer . . .

Voices. Voices . . . singing? No. Chanting. They were saying something—half-singing it in monotone unison. Susan couldn't quite make out the words.

There was a clanking sound; the voices rose in volume. Fresh air penetrated the room, and several of the candles flickered and went out.

Suddenly, there was movement. A line of silhouettes filed in from the shadows: long, black robes with droopy hoods. The chanting continued. The words were clear and distinct now. But they sounded foreign. Almost like gibberish.

The robe-clad figures formed a circle inside the innermost array of candles. The chanting fell away and one of the taller members of the band stepped into the center.

"The Master has called for a sacrifice!" a deep voice shouted.

The others responded with a phrase that made no sense. The words sounded . . . backwards or something.

"Bring the child!" the same voice ordered.

There was a clanking, another brief movement of air, then a faint gurgling. Another robe appeared out of the darkness. It stepped into the center ring with the leader. There was something in its arms: a bundle in a blanket.

The leader took the bundle and raised it into the air. The others responded with a vigorous round of gibberish.

The leader then removed the blanket. Before Susan could see what he had, she heard it: the wail of an infant. The baby was naked—a girl. Her face was screwed into an expression of pain. Her screams bounced from wall to wall, shattering the eerie mood that had settled over the dungeonlike room.

The leader set the baby on the floor. A butcher knife appeared in his hand. This was met by another chant, part of which seemed to be an established litany—of terror and death.

The gleaming steel blade rose into the air, its razor-sharp point poised over the child.

"No!"

The circle of hoods turned toward Susan, faces cloaked in darkness. The leader froze, his knife still suspended just a few short feet above the innocent child.

"Bring her!"

A trio of robes started in Susan's direction.

"She must be initiated," the leader said. "She must be taught our code of silence." He lowered the knife slowly, glaring down at the howling babe.

Susan felt hands take hold of her arms. She felt them pull her forward into the circle of candles, toward the leader, toward the child. She felt them push her down, her knees buckling. She felt the sting of the concrete floor on her palms as she tried to catch herself.

"Here, my daughter," the deep voice said.

She looked up at the madman. He was offering her the knife.

"Prove your loyalty to the Master. Sacrifice the child."

Susan's stomach churned, bile surging into her throat. "Roger!" she called. *"Roger!"*

"What's wrong?" His voice was far away.

The Satanists towered over her. She could see them smiling. No eyes, no other features. Just lips and teeth.

"Get me out of here!"

"Tell the face," Roger instructed. "Tell it you want to exit the memory."

"I want to exit the memory!"

In the next instant she was back in the atrium: marble floor, glass ceiling, birds, sun, the disembodied face hovering near a pillar. Behind her the door slammed shut with a thunderous clap that shook the cavernous room.

"That was . . . I can't . . . I can't believe . . . ," Susan stuttered, panting.

"You okay, Susan?" the unseen Roger asked.

"I'm . . . I don't . . . I'm not sure." Her lungs were still fighting for air. "How horrible! That was someone's *memory?* Somebody actually lived through that?"

"You'd have to consult Craig on that one," Roger answered. "I'm just a hacker."

"It was so—so real," she gasped, frowning up at the face. "Like it was really happening—to *me!* I fail to comprehend how reliving that ... that ... trauma would help anyone."

"Better yet," Roger added, "can you imagine someone paying for the 'thrill' of experiencing that in a VR environment? That's what Satan's Cybersex Service amounts to. It's beyond kinky. It's—"

"Demonic," Susan pronounced. She took another deep breath. "Did you get that on tape?"

"Disk," Roger corrected. "Yeah. I got it."

"Do I have to keep going in these doors in order for you to record this crud? Because I'm not sure I can stomach it."

"Too disturbing, huh?"

"*Disturbing* doesn't begin to describe it."

"Well, now that you've accessed the files, I think I can download the rest," he said. "Hang on."

Susan looked up at the face. "What are you staring at?"

"Please restate the question or—"

"Shut up," she told it. Apparently the stony-featured artificial brain understood this.

"Okay," Roger said a minute later. "I've got three other files. That should be enough."

"So I'm done? I can get out of this hellish suit?"

"You need to exit the system first," he told her. "And then we still have to access the cybersex service."

"I don't have to blunder through *that* in this garb, do I?"

"Afraid so. I could break in and start downloading," he explained, "but I wouldn't know what it was I was getting. You need to lead me to the files. Maybe we can even come up with a match—something that's in both the MRT and the Cybersex systems. It's unlikely, but it sure would go a long way toward proving a link."

Susan considered this. She had no desire to attend a second showing of the cult sacrifice. On the other hand, they needed this material for court. Craig Hanson needed it.

"Tell me what to do," she groaned.

"Tell the face you want to exit the system, then walk back through the first door."

She did. The face followed her into the entryway of the virtual environment. "Now can I quit?"

"Let me code you out, so we don't leave any fingerprints."

She could hear Roger tapping rapidly on the keyboard. "There you go. Say good-bye to Mr. Face."

"So long, Bozo."

The face smiled at her. "Good-bye, Susan."

Susan removed the helmet and looked at Roger quizzically. "Just a couple of minutes ago, it thought I was Dr. Singer. How come just now—how did that thing know my name?"

He shrugged. "Probably heard me say it. It may not be able to carry out independent reasoning, but it's not stupid." Roger reached up and pulled the helmet back down over her head. "Sit tight. I'll have you into Cybersex Land in a jiffy."

"Great," she muttered, staring at a field of pure black. "I can hardly wait."

THIRTY-SIX

THERE WAS A BURST OF LIGHT, AND A colorful scene spilled onto the visor-screen of Susan's helmet. A naked woman was prone on a bed, propped on her elbows, her legs bent at the knees, her toenails adorned in bright red paint. The front of her body was shielded by a carefully placed pillow, her backside cleverly covered with a banner of bold letters that read: Satan's Cybersex City. The woman was looking back over her bare shoulder, aiming a wicked grin at potential customers, her alluring bedroom eyes promising to fulfill their every fantasy. Above the on-line harlot stood a miniature, cartoon devil, complete with horns, a pointed tail, and a pitchfork.

"What kind of sicko would pay for this garbage?" Susan wondered.

"Good question," Roger replied, still working the keyboard. "Doesn't do anything for me, but a lot of people eat this stuff up. They say cybersex is for the Net what porn was for video."

"What's that supposed to mean?" she asked, still gawking at the obscene graphic.

"Just that smut dealers seem to have a knack for harnessing new technology. They know that sex sells, and they're continually refining their marketing strategies. Used to be, you had to patronize an adult bookstore to get your kicks. Then came video: full-color sexual excitement in the comfort of your own living room. Then came 900 lines. Then on-line erotica. The newest twist is sex in the interactive/virtual environment." He paused, clicking keys. "Just about got it. Hang on."

"You're saying this is the wave of the future?"

"No. It's the wave of the present. The Internet was originally a system of computer interconnections between military and academic institutions. It was used to exchange information and research. But a few years back, when things opened up and millions of 'newbies' came on-line, the adult entertainment industry saw the potential for profit. Today, there are thousands of cyber-sex services on the Net. You can find a list of them in the back of any on-line magazine. Or, if you've got a decent browser, you can visit the red-light district and prowl. And with these full-sensory suits—well, things can get pretty depraved."

"There," he announced. "You're in."

"No. It's still the centerfold and the little devil."

"Touch her."

"What!"

"That's how you access the service. Just—reach out and touch her hand or something."

Susan frowned, but she put a finger out and tapped the woman's foot. The woman elicited a moan, apparently to express intense pleasure, then disappeared.

"This is disgusting!" Susan said.

A wall with a dozen doors filled her vision. Each door bore a descriptive sign: Ladies Only, Gentlemen Only, Tie Me Up, The Gang's All Here . . .

"This is sick," she protested. " I can't do this."

"Look for a match," Roger told her. "Look for something involving cult activity."

"They've got homosexual stuff, orgies—ugh!" She scanned the doors, cringing at the perverse activities they implied. "Wait. What about 'Tales from Hell.'"

"Give it a try."

"Can't you just record it?"

"It's called downloading. And no, I can't. You have to enter the virtual environment in order for me to access the other files. After you've opened one, I can grab as many as we need—just like in the MRT."

"Why don't they censor this stuff?"

"Who?"

"I don't know—the government, I guess."

"They can't. For technical reasons. It's impossible. Take Satan's Cybersex City, for example. It's a virtual community with a security gate. You can only enter by password or credit card. The P8 here found the password."

"Why can't the Feds just shut it down?"

"It's not that simple. The service is hidden in the red-light district of the Net. It's kind of like trying to shut down all the prostitution services in a huge city—say L.A. You can raid them, but they just move down the street."

"I don't understand why—"

"Pick something," Roger said. "Let's get this over with before we get caught."

"Okay, okay." She extended her hand and tapped the door marked "Tales from Hell." It opened with a cackling sound. After drawing a deep breath, Susan stepped through. Inside she was met by another set of doors.

"More doors," she groaned.

"What do they say?"

"Looks like titles—like the names of some really raunchy movies."

"Pick one."

"I was afraid you'd say that." She examined them, trying to determine which "experience" would be the least horrifying. "'Debbie in the Dungeon,'" she said, tapping the door.

"I hear you knocking," a voice responded, "but you can't come in."

"Roger, the door won't open."

"It won't? Hmm . . . Let me try something." More keyboard magic. "Now try it."

Susan tapped the door again and it vanished. "Whatever it was you did, it worked. Here I go." And she stepped through the door.

For a long moment, there was nothing: black silence. "Roger, I think the thing got hung up or—" A scene abruptly materialized: a dimly lit passageway. "Never mind." It reminded her of the MRT file, except that the walls were made of earth, and a line of people was filing down the hall and through a doorway. They appeared to be normal folks: a middle-aged man in a suit, an elderly woman, a teen with long hair and faded blue jeans, a young mother carrying her baby, an old man with a cane, a preadolescent girl in shorts and a halter top—everyone had a torch in hand, these providing the only light in the rugged corridor.

Susan followed them for fifty feet, then through a door into a low-ceilinged room. It was like a bunker, or even a storm cellar. Sandbags had been stacked on one side of the space, crude metal shelves filled with canned goods lined another wall. A long wooden table sat at the far end of the room. On it was a small crate and a long-barreled revolver.

Once inside, the people placed their torches in wrought-iron stands, forming a circle of fire. The old man set his cane aside and slipped on a black robe. The man in the suit handed robes to the rest of the group and they all put them on, pulling the hoods up over their heads. Then they stood in a circle and began to chant. The words sounded to Susan like the same ones she had heard in the MRT: gibberish with a slightly familiar ring. Almost recognizable . . . but not quite.

She was about to tell Roger to do whatever it was he needed to do so that she could get out of the horrid, artificial experience and back to the real world, when the chanting stopped and the old man reached toward the mother—taking her baby.

"Not again," Susan sighed. She watched in morbid fascination and dread as the kind-looking, grandfatherly man placed the baby in the crate and shut the top. The child didn't make a peep. The man picked up the crate and cradled it in his arms. He said something—something indiscernible—in a solemn voice, before handing the wooden box to the teen.

"Bury it. For the Master," the man ordered.

For the first time, Susan noticed that there was a pit at the center of the room: a hole with a mound of loose dirt surrounding it. The teen said something—Susan thought it was the word "cool," though that seemed unthinkable—and placed the crate into the pit. He then took up a shovel and started to fill the hole. Still, the baby was quiet.

"Bring the girl," the old man ordered. "She must be initiated."

The middle-aged man took the twelve-year-old roughly by the shoulders and thrust her in front of the old man.

"Daddy!" the girl protested, trying to pull away.

"Take her clothes off," the old man said. He threw back his own robe.

"Roger! Get me out of here!"

All heads turned in Susan's direction.

"Roger!"

No response.

"A new member," the old man observed, smiling. "Wonderful. Come forward that we may initiate you as well."

"Roger!" She began struggling with the helmet, fighting to tear it off. But it wouldn't budge. The strap was jammed. She felt a tiny pinprick on her neck, in the gap between the visor and the suit. Before she could determine what had caused it, the robed figures had taken hold of her limbs and were dragging her forward, to the center of the circle.

"Roger!"

She thrashed against their grip, kicking, twisting, screaming. But there were too many of them, and her strength seemed to be fading. Her vision blurred. Her thinking slowed. Her mind grew numb. She was on her knees now. Shadowed faces glared down at her; hands—seemingly hundreds of them—poked and prodded her from every angle. The cellar had begun to spin.

Susan tried to tell herself that it wasn't real, that the ceremony was just an illusion. But these thoughts were lost in a hazy cloud of confusion and hallucination.

The old man was grinning at her hungrily. The teen continued to shovel dirt into the pit. Deep below, the baby had begun to cry. Its tiny voice sounded miles away.

Clutching herself, Susan viewed the room through a dull, apathetic stupor, her eyes searching the hoods for understanding, for sympathy, for help. But there were no faces, only empty black holes.

The door opened behind her. She turned toward it, still on her knees, staggering, drunk. She tried to focus on the door, without success. Someone was there. Around her, the robed figures bowed and took up a soft, respectful chant.

"Master," the old man said, his voice trembling. "Welcome."

The visitor approached, a nondescript, blurry blob. Susan stared, blinking, fighting to remain lucid. It was a man. A man in a white jacket—a lab coat. His features were indistinct, mouth, chin, cheeks, eyes, and ears all floating in different directions.

"Susan," he growled. "What a pleasure it is to finally meet you, face-to-face."

Susan gasped. She had no idea who this person was and could never have identified him in a lineup, but even through the gauzy veil of a drug-induced high, she recognized the voice.

"Satan."

"Please. Call me Master. After all, we are about to become intimately acquainted."

"No. Don't. Please . . . don't . . . ," she sobbed. "Jesus." For the first time in over a decade, the word was a name—a prayer—rather than a curse.

"Jesus?" He laughed at this. "What good could he possibly do you at a time like this?" He glared at her, as if he expected an answer.

"God! Jesus! *Help me!*"

The man frowned at this, dismissing it with a shake of his head. "Don't you remember our phone conversations, Susan? Don't you remember my promise? I have something special in store for you."

Susan retched, vomiting on the visor screen. She swayed back and forth, retching again, wondering why the room was suddenly disappearing from view.

The helmet, a distant voice told her. *Take off the helmet!*

She reached a weak hand up and squeezed the locking device on the strap. It gave this time, and the clasp slipped away. Pushing back the visor, she examined her new environment with wide, tearful eyes. It was quiet. No robed Satanists chanting. No torches crackling. No baby crying. The cellar was gone. She was still wearing the suit. Zipping it off, she clumsily fought her way into her pants and shirt.

"It wasn't real," she mumbled to herself, reeling as she took her purse and attempted to stand. Beside her, the P8 was still beeping and whirring. But Roger . . . where was . . .

She looked down, bracing herself against the mainframe, and saw him. Roger was lying on the floor in a lake of blood. His mouth hung open in an expression of extreme pain.

Susan retched again and stumbled to the door. *Get to Campbell*, she told herself. She made it halfway down the first hall before she tripped and fell against the wall.

The phone! She looked down at her purse, willing herself to get it out and place the call.

THIRTY-SEVEN

WAVES OF LIQUID LIGHT CRASHED OVER HER, WASHING into her eyes, flowing along a network of electric nerves, streaming down limp, heavy limbs, and pouring out in a rushing river that flooded the hallway. She was a conduit. She could feel each particle of energy as it entered, bounced about playfully inside of her, and then exited, celebrating its freedom in a dance of joy. She could see each molecule as it rocketed down from above, assaulting her mind and body with healing heat.

Suddenly, a cloud covered the sun. The light disappeared and with it the warm ecstasy of life.

"Susan?"

She stared up at the unwelcome shadow, at the large, undefined shape that had eclipsed the fountain of immaculate light.

"Susan?"

"Her eyes are open."

"Susan?"

She felt herself moving, floating lazily up into the air.

"Susan, it's me, John."

Her head turned toward him, eyes blinking. "John?"

"What happened?"

She made an effort to think, but her brain was in a freefall, taking great and extreme interest in trivial things: the smoothness of the wall, the sound—not the meaning—of words, the way air moved in and out of her lungs. She studied the large hand holding her elbow. Fingers. Such strange and wonderful creations.

They looked like something that would grow on a plant, like branches on a tree. And the hair around the knuckles—

"Susan? Can you hear me?"

Something slapped against her face. It caused a feeling. Pain? No. It couldn't be. It was too numb, too detached. Pain hurt. But this was—

Campbell slapped her lightly again. "Susan! What happened?"

Her head swung in his direction. "John . . . Where's Tony?"

Her speech was slurred, like a wino on a binge.

"He'll be here."

"But where is he?" she whined.

"I sent him for takeout, okay? He'll be here."

She swung her head in the other direction, at another figure standing in the hall. "Then who's that?"

"The security guard," he told her. "Where's Roger?"

"Roger?" She tried to think. "Roger . . . Oh, he's back there." She pointed in the wrong direction. "I think maybe he's dead." She relayed this information with a dreamy smile.

"She's been drugged," Campbell said.

"Obviously." The guard frowned.

"Go down and check those doors. See what you can find."

Susan heard the man leave, amazed that footsteps could cause such a curious sound on the carpet, like a hunter stalking a tiger in tall, dry, African grass. "Watch out for tigers!" she called after him.

"Come on," Campbell said, picking her up in his arms. "Let's get you out of here."

"It's okay, John," she replied, grinning. "You don't have to carry me. I can fly."

THIRTY-EIGHT

SHE COULD STILL FEEL THE LIGHT, STILL HEAR it pulsing and buzzing its way through her body: a raging fire of orange energy viewed through heavy, closed eyelids. When she finally managed to pry them open, she realized that it was morning, that a bright, low sun was beaming through the window, giving the room a blinding yellow glow—and that her head was exploding.

Shutting her eyes tightly, she hid beneath the pillow, willing the splitting, pounding pain to go away, willing the light to fade, willing the sun to go down.

Susan tried to remember what had happened to cause her condition, but even that attempt brought throbbing anguish. Another car wreck? Had someone crowned her with a two-by-four? Maybe she had gone on an unexpected—and now forgotten—drinking spree, and this was the granddaddy of all hangovers.

"How you feeling?" a voice asked. Each word, every inflection beat against her brain like a hammer.

"Bad," she answered in a whisper. *Bad* didn't do this affliction justice. It was far worse than simply bad, but she couldn't muster the strength to elaborate.

Peeking out from behind her pillow, she squinted at Tony.

"Here," he said, offering something.

She hoped it wasn't breakfast. Her stomach would undoubtedly revolt at the sight of anything even remotely related to pork.

"Take a couple of these," he told her.

She reached up and felt two tablets fall into her hand. Putting them into her mouth, she swallowed them without water and returned to the solitude of her warm, soft fortress.

"Doctor says those will help," Tony said. "Your hearing is in three hours. If you plan on being there, you'll need to get up in about thirty minutes."

Susan groaned at this, then wished she hadn't. *"Doctor?"* she managed to ask.

"Yeah. Apparently you were injected with a hallucinogen. The lab said it was the latest designer version of lysergic acid diethylamide."

"Huh?" she muttered.

"LSD. You were really trippin'."

"Roger," she mumbled, suddenly remembering. "What about Roger? Is he dead?" The words smashed against her skull.

"No sign of Roger."

"But I saw him," she protested, reeling against the pain. "He was hurt."

"So you said last night. But in your state, Susan, I doubt you could have seen much of anything. *Clearly,* that is."

She reached a hand up and waved him out of the room. Maybe the meds would take the edge off her headache, and they could discuss this later. In the meantime, she would lie perfectly still, trying not to breathe, trying not to do anything that might make the pain worse, wishing—only half facetiously—that she could die.

Dear God, she prayed in slow motion, *do something about my head. Either that, or take me home to heaven.*

Fifteen minutes later, she awoke from a shallow sleep, wondering if she would indeed go to heaven when she died. Had her conversion been valid?

As she remembered what Tom and Evette had said—that salvation was not a feeling but a state—she noticed that the pain had subsided. Either the prayer or the meds—or both—had worked. To a degree, at least. She now felt like she had stayed up too late, gone without sleep too long, and banged her head on a steering wheel the day before. In other words, she felt seminormal: exhausted, weak, and desperate for two weeks on the beach, far away from work. Even before the Hanson case, her mantra had become: *I need a vacation.*

After making a sincere promise to herself that as soon as the hearing was over she would indeed head for a warm, sunny locale, she rolled out of bed and into a long, hot shower. The water had a reviving effect, stimulating her skin, soothing her head, the steam magically restoring her strength. When she emerged from the stall of fogged glass and began patting herself down with a soft, thick towel, she decided that she would live, that she might even be coherent enough to plead Hanson's appeal. Her mind slowly regained its ability to reason as she dressed, dried her hair, and applied makeup. Even the bruise on her face seemed less severe.

"Good morning," she said, smiling as she entered the kitchen.

Campbell looked up from the newspaper and returned the greeting with a half-grin and a shake of his head. "Looks like the painkiller's working."

She shrugged. "I feel okay. Pretty good, actually—all things considered." She felt a rising sense of excitement: the hearing, the intricacies of the case, the judge, the DA, her first courtroom appearance—what a day this was going to be.

"Breakfast?" Tony asked. He had prepared omelets.

Susan frowned at them. The sight of food still made her slightly nauseous. "I'll just take some coffee."

Campbell's brow filled with furrows. "You sure you want some?"

"Didn't I just say I did?"

"I mean, you're already buzzing from the meds."

"I am not," she argued, resisting the urge to giggle. She was really starting to feel great.

"Maybe you should avoid caffeine."

Susan sidestepped him and poured herself a cup.

"You're the boss," Campbell muttered, returning to his paper.

"Let's go, boys," she said, gathering her satchel and pointing to two file boxes. "We've got a hearing to attend."

She hurried out to the Dodge and stood waiting as the two marshals locked up the apartment and carted boxes to the car.

"I fed your cat," Campbell grumbled, loading the files into the trunk.

"Alexander!" She had forgotten about him. She had forgotten she had a cat at all. "Thanks."

"You're welcome," Campbell sighed.

"Want shotgun?" Tony asked.

Susan shook her head, eyes slightly dilated, a giddy smile pasted on her face. "I'll sit in the back. I have work to do."

The marshals rolled their eyes at each other as they climbed in.

Susan pulled a folder out of her satchel as the Dodge sped toward I–25. Paging through the material, she found that she couldn't focus. Her mind was in overdrive. She felt anxious, like she was about to jump out of her skin.

"So you didn't find Roger?" she asked, squirming in her seat.

"Nope," Campbell replied.

"What about the disc?"

"What disc?" he asked, eyes on the road. They were heading south now, the interstate cluttered with traffic.

"We recorded everything—the Institute's MRT sessions and the cybersex operation."

Tony gave his partner a funny look, then asked, "You guys broke into the Institute's files?"

"To obtain evidence."

"It's still illegal."

"Not exactly," she argued. "It's complicated."

"How's that?" Campbell asked, sliding the Dodge past slower cars.

She explained it to them at length and in great detail, glad for the opportunity to vent the growing pool of nervous energy. When she finished, they were on highway 115 southeast of Colorado Springs, just twenty miles from Florence.

"What you're saying," Campbell clarified, "is that the Sanders kid found out that the Institute was marketing patient sessions as 'adult entertainment,' and that's what got him killed."

Susan nodded. "Right." The drug was wearing off; the frantic hyperactivity dissipating—and the pain was on the rebound.

"Got any proof?" Campbell asked.

"That's what we were after last night."

"What exactly happened last night?" Tony asked.

She paused, recalling the events, suddenly reminded that Tony was still a plausible candidate for "Satanhood." Where had he been when she was drugged? Out getting takeout, according to Campbell. How convenient.

"Roger helped me access the files," she explained. "He was recording them for use in court."

"Unlawfully obtained," Tony said, shaking his head. "The judge would have thrown it out."

"I don't think so," Susan argued. "Not this evidence. Anyway, we finished with the MRT and went to the on-line porn service. I was in this 'experience' about a satanic cult, and . . ." Her voice trailed off.

"And?" Tony prodded.

"And I couldn't get out. It was—a nightmare. So real. So horrifying—the things they were doing . . . I tried to get out. But my helmet was stuck. And Roger . . . I called to him, but he didn't answer. Then this guy shows up—inside the experience, in the virtual reality environment. And he knew me. He knew I was there and he knew my name."

"How?" Campbell wondered. "How could he?"

"Maybe the system is interactive," Tony said. "It's gotta be if Susan could go in and play a role in the experience."

"But what she's saying," Campbell continued, "is that another character not only responded to her presence, but he called her by name. Right, Susan?"

"Right."

"So that means somebody else was accessing the system at the same time she was. Somebody who knew she was going to be in there at that particular time. Who knew that, Susan?"

She shook her head, unwilling to list the principle suspects—two of whom were seated in the car with her.

"Roger did," Tony pointed out.

"Yeah, but he wasn't in the system with me," Susan said.

"How do you know?"

"Because when I finally got that stupid helmet off, Roger was lying there. And there was blood all over the place. His head was cracked open."

Silence reigned in the front seat.

"You guys believe me, don't you?"

"Ah—sure. Yeah. We believe you, Susan," Campbell stuttered. "It's just that—well, there was nothing there—no Roger, no blood—when we checked the room."

"Whoever assaulted him must have dragged the body off somewhere to hide it and then cleaned up the blood."

"How long did it take you to respond to Susan's call?" Tony asked his partner.

"Two minutes, max."

"Would you say that's enough time to ditch a body and clean up the floor?"

Campbell considered this. "It would be tight. Blood isn't easy to get rid of. It spreads when you try to wipe it up. I don't know."

"He was there!" Susan told them. "I saw Roger on the floor, in a pool of his own blood. Get a search warrant and go through the Phoenix facility. Roger's in there somewhere. Probably dead."

"The warrant's already being taken care of," Campbell assured her. "But if somebody cleaned up after a murder that quickly, I'm betting they also got the body out of there pronto. Roger's probably resting quietly in some river in Utah by now—if he's not on the lam."

"On the lam?"

"Maybe he's your Satan."

Susan scoffed at this. "He was helping me gather evidence as part of Hanson's defense. He's Craig's friend. No. There's no motive for him to harass me."

"What about the guy in the VR thing—the one who recognized you. What did he look like?"

"I was loopy by then. I didn't get a good look at him. Just a man in a—a white jacket."

"A dinner jacket—a James Bond tux?" Tony asked.

"No. More like a lab coat. Something a doctor would wear. But it doesn't matter what he looked like or wore. It was inside a computer. You could show up as Cary Grant if you wanted to."

"What did he sound like?" Campbell wondered. "Same voice as your caller?"

Susan considered this. "Pretty close. Yeah. It sounded like the same person. If we had Roger's disc, I'd show you the guy and let you listen to him talk."

"We've got a couple of marshals staking out Phoenix," Campbell said. "If Roger shows, we'll find out about the disc."

"And ask him a few other probing questions," Tony grumbled.

"We should have the warrant this morning. They'll go in and give the place the white glove. If the disc is there, our people will find it."

"It's not there," she told them.

"How can you be sure?" Campbell asked, glancing at her in the rearview mirror.

"You said yourself that Roger's body won't turn up. Neither will the disc. Not if what's on it is incriminating—and it is. Everyone and everything that lends support to my client's claim about the Institute and the frame and his innocence disappears or dies."

"Does seem a little strange," Campbell agreed.

"More than a little," Susan said, staring out the window. They were passing Penrose, approaching Florence, just forty-five minutes and a swing of the gavel away from the start of Dr. Craig Hanson's final hearing. And she was holding an empty bag.

THIRTY-NINE

THE IN-HOUSE COURTROOM AT SUPER MAX WAS SMALL, unimpressive, but complete. Along one wall of the thin, tiled space sat a judge's bench, a witness stand, a stenographer's desk, and an American flag. A row of seven chairs stood facing the bench, presumably for the attorneys, and a dozen other chairs were scattered around to accommodate interested spectators. The idea of a courtroom within the facility made good sense, saving time and avoiding the costs and security problems involved in transporting the nation's most dangerous felons to court. Still, as she stood looking at it, Susan was reminded of the magazine-laden areas that customers sat in at auto repair shops while their cars were being attended to. She was about to argue her first case—in a speedilube waiting room.

But the surroundings didn't matter, she decided, setting her satchel down and gesturing for Campbell and Tony to do the same with the file boxes. What mattered was the case itself. What mattered was doing her very best in presenting Hanson's defense. Win or lose, she would give it her all.

"We're going for coffee," Campbell said. "Want some?" He followed this offer with a disapproving look, implying that ingesting more caffeine would be unwise.

"Sure."

He shot her an expression of fatherly concern before leading Tony into the hallway.

Susan examined her watch. Twenty minutes until the hearing. She gazed around the empty room, filling the chairs with her imagination, picturing Humphries, McDermott, Hanson . . .

Her headache was back, both temples throbbing with renewed vigor. But she wasn't about to take any more of those pills. Not at the risk of rushing through the hearing like a manic mental patient.

Sinking into a chair, she closed her eyes, took a deep breath, and silently composed a sincere plea for heavenly assistance.

I realize that I've drifted away from you. And I know that after our brief reunion the other day at church, I have no right to demand anything from you. I don't feel good enough or religious enough to come to you for help. But according to Tom and Evette, you're a forgiving God. A God of great mercy. So . . . here I am.

She was interrupted by her phone. It rang two more times before she dug it out of her satchel.

"Gant here."

"Hi, Susan. It's Jack. Just wanted to wish you luck."

"Thanks, Jack."

"You nervous?"

"Yeah. Maybe a little." Her voice made it obvious that she was *very* nervous.

"Relax. Take it easy," he advised. "It'll be over before you know it."

"I hope so."

"Give me a call this afternoon and let me know how it went."

"Okay."

She hung up. Her palms were wet with perspiration. Another check of her watch told her it was just fifteen minutes to the start of the hearing. Deep breath in . . . deep breath out . . . more prayer.

I need you, God. Tom and Evette said to pray in Jesus' name. Okay—in Jesus' name . . . help! I need you to get me through this thing. I'm sweating, shaking, about to lose it. Help me to calm down and think clearly. Give me the wisdom and the . . . the insight and the . . . courage to do a good job of defending Craig. Give me—

Her phone, still in her hand, buzzed again. She flipped it open. "Yes?"

"Your first courtroom appearance, huh, Susan?"

"Who is . . . ?" She knew the answer before she could complete the question.

"Just wanted to wish you luck. Like Jack did. Except I'm more invested in the outcome than Jack is. He doesn't have a personal interest. I do."

Like Jack? she thought. How did this character know that Jack had just called? Was her cellular bugged?

"It's a real shame that you left in such a hurry last night. I did so want to make good on my promise to you. I came close, though, didn't I?" The caller paused. "You don't have a case, Susan. But if you somehow draw this thing out, if the judge doesn't set a date, I'm coming for you. Tonight. After the hearing. At your motel." There was a laugh, then a click.

Susan sat listening to the dial tone. Had the threat been a last-ditch effort to intimidate her—a final bluff—or was it, as Satan liked to call it, a promise? Either way, it had an unsettling effect on her.

"Something wrong, Counselor?"

Susan looked up and saw the district attorney and a trio of his underlings parading into the room. McDermott had a smug grin on his face, as if the hearing was just a formality and he had already won. She shut the phone and put it back into her satchel, swallowing hard. The battle was upon her.

Campbell and Tony returned with steaming Styrofoam cups, taking seats on either side of her—still functioning as jealous bodyguards, even in court.

"Looks like the enemy has arrived," Campbell observed, handing her a cup. "Never liked that guy," he said, glaring at the DA. "He's got shifty eyes."

"And he always looks so—so arrogant," Tony added. "Makes you want to punch him in the nose."

Susan ignored this. Sipping her coffee, she began reorganizing her notes for the twentieth time that morning.

Seven minutes later, when the clock on the wall read precisely 10:30, the door at the far end of the room opened. The bailiff stepped in and bellowed: "All rise." Two guards came in, followed by the judge, his black robe flowing as he marched to the bench. Sitting tall in his chair, Humphries glanced about the courtroom. Satisfied with what he saw, he lifted his gavel and proclaimed: "This court will now come to order." *Blam!*

"Bailiff, have the prisoner summoned," the judge said. He leafed through a file, pausing occasionally to peer at the attending lawyers through his reading glasses. No one spoke. They knew better. Even McDermott was silent.

Susan heard a rustling noise behind her and turned in time to see Craig Hanson being led through the door. He was surrounded by four large men, all armed, all holding billy clubs—just in case the prisoner decided to try something. He was dressed in federal-issue orange coveralls, his arms and legs bound together with manacles. A leather device was strapped over his head: a muzzle to keep him from biting someone. Susan smiled at him.

After strapping Hanson to a solitary chair midway between the attorneys and the bench, the guards backed away but didn't relax. Clubs were still at the ready, eyes still fastened on their charge.

Susan moved past them, toward her client.

"How are you doing, Craig? Hanging in there?"

Hanson nodded, his eyes sorrowful.

"Good," she said, patting his shoulder. The guards bristled at this. "Keep praying," she added before returning to her seat.

"Dr. Hanson," the judge began sleepily, "do you understand that this hearing is likely to be your last appearance in a courtroom?"

Hanson nodded.

"You have been convicted of murder in the first degree, two counts of sexual abuse against minors, and a dozen counts of cruelty to animals. In your original trial, you pled guilty to these offenses, offering a full confession. Do you wish to change that plea?"

"Yes, Your Honor," Hanson replied.

"How do you plead, Dr. Hanson?" the judge asked wearily. It was clear that he already knew the answer and these questions were just a formality—for the court record.

"Not guilty, Your Honor."

"And the confession?"

"I wish to retract it. It was the result of coercion and—"

Humphries waved him off. "We'll get to that later, Doctor. Counsel, please approach the bench."

Susan and McDermott both came forward.

"Unless new witnesses or evidence are being introduced," the judge said, "I am inclined to put the prisoner on the stand and let him tell his story. Defense?" He looked expectantly at Susan.

"Two of my witnesses are unavailable," she answered, thinking of Grant Singer and Roger Thompson. "But I do have one scheduled to appear this morning."

"New evidence?"

"Yes, Your Honor." Not much, she thought. Probably nothing that would turn the case, but evidence was evidence.

"Of what nature?"

"A diary kept by a patient of Dr. Hanson."

"Your Honor," McDermott whined with a frown, "a patient's diary is of no relevance to the crimes Dr. Hanson has been—"

"It's Ruth Sanders's journal, Your Honor," Susan clarified, returning the frown. "The mother of the boy whom my client is accused of murdering."

"Very well, I'll allow it," the judge said.

"I've also got precedent to cite, concerning the abuse charges and the way the testimonies were obtained."

McDermott's nostrils flared. "Your Honor, this is a smoke screen. The defense has nothing new to offer. Ms. Gant is grasping at straws."

Humphries didn't seem to be listening. "Enter the diary into evidence," he said. "We'll discuss the precedent later. When will your witness be here?"

"Any time, sir."

"Let's hope so."

The fighters returned to their respective corners, and Susan went through the motions of entering the diary. When she was finished the judge said, "I will go over this evidence this afternoon, after these proceedings. While we are waiting on your witness, Ms. Gant, please indulge the court with an overview. What do you hope to prove by submitting the journal?"

Susan stood and began to explain the contents of Ruth Sanders's diary, of the woman's journey from the grief of losing her son, to the horror of uncovering her own history of satanic ritual abuse.

"Your Honor," McDermott objected. "Relevance? What is the point here? Defense is stalling. Prosecution requests that Dr. Hanson be forced to take the stand."

Humphries silenced the DA with a look, then asked, "What *is* the point, Ms. Gant?"

"Your Honor," she answered. "The Sanders diary shows that this woman was led toward a diagnosis of SRA—satanic ritual abuse. She had no recollection of it until Dr. Binker—her therapist before she came under the care of Dr. Hanson—began exposing her to the MRT unit."

"MRT?" the judge sighed, adjusting his glasses. "And that is?" His patience seemed to be running out.

"Memory Reconstruction Therapy. It's a highly advanced virtual reality system that allows patients to remember and reexperience past traumas in a safe environment."

"Your Honor," McDermott whimpered. "Relevance?"

Humphries looked to Susan for an answer. "Your Honor," she said, "I intend to prove that the MRT unit at the Trinity Institute of Psychiatric Therapy has been misused—"

McDermott rolled his eyes and sighed melodramatically.

"That the Institute commonly overdiagnoses SRA—and misdiagnosed Dr. Hanson's family."

"Objection!" McDermott shouted. "The Institute is not on trial here! Dr. Hanson is!"

"That confidential MRT sessions are being marketed for profit," Susan explained, raising her voice, "via a cybersex service on the Internet."

"That's . . . preposterous!" the DA blurted out.

"That the Sanders boy discovered this scheme and was then killed to ensure his silence," she continued, matching McDermott's volume. "And that my client learned of these events and was subsequently framed for the murder of Zachary Sanders."

"Your Honor!" McDermott bellowed. "Ms. Gant has no grounds for—"

"Your Honor, I have been threatened and intimidated by—," Susan started to say.

The judged slammed his gavel down and gave both parties the evil eye. "This is a court of law—*my* court of law," he said slowly, biting off each word. "It is not a playground. If the two of you want to scream and bicker like children, take it outside." He paused, looked down at the notes he had scribbled, then groaned. It was obvious that the case was more complicated than he had anticipated.

"Your Honor," McDermott tried in a calmer voice, "the defense has no evidence upon which to base these charges. They don't even have a witness to . . ." The DA's voice trailed off as a woman entered the room.

"Sorry I'm late," Cindy whispered to Susan. "I was thirty minutes getting through security. This place is like—a prison."

"Your Honor," Susan said, glaring at McDermott. "My witness has arrived."

"Please take the stand," Humphries told Cindy. He looked at the bailiff. "Swear her in."

Cindy raised her right hand and repeated the pledge to tell the truth.

"Please state your full name for the record," the judge said without looking at her.

"Cynthia Katherine Roberts."

"Ms. Gant, please commence with your examination of the witness," Humphries said.

Susan rose and stepped closer to the witness stand. She suddenly felt a little like Perry Mason—except that there was no fawning jury, no cameras to perform for.

"Ms. Roberts," she began, "have you ever been treated by the Trinity Institute of Psychiatric Therapy?"

"Yes."

"When?"

"I was interviewed just last week. Friday. And I was seen by a doctor on Monday of this week."

"Who saw you?"

"Dr. William Bayers."

"He is the chairman of the Institute, is he not?"

Cindy nodded. "Yes."

"Why did you seek treatment?"

Cindy looked puzzled for a moment. "Because . . . to show that the Institute has a tendency to overdiagnose SRA."

"Objection!" McDermott said, springing from his seat. "Your Honor, the witness has obviously been coached."

"Sit down, Mr. McDermott," the judge growled. "You'll get your chance in a few minutes."

The DA sat back down and began conferring with his team in whispers.

"You were seen for the first time on Monday?" Susan asked.

"Yes," Cindy responded.

"Tell us about that."

"Well, I went in. Dr. Bayers talked to me for . . . I don't know, maybe twenty minutes. He asked about my background, about my emotional problems."

"What did you tell him?"

"I described myself in terms that fit the general symptoms of SRA."

"And he was convinced by this?"

"He seemed to be. He said it would take time to uncover the root of my problems, but that they could well stem from extreme childhood trauma, such as SRA."

"What happened then?"

"After we talked, he took me into something called the Memory Reconstruction Therapy unit. It's like an expensive video-game system that uses information about your past to artificially reconstruct memories, or painful events from your past."

"Did you experience a reconstructed memory?"

"Yes."

"Could you tell us about it?"

"It was weird. The technology itself is pretty bizarre—looking around, walking in, and touching things that aren't really there. My memory had to do with a vague feeling that I might have been sexually abused when I was four—an experience I made up. My description was very sketchy, but according to the doctor, the computer fills in the missing information."

"What was the result?"

She paused and shook her head. "It was . . . It's hard to describe. It was like being abused by a video game. I could feel the abuse happening. I could hear the abuser, see him—even smell his breath." She shivered.

"And this scenario was entirely fictitious?"

"Yes."

"It was not in any way based on truth?"

"No."

"Your witness, Mr. McDermott."

FORTY

Ms. Roberts," the DA said, rising to face her. "Tell us—what do you do? For a living, I mean."

"I'm an attorney."

McDermott smiled. "Is that right? How convenient."

"Objection, Your Honor. Ms. Roberts's occupation is not relevant."

"Mr. McDermott . . . ," the judge warned.

"How long have you known Ms. Gant?" the DA asked.

Cindy shrugged. "We met in college. Maybe—eight years ago."

"And would you consider her a good friend?"

"Yes."

"Your best friend?"

"Yes."

"Your Honor!" Susan said.

"Mr. McDermott, where are you going with this?" Humphries wanted to know.

"I'm trying to establish the relationship between this witness and the defense," he explained. "The defense has only one new witness in this case. And that witness is a close personal friend—a fellow lawyer—who agreed to mislead a health professional in order to discredit one of the finest psychiatric facilities in the country."

"Your Honor!"

"It's unethical, not to mention unworthy of this court!"

"Ms. Roberts's relationship with the defense—"

"I move to have this witness's testimony—"

"—is not relevant to—"

"—stricken from the record."

The gavel pounded down, echoing through the room. Judge Humphries scowled into the silence that followed. "Children, this is my final warning. If you can't play together without fighting, I'll be forced to hold you both in contempt of court. I'm willing to listen to your arguments and objections. But order will reign in this courtroom."

He looked at Susan, then at McDermott. "Does the prosecution have any further questions for the witness?"

The DA shook his head, sneering, as if Ms. Roberts wasn't worth his time or consideration.

"You may step down," the judge told Cindy.

"Thanks," Susan whispered as she passed by on her way to the door.

Cindy shook her head. "Sorry I couldn't be more help."

"Ms. Gant, you mentioned precedent?" Humphries asked.

"Yes, Your Honor." She dug the cases out of her satchel and cited them: four convictions of men accused of sexual abuse on the sole basis of recovered memories—each overturned.

Humphries was unimpressed. "As I am sure you are aware, Ms. Gant, none of those cases involved a federal offense. Furthermore, the convictions hinged upon recovered memories in the absence of hard evidence."

"But, Your Honor—"

"I realize that your client's conviction was based upon his confession. And by retracting it, the prosecution's case is greatly weakened. But having reviewed the evidence, I find that your client's fingerprints were discovered at the site of the murder. Were it not for this fact, I might be more inclined to entertain these precedents."

Susan felt a tap on her shoulder. Paul was standing next to her, holding two oversized envelopes.

"A moment, Your Honor," she said.

The judge nodded and mumbled something under his breath. "What do you have?"

"This is the info you requested from Hanson's previous employer," Paul whispered, handing her the cardboard FedEx container. "This other is something that showed up this morning. No return address. Might be junk mail," he shrugged. "But you never know."

"Thanks, Paul."

"Hey, thank Jack. He's the one who talked me into making the drive down."

After Paul left, Susan hurriedly ripped open the FedEx. It was Hanson's itinerary from last year. Setting it aside, she opened the manila envelope. She tipped up the end and a miniature compact disc slid out. There was nothing else inside. The disc had a yellow Post-it note that read: "Just in case something happens to me." The signature below was "Grant Singer."

There really is a God, Susan thought with certainty. *And he answers prayer.*

"Request permission to enter this into evidence," she said, presenting the tiny square plastic case. "And I would also like to show it to the court."

"What is it?" Humphries asked, squinting through his glasses.

"A computer disc."

"Your Honor," McDermott complained, "did the defense bring the equipment to run this disc?"

"No we did not, but—"

"As I thought," the DA said, shaking his head. "Another stall tactic, Your Honor."

"What is on the disc, Ms. Gant?"

Susan considered the question. What *was* on the disc? She had assumed that it contained the downloaded MRT files and the correlating cybersex experiences—the results of the investigation Singer and Roger Thompson had engaged in. But what if it didn't? What if it contained records from Singer's patient files? Or what if it was his personal views on Dr. Hanson? Or what if it was a computer game? There was no way of telling.

"Your Honor, I believe that this disc contains evidence linking the Institute's MRT unit to an on-line pornography service. It was not in my possession before this moment, so I did not arrange the appropriate equipment to view it."

The judge took a deep breath and let it out slowly. "What format is it?"

"Miniature CD," Susan replied.

Humphries looked at one of the guards. "Find out if there is a computer with a mini-CD available at this facility."

The guard grunted, "Yes, sir," and left.

"Your Honor," Susan said, "may I use this time to confer with my client?"

The judge nodded, his attention on his notepad.

Susan stepped over to Hanson's chair and knelt at his side. "This could be it. This could be what we've been praying for, Craig," she told him in a voice just above a whisper. Her hand patted his. "Let's just hope that Grant and Roger were able to collect the evidence we need. Which reminds me—about Roger . . ."

Hanson looked up, his sad eyes now animated. "What about him?" he asked, the muzzle muffling his question.

"We got into the system," she told him. "I saw the MRT files and the porn stuff. We even recorded it."

"But?"

"But then somebody drugged me and Roger disappeared. So did the disc."

Hanson shook his head, weighed down with despair.

"Now this shows up," she said, waving the mini-CD at him. "There's hope yet."

Behind them the guard returned with a partner. Together they wheeled a cart of equipment toward the front of the room and began tinkering with the switches and power cords. A terminal blinked to life, and metal boxes housing various peripherals began to whir.

Susan gave the disc to the bailiff, who gave it, in turn, to the guard who was now functioning as a computer tech. The guard examined the equipment for a moment, found a slot into which the disc fit, and inserted it. Seconds later an icon appeared on the screen. The guard looked at it, glanced at the CD drive, then back at the screen, puzzled. Apparently his expertise in high-tech hardware had been exhausted.

"Here," McDermott groaned. He moved the guard aside with his hand. The DA took the mouse and double-clicked on the icon. It flashed open, revealing a menu of files. Susan rose and studied the menu.

"These have already been correlated," she said.

"Huh?" McDermott perused the menu. "Your Honor . . ."

"Click on that one." Susan pointed to something marked "Burial Memory—MRT."

The DA complied, his frown growing as he waited for the computer to oblige his request. Seconds later, a picture appeared on the screen. It looked like something from a movie—vivid colors, movement, stereo sound.

The judge, the attorneys, Hanson, the guards, even Tony and Campbell watched with rapt interest. The scene depicted a dark space with a low, open-beam ceiling and a dirt floor. A single candle illuminated the backs of three figures. From their size, they appeared to be adults. Each had a short shovel and together they were digging a deep hole in the ground. Their shirts were sticky with sweat, their breath labored. Dust lifted into the air with every move of their spades.

"Your Honor," McDermott said, "I fail to see . . ." His voice trailed off as the diggers set their tools aside and donned black robes. With hoods hiding their faces, they turned toward the screen, waiting for something.

Moments later there was a loud creaking sound, like a hinged steel door opening. It clicked shut and a child appeared—a girl, about nine years old. Her face passed by in profile, looking terrified, then she turned and stood with her back to the screen. One of the adults pulled a wooden crate into view and said something. It sounded like, "Get in."

The girl began to sob, twisting away. A half-dozen meaty arms reached toward her, hands grabbing at her, thrusting her roughly into the crate. The top slammed shut and the box was pushed unceremoniously into the hole. Shovels worked to cover the crate with a fresh layer of earth. Soft, distant wails rose from beneath the dirt.

When the short movie ended, the courtroom was silent. A full minute later McDermott broke the spell with a curse. The judge admonished him with a look, then swore himself.

"I am deeply offended by the plague of sexually violent pornography that has assaulted our nation in recent years," Humphries declared. "But this . . . this is . . . it's . . ." He shook his head, unable to find the words to describe the atrocity he had just witnessed. "Ms. Gant," he finally said, "I must ask what possible reason you have for sharing it with the court."

"Your Honor, this computer file is a session from the MRT unit at the Institute, something a patient once experienced—or at least something a doctor and the computer reconstructed, based on what the doctor *thought* the patient may have experienced. At any rate, it is stored in the system at the Institute. What you are going to see now was downloaded from a cybersex service offered over the Internet."

She took the mouse from the dazed DA and double-clicked on the corresponding file: Burial Scenario—Satan's Cybersex City.

The screen flickered and a scene appeared, the same scene: a dark, cramped space, dirt floor, low ceiling, three people digging a hole. It was a rerun. The court watched as the events were reenacted.

When it was finally over, the DA started to swear, then caught himself. "That is sick," he said. "To think that people get a thrill from such unconscionable acts ... It says something about how screwed up our society is." He paused, returning to his seat. "Which is precisely why Dr. Craig Hanson must be executed, Your Honor. To prevent these sorts of atrocities from being perpetrated."

Susan's jaw dropped. The shock and dismay the DA had evidenced was all part of the act, a polished routine to ensure that the prosecution won the day. And it was apparently a very convincing, successful act. McDermott had yet to lose a case as the reigning district attorney.

"Your Honor," Susan sighed, "this disc proves that patient/doctor confidentiality has been violated in respect to the MRT sessions conducted at the Institute. It also proves that—"

"May I remind the court—and Ms. Gant," McDermott interrupted, "that we are gathered here to discuss Dr. Hanson's case, not the ethical standards or possible wrongdoing of the Trinity Institute of Psychiatric Therapy. Furthermore—"

"Enough!" Humphries barked. He removed his glasses to massage his temples, then returned them to their perch on his nose. He viewed the courtroom through dispassionate eyes. "Judging from the material on this disc," he began, gesturing to the computer, "I agree that a criminal investigation into the operation of the Memory Reconstruction Therapy unit at the Trinity Institute of Psychiatric Therapy seems to be warranted."

Susan beamed at this, shooting McDermott an "I told you so" look.

"However," Humphries continued, "as the district attorney has so thoughtfully pointed out, we have not gathered here today to argue the guilt or innocence of the Trinity Institute or those associated with it. We are gathered here to set an execution date for Dr. Craig Hanson."

An arrogant smile flashed across McDermott's face.

"Since the information presented this morning may influence Dr. Hanson's defense, I will take it into consideration. The court will recess in a few moments and I will spend the afternoon viewing the contents of the disc in its entirety to determine relevance. But I must caution the defense that proof of illegal activity on the part of the Institute, by itself, will in no way justify overturning Dr. Hanson's conviction. I assume that this is a roundabout way of discrediting Trinity Institute and thereby discrediting their diagnoses of Dr. Hanson's daughters as SRA victims." He paused, looking at Susan.

"Yes, Your Honor. But it is also meant to establish a motive for murder."

Humphries seemed confused. "Please explain, Ms. Gant."

"As I was attempting to tell you earlier—when the district attorney so rudely interrupted—the misuse of the MRT sessions is the basis for my client's defense. He contends that Zachary Sanders accidentally learned of this and was murdered. Dr. Hanson also contends that when he learned of the operation, he was framed and coerced into confessing to crimes that he did not commit."

"Yes, I remember you saying that. But your only proof toward that end is simply the link between the MRT unit and the on-line pornography service, correct?"

Susan shrugged, then opened her mouth to argue the point.

"Let me be frank with you, Ms. Gant," Humphries cut her off. "Your case is weak. Very weak. I'll look at the disc and think the matter over. I'll entertain the precedent you cited, read Ms.

Sanders's diary, and go over the testimony of your witness. But my advice to you is to have your client take the stand tomorrow. Since he has already been convicted, we are not talking about a presumption of innocence here. The 'shadow of doubt' concept disappeared when the jury handed down its verdict in the original trial. Your job in this hearing is to show that they made a terrible mistake. The burden of proof is upon you, not the prosecution. You have to prove that your client is innocent."

Susan nodded.

"And you have no other new evidence or witnesses?"

She shook her head.

"Then let Dr. Hanson tell his story."

Susan considered this. The judge was right, of course. Her case was very weak. The connections between the cybersex service, Zach's murder, and Hanson being framed were tenuous at best—all circumstantial. She had no other proof. Perhaps it was best to let Craig take the stand and fight for his life. He had managed to convince her that he wasn't a Satanist killer. Maybe he could convince Humphries.

"May I confer with my client, Your Honor?" she asked.

The judge nodded.

Hanson was staring at the floor, recognizing that defeat—and a lethal injection—were imminent.

"What do you say, Craig?"

He didn't move.

"Tell the judge what you told me. Between that and the disc and Cindy . . . and the diary . . . Well, maybe it'll be enough to turn the tide."

"I don't have much choice, do I?" he said softly.

"I'm afraid not."

"Okay."

Susan turned to face the bench. "Your Honor, my client has agreed to testify on his own behalf."

"Very well." Humphries seemed pleased. "This court stands adjourned until 11 A.M. tomorrow." He gave the gavel a crack. "Bailiff, have the prisoner returned to his cell." The judge stood and left the room, his black gown swirling behind him.

"Keep praying, Craig," Susan said in a pretense of optimism. "It's not over yet. Keep praying."

She repeated the words to herself as the guards converged on Hanson and led him away. *Keep praying, Susan. Keep praying.*

Prayer seemed to be the only hope. Nothing but the hand of God was going to save her client's life now.

FORTY-ONE

THE MOTEL 6 HAD SEEN BETTER DAYS. Built in the early sixties, it had once been a modest but clean refuge for families vacationing in southern Colorado. The years had been cruel to it, however, and after nearly a dozen progressively disinterested owners, it had become the embodiment of the phrase "cheap motel." On the outside, it looked its age: a parking area in desperate need of repaving, a neon sign that had been partially torn away by a windstorm seven years earlier, and a row of fading black doors that ran along one side of a boxy, single-level structure. The gray paint was peeling, revealing spots of dull, dry wood. A handwritten note on the office window boasted of cable TV.

On the inside, each unit was remarkably similar: mottled, gold shag carpet, dark paneling, hideous burgundy spreads covering lumpy mattresses, the lingering stench of cigarettes and beer. The phones, working or not, were bolted to the only table in each room. The bathrooms were tiny, the tubs and sinks ringed with copper stains.

Susan was oblivious to these surroundings. Seated on the floor next to the empty TV stand—a thief had apparently removed the television set—she had spread out on the carpet before her papers, folders, everything in her possession concerning the Hanson case. By getting it all out in front of her, she hoped to see something she had hitherto missed. Some detail. Some small but significant point. Some minute piece of this confusing mess.

In her lap was a legal pad. On it she had scrawled her thoughts: Someone was profiting from the MRT records—selling them as entertainment. Zach found out. Zach was killed. Ruth Sanders was diagnosed SRA. Hanson became her new doctor. Hanson got curious about the MRT business. Hanson and Roger Thompson investigated. Hanson's family was threatened. Hanson was framed. Questions: (l) Who was profiting? (2) Who killed Zach? (3) Who assigned Ruth Sanders to Hanson? (4) Who threatened Hanson's family? (5) Who framed Hanson? (6) Who wanted him to be executed? (7) Who was trying to scare his lawyer off the case?

Below this, she had drawn an oversized question mark. Then she had written: SATAN—doodling in and around the letters as she considered the puzzle.

She hadn't bothered to list suspects. There didn't seem to be any. Nobody fit the profile. And at the same time, everyone fit it. What if it was a conspiracy? Doubtful, but that was the only way she could explain it. Someone at the Institute might profit from selling the MRT sessions over the Internet. The rest of the questions revolved around Satan's identity. This Satan had probably killed Zach, framed Hanson, and was now making her life miserable. And almost everyone she had been associated with in the past week was filed in the "probable" category when it came to her stalker's identity. Campbell had had the opportunity. So had Tony. Roger—where was he, anyway? What about Dr. Bayers? For that matter, what about McDermott? The guy was ruthless. And he had political aspirations. But was he that desperate? Would he frame a man for murder, just for the publicity involved in sending a "dangerous Satanist" to death row? What about Clint O'Connor? After all, he was a member of Trinity Fellowship. Why not Humphries? The mean old poop. And don't forget Cindy. And Paul. And Jack. When you started assuming that people were hiding things, secretly making creepy calls in the middle of the night, logic took a backseat to paranoia, and everyone and their dog became suspect.

None of that mattered, of course. In just sixteen hours, Dr. Craig Hanson would take the stand. And if she didn't come up with something—anything—before then, it would be Hanson's word against his own previous confession. A death-row inmate's sudden decision to void his confession was ever so slightly predictable.

Maybe she could put Tony and John on the stand. If they testified about the threats that had been made against her life, wouldn't that at least suggest that there was someone running around out there who didn't want Craig exonerated? She made a note to talk to the marshals about that in the morning.

Setting her pencil down, Susan gazed at the stacks of information on the floor around her: court records, witness testimony, notes, forms, files . . . Where was it? Where was the key that would unlock that prison door and set Hanson free?

"God only knows," Susan muttered. It was a phrase she used quite often, out of habit. But this time, the words took on new meaning.

"God," she said, shifting into a more reverent attitude, "I can't rescue Craig from the needle. I can't turn this hearing around. Only you can do that. Please. Have mercy on this guy. I know it's a cliché, but he needs a miracle here. And if he doesn't get one—"

There was a knock at the door. "Susan?" She recognized Campbell's voice.

"Just a second." She struggled to stand, her knees stiff. "I'm coming." When she opened the door, Tony and John were both there.

"You watching TV?" Tony asked.

She smirked at him. "Very funny." She pointed at the empty platform where the television was supposed to be.

"Come down to our room," Campbell said. "You've got to see this."

"What? What's wrong?"

"Hurry," Tony insisted. They each grabbed an elbow and ushered her down the sidewalk to the next door. Inside, the TV was blaring.

"Look," Campbell said, pointing at the set.

Susan stared at the screen. It was a newscast. A female reporter was standing in front of a large, impressive home.

" ... discovered by his wife, Patricia, at around 5:30 this evening," the woman told the camera. "She is currently being questioned by police. Authorities tell us that it appears to be a suicide."

"What's going on?" Susan asked.

"Shhh!" the two marshals admonished in unison.

"To recap," the report said, "Dr. William Bayers, chairman of the Trinity Institute of Psychiatric Therapy, was found dead in his home tonight ..."

"Dr. Bayers?" Susan wondered aloud. "Dead?"

"Killed himself, according to this," Tony told her, aiming a thumb at the TV.

"Let me see what I can find out," Campbell said, reaching for the phone. He placed a call, then another, and another. On the fourth, he reached someone willing to answer his questions.

"Uh-huh ... Yeah ... Anything to suggest foul play? Uh-huh ..."

Tony was flipping channels, looking for another newscast. Susan sank to the bed, dazed, unable to decide what this meant— what effect the event might have on her client. Dr. Bayers had committed suicide? Why? It didn't make sense.

Campbell replaced the receiver and shook his head. "Well, I'll be."

"What?" Tony demanded.

"You'll never believe it," he said, a faraway look in his eyes.

"Try us," Susan urged.

Campbell took a deep breath. "Well, according to Colorado Springs PD, it's a confirmed suicide. Bayers hung himself."

"Yeah, but why did—," Susan started to object.

"And he left a note," Campbell added. "Sounds like it explained everything."

Susan and Tony stared at him, waiting.

Campbell took a seat on the bed before continuing. "He confessed to killing Zach Sanders."

"You're kidding!" Susan said, mouth agape.

"He also confessed to framing Hanson. In the note, Bayers said the cybersex business was his idea. Guess it was pretty profitable too. Anyway, Zach found out, Bayers killed him. Then when Hanson got curious, Bayers set up an elaborate frame."

"That's . . . that's . . . incredible!" Susan stuttered.

Campbell nodded his agreement. "It gets better. He also confessed to killing Grant Singer. Same reason—the guy started snooping around. Oh, and listen to this. The cops found all sorts of interesting items in the crawl space under Bayers's house: a voice modulator, one-pass audio/video equipment, phone bugs, miniature surveillance cameras . . . They even found a stash of LSD."

"Dr. Bayers?" Susan said. "*He* drugged me? *He's* the one who's been spying on me and making those calls? He's—he's Satan?"

"Was," Tony clarified. "The greedy little pervert."

"Don't forget coward," Campbell added. "When he saw that his scheme was falling apart, that Hanson was blowing the whistle, Bayers took the easy way out."

"Saves the taxpayers the cost of one lethal injection, I guess," Tony noted.

Susan stared at the bedspread like a zombie. She had the feeling that everything was happening in slow motion, that the normal rules for time had been suspended, that someone had suddenly flipped on a brand-new light that revealed things previously unknown—and revealed them with great clarity. "That means . . . That means . . . my client . . . That means, Craig . . . he . . . he'll . . ."

"He'll walk," Campbell said. "No doubt about it. I'll have them fax a report of the investigation over to Super Max—for the judge."

"Man,"Tony chuckled, "talk about an unlikely turn of events."

Unlikely wasn't the right word for it, Susan decided. *Miraculous*. That was it. This was downright miraculous. She aimed a silent "thank you" at the Miracle Worker, rose shakily, and bid the marshals goodnight.

Back in her room, she struggled to comprehend what had just happened. In the space of a few short minutes, everything had changed. Everything! The puzzle had been solved, she was safe, her client was on the verge of freedom . . . She felt numb, light-headed, disoriented.

She began cleaning up the mess she had made, stuffing folders and documents back into the boxes. They were unnecessary now.

Bayers was Satan. Bayers had exploited a new therapy technique, then had sold patient memories over the Internet.

The Satan part made sense. If Bayers was responsible for the cybersex operation, then he would do whatever it took to keep it covert—eliminating a snoopy teenager, framing a snoopy psychiatrist, killing another snoopy psychiatrist, threatening a snoopy attorney. But the part of the equation that didn't quite click was: Why? Why would an imminent health professional, a man at the top of his field, a man with an international reputation, at the helm of a prestigious institute—why would he risk losing all that by marketing cheap, depraved pornography? Susan could only think of one viable answer: Greed. The man wanted more. Nothing novel about that. Greed had brought down many powerful, intelligent, and gifted men and women over the course of history.

Susan was suddenly exhausted. Happy, even giddy, a sense of elation washing over her. But dreadfully tired. When the floor was clear, she brushed her teeth, threw on an old nightshirt, and slid into bed.

Tomorrow will be . . . unreal, she thought as her body relaxed beneath the stiff, yellowed sheets. Today had been something. But tomorrow—tomorrow she would win her first case, rescuing a man from death row. Of course, it wasn't her doing. It was God's. But like a starting baseball pitcher whose losing effort had been saved by a supremely talented reliever, she would celebrate the team victory. Yes, tomorrow. Tomorrow would be . . . heavenly. Outstanding. Incomparable.

She fell asleep trying to find the right words to describe the day that awaited her.

FORTY-TWO

WHEN THE HEARING RECONVENED THE NEXT MORNING, it was plain from the faces gathered in the small courtroom that everyone was privy to the events of the past evening. District Attorney McDermott was noticeably subdued, his eyes downcast, the smug grin replaced with a frown of resignation. He looked like a mourner at the funeral of a good friend. Judge Humphries was his usual serious, all-business self: lips twisted into the scowl that had become his trademark. But there was something different. Something about his eyes. The intensity was gone. So was the anger. He actually seemed pleased that the proceedings were about to come to an abrupt, unforeseen halt.

As the guards led the prisoner in, manacles tinkling on the tile floor, Susan realized that he didn't know. Even behind the muzzle mask, it was clear that her client was downcast, sure that he was facing imminent doom. Maybe he had missed the newscast. Maybe he had been too depressed to watch television. Maybe he wasn't allowed to. Whatever the reason, Craig Hanson was totally unaware that he was about to become a free man.

Susan was about to request a conference with him when the judge spoke.

"Counsel please approach the bench," he said.

She and her disappointed counterpart went forward.

"I assume you both know about Dr. Bayers," Humphries said. They nodded.

"The preliminary investigation of his suicide lends great support to the defense's argument that Dr. Hanson was framed. Do you agree, Mr. McDermott?"

The DA grunted, "Yes."

"Are you ready to drop your case against Dr. Hanson?"

McDermott looked pained. He paused, unwilling to answer. Finally he uttered a quiet, "Yes, Your Honor."

They returned to their seats, and the judge addressed the prisoner.

"Dr. Hanson, will you please rise."

Hanson stood, his head drooping forward, eyes on the floor.

"Doctor, as you may have heard, the chairman of Trinity Institute committed suicide last night."

Hanson's head jerked up. "What?"

"Dr. Bayers killed himself. And he left a note confessing to his role in the pornography service and the murder of Zachary Sanders. In other words, Dr. Hanson . . ."

Hanson stared at him in disbelief.

"You have been exonerated."

His knees buckled and he sprawled to the floor.

"Help him up," the judge muttered to the bailiff.

When Hanson was upright again, the judge continued. "I must caution you, Dr. Hanson, that Dr. Bayers's suicide is still under investigation. According to a handwriting expert, the note was indeed penned by his hand. Still, if his death turns out to be the result of foul play, you will be incarcerated and face this court again. Do you understand that?"

Hanson nodded. He had begun to weep.

"Also, there is the matter of your fingerprints. They were found inside Ruth Sanders's house."

"I broke in. I was trying to figure out why Zach had been killed."

"So Ms. Gant has informed me. At any rate, you now stand charged with breaking and entering. How do you plead?"

"Well . . . I . . ." He hesitated, looking at Susan.

"Your Honor," Susan said, "my client and I have not had a chance to confer this morning. If we might—"

"Plead guilty," Humphries advised. "You've already served two years. I think the prosecution will agree to parole. What about it, Mr. McDermott?"

The DA closed his eyes and nodded.

"Guilty," Hanson chimed through the tears.

"Very well, then. Bailiff, make the necessary arrangements for Dr. Hanson's release." The gavel banged down. "This court stands adjourned." The judge gave the room one last scowl, then gathered his gown and marched out.

Hanson crumpled to the ground again, sobbing. "Praise God! Praise God!"

Rushing to his side, Susan hugged him. "God heard you, Craig," she told him, starting to cry herself. "He heard you and he answered."

"Us," Hanson said, his body shaking. "He heard us."

"Pardon me, ma'am," the bailiff said. He pulled Hanson to his feet, unlocked the manacles, and unstrapped the muzzle. "We'll have the paperwork completed in about two hours. If you'll follow me, Doctor, we'll get you some street clothes."

"I'll wait for you in the visitor's area," Susan told him.

He nodded, then gave her hand a long, firm squeeze. "Thank you. Thank you for believing in me."

She smiled back at him, watching as the bailiff led him out. The emotion of the moment seemed to solidify the bond between them.

"Looks like the defense kicked butt," Tony commented.

Susan wiped away a stray tear.

"Congratulations," Campbell said. "Guess I owe you an apology."

"Huh?"

"For bad-mouthing your client. If it had been up to me, I'd have put the needle to an innocent man."

"Me too," Tony agreed.

The marshals began helping Susan repack the case files. A few chairs away, McDermott's crew was doing the same. The room was unnaturally quiet. When the boxes were closed and the two groups made ready to leave, the DA looked up at Susan. His mouth opened, then closed again. He shook his head and muttered something, gesturing for his underlings to follow him out.

"Nothing like a sore loser," Tony observed.

They spent the next two-and-a-half hours in the visitor's waiting room—waiting. They were fed lunch and coffee. Tony read and reread tattered issues of *Sports Illustrated* from cover to cover, then resorted to leafing through ancient *Newsweeks*. Campbell focused his attention on a Martin Cruz Smith novel he had brought along for just such an occasion, dozing off periodically and snoring himself awake.

Susan was too wired to nap or read. Fueled by the unexpected victory and three cups of coffee, her mind was racing, her body tense. She couldn't sit still. Pacing back and forth in the tiny room, she mentally relived the events of the past week with a mixture of elation and awe. Her first case . . . A death-row no-winner . . . A likable family man falsely accused . . . Threats against her life . . . A "fox-hole" religious conversion . . . The resurgence of a faith long forgotten . . . A frantic, desperate search for new evidence . . . Then the sudden suicide of the man responsible for framing her client . . .

She had prayed for a miracle. And she had received a miracle. Nothing else could explain today's hearing: Judge Humphries granting the release of convicted murderer Dr. Craig Hanson. It was amazing, it was—

The door swung open and Hanson entered the waiting area. He looked like a new man. The prison coveralls were gone, replaced by slacks and a sports shirt. The sullen eyes were now bright and alive. His smile was broad, evidencing a deep and abiding joy. He was free. And every part of him, his expression, his stance, his mood, seemed to proclaim that truth.

Susan stepped toward him slowly, her eyes tearing up, and offered a comforting hug. "Welcome back to the land of the living, Craig," she whispered.

"I can't tell you how much I appreciate . . . ," he started to say. But his voice cracked and he began to cry.

Susan shook her head at him. "Don't thank me. Thank him." She aimed her pointer finger toward heaven.

"Anytime you're ready," Campbell prodded.

She turned and introduced the marshals to Hanson.

"Guess you could use a lift, huh?" Tony joked.

"Yeah," Hanson grinned. "I sure could."

Once in the car, Campbell and Tony tuned in a Rockies game on the radio and did their best to pretend they weren't there, allowing Susan and her client a modicum of privacy.

"This is unreal," Hanson was saying. "I got so beaten down. I've always believed in God and in the power of prayer, but after two years, and facing a lethal injection, I just—I guess I lost hope."

"What's that verse about God making things work out for his children?"

"'In all things God works for the good of those who love him, who have been called according to his purpose,'" Hanson quoted. "And it's true. I'm a walking testimony of God's faithfulness." He paused and sighed.

"Still think you're a modern-day Job?" she asked.

"Actually, yeah. This whole experience mirrors Job's life: unexpected tragedy, the loss of everything followed by a time of intense testing, and ultimately vindication and a wave of divine restoration. It's been extraordinary. I wouldn't do it again for all the money in the world. But it certainly does strengthen your faith."

"Strengthened mine too," Susan said. She went on to tell him about her encounter with God at Trinity Fellowship. When he finished commenting on it, she asked, "What are you going to do now?"

He shrugged. "I don't know. I doubt the Institute will take me back. Not sure I'd want to go back. Sam's gone. The divorce will be final in a few weeks." He paused, looking out the window. To the left, the snowcapped pinnacles of the lower Front Range were glowing a brilliant white in the afternoon sun. "I guess I'll start over. Take it slow. Probably move to a new city—somewhere that my past won't be a problem. Then just take it a day at a time." Another contemplative pause. "What about you? Will you get a promotion or something for saving my skin?"

Susan snorted at this. "No. And besides, I didn't save your skin. God did."

They were still discussing the case, their futures, and their spiritual/emotional states, when the Dodge exited I–25 and pulled into the parking lot of the Hampton Inn.

"Sorry to break up the party," Campbell said, glancing back over the seat. "But this is your stop, isn't it, Doctor?"

Hanson looked out the window at the hotel. "Yeah. This is it. Compliments of Super Max. Thanks a lot, guys."

Susan gave him a final smile. They embraced and for a brief, awkward moment, their faces came dangerously close to one another, lips poised for a kiss. Then Hanson climbed out of the car.

"I'll call you in the morning," Susan promised.

"Okay."

The door slammed and Campbell started back toward the interstate.

"You like that guy, don't you?" Tony asked.

"Sure. He's likable. And he was my client, so—"

"You know what I mean, Susan," Tony prodded.

Susan didn't respond. On the way back to Denver, she considered the implication. The answer was yes, she did like Craig Hanson. She wasn't supposed to. As a lawyer, she was supposed to keep a distanced objectivity, to not allow herself to become personally involved. Yet somehow that was rather difficult when the client was facing the death penalty, claimed to be innocent, and was depending upon her for his very life. Add that to the stress of handling her first case, the terror of the looming possibility that she might be attacked or even killed by an anonymous assailant, and ethical issues began to blur—black and white merging into a confusing gray. Experiences like this tended to draw human beings together. That was natural. When the smoke settled, their emotions would return to a more even keel. The infatuation would quickly wear off.

And even if it didn't, even if a lasting connection had been forged between her and her client, it didn't matter. He was going his way. She was going hers.

It's too bad, really, she thought, gazing out the window at golden slopes racing up toward ivory peaks. Dr. Craig Hanson was quite an attractive man—in more ways than one.

FORTY-THREE

"I GUESS THIS IS IT."

"I guess it is."

The three of them looked at each other, unsure of what to do, what to say, or how to act. It was one of those awkward situations. How were two U.S. marshals supposed to say good-bye to a person they had spent a week protecting—a person they had eaten with, talked with, flown with, even slept with (so to speak), and in the process grown quite fond of? Conversely, how was a public defender supposed to bid farewell to the two brave men who had guarded her life with their own, staying up until all hours, gulping down fast food in the front seat of a Dodge, in order to keep a lunatic from killing her?

They stood in front of Susan's office building for a long moment, none of them able to think of the right way to go about parting. Finally, Campbell stepped forward and enveloped her in a bear hug.

"It's been—a unique experience, Susan," he said. "I hope your future cases are less dangerous—but just as successful. Good luck."

"Thanks, John."

Tony started to hug her, then changed his mind and offered his hand. "I'm not good with this 'good-bye' stuff," he said.

"I understand." Susan smiled at them. "Thanks, guys. You were great. If it wasn't for you . . ."

"Just doing our job, ma'am," Campbell said with mock formality. "Take care, Susan." He turned and started for the car.

"Say," Tony whispered. "Now that we're not involved in a case
... I mean ... I'm not assigned to you anymore—well, I was
wondering if maybe ... you know ... sometime the two of us
could—"

"Come on, Casanova!" Campbell growled. "Quit bothering
the lady."

Tony shrugged, a little embarrassed and clearly disappointed,
and followed his partner.

Watching the Dodge pull away from the curb, Susan decided
that she would miss them: Campbell's fatherly concern, Tony's
youthful enthusiasm. They had been through a lot together. Sadly,
their services were no longer needed. *Thankfully*, their services
were no longer needed.

It was ten minutes after four when she reached her office. Setting the last of the case files down, she sank into the chair behind
her desk just in time to answer the phone.

"Gant here."

"Congratulations!"

"Jack?"

"Yeah. I just heard. Wow! I'm impressed. I give you a loser and
you turn the thing around—in a week!"

"Well, I didn't—"

"Come on now, Susan. Don't be modest. You're a seasoned
lawyer now, batting 1000. Might as well strut. I would—no matter how the case was turned."

"I'm just glad it's over."

"I wouldn't say it's over, exactly."

"What do you mean?"

"There's still the press. They'll mob you when news of Hanson's release is leaked."

"Great," she groaned.

"Comes with the territory. Tooting your own horn for the
cameras is part of the job. You'll get used to it."

"I sincerely hope not."

"Anyway, all kidding aside—job well done!"

"Thanks, Jack."

"Now go home, and don't bother coming in tomorrow. Take the day off. You deserve it."

"Thanks, Jack," she repeated, knowing that she would be in bright and early the next morning.

As she was hanging up, Paul appeared at the door, a gleam in his eye. He pumped a fist in the air. "Yes!"

Susan laughed.

"Congratulations!"

"Thanks, Paul."

"Tell me something, though. The packets I brought you, they were the key to overturning the conviction—right?"

"They helped," she said, trying not to dash his hopes.

"Helped?" he said, frowning.

"One of them really did help."

"And the other?"

"I haven't really looked at it yet," she admitted.

"Mmm. Oh, well."

"But I appreciate all your effort and support, Paul. I couldn't have done it without you."

He rolled his eyes and disappeared down the hall.

Still high from the judge's verdict, Susan found it impossible to collect her scattered thoughts. What was she supposed to do now that it was over? Surely there were loose ends to tie up or something. Then it dawned on her: Samantha Hanson. Craig had asked her to notify his wife.

After consulting her Rolodex, she placed the call. It rang and rang. On the sixth ring, someone picked up.

"Samantha?"

"No. This is Mrs. Mitchell," an unpleasant voice responded.

"Oh, I'm sorry. Could I please speak with Samantha?"

"May I ask who's calling?"

"Susan Gant, Dr. Hanson's attorney."

"She doesn't want to speak with you, Ms. Gant. But I will be happy to give her a message."

Susan doubted that Mrs. Mitchell would be happy to do anything. She was a bitter old woman. She also doubted that Sam refused to speak to her. Mrs. Mitchell seemed to have taken on the role of self-appointed censor for her daughter.

"Well, her husband's hearing started yesterday."

"Soon to be ex-husband," Mrs. Mitchell reminded her. "The divorce is in the works."

"Yes, I know. But I thought that Samantha would be interested to know that her—that Dr. Hanson's conviction was overturned."

Mrs. Mitchell was silent.

"Hello? Are you still there?"

"I'm here," she muttered. "Is that all?"

"Well—ah—yes, I suppose it is. Just tell her that Craig has been released. And that the man responsible for the Sanders murder and for all the harassment and threats is . . . he committed suicide."

"Harassment? Threats?"

"Of Samantha and her daughters. And me."

"What are you talking about?"

"Would you just give her the message, please?" Susan asked. She was getting irritated.

Mrs. Mitchell sighed into the receiver. "All right." Then there was a click and a dial tone.

Susan shook off the odd conversation and surveyed the office. It was a disaster area: stacks of paper, files, and folders spread everywhere. She tried to think of what else needed to be done before she started cleaning up. Unable to come up with anything, she rose and was about to start shoving piles around when it hit her: Roger!

Picking up the phone, she gave the Rolodex another flip and dialed Roger's home. No answer. She tried his work number. They hadn't heard from him in two days. Finally she punched in Campbell's number.

"John?"

"Susan? Long time no see," he chuckled. "What's up?"

"I'm still worried about Roger. Any news?"

"Nope. No sign of him at Phoenix. Colorado Springs PD hasn't turned up anything."

"John, I have a bad feeling. I swear to you that I saw him on the floor, unconscious—if not dead."

"Yeah, I know." He paused. "Let me make a few calls. I'll get back to you."

"Thanks."

She stood up, stretched, and began sorting through the briefs and records littering the floor. Some of the files had to be returned to the DA, others to the records department. A few could be tossed out. Like the packet from Hanson's previous employer. It was worthless now.

Picking it out of the clutter, she threw it Frisbee-style toward the trash can near the door. As it sailed across the room, the cardboard envelope separated from the contents. The envelope landed in the waste can, but the papers drifted to the floor. Gathering them up, she glanced at the itinerary printed on the top sheet. It was a gridlike table listing dates, cities, and engagements. Hanson had attended a convention in Indianapolis in November, spoken at a conference in Seattle in October, given a presentation at a college in Chicago in September, been part of a committee at another convention in Washington D.C. in August—the locations seemed vaguely familiar. Perhaps she had seen the itinerary before. It didn't matter.

She was crumpling the sheets and shooting them into the garbage like little basketballs when she realized why the cities listed rang a bell. Smoothing out one of the pages, she rummaged through the file boxes. Two minutes later she found the folder containing information about the cruelty to animals charges leveled against Hanson. Flipping it open, she ran down the counts: a calf mutilation, a sheep mutilation, another calf, a dog, another sheep, a goat, another goat, two cats . . . She checked the locations. One of the goats had been dismembered and disemboweled just outside of Washington. When? August. A calf had been found slaughtered and drained of blood in a suburb of Chicago in—September.

Susan retrieved the mangled itinerary balls and sank to the floor. Smoothing them out, she began searching for corollaries in the cruelty to animals file. Her eyes darted from one list to the other. There were a few matches. Hanson had been in the right place at the right time on about five occasions—five out of thirteen mutilations. Coincidence, she thought. That was how the prosecution had steamrolled Hanson in the first place. Drawing on his confession, they had loaded up the list of offenses with the cruelty to animals charges in order to make it a federal case. And the fact that some—though less than half—of the events happened to correspond with Hanson's travel schedule had made it that much more convincing.

She shook her head at the nerve of the DA. McDermott would do anything to gain publicity and win a case—even manipulate charges.

Recrumpling one of the sheets, she tossed it at the can, missed, and started to do the same with the next one. Then something caught her eye. She froze. Beneath each of Hanson's engagements, the itinerary listed further information: a brief description of the event, what hotel he was booked into, and who his traveling companions were. The first entry on the sheet noted that Hanson had attended a lecture series at the University of Miami in May. The fine print beneath this listing explained that he had stayed at the Marriott and that another doctor from Therapy Inc.—Hanson's former employer—had attended the series with him. Nothing strange about that.

But it was the second entry on the page that caused a shiver to run up Susan's spine. Hanson had attended a conference in Albuquerque in April. This conference corresponded with the mutilation of two goats just outside of Santa Fe. Three other people had attended with him: two doctors of psychiatric medicine, and a computer tech referred to as R. Thompson. *Roger?*

Retrieving the other sheets, Susan examined them with trembling hands. R. Thompson had been on hand at every speaking engagement and conference that coincided with an animal mutilation. And R. Thompson had also attended the event in Denver—the one that coincided with the murder of Zach Sanders. *Roger?*

Susan suddenly felt nauseous.

The phone rang. It was Campbell.

"No luck on Roger, I'm afraid," he told her. "Nobody's seen him in the last couple of days. He hasn't been arrested or admitted to a hospital. At least, not under his legal name. Springs PD says his car's at home."

"His car? It can't be. I wrecked it."

"No, not the one you totaled. The other one."

"What other one? Roger only has one car. He told me he had to bum a ride to work after I demolished his Toyota. Why would he need a ride if—"

"You got me. But according to the DMV, there are two cars registered to Roger Thompson: a blue Cressida and a brand-new Porsche."

"Porsche?"

"Is there an echo on this line?" Campbell joked. "Yeah. A Porsche. Got a problem with German cars or something?"

"I don't suppose you've got a color on the Porsche."

"Hang on." Papers rustled in the background. "Um . . . Let's see . . . Here it is: black."

"Black?"

"I'm gonna have to have the phone company come out and fix that echo," Campbell laughed. "Is something wrong?"

"I—I don't know, John. I'm not sure."

"Well, listen, give me a holler if you need anything, okay?"

"Okay."

She pressed the button, waited for a dial tone, then she called information.

"What city please?"

"Colorado Springs. The Hampton Inn."

"I have two listings."

"I need the northern location—the one near I–25 and Woodmen."

There was a click, after which a mechanical voice provided her with the number.

Susan punched it in.

"Hampton Inn. How may I direct your call?"

"I'm trying to reach Dr. Craig Hanson."

There was a pause. "He's in room 217. I'll buzz it for you."

After a series of clicks, there was a busy signal.

"His line is busy."

"I'll try again later."

She hung up, thought for a moment, then entered Samantha Hanson's number.

"Hello."

"Mrs. Mitchell?"

"Yes," came the guarded reply.

"This is Susan Gant again. I'm sorry to bother you but—"

"What is it?" she groaned, obviously put out.

"I need to speak to your daughter."

"As I told you, she doesn't want to speak with you."

"Mrs. Mitchell, it's urgent."

"It may well be, but even if it was an emergency, it wouldn't matter. Sam is out of the house this evening. She's attending her group therapy meeting. If you really *must* speak with her, call back in the morning." Her voice was laden with cynicism.

"Maybe you can help me, Mrs. Mitchell."

"I doubt that."

"It's about Roger Thompson."

"What about him?"

"Are you familiar with the name?"

Mrs. Mitchell blew air into the receiver. "Of course."

"Did Roger work with Craig in St. Louis?"

"He's worked with Craig nearly everywhere."

Susan considered this.

"Roger is one of the many reasons Sam is divorcing Craig."

"Huh?"

"Craig and Roger have been inseparable since childhood. They grew up just a few blocks from us in St. Louis. Roger was always a bad apple. A bad influence on Craig. It's no surprise that Roger grew up to be a drunk. Anyway, when Sam married Craig, she got Roger in the deal. He's been a third wheel, hanging around, weighing them down, fouling up their relationship. And the problem is, Craig puts up with it."

"I thought Craig and Sam were happy."

Mrs. Mitchell laughed out loud at this. "Sam hasn't been happy for a single moment since she married Craig. She never really loved him, you know. My poor baby's been depressed and lonely ever since: neglected by her husband and pestered to death by his ever-present buddy. She would have left him anyway, eventually, even if all of this murder and mayhem hadn't come up. And I say good riddance." Mrs. Mitchell took a deep breath. "Now, is there anything else?"

"No," Susan said. "You've been very helpful. I'll be in touch."

She replaced the receiver and stared at the desktop. What was all this? Was it possible that Roger . . .

No. Her tired mind was jumping to erroneous conclusions again. Just as it had a few short days earlier when she'd convinced herself that John Campbell was the enemy. Look how far off that assessment had been. And that was before taking a trip on a hallucinogenic drug. Maybe this line of thinking was the result of a lingering LSD-induced psychosis.

Still, what if . . .

What if Roger had drugged her at Phoenix? He'd had the opportunity—before mysteriously disappearing. What if he had faked his own death? And what if it was *his* black Porsche that had nearly got her killed on I–25? What if he had murdered Dr. Bayers and made it look like a suicide—just as Zach Sanders's murder had been made to look like a suicide? Dr. Bayers's posthumous confession certainly was convenient. It brought a neat, tidy end to the case. And it got Craig Hanson, Roger's best friend, out of prison.

Except—if all that were true, it meant that Roger and Craig were no longer buddies. Whoever killed Bayers—if he had, in fact, been murdered—was also responsible for framing Hanson. Setting someone up for a murder rap and a stint on death row wasn't the usual way of displaying friendship. And if Roger had framed Craig in the first place, why would he help set him free?

Unless . . .

Maybe when Craig retracted his confession and exposed the cybersex operation, Roger panicked. He needed a plan B—a new scapegoat: Dr. Bayers. If that were true, then Roger had one loose end to tie up, one last person to silence in order to ensure that he was not implicated: Craig Hanson.

Was Craig's life in danger?

Susan tried the Hampton Inn again. The phone in room 217 was still busy. Grabbing her purse, she hurried out of the office.

Calm down, she told herself as she jogged to her car. *Quit assuming the worst. Head back down to the Springs. Check Roger's car. If it matches the one you encountered on the interstate, then you can start making wild accusations.*

FORTY-FOUR

THE SUN HAD DISAPPEARED BEHIND THE PORTENTOUS PRESENCE of Pikes Peak and dark shadows were quickly descending by the time Susan reached Fountain. Just south of the Springs, east of Cheyenne Mountain and Ft. Carson, the community of Fountain was home to an Apple Computer factory. And home to Roger Thompson.

Roger's house turned out to be a modest sixties-era ranch, part of a subdivision that had housed middle-income families several decades earlier, but was now occupied by people struggling to rise above poverty. The surrounding houses were in disrepair—in need of paint, shingles, new windows. An optimistic real-estate agent might have called them "fixers." To anyone else, they were just run-down, and the neighborhood less than desirable.

Susan made a slow pass to confirm the house number, rounded the block, and parked at the corner. As she shut off the engine and prepared to make a furtive search for the black Porsche, she wondered if her car would be safe. A thumping bass emanated from the nearest home. There were four cars crammed in the tiny driveway, all low-riders. This looked like gang territory.

She climbed out and locked the doors, prayed for her own safety, as well as that of her car. Why was she doing this? And why did Roger Thompson live in this part of town? The answer to the former was simple. She was either foolish, stupid, or crazy—perhaps all of the above. The latter question—she wasn't sure. Working for Phoenix, surely he earned enough to afford something better. And if Roger was, in fact, behind the cybersex service, he had to be raking in big dollars. Why the run-down old house? Maybe he drank away his money. Or maybe it was a ruse to fool the IRS. He could have been pigeonholing his windfall, hiding the illegal profits from the federal government. He could afford a Cressida *and* a Porsche. That said something about his financial status.

When she reached his driveway, she paused, looking for signs that someone might be home. But the house was dark, the window blinds closed. Everything was quiet. Roger and his sports car probably weren't there.

Slinking up the side yard, she reached the garage and peered inside the wide window that ran across the top of the door. The glass was opaque—to guard against prying eyes, she guessed. Further down the side yard, a six-foot fence with a locked gate kept the curious from venturing into the backyard. Susan surveyed the street for witnesses, then approached the fence. Between the slats she could see a piece of the backyard and a door that she supposed led into the garage.

There was a brief moment of indecision as she tried to decide whether to hop the fence. So far she was guilty merely of being overly nosy. But once she went over that fence, things would get much more serious. She thought of the possible consequences: arrest, prosecution—or worse, vigilante justice—she might get shot.

Then she thought of Satan—harassing her, framing Craig Hanson, possibly even murdering people. And all this time, it might have been Roger. Only one way to find out.

Pulling herself up with her arms, she threw one foot up, as if mounting an oversized horse. The other foot followed. Unfortunately, her weight shifted a little too quickly. She lost her balance and slid over the top and down the other side, ripping her pant leg and picking up a handful of splinters before landing on a concrete pad. Pain raced along her skinned shin and bruised kneecap. Before she could cry out, she heard something: a deep, guttural growl.

Lifting her head, Susan's eyes met the hard, cold glare of a huge, vicious-looking rottweiler. It was standing at the back corner of the house, a mere ten to twelve yards away. The dog looked at her, unwavering. She looked back, stunned, paralyzed. The growl intensified and the dog's mouth formed a smile, revealing an impressive set of sharp, yellow teeth.

Susan glanced at the door. It was only a few short steps away. But there were two serious problems. First, it might be locked. If she made a break for it and the knob didn't turn, the dog would maul her. Second, she had to reach it before the animal, who was undoubtedly much faster than she was, reached her. Going back over the fence was out of the question; she would never have time to clear it before the dog grabbed her and pulled her down.

The dog took a step toward her, slobber trailing from its grinning mouth. Now was the time to check on the status of that door, she realized.

In a sudden, jerky motion, she jumped to her feet and dashed for the door. At the same instant, the rottweiler sprang, fangs bared. Susan's hands grasped the knob. The dog left its feet, its muscular body soaring toward her in a lethal, lightning-quick pounce. The knob turned just as Susan's eyes focused on an impressive set of teeth, powered by nearly one hundred pounds of muscle, rocketing toward her neck.

The door creaked open and she slid through the opening, slamming it shut behind her. There was a sickening thud as the animal crashed against it and gave a pathetic yelp.

Thank God, she thought, panting in the darkness. *Thank you, God.* A split second's hesitation, one little stumble, and she would have been dog chow.

She felt along the wall for a light switch. There didn't seem to be one. Just as well, she decided. Turning on the light might alert Roger—if he was home. She took a dozen blind, halting steps before she kicked something. It was solid. Her hands told her it was a table—a workbench probably. Yes. There were tools on it: several small hammers, tiny screwdrivers. A vice was attached to one end of the table.

The dog had apparently recovered now. She could hear him barking and scratching at the door. Time was running out on her little sleuthing adventure.

Her fingers fumbled with a row of undersized wrenches, more little screwdrivers, a cardboard box filled with wires and squares of plastic. Then she happened upon a treasure: a thin, four-inch tube. She toggled the switch with her thumb, and a miniature shaft of light shot across the workbench.

Careful to keep the penlight's beam away from the window, Susan surveyed her surroundings. The garage was smaller than she had expected: a low roof with rotting wooden beams, and close, open-studded walls. Most of the garage was taken up by the work-bench and the boxes stacked around it. Susan glanced in one of the boxes and saw what she assumed to be computer cards or chips of some kind. There were more of these on the workbench. The tools, she now realized, were for performing electronic diagnostics.

In front of the bench was a section of concrete floor bordered by more boxes, many of them marked with computer logos. The space was barely large enough for a car—a compact car. And at the moment, it was empty. Roger wasn't home. Or at least his car wasn't.

The rottweiler was going nuts, barking as if it were rabid, attacking the door with its claws. Well, she was done here. She had come to see the car, and it was gone. She switched off the pen-light and started for the main door of the garage, intending to roll it up and escape. It would be noisy, but with the dog waiting to greet her at the other door, she had little choice.

Just before she reached the door, she bumped a column of boxes. They groaned as they leaned, then one of them brushed her shoulder as it tumbled from its perch. There was a crunch as cardboard met concrete, and something clattered out onto the floor. It sounded like metal. She thumbed the penlight on again. It was a license plate, upside down in the middle of the garage.

Holding the penlight with her teeth, she righted the box, picked up the plate, and tossed it back in. The dog was furiously trying to break down the door, its barking frantic. Susan hurried to replace the box. Lifting it she noticed the contents: more wires, more circuit boards, more chips. In the middle of the computer hardware, the plate sat face up, illuminated by the tiny, brilliant beam. It read: SATAN.

Susan's mouth fell open. The penlight dropped. The bulb gave a crack as it bounced on the concrete. Darkness reigned. She let the box slide to the floor and felt for the plate. The dog was possessed now, digging at the door, pulling it apart sliver by sliver.

The main garage door wasn't locked. Susan fought with the mechanism, heard it click, and yanked with all her might. The door lurched upward, exposing a few feet of driveway bleached white by the cold rays of a nearby streetlight. Susan fell to her knees and rolled out. It was only as she performed this maneuver that she noticed a tiny sensor at the side of the door. The alarm sounded. It was loud and obnoxious—enough to bring even an inattentive neighbor to the window.

She jumped to her feet and ran, plate in hand, to her car. Holding the key between trembling fingers, she poked at the lock, missed, and poked again. She dropped the key ring, picked it back up, and jabbed at the door, scratching the paint before she felt the key enter the lock.

The dog was having a fit now, barking itself sick in Roger's backyard, spurred on by the alarm. Between the siren and the hound, the entire block had been aroused. Curtains were being pushed back, heads were poking out doors, and several people had stepped onto their porches to see what all the racket was about.

Susan pulled the door open and dropped into the seat, throwing the plate into the floorboard on the passenger's side. She managed to hit the ignition hole with the key and twisted, summoning the engine to life. Flooring the accelerator, she ground the stick into gear and was about to breathe a sigh of relief. But instead of squealing tires, there was only a sputter and then silence. She was in third. The engine had died.

The street was alive now. More people were outside, standing on their stoops and driveways, calling to one another, staring in her direction. Two men emerged from the closest house, eyed her car, then walked toward her. They looked like gang members.

Susan gave the key another twist. The engine made an effort, but failed to start. She could smell gasoline. It was flooded. Great!

The men were nearly upon her. They were smiling, laughing. They had found a sitting duck.

Susan uttered a half-prayer/half-curse and tried again. This time the Subaru responded with a roar and after a brief, panicked grinding session, she found the right gear.

Mashing the pedal to the floor, she screeched off, leaving the two hoodlums, the suspicious neighbors, and the blasted dog in a cloud of burning rubber.

Six blocks later, in view of the comforting lights of a strip mall and convenience store complex, she rolled down the window and drank in the night air. Her heart was still pounding, her breath coming in gulps. Her shirt was stuck to the seat with perspiration.

Glancing down at the plate, she found that she couldn't think straight. The adrenaline was still pumping; her "fight or flight" response was in full swing.

Pray, she told herself. This turned out to be more difficult than she had anticipated. Words failed her. The rush of emotions made cohesive thought almost impossible. She couldn't even remember the 23rd Psalm. Finally, she shook her head and muttered, "I need help."

By the time she reached the interstate, a simple but effective plan had begun to materialize. Call in the marshals. Then find Craig. Before Roger does.

FORTY-FIVE

"ARE YOU NUTS? WHAT WERE YOU THINKING?"

"I don't know. I just—I guess I *wasn't* thinking."

"I guess you weren't." The voice on the other end of the line cursed softly. "You actually burglarized Thompson's garage?"

"Well, I wouldn't say that. I mean, the garage door was unlocked, and I—"

"The gate to the side yard was locked, right? You said you had to jump the fence."

"Right."

"And you were not invited into the garage by the owner, right?"

"True, but—"

"And you removed property from the premises without permission, right?"

"It wasn't like I was stealing or anything."

"Hopping the fence—that's trespassing. Snooping in the garage—that's what we call breaking and entering. Taking the plate—that constitutes burglary. You could go to jail for this little escapade, Susan."

She sighed into her cellular phone. Campbell was correct on all accounts. It had been a foolhardy thing to do, and yes, technically, she could be arrested.

"Where are you now?" he grumbled

"Sitting outside Hanson's hotel."

Campbell cursed again. "Why?"

"Because Craig may be in danger."

"Maybe so. But what business is that of yours?"

"He's my client."

"*Was* your client. And since when were you deputized as a law enforcement agent?"

"I just thought that someone should warn—"

"There you go, thinking again. Listen, Susan. Leave the cops-and-robbers stuff to the professionals, okay?"

"Fine. Then you and Tony need to get down here. Because I'm telling you, Roger is Satan."

"So you said."

"It all makes sense now. Roger's a computer whiz. He's the one who set up the cybersex thing in the first place. He murdered Zach and Singer and Bayers, and he framed Craig Hanson, all to keep from getting caught. And he's the nut who's been trying to kill me. Remember when he got drunk and had to take a cab home? Remember that I drove his sabotaged car back to the Springs for him? It was a setup, John."

"Yeah. Does kind of fall together, doesn't it?" Campbell admitted.

"And now with this plate, we've got the guy, dead bang."

"I wouldn't say that, exactly. But a case against him does seem to be presenting itself." There was a pause. "We'll put out the flashing light and be down in forty-five minutes. In the meantime, I'll have some local cops come over and keep an eye on Hanson."

"Great. I'll tell him."

"No. You won't tell him anything. You should never have gone in Thompson's garage in the first place. Lucky you didn't get yourself hurt. Now it's time to hang up your P-I badge and call it a night. Got that, Susan?"

"Yeah."

"If Dr. Hanson's life is in danger, yours may be too. Go home, Susan. Let us handle it."

"All right."

"I'll give you a call in the morning and let you know how things turned out."

"Okay. Goodnight, John."

She flipped the phone shut and stared across the quiet parking lot. Once again, John Campbell was the voice of reason. She had no business being on what amounted to a stakeout. She was a lawyer, not an undercover police officer. Her place was in the courtroom, not the streets.

Starting the car, she composed a short, silent prayer for Hanson's safety, then reached for the gearshift. The marshal was right. Time for her to call it a night and go home.

She had exited the lot and was heading down a side street, wondering what traffic on I–25 would be like at this time in the evening, when she saw it: a jet-black Porsche. It was nestled between a pickup and a minivan, only two rows from where she had just been parked. Pulling back into the lot, she rolled by it, taking in the car's shape and curves. Yes. It was the same model that had run her off the road, that had been wearing a S-A-T-A-N plate. But a streetlight backlit the dark, tinted windows, showing her that it was empty. Roger Thompson was prowling around the hotel somewhere.

Pulling into a handicapped slot near the main office, Susan unfolded the phone and called the hotel desk.

"Room 217, please."

The operator attempted to ring Hanson's room.

"I'm sorry," the kind voice said. "The line is busy."

She hung up. Why would Hanson's line be busy for hours? Was he calling his friends and family, sharing the good news of his release? Maybe. Or maybe he was exhausted from the stress and had taken the phone off the hook to get some rest. That made sense. What Susan found herself doing next did not.

She was out of the car and in the hotel before her rational mind could object. When it did, citing Campbell's order to stay out of the way, she answered with a quick review of the situation: Roger was Satan. His car was in the lot. His plan to frame Hanson and see him executed had failed. Craig needed to be warned. The marshals were still in Denver. She was here. She had to act. She couldn't just walk away. She would inform Craig, then facilitate an escape to ensure his safety.

The lobby was quiet, the front desk deserted. A television offered a newscast to a lounge of empty chairs and sofas. Susan took the stairs to the second floor. The carpeted halls were silent, the guests either at dinner or already retired for the evening.

She glanced at the doors, counting off the numbers: 207, 209, 211 ... Down at the end of the corridor, next to an emergency exit, she located room 217. She stopped and listened. Nothing. Not even the mechanical sound of an ice dispenser or a soda machine.

For a moment she hesitated, wondering if Campbell might have been right. She was out of her league. What if Roger was behind that door? What if he had already done away with Hanson and was waiting to do the same with her?

Forcing herself to take a deep breath, Susan prayed for courage and lifted a shaky fist toward the door. She gave it a sharp rap.

Ten seconds later, a muffled voice responded. "Just a minute."

She heard a rattle—the chain being removed—then a thunk as the bolt slid back. The door opened a crack and a face peered out. It was Hanson. His hair was wet.

"Susan?"

"Hi, Craig. Mind if I come in?"

"Uh ... well ..."

"It's important."

His cheeks flushed slightly. "Okay." The door swung back to reveal Hanson wearing nothing but a towel. He was dripping on the carpet, holding the towel around his waist. "Just got out of the shower," he apologized, embarrassed. "Come on in. What's up?"

"It's Roger. He's a murderer," she blurted out.

"What?"

"He killed Dr. Bayers."

Susan closed the door and bolted it shut. When she turned back toward Hanson, his eyes were wide.

"Roger?" He shook his head in disbelief. "Impossible. Dr. Bayers committed suicide. Besides, he confessed."

"It was another con," she told him. "Roger killed him and made it look like a suicide. Same story with Zach Sanders and Grant Singer."

"How do you know all this? Do you have any proof?"

Susan handed him the license plate.

"This was on the car that tried to run me off of I–25. I found it in Roger's garage. And his car—his Porsche—matches the one I saw."

Hanson's mouth was hanging open now. *"Roger?* But we've been friends forever. He would never—"

"Maybe you don't know him as well as you think you do." Susan glanced around the room. On the nightstand, the phone was off the hook. "Get your clothes on. We need to get out of here. I saw Roger's car outside."

"You did?"

"The marshals are on their way. Cops, too. But if Roger's on the loose, we can't take any chances."

Hanson was frozen, clutching the towel, staring at the plate.

"I know it's a shock, Craig, but let's go. We could both be in danger."

Hanson tossed the plate on the bed and swore. "I was really hoping it wouldn't come to this, Susan."

She looked at him, confused.

"I thought you were different," he continued. "I thought you would know when to leave well enough alone. But you're just like Ronald."

"Who?"

"My last lawyer. The one I had to fire. Ronald Evans."

"May he rest in peace," a familiar voice added. It came from the bathroom.

Susan jumped, twisting, and saw Roger Thompson stepping into view.

"Oh, God!" she gasped, backing away.

"Ron never liked Craig's case," Roger said, pausing to sip from the tumbler in his hand. It held several ounces of light brown liquid and a half-dozen ice cubes. "Didn't believe Craig. And he got to snooping around. After Craig fired him, old Ron went on a vacation with his family. Hawaii, I think it was. Had an accident. His head was cracked open by the grill of a Sable. Hit and run. Never caught the driver. A real tragedy. Poor old Ron."

Stunned, Susan looked to Hanson for an explanation, glanced back at Roger, then at Hanson again. "I don't understand."

"Sure you do, Susan," Hanson smiled. "Think it through."

"But Roger . . . he's . . ."

"Oh, that's right," Hanson laughed. "You two haven't been formally introduced. Susan, meet Satan. Satan, Susan."

"Charmed, I'm sure," Roger grinned. Rattling the ice in his glass, he took another gulp of booze. "Another drink, Roger?" he asked himself. "Don't mind if I do." He disappeared into the bathroom for a moment and returned with a bottle of Jack Daniels, pouring himself a generous helping. "Craig?"

"No, thanks, Rog. Gotta keep a clear head for this one," he said, aiming a thumb at Susan. "You might want to ease back, too."

"Good idea," Roger agreed, swigging.

Susan tried to comprehend what was taking place.

"You're right about getting out of here, Susan," Hanson nodded. He dropped his towel and proceeded to get dressed, apparently unconcerned about who was present. "If the marshals are on the way, we'd better take an earlier flight. Let's see—how about that nonstop to Mexico City? We can make that, can't we, Rog?"

Roger burped, then shrugged, reaching for the bottle again.

"Who killed Zach Sanders?" Susan asked.

"Doesn't really matter, does it?" Hanson responded, pulling on his pants. "Dead is dead."

"I'll tell you one thing, though," Roger beamed. "Ruth Sanders may have been a bona fide SRA victim, for all I know. But the devil did *not* take her son. Trust me on that one." He punctuated the statement with a hiccup.

Susan was aghast. "You told me you were innocent, Craig. You said you were framed."

Hanson offered a boyish grin. "I lied."

"But I believed you."

"I'm a good liar."

"He is," Roger agreed.

"The threats, the conspiracy, the accusations against the Institute, against Bayers—those were all lies? That whole long story?"

"Mostly," Hanson admitted.

"What about your confession?"

Hanson cursed at this. "Speaking of lying, the DA's office did their share of that. Plea bargain, my eye." He swore again.

Susan realized that she was trembling. "Why did Zach have to die? Why did Singer and Bayers have to die?"

Frowning, Hanson groaned, "As if you didn't already know." He pulled on his shirt and began buttoning it up.

"To keep them quiet?"

Roger belched an affirmation.

"So you and Roger are behind the Internet porn stuff?"

Hanson sighed, wearying of the third-degree.

"That's worse than criminal," Susan observed. "That's sick."

"We're artists," Roger argued proudly, eyes glazed. "Filmmakers turned cyberspace entrepreneurs." He took a swallow of whiskey and grimaced. "We got our start in child porn. You know, black-market videos of little kids doing nasty things. We used Craig's patients. Low overhead—good money."

"What about the SRA stuff?" Susan asked in morbid fascination. "Are you two Satanists?"

Roger laughed at this, spilling most of what was left of his
drink. "No," he said, pouring another. "That was the next step. We
saw how popular the occult was, how teenagers were getting into
devil worship, you know, heavy metal and all. Satanism's hot. Read
an article that said it has something to do with the upsurge in hallucinogenic drug use. Anyway, whatever the reason, devil worship
sells—big time.

"So we staged some ceremonies with animals, filmed them.
Voila! Instant success. Between our kiddie flicks and our bloody
rituals, we were making a bundle."

"When did you start offering this smut via computers?"

"That was my idea," he announced, smiling. "When the Net
started opening up back in the early nineties, I saw the potential:
Interactive pornography. It's anonymous. It's accessible twenty-
four hours a day. It's absolutely risk-free. No VD or AIDS to worry
about. And you don't have to leave home to get it. Talk about convenient. Dirty old men give us their credit card numbers. We give
them Jack and Jill having an orgy. Antisocial teens hook up with
us on-line—with Daddy's credit card. We give them animal sacrifices. Who could ask for a better arrangement?"

"Roger, I think you've had enough to drink," Hanson said,
tying his shoes. "It's time to shut up. We need to get out of here."

"Aw, can't I tell her about the MRT?"

"She knows about that. She knows everything," he mumbled,
stepping into the bathroom to comb his hair.

"The MRT unit," Roger began in a lowered voice, "gave us
more product than we knew what to do with. All those weirdos
having bogus memories. And the MRT created these wonderful 3-
D, full-color, stereo-sound movies. That was our final jump in technology: virtual reality. It's the ultimate medium for adult
entertainment. Full sensory, vicarious experiences. Safe sex and safe

satanic ceremonies—on-line, at the touch of a button. And we got in on the ground floor. You're looking at a couple of visionaries."

"But now you're fleeing the country," Susan noted. "Looks like the goose is done laying golden eggs."

Hanson returned, smirking. "We can operate from anywhere on the planet, Susan." He picked up a small suitcase and checked the contents. "All we need is a modem."

"You both mutilated animals," Susan said, taking a baby step backward, toward the door.

"For creative purposes only," Roger stipulated. "We weren't being cruel. We were being auteurs."

"You both murdered people," she said, sneaking another tiny step. The door was still ten feet away.

"Only to protect our business concerns," Roger smiled. He hiccuped again, nearly fell over, then staggered to the bed and sat down. "We did, however, videotape the events, for possible mer-chandising."

Susan cringed at this, but managed to slink backward another half yard. "What about the SRA charges? Craig, did you abuse your kids?"

Hanson closed the bag. "No. SRA is a crock. I told you that. Hardly ever really happens. Singer—the putz—he was just like the rest of them at the Institute, always ready to dig for repressed memories, always looking for signs of ritual abuse. I never laid a hand on my girls. Never even used them for our movies."

"We could have," Roger said, raising his eyebrows. "They would have been perfect. Couple of great-looking—"

"Shut up!" Hanson told him. "They're my daughters, my flesh and blood. I may be greedy, but I'm not a pervert."

Susan slid two more feet back. Roger had his eyes closed now—probably on the verge of passing out. Hanson was busy with another bag. This was her chance. She eyed the door, took a step. It was three long strides away.

But Hanson was no fool. He smiled. "Ready to go, Susan? Me too." He pulled a long knife from the suitcase. "If you get any wild notions about running out on us—don't. I've gotten rather good at using one of these things. I can slit a calf's throat and skin it in a few short minutes." The blade zipped back and forth through the air in a threatening manner. "Come on, Roger. Get up and grab a bag."

Roger cursed, groaned something indiscernible, then got up and took hold of one of the suitcases.

Susan backed away cautiously, reducing the distance to the door. "I'm not going with you."

"Sure you are, Susan," Hanson said. "We need you. For insurance."

"You know too much," Roger grunted, red-nosed.

"Besides, you'll love Mexico." Hanson picked up the bag. "If you behave yourself, it could be fun. Just the three of us—sand, surf, tequila—one long party."

Susan took a deep breath, then stared into Hanson's eyes. "I was serious when I told you that I gave my life to Jesus. He's my Lord."

"Bully for you, Susan," Hanson deadpanned. "But unless you want an express trip to see that Lord of yours, I'd stop right there. Move another inch toward the door and I'll cut you."

"I also read up on spiritual warfare, just like you advised." She stared Hanson in the eyes, took a deep breath, then said, "In the name of Jesus, stop!"

Hanson froze. A pained expression spread over his face. He dropped the bag, then clutched at this heart. "Roger! Roger, help—I'm—I'm—melting!"

Roger swore under his breath. "Quit messing around, Craig."

"No, wait, that was the wicked witch in *The Wizard of Oz*," Hanson chuckled, picking the bag back up. "Knock it off, Susan."

"In Jesus' name, stop!" she tried again.

Hanson rolled his eyes. "Quit with the mumbo-jumbo, will you? You're going with us, and there's nothing you can do about it. Relax. Consider it a vacation."

Susan fumbled with her purse, hands trembling. Hanson started toward her, the blade lifted high. She tossed out makeup, keys, credit cards—where was it?

"I'll open you up, Susan," Hanson promised. "If I have to, I'll do it right here."

She glanced up at him, at the knife blade, then swallowed a scream as her fingers found what they had been frantically searching for. With a firm grip on the handle, she jerked the gun out of her purse.

Hanson stopped and stared at it, the knife still poised to strike.

Roger tripped backward, onto the bed, cursing, his eyes wide in terror.

"Susan. Come on, now. It's me, Craig. Your client. There's something between us, remember? Something special. A connection. Tell you what, I'll put the knife down, okay?"

He laid the knife down on the TV set in slow motion, eyes glued to Susan. But his hand never released its grip on the handle.

"Everything's going to be fine," he told her with a pleasant smile. "Let's just talk this over."

They stood like warring statues for nearly half a minute, each studying the other. Then suddenly, without warning, Hanson lunged forward. Light glinted from the blade as it slashed through the air, toward Susan's throat.

Without conscious thought she pointed the barrel at Hanson's heart and gave the trigger three gentle tugs.

Roger swore hysterically, then began to retch.

FORTY-SIX

Y OU SHOULD HAVE GONE HOME."

"Yeah. I should have."

Campbell muttered something under his breath as he surveyed the scene. Dr. Craig Hanson was sprawled on the floor, eyes open, mouth agape, a look of shock frozen on his dull, gray face. There were three neat holes clustered in the upper right section of his abdomen. Beneath him, the carpet was stained a dark red, blood having pooled in a wide, jagged circle. A photographer was pacing around the body, stepping over the knife, avoiding splayed limbs and blood-soaked carpet, recording the scene with clicks and flashes. The coroner stood to one side, waiting for his turn. Next to him, two plainclothes homicide detectives conversed in hushed tones.

Hanson's partner in crime, Roger Thompson, was sitting on the bed, hands cuffed behind his back, crying like a baby.

"You have the right to an attorney," an officer was saying, "if you cannot afford one, one will be appointed for you."

Roger wasn't listening. "I don't want to go to prison," he wailed between sobs. "I'd rather be dead." Still drunk, his flushed face looked up at Susan. "Why didn't you shoot me too? I don't want to go to prison."

Campbell sneered at this, then led Susan out of the room. Tony was standing in the hallway, flanked by a half-dozen members of the Colorado Springs Police Department and several representatives from the local sheriff's office. They were milling about, shooting the breeze, trading murder scene stories. Tony saw Campbell and Susan coming and walked toward them.

"Talked to Springs PD," Tony said, nodding his head back in the direction of the officers. "They're willing to forgo charges—considering the circumstances."

"You dodged a bullet there, Susan," Campbell said. "They could press if they wanted to, cart you off to jail, and try to have you indicted."

"But they're not going to. You're free to go," Tony explained. "You can't leave the state until the investigation is closed, however. And you have to make yourself available for questioning."

Susan looked at them through weary eyes. She still felt sick. Repulsed by what she had discovered, horrified by what she had done—what she had been forced to do. Even in self-defense, even when fending off a murderer, ending a human life is a terrible act, something she was certain would haunt her the rest of her life.

"Don't worry," she managed to say. "I don't plan on going anywhere."

"Good thing I took you to the range and taught you to use that gun," Campbell noted, glancing back in at Hanson's body.

"Good thing you made me carry it," Susan said. Seconds later she broke, frayed nerves, fear, stress, shock, and sorrow combining to produce a bout of shakes and uncontrolled crying.

"I—I killed him," she sobbed. "I killed my client—I killed Craig!"

Campbell placed a comforting arm over her shoulder. "It'll be okay, Susan. It's over now." He glanced at Tony and shrugged, unsure what to do.

Tony shrugged back, equally puzzled. Consoling a crying woman was obviously one of the greatest mysteries ever to face the adult male.

"How about if we give you a ride home?" Campbell tried.

"I've—I've got my—my car," she bawled.

"I know. But I thought maybe you could use some company. We could have the car driven up later."

She nodded and mouthed, "Okay."

Each marshal took an arm as they led her down the hall, into the elevator.

When the elevator opened on the ground floor, they were met by a lobby full of press: TV cameras, lights, reporters, microphones. Campbell glared at them, growled something, then set out to blaze a trail through the crowd. A pathway opened as journalists drew back, intimidated by the hulking form. Behind his blocking, Tony helped Susan along, shielding her face from cameras and shoving away obtrusive mikes.

When they were inside the Dodge, safe from the prying eyes and ears of the press, Campbell offered a handkerchief.

"Thanks," Susan sniffed. The tears were flowing with less vigor now. "Listen, you guys, I want you to know how much I appreciate all you've done for me."

Campbell and Tony shrugged this off. "Just doing our job," they chimed.

"Well, thank you anyway. You guys are the greatest." With that she spread out on the backseat and closed her eyes. The sadness and shock of what had just occurred had already begun to give way to exhaustion. As her body relaxed, as her conscience let go of the event—if only temporarily—the comforting words of Psalm 23 wafted through her depleted mind: *The* LORD *is my shepherd, I shall not want. He leads me to lie down in green pastures.*

Susan saw herself standing in a pasture, soft fields and meadows of deep green grass climbing hills that rolled toward the horizon.

He leads me beside still waters.

She sat down next to a pristine pond, fed by a clear, rocky brook.

He restores my soul.

She realized that she was not alone. *He* was with her.

Yea, though I walk through the valley of the shadow of death, I will fear no evil.

The air was sweet, the light alive. Susan could feel *his* hand in hers. And she was no longer afraid.

For thou art with me. . .

––––––––––––––

"It's not like we made any great sacrifices," Campbell was saying as they accelerated toward the interstate. "Protecting people, apprehending dangerous felons, investigating illegal activity—it's all in a day's work for a U.S. marshal."

Tony laughed. "You sound like an advertisement—a corny advertisement."

"Yeah, well, it's true. The job's demanding, but it has its own rewards."

"Maybe. But we *do* make sacrifices," Tony argued.

"Such as?"

"What would you call Bambi?"

"You really want to know?"

"I blew that relationship because of this 'rewarding' job."

"Life's rough, Tony."

"*Rough?* Do you really understand what I missed out on?"

"No great loss, trust me."

"And now Jessica—"

"Wait—who?"

"Jessica. She's Bambi, only brunette: beautiful dark eyes, full lips, and legs that—"

"I get the picture."

"Anyway, I was supposed to take her to dinner tonight. In fact, I was just leaving my place to pick her up when you called."

"You told me you were staying home to work on your report tonight."

"Yeah, well—it's a moot point now. I had to break the date at the very last minute. And she wasn't exactly pleased about that."

"The trials and tribulations of Don Juan," Campbell commiserated.

"I'll be lucky if she talks to me again."

"If she's the right one for you, she'll understand."

"Sure. That's easy for you to say—Mr. Married for a Quarter of a Century."

"Not quite. Next year will be our twenty-fourth. And just because I'm married doesn't mean I'm dead. I'm still a good judge of people. For instance, let's assess your situation. This Jessica—body that won't quit," Campbell reviewed, grinning. "Bedroom eyes, kissy-kissy lips . . . No mention made of personality, sense of humor, or intelligence. Nothing even remotely suggesting commitment. Sounds like another bimbo to me."

"Hey!" Tony objected. He slugged Campbell in the arm.

"What do you think, Susan?" Campbell chuckled. "Bimbo city?"

There was no response.

"Susan?"

Tony twisted to see behind him. "Susan?"

The occupant of the backseat was curled into a ball, breath escaping in rhythmic hisses, like air from a bicycle pump. Public Defender Susan Gant was fast asleep.

Also available from award-winning author Christopher A. Lane and Zondervan Publishing House

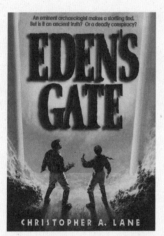

Eden's Gate

Eden's Gate pits the political, intellectual, and monetary powers of the world against the Maker of the Universe—with explosive consequences.

When Dr. Richard Grimm, a noted archaeologist, disappears in the Middle East under mysterious circumstances, Dr. Ben Lawrence is called in to take his place. A Christian and a creationist, Ben is used to being pushed aside and ridiculed. This dig is his big break—the chance to discover the birthplace of humankind. But the trail of Dr. Grimm leads straight into enemy territory: Northern Iraq.

Meanwhile, Jennifer Rogers is none too thrilled about her new boss on the dig. As the rebel daughter of Chinese missionaries, she considers Ben Lawrence as not only her opposite, but also her enemy. So why does she find herself so attracted to him?

Unknown to Ben and Jennifer, more than one person has a stake in this obscure Babylonian dig. A high-powered businessman, a TV news celebrity, FBI and CIA agents—all of them have an interest in the operation. Power, money—even lives—are at stake. And Jennifer and Ben are caught in the middle, battling forces beyond their control.

We want to hear from you. Please send your comments about this book to us in care of the address below. Thank you.

ZondervanPublishingHouse
Grand Rapids, Michigan 49530
http://www.zondervan.com